Alan Dunn lives on the fringes of the Lake District. He has worked as a hospital administrator, insurance salesman, company director and work study officer. He is also a folk dancer, singer and musician, and leads a folk dance band which performs throughout Cumbria. In 1991 his short story 'French Kisses' won second prize in the Ian St James Awards and was published in the anthology *Midnight Oil*. His first novel, *The Collier and His Mistress*, was published in 1993.

Also by Alan Dunn:

The Collier and his Mistress

The English Dancing Master

ALAN DUNN

being a

Most Elegant Musick of Sixteen Bars in Length in
the Traditional Manner of the Dancing Masters of
the North of England

WARNER BOOKS

A *Warner* Book

First published in Great Britain in 1995
by Little, Brown and Company
This edition published in 1997 by Warner Books

Copyright © Alan Dunn 1995

A CIP catalogue record for this book
is available from the British Library.

ISBN 0 7515 1753 4

Typeset by Palimpsest Book Production Limited,
Polmont, Stirlingshire
Printed and bound in Great Britain by
Mackays of Chatham PLC, Chatham, Kent

Warner Books
A Division of
Little, Brown and Company (UK)
Brettenham House
Lancaster Place
London WC2E 7EN

Dedicated to my mother, Thelma, with love; and in memory of my Uncle Bob.

Thanks to Jan, who has always given me the time, the space and the inspiration to write. To Stuart and Chris Hetherington, for being there. To Diana Tyler. And to my sons, Michael and Peter, who show me how to jump at the sun.

Prologue

Tuesday, 1 June 1830

In which a tune enters a young man's mind and will not disappear, though his need for sleep is greater than his need for music.

Rob Tweddle lay on his bed and stared at the stains on the ceiling, trying to make them into new, interesting shapes. He was still fully clothed, as if anticipating that sleep would be no close companion that night. It was the tune, that damnable tune, it wouldn't leave him alone, it danced in his brain complete with variations in different keys, he could hear it played on the fiddle, the piano, the flute; a whole band had taken possession of his head. He sat up abruptly, and a rat scuttled away through a hole in the skirting.

'I'll chase it away,' he said, reaching to light the stub of a candle, 'I'll get rid of it.' In the dim light he found a pen and ink, scrabbled in a box beside his bed for a piece of paper and a rule. He drew two sets of five parallel lines, then a treble clef and three sharp signs.

'It's a good tune really, that's why it's in my mind. So if I write it down, there'll be no need for it to be there, and I'll be able to sleep.'

He added notes to the paper, and bar lines. It was a short

tune, only sixteen bars, though it took him almost twenty minutes to write it out to his satisfaction. He looked at the page and yawned, set it down and returned to his bed.

'Trouble is,' he said, 'I can't remember the name. What the hell was the name?'

It must have mattered little; his heavy, easy, rhythmic breathing soon filled the room. Sleep and the night claimed him.

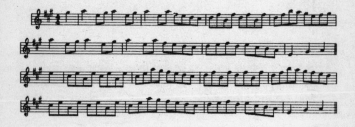

The First Bar of the Musick

―――◆―――

Wednesday, 2 June 1830

In which Mr George Taylor and Mr James Playford meet and connive to dismiss Mr Playford's clerk, Mr Rob Tweddle, who does not seem dismayed at the prospect.

'The chord is A major, reasonably straightforward on the pianoforte, Miss Marjorie, but requiring a little more attention on the violin, Miss Priscilla.'

The voice was well modulated, that of someone who has spent a lifetime aspiring to but never quite attaining the position of gentleman. It reached stridently into the street from the upstairs window of a tall, narrow building bullied on one side by a squat public house and on the other by a fat, flyblown butcher's shop.

'Now then, Miss Priscilla, you must play an arpeggio of the notes A, C sharp and E, and you must do so in a specific rhythm. The music is in common time. It is a reel, and in playing the chord, in sustaining the chord, and in beginning the piece itself, you must give your dancers a clue to the pace at which you expect them to begin dancing.'

The day would be hot again. It was early, no later than ten in the morning, but the eager sunlight was already hunting

wary shadows, sending them scurrying deep into the dark
courtyards and dank alleyways which snaked down to the
Tyne. The steep street was busy with noise. Horse-drawn
carriages and wagons laboured up its cobbled slope, while
those beasts passing in the opposite direction stepped stiff-
legged, braked and wary, down to the quayside. A drayman
was sweating, unloading heavy barrels into the inn's dirty
basement. A butcher boy scurried past him without a glance,
his eyes fixed on the woman in the top room of the inn as she
flung open her attic window and yawned her belated greetings
to the new day. He yelled to her and rolled his tongue round
his lips; she spat her reply and missed. The gobbet landed, to
the butcher boy's great delight, in a cart carrying fish uphill
to the market. The boy danced on his way to the sound of
violin and piano tormenting an unrecognisable tune.

'That is very good,' came the same rounded tones as before.
'Very good indeed, we shall have you performing in public
within a week. Two weeks at the outside, that much is
certain, or my name isn't James Playford. Now I'd like to
hear the piece just once more. Let us begin with the chord,
Miss Priscilla, will you count in please?'

The costermonger and knife grinder, the barrow boy and
fishwife, the keel man and stevedore and clay seller, all those
who passed along or plied their trades in this winding road
joining town to river sported his or her sense of belonging like
a cockade. The clothes they wore, the tools they carried, the
wares they sold blended with and became part of the street.
Even those wearing the uniforms of businessmen (checked
trousers and double-breasted waistcoats, tight jackets, and
high cravats which would soon be loosened as the day's
heat intensified) walked and talked with a purpose. They
had their duties to attend to, offices to visit, goods to inspect;
whether merchants or bankers, lawyers or accountants, they
all had their work to do and seemed intent on carrying out
that work conscientiously. Amidst the noises and tastes and
smells, the cries of enticement and warning, the rumblings
of iron-framed wheels on uneven sets, the pressing of flesh

both formal and less so, the aromas of coffee and bread and smoked fish, the stench of bad meat, only one man seemed to have no purpose. True, he did have the air of someone looking for something, a place or a person, but if he was searching then he was ambivalent in his task, almost indifferent to the outcome, uncomfortable in the quest itself.

His puzzled glances up and down the street marked him as a stranger to the area, and his clothes told that he would normally be found in the gaming houses and salons and drawing rooms of a more elegant part of the town, not amongst these warehouses, yards and brothels. The cloth of his suit was well cut; the trousers, with their braided seam, could have been made for no other than their occupier; the jacket was trimmed with buttons at the tail as well as at the sleeves; and the hat (carried in the hand in deference to the heat of the day) was unfashionably though elegantly tapered towards its tall crown. The style was slightly awkward, as if a conservative tailor had been asked by a young wife to provide a modern suit for her elderly, unfashionable husband and between them the three had managed to convey only a sense of compromise and incoherence. But this gentleman was not entirely elderly, having seen no more than forty-five summers, nor was he married, despite being handsome in a square-faced, heavy-eyebrowed way. He could confess (but had never felt the need to do so) to having had many liaisons with women who would have consented to marriage had the proposal been put to them, and he had enjoyed what he considered the benefits of marriage without the obligations normally imposed on a gentleman by such a state. And his clothes were his own choice, their incongruous style selected specifically to persuade women that his reputation was undeserved, that he was no predator, that he was a man who needed to be cared for and cosseted. His air of apparent helplessness had lured more women to his bed than he could remember, and his memory was normally keen.

On this hot June morning George William Frederick Taylor (he always insisted on initial introductions granting him the honour of his full name) was not seeking a new liaison. He had recently invested both time and money (though the latter was of little importance to him) on a young widow of twenty-one. The loss of Lady Montague's beloved husband had required some consolation which he had been in an ideal position to provide, and he suspected that he would soon be able to enjoy the benefits of his careful husbandry. But there was other work to be done, and his task this morning was an unwelcome diversion which he felt unable to delegate to some other member of his household. A favour such as this, requested personally by a member of his family, albeit one whom he disliked, ought to be carried out personally. And besides, favours could be stored, banked; interest could be accrued on favours; the return on favours could be considerable. For that reason alone he was abroad at this unreasonable hour in an area of the town he would normally avoid (even those women who were clearly not prostitutes were unattractive), searching for an address recommended to him by an acquaintance he barely knew, and clutching a letter bearing the broad, simple and illogical spelling of his elder brother.

The voice he'd heard minutes before but which had not registered, the mellifluous over-ornamented tones of the music teacher, reached down once more into the street.

'No, no, no! Please, allow me to demonstrate, Miss Marjorie.'

A keen ear would have heard the sound of a chair being pushed back on an unpolished wooden floor, and any passer-by who had heard the pupil would be under no illusion that anyone but the teacher was now at the keys of the piano. A trained ear would perhaps have noticed that the playing and the voice were similar; the simple melody was not improved by the addition of superfluous grace notes, the tone was strident throughout, the fingers had no touch of delicacy, no understanding. But that morning there was no listener able to apply such discrimination, nor was there ever likely to be in such an area of the city. Only George Taylor was there, and *his* knowledge of music was as great as his wish to linger. Led on by the music and the voice, he had noticed the name on the brass plate and matched it to that scribbled by his informant. It was a comparatively new plate, untarnished, the letters not worn away by too frequent polishing, and he touched it gingerly as if to confirm that this was the place and the person he sought. 'James Playford, Dancing Master, Professor of Music,' he read again, then marched forward, up two worn stone steps, and through a door which creaked as he opened it. So bright was the morning outside, so dark was it inside the hallway, that he stood for more than a minute before he could see properly again. During that time the music, which had at least been confirmation that he was in close proximity to his quarry, ceased. He blinked in the coolness and waited. The voice spoke, and the music began again.

'You see? That is how the tune ought to be played, the right hand providing the melody and a subtle ornamentation, the left providing a simple chordal accompaniment. And meanwhile the violin may add its part. The harmonies are, I assure you, entirely in keeping with the piece. Allow me.'

The same tune, with slight variations, was elicited from a violin. The sound came from above Taylor's head. Noticing ahead of him an uneven narrow staircase, he climbed slowly. He ignored the door to his right, which was slightly ajar but showed no sign of activity behind it.

'The dancers,' continued the voice, 'ought to be able to step with the tune, and *you* should be able to supply the constancy, the consistency of pace which will allow them to become part of *your* music. Like this.'

The tune was played again on the violin, but more roughly and accompanied by a brisk clatter which George Taylor assumed was one of the pupils beating time inaccurately on the lid of the piano. The rhythm and the melody did not quite fit together, and as he turned a curve in the stairs he saw the reason. As the top step came into view, and beyond it an open door into a room larger than the outer dimensions of the building would seem to allow, a pair of feet announced their noisy presence, dancing in a shaft of bright sunlight and raising scuds of dust each time they hit the floor. They were shod in light leather pumps with flat heels, and the trousers, which ought to have been captured by straps beneath the soles, flapped loose halfway up a pair of thin ankles clothed in dull red stockings; both stockings and legs looked in need of a wash.

These feet were the source of the noise; these feet were attempting bravely but unsuccessfully to mark the irregular passage of the tune; these feet undoubtedly belonged to the teacher's voice which had been spilling out into the street with the power of overcooked cabbage. George Taylor took a further step, and the portions of that gentleman lying between feet and voice came into view. Brown trousers were unpressed and hung like folds of skin about legs which seemed too narrow to be used so energetically. A waistcoat of a similar autumnal hue but striped with a narrow thread of muted red was buttoned tightly over a large belly which seemed intent on moving in many different directions all at the same time. Beneath the waistcoat a shirt which had once been white was topped by an untidy bow of flamboyant blue, and this alone appeared to be keeping the dancer's wing collar in reasonably close proximity to his shirt. Above the bow an unkempt mop of overlong, straggling white hair couldn't hide a thick, corrugated neck; its salmon-pink skin was matched by the neat dome of flesh which formed the larger part of the man's head. The man's jacket was thrown over the back of a crippled old chair; its owner, so intent on playing the violin and dancing at the same time, failed to notice that he and his apparel had been observed by a stranger.

As Taylor reached the top step, elegantly and silently, he came into the view of the Misses Priscilla and Marjorie, sitting patiently in front of an antique piano decorated with candelabra and bearing a sleeping cat. Their glances drew his attention and he immediately doffed his hat to them, gave a brief bow which assured them of his position as a man of quality, and waited.

'So now . . . you can see . . . how you must start and

... then play the piece,' panted the teacher, his feet finally coming to a halt. 'And then, to signal that you have come to a close ... another chord, usually the same as that which ... started the piece. And there we have it. My goodness me, ladies, such value. Music *and* dancing; two lessons for the price of one! But it's nearing finishing time, and I'm sure you would benefit ...' he slowed, becoming aware that his pupils' attention was not entirely on him, '... you would benefit from playing the whole piece through again, copying the points I've mentioned, and then we can ...'

He whirled suddenly. The speed of the manoeuvre took all, himself included, by surprise, he hadn't realised that the floor was quite so well polished. But there was a need for speed. He suspected that his clerk, a young man too clever, too smart, too damn polite for his own good, had been ogling the young ladies; he'd caught him doing that before and threatened him with dismissal if it should happen again. So certain was he that he'd guessed the true nature of the intrusion that his lips were already forming the yell of castigation as he spun around. His lungs were already drawing in the huge volume of air necessary to throw a selection of his choicest insults across the room; his fingers were flexing and stretching, ready to seek the nearest portable object (a book, the cat, a chair perhaps?) to hurl at the miscreant. When he saw that he'd been interrupted by a stranger, and a stranger who appeared to be a gentleman at that, his dervish turn subsided into an ungainly pirouette culminating in a deep, formal bow, during which he took the opportunity to release the air in his lungs with a too audible hiss.

'My dear sir,' he began sibilantly, 'please accept my apologies. Had I known that my clerk had permitted anyone to ascend then I would surely have ceased my instruction.' His eyes, nose, mouth and ears were all too small for his large face, when he spoke they took on a life of their own and circled each other warily. Even when he was silent they twitched in anticipation of their next adventure.

'I saw no clerk, sir,' protested Taylor, 'I merely entered and followed the sound of music. I trust, however, that you will be able to help me. I am seeking the premises of a . . .' he pretended to consult the piece of paper in his hand, '. . . a Mr Playford, who has, so I am told, the reputation of being a dancing master. I saw the nameplate. And it is I who should be seeking forgiveness, I fear that I have interrupted the lesson of these two charming young ladies. Please, do continue.'

The two voices provided an interesting contrast. Both appeared keen to hide their origins, but Taylor's was more successful. Acknowledging the competition lost, the dancing master's tones regressed to the south, to the less fashionable parts of London.

'The young ladies were about to depart,' he announced. 'Their lesson is over for today.' He turned and flapped at the girls, motioning them away.

Taylor noticed, as his eyes became more used to the patches of gloom interspersed with bright sunlight, that the girls were exactly that. He had thought them at first to be in their early twenties but, as he watched them gather together their music and their purses, one putting her violin carefully away in its case while the other folded up a music stand, he realised that they were considerably younger than that. If he found it unusual that such young girls should be left in the presence of a man without a chaperone, then he showed no sign of his opinion. These were, after all, swiftly changing times. No doubt there would be some explanation.

He turned his attention from the girls to the fussing hen of their teacher. The man was clearly incapable of doing his job, whether teaching music or dancing, George Taylor was certain of that. Had he been seeking the services of a dancing master for himself or for a close friend then he would not have ventured this close to the quayside. But this was for Samuel, his brother (of whom he was not fond), a man with no taste, no business sense and little money. He remembered part of his letter. 'I require a dancing master, an *English* dancing master, for a two-week period during June. He must be able to attend at that time. And I implore you, my dear George, he must be cheap.'

The words had stayed with him. 'He must be cheap.' Not 'he must be good' or even 'he must be the best available at the price'. Only 'he must be cheap'. Taylor reached into his pocket and brought out his watch. There were many other things he could be doing instead of wasting time as a messenger boy; he could only pray that this fellow, this unkempt, ragged mongrel of a dance teacher, would be free to carry out his brother's wishes. He stepped to one side as the two girls passed, nodded to them and noticed that one – was it Miss Priscilla or Miss Marjorie? – was particularly good-looking and carried herself well despite being, so far as he could tell, the younger of the two. Was she yet even fifteen? he wondered. She smiled gracefully and graciously at him, while her companion turned down her head and blushed.

'Such very pleasant young ladies,' he said softly as he watched them descend into the gloom of the staircase, 'so polite, and so talented. And I heard you mention their names, Mr Playford. Miss Priscilla and Miss Marjorie?' He waited for the acknowledgement which duly arrived as a brief nod, cloaked in the dancing master's urgent curiosity, his need to know why this gentleman was here.

'I seem to recognise one of them, she could be the daughter of a business acquaintance of mine. The one with the smile, such a happy smile. Miss Marjorie?'

'No, good sir, Miss Marjorie Allen is the more shy of the couple. Miss Priscilla Allen tends to have the more open countenance. But I pray, tell me of your business here. How may I help—'

'Allen? Allen? Surely not Allens the millers? I'm aware that their youngest daughter is considered a charming girl but I did meet her, many years ago, and I feel sure I would have recognised her.'

'No, sir, the Misses Allen are the daughters of Messrs. Allen and Allen, stationers, of Market Street. Now, good sir, if I may be so bold, you wished to see me on some matter to do

with music? Or dancing? Or perhaps both. I can assure you
that my services . . .'

Taylor was not to be distracted. He wandered away from
the dancing master, headed to the window to gaze down into
the street, leaving his companion fluttering like a wounded
bird. Through the open sash he could see the two girls
climbing the hill, and he considered leaving immediately to
pursue them. But no, he did have business here, and he now
knew their address. Merchant stock, the easiest to deal with
for a man of his nature, his quality. He smiled in anticipation
of the chase, and even as he did so the younger sister looked
back, looked up at the window. She could not have seen him;
he wished that she could have.

He turned back into the room to find Playford close behind
him, determined not to let him escape. He backed away,
Playford drew closer, his face earnest, his manner obsequious,
his thirst for information overcoming his cultivated, over-
bearing politeness. As Taylor retreated further, so Playford
followed, one circling the other in a painful gavotte around
the dusty room, their musical accompaniment the dancing
master's plaintive, inquisitive bleating.

'Now, sir, how may I be of assistance? I assure you that
I shall do all I can to assist you in whatever you feel are
your needs in whatever of my fields I can most, uh, that
is, assist you in, if you understand, Mr . . ., that is, I don't
believe you gave your name, but I'm sure that I can, uh, that
I can—'

'That you can assist me?'

'Yes. Quite. Mr . . .?'

Having completed a round of the room George Taylor
was not willing to submit to a second trip. 'I shall explain,
Mr Playwell, but, forgive me for asking, is there somewhere
a little more comfortable where we may talk?'

The dancing master threw up his hands in mock horror,
his face twisted into a mask of distraction. His mouth flew
wide open to show a large tongue, vast gums and few teeth.
'But of course, of course. We may use my office downstairs, I

should have thought. Please follow me. And my name, forgive me for reminding you, is "Playford."'

He led the way down the stairs and opened the door which Taylor had ignored when he came into the building. They entered a small anteroom, nothing more than a wide corridor leading to a room beyond. It had one high, dirty window, below which a young man was seated at a desk, poring over a ledger and whispering a litany of figures as he added a column. He looked around, saw who had entered and scribbled the total on a piece of paper, marking the ledger with a pencil.

'Mr Playford,' he said, nodding his head at his master and rising to his feet. 'Morning, sir,' was tossed gently at the stranger, and even in those few words his birthplace was pinpointed: east of the town, riverside, north bank, Willington Quay, perhaps? He was taller than the other two, though not too thin, and he held his shoulders forward and his knees slightly bent as if afraid that his height might offend. He waited for his instructions.

'Tweddle, refreshments. What may I offer you, good sir? Coffee perhaps, or tea? Or wine, a glass of sherry, port? Some cool lemonade perhaps?'

Taylor pulled out his watch again, examined it carefully. 'I have very little time, so perhaps ... Yes, a glass of good sherry would prove very welcome.'

'And I shall have the same. In my room, Tweddle, jump to it!'

The clerk seemed unsure of himself. He waited until his master had ushered the stranger past then hissed urgently, 'Mr Playford, sir, we haven't any sherry. Nor port, nor wine. We've only tea, and that's mouldering, I believe.'

'Then go and get some, Tweddle, there is a public house next door, another within staggering distance. A young man, even one with as few mental resources as you, ought to be able to procure two glasses of sherry. Use your initiative lad!'

'Yes, sir. But they won't give credit any more, last time the landlord threatened me with a beating. I did tell you.'

The clerk looked down on his master's pate. His face held a wry smile which seemed to combine sympathy with humour and concern but without the obsequiousness that characterised the older man's bearing. He was in his twenties; no one who met him would be able to make a better estimate. If he was described as handsome, particularly when he smiled, then it would be a lady speaking; and his friends (or those he called friends – the other young men he drank and caroused with) would have acknowledged that the ladies found him attractive and would have admitted that they enjoyed his company because of this. His hair was long and dark and well groomed, his eyes were deep brown, and he wore his patience like a badge of office. That his employer treated him poorly and castigated him freely and frequently he accepted as part of his lot, certain that it wasn't due to some shortcoming on his part. The work he did was always carried out neatly and accurately. He always behaved politely, even to those who were rude to him. And so he waited for his master's due reaction, smiling confidently, and was justly rewarded.

The dancing teacher's eyebrows lowered so that his forehead took up the entire top half of his face. His mouth grew smaller as he sucked and pinched at his lips. 'There's no money in the place?' he asked.

'Your son-in-law, Mr Patterson, that is,' he said, as if there was some choice, 'he emptied the pot earlier this morning, to the last farthing. He said he needed some new dancing shoes.'

'The scoundrel! He had a pair only last month and . . .' he realised he had raised his voice, that his words might be overheard, and lowered his voice to a whisper '. . . I warned him of our financial position! And now I have a gentleman to see me and no means of entertaining him. He's a spendthrift, that young man, a spendthrift and a profligate and . . . and a dummy. That's what he is – a dummy. What my daughter saw in him, I've no idea. Even you have more brains than him!'

The clerk seemed to take neither pride nor offence at this. He lowered his head, as if thinking, then nodded to himself.

'I know what to do,' he said. 'If you go and have your meeting with your gentleman, I'll find you some sherry.'

'You will?'

'Have I ever let you down before, Mr Playford?'

The question was answered with a face of wrinkled suspicion.

'You'd better hurry, Mr Playford, I don't think your gentleman has too much time to spare.'

'Yes. Quite. And you'll see to—'

'I'll be in there before you can say . . .' He paused, then smiled broadly as the dancing master hurried into the inner chamber and closed the door firmly behind him. 'Before you can say, "Rob Tweddle's the best clerk a man could hope to employ",' he added to no one but himself.

He was as good as his word. The sherry was good, the glasses were clean, and both had been handed over without the need for cash to be offered in exchange. True, there'd been a little bartering. The landlord wasn't an easy man to bargain with, but the clerk had seen the way he'd looked at Playford's daughter when she rolled up the street (though only when his thin, bony wife was servicing one of her customers in the rooms above), and he knew that the landlord sang a great deal while he was at his work. What greater attraction could there be than a singing lesson from young Mrs Patterson? And if that was worth more than a single bottle of sherry, well, who would begrudge an enterprising clerk the bottle of claret which was even now hidden in his cloak? There would be satisfaction all round.

He entered the room bearing a tray containing the bottle and the glasses and poured from one to the others. He offered the tray to each of the two men, slowly and graciously, taking his time, listening carefully to what proved to be his master's monologue.

'So, Mr Taylor, you've been asked by your brother, who lives in – no, don't tell me, it's some forty miles away, you said, to the northwest. Bellingford? Yes, Bellingford, I have a good memory for names, although I must confess that I don't know the place. But I digress. Your brother has asked you to procure the services of a dancing master for two weeks prior to his daughter's wedding in order that she and her fiancé and their respective families, and the local gentry, may learn certain dances for the wedding celebrations? Now then, if I understand correctly, a dancing teacher visits the area each summer, but he travels down from Scotland, yes? And your niece, spending some time in Edinburgh recently, was introduced there to *English* dancing, and wishes to learn specifically from an English dancing master. An entirely reasonable request, I assure you, the Caledonian teachers are a little behind the times when it comes to knowledge of what is and is not *en vogue* each season, whereas I have regular correspondence from colleagues in London who tell me of all the fashions in society dancing, and I can assure you that . . .' He paused, for breath and because he'd forgotten how he'd started the sentence, and made do with gathering the amorphous mass of his thoughts together. 'I feel sure that I can help you, and I know that you will enjoy the celebrations as much as your brother and his family—'

'Mr Playford?' The interruption came from the clerk, who had been on the point of leaving the room.

'Yes, Tweddle?'

'Would you like me to fetch you your engagements book? So that I can note down details of any obligations you may wish to undertake?'

'Of course,' the dancing master said harshly, 'I was just about to ask you to do that. I would have expected you to anticipate the need more swiftly than you did.' He turned back to his customer, his client. 'Now then, Mr Taylor, would you like another glass of sherry? And was I correct in my summary of your, or should I say your brother's, requirements?'

'Yes,' came the weary reply, 'you seem to have made an excellent job of turning a penny broadside into a four-act drama. Nonetheless, you have the facts at hand, save for my presence at the . . .' he paused and smiled, '. . . the event. A previous business engagement. I simply won't be able to cancel it. But you have my brother's letter, there is really little else to discuss. Your fee, forty guineas plus expenses in travelling, plus your board and lodgings for the fortnight in my brother's own house, would, I think, be acceptable. I take it that you can do the job within the given period of time?'

Playford's voice became businesslike. 'Yes, I'm sure that, given such a fee, given a deposit of twenty-five percent, the balance payable, in cash, on departing your brother's house, given teaching time of three two-hour sessions each day in the morning, afternoon and evening, such sessions to include instructing musicians and, where necessary, writing out fair copies of music, given all of this I am sure that I can accommodate your brother's requirements.'

'Good. In that case I shall arrange a draft for the deposit and—'

'Excuse me, Mr Playford.' It was the clerk returning to the room, carrying a red-bound book, smaller than the ledger, though with entries in the same copperplate hand. 'Your diary shows that you have engagements throughout the period from early June to late July. Preparations for the Lord Mayor's ball occupy one of those weeks, and you have teaching commitments in both music and dancing, and you've agreed to play at several evening dances.'

The dancing master said nothing, but his face showed disbelief. He'd known, of course, that he would be busy during the early summer. It was the anticipation of this which allowed him to defray his family's considerable living expenses during the lean spring months. He was also aware that these commitments might conflict with this potential journey to the wilds of Northumberland, but he'd hoped, optimistically but unrealistically, that they would have fallen either side of the new work. It was encouraging, of course, to know that his services were in demand, but both he and the clerk knew that the engagements were to be carried out cheaply, or as favours, or as payment for debts already incurred.

'Well, I'm sorry that my time has been wasted,' said Taylor, rising to his feet and draining his glass. 'I too have my obligations, however, and tiresome as it is I must carry out this duty for my dear brother. I shall therefore seek out another dancing master. Good day, sir.'

His speedy march across the room was halted by the clerk still standing in the doorway, unwilling, it seemed, to let him pass. He took a deep breath and scowled; he was not used to behaviour such as this from the employees of the lower classes and was about to express his discontent with both servant and master when the clerk spoke.

'What about Mr David, sir? Could he not help?'

'And who, may I ask, is this David person? And exactly how would he be able to help? I warn you, Mr Playbill, I am not a patient man and I find the way in which you and your hireling behave to be most unacceptable. Come on, man, speak up!'

'David?' Playford stuttered, 'David? David is my son-in-law, that's who he is. Married no more than three months, to my daughter, that is, as he would be to make him my son-in-law, of course. He used to be a pupil of mine, dancing and music both. He met my daughter through that, and she was impressed with his ability, but—'

'What Mr Playford is trying to say, Mr Taylor, sir, and I hope you'll accept my apologies for butting in like this, is that his son-in-law, Mr David Patterson, is also a teacher of music and dancing. I'm sure that Mr Playford can vouch for his knowledge of the subjects, and it occurred to me that he might be able to help your brother out.'

Taylor seemed unimpressed. He spoke quickly, moving around the clerk as he did so. 'Thank you for your concern, Mr Twaddle, I believe that is your name, but I've had quite enough of your master and his dithering, and you and your interruptions, and I believe that I shall attempt to secure the services of another teacher, even if I do have to pay a little extra on my brother's behalf. I feel sure that it will be money well spent. Now if I may pass? Good day to you Mr Playfair.'

'Wait!' Playford's voice rang out high and piping.

'My mind is quite made up.'

'But Mr Taylor, my clerk is speaking the truth, I assure you. My son-in-law is a competent enough teacher. He could carry out the task, if given the opportunity.'

'No, Mr Playford. And now I must be going.'

'It will do you little good, Mr Taylor.' It was the clerk again.

'I beg your pardon? I am not used to being addressed in such a manner by a mere clerk, and nothing you can say will persuade me to reconsider. Now out of my way!'

'I'm sorry, Mr Taylor, I can't let you pass.'

The characters froze like players at the end of a melodrama, all that was needed was the ripple of applause from a hidden audience. If George Taylor was shocked by the impropriety of the situation, then James Playford was aghast. The eyebrows which earlier had taken up residence near the bridge of his ample nose became suddenly animated, twitching their way up through the furrows of his forehead in an attempt to hide in his meagre scalp. What small chance there might have been of saving this commission was now surely lost, and word of this outrage would spread quickly. This Taylor looked like a man who enjoyed his revenge.

'Oh, Mr Taylor, I'm so sorry, my clerk had no right to speak ... He was completely ... I don't know what to say, I can't ...' He stumbled to a halt, then found the necessary words. 'Tweddle, your employment has ceased! Leave immediately!'

'I'm sorry, Mr Playford, I can't do that.'

Once again the simple words brought silence, but this time it was brief as the clerk continued, aware of his misdemeanour and eager to explain himself before further retribution struck.

'My apologies to both of you gentlemen for speaking out so rudely, but I feared that unless I did so you would both suffer. Mr Taylor, sir, I meant no harm, but you obviously aren't aware there'll be no other dancing masters free in the city at the time you need, the engagements in my master's diary will be matched by those in other teachers' diaries, the season of balls and dances is almost upon us. And Mr Playford, I'd no wish to behave so insolently to a gentleman, particularly one you value so highly, but I could think of no means of persuading him to stay other than speaking out as I did. Please forgive me, gentlemen. I'll leave now and wait outside at my desk, and I trust you'll both be able to reconsider your thoughts and feelings on the matters which have just passed. If you, Mr Taylor, still wish to attempt to secure the services of another dancing master then I'll say nothing else to stop you. And if you, Mr Playford, still wish me to relinquish my position, then I'll do so immediately. I await your decisions.'

He bowed sharply and left the room, closed the door behind him, and waited until the dull murmur of reluctant conversation had recommenced. He then moved quickly to his desk and pulled open the bottom drawer. From his pocket he took a key, from the drawer he took a wooden pencil case held shut with a metal clasp and small padlock, and he married the two. He fished inside and took out a handkerchief, opened it quickly and inspected the contents. They were coins, small change in copper as well as thicker golden coins. He rewrapped them carefully. This was his insurance. He'd been with Playford only a year, but in that time he'd come to realise how easy it was to deceive him. The clerk was responsible for all correspondence and for keeping all accounts, detailing income and expenditure, and he was, in theory, entrusted with all money coming into the business. But he'd soon found that theory and practice were ill at ease in each other's company. Sometimes customers paid James Playford direct, and he neglected or forgot to pass money over to his clerk. Often the money that was received (and kept in a small safe) was taken (from the small safe; the key was hidden in the second drawer of James Playford's desk) by Playford himself, his daughter, or his son-in-law. Despite Rob Tweddle informing his employer of the inadequacies of the system, no attempt was made to improve matters, and

one day, when searching for some papers, he found, lying at
the back of his desk drawer, two sovereigns. He didn't know
why they were there and, since his master was teaching at the
time, he took the safe key from the desk and put the money
away. It took him an hour to come to the conclusion that, if
the money hadn't been missed in the first place, then there
was no reason to assume that it would be missed now. He
took the money back and placed it carefully in his own pencil
case. Caution made him keep the coins in his desk; while
they were still there he couldn't be accused of stealing. But
his wages were low, and there were times when he felt he
was the only one who really cared that the business should
succeed. Hadn't he once, in Mr Playford's absence (when
David Patterson was meant to be taking a class but had spent
the afternoon bedding a middle-aged soprano) taught a mixed
group of sixteen children how to dance the Eightsome Reel
and the Cumberland Square Eight? And whose sweet words
had often persuaded parents to send their children to learn
to dance, and husbands to send their wives to learn to play
the piano? It required little argument for him to persuade
himself that the money was his, that he'd earned it, and it
grew in quantity as he found the opportunity to divert a little
more each week to its secret hiding place. One day, he told
himself, when the need arose, he would take it all away. And
as he put the handkerchief back in the case, and the case in
the drawer, he wondered whether the need had already crept
into his company.

From the inner office the voices continued to talk, but
their rumble was indecipherable. Minutes passed, however,
without any sign of Taylor leaving abruptly. Rob returned to
his work, checking columns of figures, making the cash and
the ledgers agree with one another. He felt that there was
an elegance in his book work which was easily comparable
with that of dancing, and since coming to work at the school
he'd spent what time he could watching and listening to his
master in an attempt to learn the dances (though Playford, on
discovering him, had put his curiosity down to lechery) and

also to find out why people would pay Playford for teaching something which, so far as Rob was concerned, was a natural ability. Yes, he could see that movements and steps had to be taught and learned, but he felt that the world was divided into those who were dancers and those who weren't. James Playford was, or had been, a dancer. So, despite his lack of both practice and experience, was Rob himself; he knew that. And David Patterson? He was not, never could be, a proper dancer. He knew the steps, he could even demonstrate them, but he danced with his head, not his heart. And his partner in dancing and in life, Emily Patterson, had inherited none of her father's grace of movement. She was nothing more than a pretty face, a jiggling body (it was hardly surprising she had difficulty in the more energetic dances) and a voice which the hard of hearing might consider almost operatic. And if there was a touch of jealousy in any of these emotions, because Rob had once considered that Emily Playford (as she had been when he first came to work for her father) might smile a little more favourably on him, then that jealousy was partly assuaged by the dream in which she came to him, diaphanous as night, and confessed her love for him, and gave herself to him. The balance of his jealousy was as easily dispersed by his other dream, the one in which he became the dancing master and David Patterson was the hopeless, continuously failing pupil. Best of all was when both dreams coincided.

His reverie was interrupted by the door opening, but he kept his head immersed in the ledger and waited to be summoned.

'Tweddle.' It was Playford's voice, but even in that single word he could tell that the menace had not disappeared. He turned round, a mask of submissiveness on his face. 'Yes sir?'

'Come into my room.'

He felt like a schoolboy. His hands itched again with the pain of the leather tawse, and he relived the humiliation of repeated ridicule on account of his name, or his lack of a father, or his patched clothes. He'd always feared the summons of authority, even when he was innocent of any wrongdoing. Authority had neither logic nor reason; authority had only power – the power to hurt. He entered the room.

'Mr Taylor and I,' announced Playford regally, 'have had the opportunity to discuss further the matter of his brother's request for a dancing teacher. We have decided that my partner and son-in-law, Mr Patterson, will certainly be capable of carrying out the duties specified and that he will attend Mr Taylor's brother's home at . . .' he paused. 'Forgive me, dear sir, the name of the place again?'

'Bellingford.'

'Yes. He will attend at a mutually convenient date for a period of two weeks.' He handed his clerk a piece of paper. 'Here is the letter giving details of both address and requirements. You will write a response confirming the dates for Mr Patterson's attendance and inform me of the reply. Do you understand?'

'Yes, Mr Playford.' He made to leave.

'And Tweddle.'

'Yes Mr Playford?'

'Your behaviour earlier was inexcusable. You were rude and discourteous to the point of insolence, whatever the reason, no matter how extenuating the circumstances. I'm afraid that I must give you one week's notice of termination of your employment.'

The clerk's face clouded with disbelief.

'And I must insist that you apologise to Mr Taylor in person and confirm that apology in writing. I consider in doing this that I am acting with justification, and many employers would feel that, in allowing you to work an extra week, I am showing myself to be kind in the extreme. Do you accept this action? Or do you perhaps wish to leave immediately?'

The clerk found his voice. 'No, sir. I must agree with all you've said. And I agree to write the most abject of apologies to Mr Taylor in the hope that my apology, and the fact that I must lose my job, will provide a measure of recompense for the hurt I have caused him.' He sank to his knees in front of George Taylor and lowered his head further. Only the mass of dark hair on the top of his head could be seen. His body was shaking with what the two onlookers took to be remorse.

'Very well,' said Playford. 'Very well, Tweddle, that will do. Go outside, please, I detest seeing a man cry. Mr Taylor and I will have another sherry—'

'No,' said Taylor, 'I must decline. I have business elsewhere; pressing business. An order for some stationery which simply must be placed today. I shall trust you to write to my brother to confirm that arrangements have been made. Goodbye.'

Playford sprang to his feet. 'But Mr Taylor, you mentioned, that is, we negotiated a deposit. In good faith of your brother agreeing to our arrangements. Ten guineas was the agreed sum.'

'Ah, Mr Playhouse, you have a good memory. Not, alas, as good as mine. The agreed sum was twenty-five percent of the total, and the total we negotiated, or renegotiated, I might say, was thirty guineas. Your deposit is therefore, let me see, eight pounds and sixpence precisely. Less my commission, to be deducted in full from the deposit. The balance is, according to my calculations, four pounds seventeen shillings and sixpence. Here is five pounds. You may give me the difference at some convenient time.' He placed a note on the table, turned with a flourish, and left.

The dancing master looked at the money, looked guiltily at his clerk, then stuffed the note directly into his pocket. He stared at the floor, and when he spoke his words were a mumble. 'Tweddle, you should not have spoken to him like that. Mr Taylor is a powerful man. He is a rich man. Quite apart from gaining me the position with his brother he may bring further business my way. I could not afford to offend him.'

'Yes, Mr Playford, I can understand that.' The clerk's voice held no emotion.

'He's taken a dislike to you. He was insistent that I terminate your employment. He warned me not to have pity on you. He said that he would know if I kept you on.' The dancing master seemed desperate to imply that the dismissal was nothing to do with him. 'He said that if I did keep you on, or even took you back after a short while, then he would cancel his brother's work and everything else as well. And I need the money, you especially should know that. I need the money.'

'You do, Mr Playford, you certainly do.'

'I had no choice. My hands were tied.'

'Tied as tight as a noose round a murderer's neck, Mr Playford.'

The dancing master was about to speak but was halted by the comparison. His mouth opened and closed like that of a fish, he even seemed to be making swimming motions with his hands.

'But what could I do?'

'You did it, Mr Playford. You dismissed me, giving me one week's notice, and I suppose I should expect no better in the circumstances. But *you* know what I did, the way I spoke, I did it for your good, and your family's good.'

'But what will you do? Where will you seek work?'

'I'm not without ambition, Mr Playford, nor experience, nor contacts. I'll find a suitable position, I've no doubt of that.'

The dancing master seemed surprised, as if he'd expected a plea for mercy, for the decision to be reversed, at the very least for a stay of execution beyond the allotted week.

'Oh,' he said, 'I see. In that case . . .' He turned away, then turned back. 'I don't suppose . . .?'

'Yes?'

'I don't suppose,' Playford said quickly, as if the words caused him pain, 'I don't suppose you know of someone who might be able to take up your old duties?'

Rob smiled. The money in his pencil case was already on its way to his pocket and he had plans to make. 'I might be able to find someone suitable, Mr Playford. I might just be able to find someone who would suit you and your business right down to the ground.' It was only with a great effort that he was able to keep a smile from his face.

The Second Bar of the Musick

Monday, 14 June 1830

In which we learn that Mr Rob Tweddle is a thief and a fraud who intends ridiculing those who have crossed him and seducing the innocent niece of Mr George Taylor.

'Where the hell has he got to? Why *I* had to come and fetch him I don't know, after all, why does the old man keep servants? But if there's a job to be done, anything that needs the slightest touch of common sense, well, just call for Danny Taylor. He's the boy. He'll sort it out for you.'

The source of this bad humour was no boy. Daniel Taylor had said farewell to childhood many years before and had exceeded his father's height and girth for some ten years, since he had just turned fifteen. He was stronger than any boy, there was no doubting that, but he remained childishly fond of displaying that strength. Other young men of his age feared him and his bad temper but didn't respect him; they were pleasant to him from necessity rather than volition.

He was talking to his dog, black and lithe and panting in the breeze. Both of them appeared to be searching for someone as their cart passed the abbey doors and rattled through the streets of the busy market town. Ahead of them a shepherd was driving his small flock, no more than a dozen beasts, and the dog tensed at their sight and smell. The dog's master saw this, said softly, 'Down, lass.' The dog subsided, its frustration expressed in the stare it threw at the sheep as the cart passed them by.

They were travelling fast, faster than any of the other road users, and their passage drew glances of disapproval. Heads were shaken. One man spat on the ground, another had to leap to one side to avoid being knocked over and then stood in the middle of the road, shaking his fist and cursing. Danny Taylor looked back, he knew the man; he would seek him out next time he was in Hexham and show him why he should never cross Danny Taylor. He laughed in anticipation, but the laughter was short-lived. Ahead of him, unexpectedly, he saw the Newcastle to Carlisle coach. The road was narrowing, and what little space there was had been reduced by the presence of stalls selling vegetables and pies and pastries, chickens and fresh fish, cheeses and fruit and flowers. He knew that the coach wouldn't give way. The four bays pulling it danced as they headed towards him, the coach was wider and taller and stronger than his dogcart, and the coachman was urging his steeds onward with a flick of his whip. Danny Taylor pulled hard on the brake, hauled on the reins until he thought that the bit would tear his pony's mouth in two and still was certain there would be a collision. His pony reared in its traces then saw a gap between two stalls and forced itself in there. The dogcart followed part of the way but spun as it did so, the pony reared again, and carrots and potatoes and onions were hurled into the road beneath the wheels of the passing coach. Danny Taylor was thrown forward against the pony, then slid down its rump and onto the dusty ground. He lay blinking beneath the vegetables and abuse of the stallholder. Sympathy for his plight, concern for the possibility of his injury, came from only one direction; the dog that had sat beside him was now capering around his body, darting its head at him, licking his face with its wide, wet pink tongue.

'I've never seen the like,' one woman exclaimed, 'he came down that road as if the de'il himself was after him!'

'Don't you know who he is?' muttered a second woman, older than the first, clad in what looked like sacking but was merely very dirty linen. She was scrabbling in the dirt to pick up some carrots without the stallholder seeing. 'It's young Taylor, him from Bellingford. They say the de'il's in him, let alone after him!'

'Hey you!' screamed the stallholder. Half of his produce had been ruined and the rest was being spirited away even as he watched. He ran at the old woman, who showed a nimbleness at odds with her age. She cackled as she ran away and pointed behind him to where a young boy was thrusting onions into an old sack. The stallholder turned again but the boy was already gone. 'Someone,' he said slowly, 'is goin' to pay for this!'

His attention was turned to the cause of the injury, the still form of Danny Taylor. The stallholder was no small man himself, and he was filled with indignation made strong by his anger. As he rolled towards the wreckage of his produce he saw a beam of wood before him, it had once been the leg of the rough table that had borne his vegetables, his own vegetables, sweet and early season and worth . . . But no, the value was unimportant now, it was honour that was at stake, and pride, and a need for vengeance. He picked up the stave, and the crowd which was beginning to form drew a single breath. Danny Taylor was shaking his head and rubbing his eyes and groaning, and the dog was barking at his feet as if trying to draw his attention to the danger approaching. The stallholder drew closer, rapping the length of timber against the palm of his hand.

'Go on, George, let 'im 'ave it!' came a yell of encouragement.

'He'll need a damn sight bigger stick than that to beat any sense into Danny Taylor's head,' said another.

'Better hit him when he's down, George,' shouted a third, 'if he gets up you won't have a chance!'

The stallholder stopped and looked around him. He'd never
met Danny Taylor but he'd heard about him, and he didn't
like the sound of those tales. But the horseshoe of jeers
and yells was pushing him on, he knew that he couldn't
back down now. He steeled himself and stepped forward,
it wouldn't be the first time he'd hit a man when he was
down. He'd do it quickly, while he was still dazed, if he
hit him hard enough he might not be able to remember
who'd done the deed. And Taylor, old man Taylor, he
had money, his son would have money, he'd be able to
take some of it to cover his expenses. Come to think of it,
the attack was justified, everyone would agree with him, no
one liked young Taylor. Reassured, he raised the stick high,
was about to bring it down hard and sharp when a dart of
black hair and strong white teeth hurled itself at his arm. It
missed, but he pulled back and succeeded only in rapping
himself on the ankle with the beam. He cursed and whirled
around, but the dog was quicker. It nipped behind him and
harried his ankles, when he flapped at it with his stick it easily
avoided the clumsy thrust and arrowed in to bite at his hand.
It drew blood.

'Bastard dog!' screamed the stallholder and kicked at it.
The dog had been watching its attacker's hands and the kick
came as a surprise, caught it on the flank, lifted it, turned its
snarl into a whimper.

'Here, George,' yelled a voice, and a knife was thrown to
the ground in front of him. The stallholder bent to pick it up,
eyes fixed on the wary animal now circling him. He smiled
as he felt the polished handle, hefted the knife to feel the
balance of its blade, and moved after the dog. There was no
easy escape for the animal; a forest of hostile legs surrounded
it. If it crept too close, feet lunged out to kick it closer to its
adversary. Its attention was on the knife in the stallholder's
hand, it could see the danger which lay there. So intent was
its gaze that it could do nothing to avoid the net thrown
suddenly from the crowd. It was a coarse net, not one used
for fishing, but for carrying, and it wound itself around the

dog's body, tangled its legs as it twisted in an attempt to escape, turned it helpless onto its side.

'I'll teach you, hound, I'll gut you!' yelled the stallholder. They were the last words he would speak for some time. So intent was he on the animal he failed to notice the dog's owner, and yells of warning from friends in the mob were drowned by others who sympathised with the beast. Danny Taylor moved easily for a large man, he moved swiftly, despite having just regained his senses. It required only one blow to the back of the neck to knock his opponent to the ground, but that blow was followed by another, and then a kick, and then another, and another, to the stallholder's back and legs and head. He paused only once, and that was to growl a warning at some of those watching who might, he suspected, have tried to hold him back. There was no doubt that he would have killed the man. Blood was oozing from his nose and mouth and ears, his arm was bent at an unnatural angle and he'd ceased groaning. His only movement was in the aftermath of each kick, an involuntary spasm that seemed to encourage his attacker further. The screams and yells of the crowd became an angry muttering, then a muted whisper, then complete silence. The world still passed by beyond. There were sounds of singing and the calls of street traders; sheep bleated and cattle lowed, carts rumbled along the rutted street. But these noises were alien, they seemed unable to overcome the soft slap and thud of leather on flesh and bone. It took a voice to do that, a quiet voice, but a voice of authority. The voice of a woman.

'Mr Taylor! Daniel Taylor, I think you'd better stop that now. I think you'd better stop before you kill him.'

And Danny Taylor did stop. He stopped because he recognised the voice, and he looked up for confirmation that his memory was correct. The woman, no more than eighteen years old but certainly a woman, despite the slightness of her stature, had been standing outside the circle of spectators when she spoke. She had obviously observed the one-sided fight from a flight of stone stairs descending from a seamstress's rooms bordering the marketplace. Her lack of height was more than balanced by her self-confidence. As she moved forward the crowd stepped to one side to let her pass. Women curtseyed, men doffed their hats or, if they had none due to poverty or forgetfulness or the good weather, touched their foreheads in deference. The young woman ignored this. Her eyes were fixed on Danny Taylor. She bent to untangle the whining, twisting dog from its net (it calmed at her approach, lay still as she unwound the coarse threads from its legs), and spoke clearly as she carried out her task.

'My father is due to meet me here. I would suggest that before he arrives some of you take this man away to the doctor's house, he seems in need of assistance.' Her voice held none of the local burr. If she was from Hexham then all trace of accent had been removed by either education or isolation; but her words needed no repetition. The stallholder was lifted quickly onto a swiftly procured cart and trundled away by his friends. 'And have the rest of you no work to do? There is nothing more to see.'

The crowd dispersed slowly with many backward glances, leaving only the woman and Danny Taylor. She finished untangling the dog which leapt to its feet and licked her hand gratefully then circled its owner and lay down, panting, watching his eyes. They were cast down, as if he was searching the ground for a lost coin.

'What happened, Mr Taylor?' the woman said. She was close to him now. The difference in their size made her confidence and his subservience faintly ridiculous.

'He ... That is, I was coming into town, I was to meet the coach, from Newcastle, and he ... I upset his cart. It was an accident!'

'Were you driving fast? I hear that you do drive fast. My father has told me so.'

At the mention of the woman's father Danny glanced anxiously around, but his gaze soon returned to his feet.

'I was in a hurry, Miss Stephenson. I'd to meet the coach, but I was driving no faster than I ought, I swear it!'

'Then I shall believe you, just as you always believe me.' Her voice held what might have been a trace of mockery. 'You do believe everything I tell you, Mr Taylor, don't you?'

'Why, Miss Charlotte, of course I do!' He lifted his eyes to stare at her, shocked that she should consider the possibility of him thinking that she might tell him a lie.

'Mr Taylor!' she protested. 'You may address me as Charlotte in private company, in the surroundings of our own homes, just as I may call you Daniel, or even Danny. But this is not private.'

'I'm sorry,' came the sullen reply.

'I should think so too,' continued the woman. 'What would people say if they were to hear such familiarity? They might feel that there was some degree of attachment between us, possibly even of an emotional nature. You know how parochial tongues wag in this place.' She wrinkled her nose distastefully to emphasise the point and did it, Danny Taylor conceded, most attractively. She went on. 'And a girl must think of her reputation.'

'I said I was sorry, Miss Stephenson.'

'Then I forgive you.'

'Thank you, Miss Stephenson.'

'You're welcome. By the by, is that your pony over there, eating all that poor stallholder's vegetables? I think you ought to bring him under control. I shall wait here, and then you may tell me the rest of your story.'

She hurried him away with a flick of her wrist and watched as he checked both horse and dogcart for damage. He in turn kept looking across at her as she waited, unaware that his eyes bore the same expression of devotion as that worn by his faithful, fawning dog. He'd known her for some years. She was a friend of Annie, his younger sister, and he'd considered her an obnoxious child, alternately chiding him, then sulking when he refused to do as she asked. Then she'd gone away, to stay with relatives in London, and in those brief six months had grown into a woman. And now she could do no wrong.

She wasn't beautiful in the sense that Annie was beautiful, or even that his mother was beautiful. *They* had a classical grace, a delicate poise, a balance of features and movement which was, to him, perfection and which made him consider himself in comparison to be boorish and clumsy and ugly. His other sister, his elder sister, Frances, was somewhere between him and Annie in everything. She was plain and stolid; she wasn't good at anything in particular, but neither did she have any failings. But Charlotte Stephenson, she was different to them all. She was fiery and opinonated to the point of rudeness. Her dark hair and heavy eyebrows topped a heart-shaped face, and she had a natural pout which lifted as soon as she smiled. She was unafraid of argument. She flirted and yet, so far as he knew, was being courted by no man. She knew of his affection for her; he swore that to be true although he'd never dared breathe a word of it, not even to Annie. He was, in truth, an uncommunicative man and didn't recognise that what he termed affection would be called in others love. Even had he known it to be so he would have been unable to declare it, certain that he would be spurned by one he considered so much his better. As he led horse and dog to her side he was pleased merely to be in her company.

'Would you care to ride, Miss Stephenson?' he offered. She shook her head firmly.

'No thank you, Mr Taylor. But I am due to head home from the coach house, and the tale you were telling before mentioned that you too were heading in that direction, so I would welcome your company. And you may also, if you wish and if there is time,' she paused for breath, and the pause almost became a sigh, 'tell me how the arrangements are progressing for Annie's wedding.'

They strolled leisurely round the perimeter of the market-place and past the old gaol house, Danny dictating the slow and measured pace. The distance to the coach house wasn't great and he wished to extend as much as possible the time spent with his companion.

'So you collided with that poor man's stall,' she asked innocently, 'despite not travelling at an excessive speed? No doubt it was extended into the roadway too far. You couldn't have avoided it. You were probably doing us all a favour by demolishing it in the way you did.'

'Pardon?' He seemed puzzled, suspecting sarcasm but certain that she wouldn't stoop to using it against him.

'The stall. It was blocking the road, surely, for you to hit it with such force. And no doubt it was a ramshackle affair. It probably would have fallen down anyway from the weight of vegetables stored on it. You merely hastened its demise.'

'Yes,' he reassured himself. 'Yes, that's it. It was in the way, and it wasn't strong anyway. He deserved it, it was dangerous, could have injured someone.'

'But why then, Mr Taylor, was the stallholder attacking your dog with such intent to kill? Had your dog attacked him? Bitten him? If so, why?'

'I'm sure I don't know.'

'No, I'm sure you don't, Mr Taylor. Your dog is so gentle. What is he called?'

'She, Miss Stephenson. She's called Bess.'

The dog, riding once more in the cart, looked across at the mention of her name, ready once again to leap to the aid of her master.

'Bess. She is gentle, though, isn't she?'

'Yes, of course.'

'She wouldn't harm anyone?'

'No. Unless . . .'

'Unless?'

'Unless someone attacked me. Or Annie, I've trained her that way. She'd defend us with her life.'

'So if she attacked the stallholder, then it could only have been because the stallholder attacked you. While you were unconscious. That would explain the matter, would it not?'

'Well, yes, but I can't be certain. I was . . .'

'You were unconscious. After falling from your dogcart, which was, as you've already told me, travelling very slowly.'

Daniel Taylor nodded, unsure where this was leading.

'But despite your travelling slowly, you were unable to control your horse and cart, and you were rendered unconscious when you were thrown from the cart. Is it not possible that you were travelling a little faster than you might care to admit?'

'No!'

'And could it be that the stallholder was under the impression that the fault lay entirely with you, that his stall was soundly built and correctly placed, and that he was advancing upon you to exact revenge, rightly or wrongly, when your dog sprang to the defence?'

'No, I swear it!'

'Be calm, Mr Taylor, this is not a court and I am neither judge nor jury. I am, however, the daughter of a justice of the peace who takes a great interest in the wellbeing of his townsfolk. I have no need to point out that my father is also the mayor. And should he hear of this afternoon's accident, or quarrel, altercation, call it what you will, then I am certain that the questions he and his constable will ask of those present will be far less gentle than my delicate queries. Do you understand?'

The couple had stopped walking. Harold Stephenson's position in the town was indeed powerful, Danny Taylor needed no reminding of that fact. He was businessman – the owner of several hat and glove factories – and banker, a philanthropist but a stern master, and when he frowned upon someone, that individual would do well to move from the shadow of his gaze. More than once Daniel Taylor had had the wrath of the mayor directed at him and was lucky that his father had been able to plead friendship on his own part and youthful, alcohol-induced high spirits on behalf of his son. And even on those occasions reparation had been necessary.

'You don't think that your father might be persuaded that the blame was mine?'

'I was no witness,' came the reply, 'but the stallholder

probably had friends in the crowd. Friends who might speak against you.'

'What can I do then? Last time I . . . That is, I've appeared before your father previously, informally, but he told me that—'

'I'm aware of what my father has said in the past.'

Daniel Taylor turned. The gaol loomed behind them, foursquare, bleak despite the blue skies above it and the house martins darting from beneath its eaves.

'Miss Charlotte, what should I do?' he asked pitifully.

She smiled at him, suddenly ready to forgive the slip in his manners, prepared even to reply in kind.

'Daniel, the stallholder is at the doctor's house, and I suspect that you ceased the beating before any lasting harm was done. But I fear he may have a broken arm and will be bruised and unable to work for some time, and the doctor will require paying for his labour. Then there is the matter of the stall itself, and the produce. I feel that if you were prepared to acknowledge that you played some part in the incident and demonstrated your remorse by helping the stallholder over what may be a hard time, then public reaction would be favourable. And *I* can ensure that my father's private reaction will be favourable. Perhaps a sum of, let me see, five pounds might be—'

'Five pounds? Five pounds? I'd no sooner pay five pounds to that rascal—'

'Then I can see little point in continuing our conversation. Goodbye, Mr Taylor.'

Charlotte Stephenson turned on her heels and marched away with a speed surprising in one cocooned in such an encumbrance of a dress. The lace and tucks of her hem were held high to show the silk boots beneath, tiny heels clicking as she hurried away. Daniel Taylor ran after her.

'Charlotte, I . . . Dammit! Miss Stephenson, wait! Please, wait!'

She stopped abruptly but did not turn round. He caught up with her.

'Miss Stephenson, do you not consider that three pounds . . .'

She set off walking again.

'Very well then, Miss Stephenson, your stallholder shall have his precious five pounds, damn his eyes!'

She turned and smiled sweetly.

'I shall be driving past the doctor's house, Mr Taylor. If you give the money to me I shall ensure that it reaches the injured man.'

'But—'

'You do have sufficient money, Mr Taylor?'

'Why, yes, but—'

'Oh good. I assure you, it will be in safe hands.'

Daniel Taylor reached into the pocket of his jacket and drew out a wallet, extracted from it a large piece of paper. He handed it over.

'Drawn on my father's bank, I see. I need have no fears as to the note's veracity.' She folded it up and placed it neatly in her purse. 'Now then, Mr Taylor, you never did explain why it was that you were in such leisurely haste to meet the express.'

'I didn't?'

'You did not. And . . . Ah, alas, it must wait until another day, I fear. There is my mother and her coach. Look, she's waving at us. Do wave back, Mr Taylor.'

He did as he was told, begrudgingly.

'And your father, Miss Stephenson, is he not here also? You said earlier—'

'My father? He is in Newcastle for the week, Mr Taylor.'

'But . . . But you told the crowd. You said that your father was due to meet you, I swear it!'

'Did I?'

'You did indeed, Miss Stephenson.'

'Oh. My goodness me.' She pursed her lips and raised her eyebrows and glanced heavenward, as if seeking forgiveness. 'Well, Mr Taylor,' she continued, 'it just goes to show that you should never, ever believe everything that everyone tells you. But I must go now. Goodbye.' She smiled and nodded, then turned away.

'But I haven't told you about the dancing master!' he called after her. If he'd deliberately tried to halt her retreat he could have found no better way of doing so. She turned, head on one side.

'A dancing master?'

'Yes, a dancing master. Father has hired him to teach Annie and the rest of the family and her friends the latest steps, for her wedding. I'm due to collect him from the coach. That's why I was hurrying . . .'

She raised her eyebrows at the confession but made no comment.

'That's why I came into town,' he corrected himself. 'To collect him.'

'I thought that Scotsman came to Bellingford every summer. What's his name, McManus? At least he calls himself a teacher of dance. Is he out of favour?'

'He's out of fashion. Annie decided that she wanted to do *English* dancing. Two months ago, while you were in London, she visited Edinburgh, of all places, and everyone dances the English style there, or so she says. So McManus is out and this teacher, his name's Patterson I'm told, David Patterson, son-in-law of someone called Playford, who's meant to have a good reputation, he's to stay right up to the wedding and teach them all to dance.'

'Them, Mr Taylor? Are you not included in this instruction?'

'Me? Dance? I'd sooner dine in hell with the devil.'

'Mr Taylor!'

'I'm sorry, Miss Stephenson, but I'm not a dancer, I'm not made for dancing. I can only understand a fraction of what I'm told, and even then my feet won't obey the instructions my brain sends them.'

'Oh, that is indeed sad, Mr Taylor, because, as you know, your sister has invited me to her wedding, and I would welcome the opportunity to learn some new dances. I do enjoy dancing. I feel sure she would ask me along for a day or two of instruction if she knew that I felt that way.' She opened her eyes wide as she cast the line. 'But I would need a partner.'

There was no doubt that the angler would be successful, but even she was surprised at the speed with which her prey was hooked.

'I suppose,' said Danny Taylor, not recognising the lure as such, 'I suppose I could – if you felt able to accept me, knowing by my own admission how poor I'm likely to be . . . And didn't mind the fact that I have so little experience in this area . . . Then I'd be more than willing to partner you.'

The response was swift; the fish was caught, reeled in and netted with consummate skill.

'Very well, Mr Taylor. Or perhaps Daniel would fit the occasion better. Perhaps you would ask your sister and your mother the best day to attend and send word to me. Or perhaps you would care to carry the message yourself. I would be pleased to see you.' There was a shrill bleating from the direction of Charlotte Stephenson's coach. She turned anxiously. 'Oh Lord, I must go, my mother is calling, and you must find your dancing master. Goodbye, Mr Taylor.'

'Goodbye, Miss Stephenson.'

He watched her as she walked, almost skipped over to the waiting carriage and was helped into it by the footman. He watched as she kissed her mother and expected at the least a wave from her as the carriage rolled past, but she was looking away from him, deliberately, he felt. He cursed, and his dog shrank from him, unaware that her master's frustration was directed against females of the human race only. He shook his head, forced her from his mind.

'Alright then, Bess. I suppose we'd better find that damned dancing master. Lord knows where he'll be, I should have been here near an hour ago.' He peered about him. There were too many strangers in town on market day, finding one in the multitude would be difficult. And then he heard the sound of a cheer from within the tavern opposite, and the faint sound of a fiddle being played. He smiled down at the dog.

'This could be him, lass. Come on, let's take a look.'

He shambled bear-like towards the doorway, and the music grew louder. It was always like this on market day, the alehouses would fill to overflowing with farmers spending their profits; there would be gamblers eager to help them lose their small change, and some of the women were none too particular about their bedfellows. There would be fighting as well, and the constables, both of them, would be on duty, though willing to ignore an incident if sufficient coins were pressed into their hands.

Children were climbing on the stone sill of the inn's single, large window, peering in over panes which had been slid open at top and bottom. Danny Taylor paused on the threshold, as if to gain strength, ordered the dog to stay, then pushed his way inside. There were bodies everywhere, sitting, standing, jammed against walls, leaning on shelves and tables. Two serving girls were pushing their way through the crush, trays holding tankards of beer held high above their heads and slopping their contents over uncomplaining customers. There was a smell of sweat and animals, of smoke and roast meat, of cheap small beer, and above the sound of laughter and loud conversation, of yelled orders and high-pitched giggles, a fiddle was being played – badly. Danny Taylor followed the sound. It was coming from beyond a partition in the main room. There was an accompaniment of sorts; the beating of hands on wooden chairs and tables, someone was playing the bones, and a piccolo was trying vainly to carry the tune along at a regular pace, but the fiddle was the loudest instrument and the most obtuse. It seemed to have a life of its own, it didn't quite reach the notes it was meant to, and if it did, it let them escape too soon or it held onto them too long. This meant little to most of the customers. They'd been drinking for so long and their senses were so dull they would have applauded if the violinist had been able to play only on the open strings, untuned, with a slack bow. This was at least an attempt to play recognisable tunes.

The music came to a rousing if ragged end, and from the depths of the ragged though rousing applause someone shouted out, 'Give us "Hexham Races" again, bonny lad!'

'How doesh tha' go?' asked a wavering tremolo of a voice.

'You knaa, "Hexham Races". Ev'rybody knaas "Hexham Races". I bet even His Majesty Fat George knaas "Hexham Races"!' There was a roar of laughter.

'Aye he does that. After all, it's a jiggy-jig, and we knaa how much he likes that kind o' thing!'

'But tell me how the tune goesh. How ... How ... Will shomebody shing the damn tune?' There was more laughter, then someone began to sing raucously, and the violin picked up what little melody there was. Daniel Taylor fought his way through the crowd and, through judicious use of his elbows and weight, was able to peer round the corner. Squashed into a seat was the violinist surrounded by a travelling bag and a large chest. His clothing was garish: red and blue checked trousers and waistcoat, a bright red silk cravat; over the back of the chair a dark-blue coat was slung. He was in his early thirties, a small man. His hair was beginning to turn grey and was tight-curled, and he seemed to have difficulty in focusing both his eyes and his attention on his instrument. This was not entirely due to the amount of alcohol he must have consumed, for draped around him was one of the more attractive (at least Danny Taylor found her so) coach house doxies, her hands wandering over and around him. He was obviously the centre of attraction. Danny couldn't even see the piccolo player, and the rhythm on bones might have been provided by any of the belching, cheering worthies around the table.

'Mr Patterson,' he began, raising his voice over the hub-bub, 'my name's Taylor. I've come to take you out to Bellingford.'

The violinist looked askance at him. Danny Taylor shook

his head, the man was obviously further gone than he'd estimated.

'Bellingford,' he mouthed slowly, as if to a halfwit. 'Dancing. You're to teach there, for the Taylors.' The violinist was looking straight at him now and smiling, he must surely have understood. He smiled his relief back again and went on. 'I'll just get your bags. If you want to put your instrument in its case, the dogcart's outside.'

He reached for the case and the man's eyes widened. He yelled and dived for his luggage, throwing the doxy from his lap to one grateful neighbour, the violin and bow going in the opposite direction to the drinker on his other side.

'Thief!' he screamed. 'Thief! You all saw him. He wants to steal my belongings!'

Danny stood up again. Those around the table looked at him. He was sure that one or two recognised him, certainly they didn't seem willing to join in the argument.

'But Mr Patterson,' he said, almost pleading, he'd been in enough trouble already that day, 'I've come to take you out to Bellingford, where you're meant to be.' He reached out his hand again, but the violinist grabbed back his bow and tried to hit Danny with it. His aim was poor, instead of striking him on the head as he intended he merely whipped his hand, and the musician ended up catapulting himself back into his seat. But the blow had wounded Danny Taylor's pride.

'Damnation!' he yelled, 'I've come to fetch a dance teacher and I won't leave without one!'

His intention was clear. His arms shot out, he was going to pull the little violinist to him and carry him out of the tavern by force if necessary. He felt someone take hold of one of his arms but he shook himself free, only to find the grip renewed. He dug down with his elbow, it sank into the flesh of his assailant's stomach and he heard the whoosh of breath unwillingly expelled. He turned to see someone sink to the ground before him and was about to bring his knee up into the man's face when he noticed a piece of paper fluttering in his hand, being waved like a flag of surrender.

He postponed the blow and grabbed at the paper, despite those around him urging him to a bloodier conclusion. A frown crept across his face. The paper was a letter, written in a neat copperplate, and he could read the first few words.

'Dear Mr Taylor,' it began, 'allow me to introduce the bearer of this letter . . .'

The man on the floor was looking up at him now, though his arms were crossed over his stomach. He was in pain. Rob Tweddle hadn't felt such physical pain for many years, he normally relied on his wit to keep himself clear of taproom brawls such as this, but now his plans had brought him to his knees in front of the man who had been sent to meet him.

'My name . . .' he hissed through clenched teeth, '. . . is David Patterson.'

The journey to Bellingford passed pleasantly enough once Rob had caught his breath and regained his senses. His assailant had proved immediately and overwhelmingly apologetic, had helped Rob to his feet and dusted him down, almost carried him outside, and then insisted on loading the dogcart with his luggage. Rob sat and watched and stroked the ears of the dog now sitting on top of his small, worn, unkempt trunk. His only other bag, a coarse sack, its neck closed with a piece of rope, sat beside him.

'Is that it, Mr Patterson?' asked Danny Taylor.

'Yes, that's all Mr Taylor.' There was an embarrassing silence. Danny Taylor looked around him as if certain that he'd missed something.

'I like to travel light,' said Rob as an explanation.

'But your violin, I can't see your violin anywhere. Is it in your travelling chest?'

'No, I don't play the violin.'

'But . . . But I thought all dancing masters played the violin.'

'Not me. I do play, but not the violin. I play the flute. It's here with me, in my bag.'

Danny Taylor accepted the explanation and climbed up beside his passenger.

'Are you sure you're alright to travel? We can wait a little while if you need more time to recover.'

'Thank you, Mr Taylor, but I'm quite well. I was winded, nothing more. Please, drive on.'

'Very well, Mr Patterson.' Danny Taylor lifted the reins and clicked his tongue. The pony moved gently away at a pace far more sedate than had been used only two hours previously, though whether this was because Danny felt that his passenger's injuries would benefit from the softer ride or because he feared another accident only he knew. Or perhaps it gave him time to think. Certainly he said nothing, nothing at all, until the streets of the town were behind them and they'd reached the open countryside. And even then, when he did speak, the words didn't come easily.

'Mr Patterson?'

'Yes, Mr Taylor.'

'I should like, if I may, to ask you a favour.'

'Asking favours costs a man nothing, Mr Taylor. The same cannot be said of granting them, but if it is within my power to do so, then . . .' He spread his hands and looked to the broad, blue, lark-strewn sky above, as if to imply that, given the Almighty's compliance, the favour was already in Danny Taylor's possession.

'Thank you, Mr Patterson.'

'And what is the favour?'

'Well . . . it's just that I'd appreciate it if you didn't, at least not to my family, especially my father, he wouldn't understand . . . That is, I always seem to be in trouble, and I was only trying to help. Annie, my sister, she would understand, at least I think she would. But she might let slip to someone else, and who knows what might happen then. And . . . I'm not really making myself clear, am I?'

'No, Mr Taylor, not at all.'

'I'm sorry, I'm not good with words. But the favour I'm asking is that I'd appreciate it if you didn't tell anyone I knocked you down. It would cause such trouble, and I already have that aplenty. I know that I embarrassed you, hurt you even, but . . .'

'Mr Taylor, I shall mention the incident to no one. It didn't occur. Will that suffice?'

'Why, Mr Patterson, you're a real gentleman. Thank you, sir, thank you so much!'

Rob Tweddle nodded, closed his eyes to the warmth of the sun and relaxed. He needed to think, his plan wasn't yet firm, he wasn't sure whether he'd covered every eventuality. By anticipating problems he could design a strategy to cope with the more easily seen difficulties; those that were better hidden would have to be dealt with using his imagination, his flair for deception. He smiled as those very words crossed his mind, 'a flair for deception'. If he had any such attribute then it would be tested fully during the coming days, and he had to admit that he was looking forward to the challenge.

'Mr Patterson?'

'Yes, Mr Taylor?' He tried to hide the weariness in his voice.

'Forgive me being presumptuous, but you seem very young to be a dancing master. And you certainly don't sound like a dancing master.'

Rob smiled to himself. He could remember James Playford's response to objections voiced by potential customers to *his* frail and elderly appearance. It could be used as a riposte in both circumstances.

'A wise man once told me, "Age is no bar to skill, or knowledge, or a determination to teach, to excel, to triumph over adversity!" ' He raised his finger skywards. 'I have the skill and the knowledge, Mr Taylor. I'm also informed that I have youthful looks for my age, so don't be deceived by appearances – all is not necessarily what it seems. And as for the way I talk, I can't and won't deny the background that gave me this accent. But I speak well enough to make myself understood. What more can a man want? You may rest assured that I can teach you and your family to dance.'

Rob smiled in what he hoped was not too condescending a manner. 'You see, that's my profession, Mr Taylor, music and dancing. There are many things about which you must know far more than me, such as . . .' he searched for the compliment '. . . well, such as farming and rearing stock, hunting no doubt, the ways of wild creatures and their identification. Do I speak the truth?'

'Possibly, Mr Patterson, possibly. But even if it is so, these aren't the types of skills and learning some folk like. Do you understand me?'

'You mean that some people don't like the fact that you know about farming? I can't see who might be offended at that. I would think it a very useful skill to possess.'

'No, Mr Patterson, I don't mean it that way. I mean that some folk, especially some lady folk, like a man to know more than is necessary to earn a living, even if he might be no good at these other things that they, that is the ladies, like.' He came to a rambling halt. 'You don't understand, do you?' So certain was he that the question became a statement of fact.

'You mean that some women like a man to be able to dance,' suggested Rob, 'even though some men dislike dancing.'

'That's it. That's exactly it!'

'But very often the reason men dislike dancing isn't because it's unpleasant but because they feel uncertain of their abilities in that area.'

'Yes, yes!'

'And you're one of those men?'

'Well, I can't dance. I never could dance, I never wanted to dance. That is, not until now.'

'But now you want to learn to dance in order to partner some young lady who's taken your fancy, am I right?'

'You are so right, Mr Patterson. You can read my mind, I swear it.'

'Then I'm your man, Mr Taylor. If you wish to learn to dance, then I'll teach you to dance.'

'I'm no good. I can't figure out the steps.'

'You will, Mr Taylor, you will.'

Daniel Taylor smiled, his big red face creased and dimpled, he clutched the reins in triumph as he saw himself whirling and twirling round the room with Charlotte Stephenson gazing adoringly up at him. His reverie was interrupted.

'But, Mr Taylor, there are two things I'd ask in return.'

'Anything, Mr Patterson, anything at all.'

'The first is that you allow me a little time to think during the balance of the journey. I need to consider how to approach my lessons.'

'I shall be quiet as a church mouse, Mr Patterson.'

'And the second is that, since we're to spend time in each other's company, you'd do me the honour of addressing me by my Christian name, David.'

'Mr Patterson, the privilege is mine. And you must call me by my first name, Daniel. But my friends call me Danny, and I'd like to count you as one of those.'

'Thank you very much, Danny.'

'Thank *you*, Mr . . . I'm sorry. Thank you, David.'

The remainder of the journey passed in comparative peace. Rob was able to collect his thoughts, to summarise what he'd done and what he hoped to do. He was sure he'd covered his tracks well. He'd told no one at his lodgings that he was leaving, no one on the coach had asked his name, and he'd spoken to none of the other passengers. Playford would be hard put to trace him, though he'd try, he'd certainly try. There was the matter of the safe being emptied, that in itself would be no small annoyance. And David Patterson, the real David Patterson, would find it difficult to teach dancing when his instruction books had gone missing, music as well. Both of those matters would be discovered quickly, and no doubt the Newcastle constables would already have been informed. But that meant little; he was far away from their justice.

It would take the Playford family a little while longer to discover the mistakes he'd entered in the ledger, but if the weather stayed fine they'd soon become aware of the dead cat hidden beneath their floorboards. And then there was Arnold, his replacement who had come with such good references (Rob had written them himself) but who couldn't add two figures together, let alone total a column. His love of alcohol and plump young women wouldn't endear him to David or Emily Patterson, and his dislike of washing would be sure to offend even the staunchest of Playford's customers. Such revenge was, of course, petty; it had no part in Rob's larger plan, but it was no less sweet because of that. It was ironic that, if this venture succeeded, it would do so because of Playford's inability to carry out any mundane task for himself. He'd given Rob the task of organising his son-in-law's visit to Bellingford, and this Rob had done by means of letters signed with a fair imitation of Playford's own hand. Details of David Patterson's forthcoming trip were still held by Playford. He would only discover they were wrong when he turned up on the day of Annie Taylor's wedding, a fortnight too late, to find what mischief Rob had made in the Playford name. But the beauty of the deception was that he would also be paying back George Taylor for having him sacked in the first place. He would spoil the wedding and, to cap it all, be paid for it. He wasn't yet sure how he would do all of this. The details he would work out as he went along. So much depended upon the Taylors themselves, and if they were anything like this bumpkin of a son then they would be no challenge to him, no challenge at all. He would play merry hell with their cosy little village and their happy country wedding. By the time he was finished they would think the devil himself had been their dancing master.

The village seemed a long time in arriving. The road wasn't particularly good; the ground was dry and the wheels bumped and jarred through every single rut. The route seemed to have been designed by a madman. It rose straight over and down the many hills that stood in their way, refusing to skirt them for a more gentle gradient, so progress upwards was slow and downwards was dangerous. The scenery, Rob was prepared to admit, was pleasant enough. There were many green fields, newly hedged or fenced, stretches of woods and smaller copses and spinneys, a large house or two to which Danny Taylor made obeisance and muttered the name of the owner in grudging respect. There were lesser dwellings too; farms, most of them well kept, villages and hamlets, cottages in groups too small to be honoured with a name, individual homes nestling beside streams. Not all were neat and tidy, and Rob was surprised to find that some, which he considered, from a distance, had been long abandoned, proved upon closer inspection to have tribes of ragged barefoot children rattling around the door, and old women spinning or carding or knitting in the road. All of them looked on with suspicion as the dogcart passed by. No word of greeting was thrown by either party.

'Who are they?' Rob asked innocently, breaking the silence.

'The families of labourers,' answered Danny. 'Unskilled people. They breed too fast, they can't care for themselves; they depend on the parish for their living.' He spat into the roadside to end his comment with the punctuation he felt it deserved, indeed, his affection for the countryside seemed limited to the beasts upon it rather than the people who lived and worked there.

As the miles crept by, the fields of wheat, already beginning to brown, were replaced by larger expanses of rough hilly ground, and where sturdy heifers with weak-legged, big-eyed calves had stared at them without curiosity there appeared skittish sheep and their carefree wastrel lambs. They looked up at the rattle of the cart and then were off, the dog imagining herself following them, tense in every muscle, but remaining locked in her place by her master's unspoken command. Danny Taylor pointed out the good beasts and the poor, told his companion the breeds (there weren't many; the only ones Rob could remember were Blackface and Cheviot) and showed him the places where the stupid animals – he somehow inferred respect with the adjective – would become snowbound in winter. The unremitting green of the grass and trees, the stifling warmth of the flower-scented breeze, the

repetitive warbling of hidden birds all combined to make
Rob long for the dirt and noise and smells of Newcastle.
He felt nervous, sick even; the sky was too blue, too big,
too oppressive. He closed his eyes again but this just made
matters worse, he was forced to concentrate on the jolting
and rolling of the cart. And then they stopped.

Rob opened his eyes. They were on the crest of a hill where
the path, for it was now no more than that, wound its way
between clumps of bright-yellow, bee-droning gorse. Below
them was a small valley, a shallow river curling through
its midst, and there were at last signs of habitation. Rob
could see a church tower, foursquare with battlements,
no spire, and a millwheel turning; smoke was rising from
some buildings. There was a faint, distant sound of children
playing, and he swore he could smell roast meat. He suddenly
realised how hungry he was.

'That's Bellingford,' said Danny as he urged the pony
forwards. 'That's where I was born, that's where I live, and
that's probably where I'll die.' And with that air of finality
they descended to the village.

If Rob had been expecting some reception, a warm welcome, then he was disappointed. Danny drove the dogcart
down the hill but veered away from the village itself and
headed towards the manor house. It was less grand than the
others they'd passed that day, but still impressive. No single
architectural style dominated as they approached; it appeared
to have been put together at the whim of generations of
Taylors. The drive led past the oldest part first, a grey
stone peel tower decked with ivy, its steeply pitched roof
crowned with squawking jackdaws. A wide staircase of the
same warm stone angled up two sides to a strong, tall door
set some fifteen feet above ground level.

Joined to the tower, butting squarely on to one of its sides,
was what would elsewhere have seemed nothing more than
the home of a yeoman farmer, a simple two-storey building
with small windows and a roof bowed with the weight of
years. Yet attached to this, at the end furthest from the

tower, they came across the largest part of the house, neither
a palace nor a castle but combining aspects of both. It too
was built of local stone, three stories high, but each block
had been carefully dressed and shaped. The windows were
tall rectangles with angular pediments above and ornamented
uprights to both sides, and as they rounded the corner Rob
saw the front of the house, stately and proud and looking
over sheep-flecked fields which rolled down to the river. The
double doors were wide and filled with glass, and to either
side four huge columns supported a third-floor balcony. On
the roof itself was a stone railing, its uprights straight and
simple, and at regular intervals behind the rail stood statues
of soldiers and knights, bowmen and spearmen, all gazing
down at Rob with stony disdain. As Danny pulled the reins
to draw the trap to a halt, a similar granite-faced apparition
came through the doorway, stiff and straight, arms fixed to
his side.

'Andrew,' called Danny, 'is there no one else about? Are
you the welcoming party?'

'Aye, Mr Daniel sir,' came a deep, sweet Northumbrian
voice, far less sharp than that of Newcastle, thought Rob,
a voice which should have been singing its response. 'I'm
the welcoming party sure enough,' he continued, 'the family
have gone out. Your father's taken them to see the kingfishers
down by the millpond.'

'All of them?'

'All of them. They waited to have dinner with you, but then
they thought you'd stopped to have a meal on the way.'

'And so they ate without us?'

'They did, Mr Daniel, they did indeed. But there's a good
selection of cold meats and potatoes and vegetables waiting
for you, and they said they'd be back before dark.' The
servant turned towards Rob. 'They were most curious to
meet you, Mr Patterson, so I doubt they'll be late.'

'I'm sorry, Andrew,' said Danny, leaping from the cart, 'I
forgot my manners. David Patterson, this is our . . . Andrew,
what is your position in the household? I know I call you

a butler and sometimes a manservant, but you're more than that, aren't you?' He whispered in an aside, 'Andrew predates most of the building, let alone its inhabitants. For the first few years of my life I spent more time with him than with my mother and father put together.'

'I'm nothing but a servant, Mr Daniel, and I have no wish to be other than a servant.'

'Andrew, you're as much a part of the family as I am. Now then, tell me where I'm to put Mr Patterson's luggage. It's far too heavy for you to be heaving it about.'

Rob noticed that his host's attitudes and manners had changed during the journey. The brash, almost juvenile antagonism had been discarded to leave a young man who was almost pleasant, who seemed content in the familiar surroundings of his home, proud to show it to his new companion.

'Mr Patterson has been placed in the guest wing,' said the servant. 'His bed has been aired and his fire laid, though I doubt he'll need it lit. There's fresh water in his bowl and jug, flowers on the table, a selection of books for his diversion. If he should need anything else . . .' He held out his hands as if to show that he doubted anything else could be required, but if it was then he would certainly be willing and able to provide it.

'Thank you Andrew,' said Rob. 'I'm sure everything will be perfect.'

'Right then,' laughed Danny, 'let's go in. First we'll eat, and then we can drink, and then I'll show you to your room and we can wait for the others.' He skipped through the door held open by the servant, who shrugged at Rob, as if to disclaim any responsibility for his master's behaviour. 'What more do we need from life,' sang Danny Taylor, 'than food, wine and companionship!'

Certainly the first two of these were present in profusion, but there was no sign of the rest of the Taylor family as the young men ate and drank, then drank a little more, and then a little

more. It began to get dark, and Danny Taylor's impromptu
tour of the house turned into a staggering, laughing, belching
joke of a journey. Only once did he take on a more serious
air, when he took Rob into the ballroom. It wasn't excessively
large or overly grand; perhaps a hundred people could have
danced at once in comfort, and in the deep red shadows of the
setting sun the colours of wall and ceiling seemed dusty and
faded; even the air in the room seemed centuries old. Along
one wall hung paintings, poor affairs, Rob decided, stilted
and unimaginative in both style and execution – man with
horse, man with hounds, man with wife, he didn't bother
listening to his guide's explanation of how each was related
to the other. But there were two small portraits displayed
away from the others, and they attracted Rob's attention,
not because of the quality of the paintings, but because of the
beauty of the subject. It was the same woman, Rob decided
as he stood in front of the pair. She had dark brown hair and
chestnut eyes; her lips were red and slightly parted, and she
was smiling directly at him; and she was very beautiful.

'Who's that?' he asked reverentially.

Danny Taylor smiled. 'The one on the left is my mother,
painted when she was a young girl. And the one on the
right is my sister Annie, and that was painted just over a
year ago.'

'Your mother? And your sister?'

'Yes. Don't be concerned that you thought they were the
same person, everyone does. And you're not the only one
to think they're beautiful. Annie most certainly is. And my
mother, well, when she smiles, you can see her as she was.'
He put his arm round Rob's shoulder, the wine had made
him over-friendly. 'I love them both,' he confided, 'and I'd
kill anyone who tried to harm them.' He whirled clumsily
around the dance floor, bottle in one hand, flickering candle
in the other. 'But I'm tired of waiting. Come on, they can't be
far. I want you to meet them all. We'll go look for them!'

The moon was high when they crept back into the house,

and their shoes were wet with a heavy dew. Bats hawked
the still air, and far across the valley a pair of lovesick
tawny owls haunted the night. Sure enough, they'd missed
the other members of the family. The two parties had
danced circles round each other as the day slowly slipped
away. And so the young men whispered goodnight and
found their rooms, and Rob realised how tired he was,
yet sleep wouldn't come. Instead thoughts of dark eyes
chased him, and even beneath a single sheet the heat of
the night was too great. He sprung from the bed to check
that the windows were open, throwing his shift to the
floor as he strode across the room. He flung the curtains open and rested his elbows on the sillboard to let
the cool darkness wash over him. And then he saw, or
thought he saw, down below in the garden, a flicker of
something white moving. He watched more closely. The
moon wasn't half full, but the light was strong enough
to cast shadows, and it was a shadow he saw first. It
moved across the rough grass from beneath an old yew
tree, and it took form and shape, and it was a woman.
Rob didn't move, so frightened was he that the wraith
would disappear if he broke the spell. The woman moved
this way and that, dancing, yes, dancing to some private
tune, arms outstretched and then raised above her head,
bare feet leaving a trail of deeper shadows in the shadow
of the lawn. Rob moved to one side to ease the imminent
cramp that tensed his arms and in doing so knocked a small
wooden wedge, placed there in case the windows should
rattle, to the floor. He barely heard the noise himself,
but the woman suddenly ceased her movement and looked
straight up at him, though he knew that she wouldn't be
able to see him in the darkness. She had dark hair and dark
eyes. Her beauty was indeed as great as her brother had
stated, and no artist, no matter how great or gifted, could
have captured that beauty on canvas. Rob realised he was
looking down at Annie Taylor, and when she smiled, just
before she ran off, he knew he would have to have her.

He *would* have her, and that would add to his revenge, that would be the fitting glory to crown his masquerade. And so, content, he returned to his bed, and slept, and dreamed.

The Third Bar of the Musick

<hr/>

Tuesday, 15 June 1830

In which Mr Rob Tweddle plays the part of dancing master, fails to impress Miss Annie Taylor and her sister, Mrs Frances Arnison, and learns that enthusiasm can sometimes impress more than knowledge.

Rob woke to a persistent rapping at his door. He'd willed himself to dream of a dark-haired maiden with smooth white skin who longed to dance with him, and that was how the dream had started, but somehow the ballroom had turned into James Playford's practice hall, and the maiden had metamorphosed from the slim sylph Annie Taylor into the plump termagant Emily Patterson. The sharp, shrewish tapping of her prim little feet on the floor, the imperative of her summons, the urgency of her lascivious grin (even in a nightmare he retained some degree of control) all vanished as he struggled into wakefulness. He allowed his senses to impinge on his dreamworld, expecting to see the familiar damp, mottled walls of his lodgings, to hear the mechanical rumble of quayside winches and fishwives' squawking, to smell rotten vegetables and overcooked broth and the miasma of thousands of night closets flowing into the murky Tyne. Instead he saw daylight strained through thick curtains, stippling an ornate plaster ceiling; he heard birdsong and the distant bleating of lambs seeking misplaced ewes; he smelt flowers and late apple blossom. And he felt the sweet warmth of a wide, soft, comfortable, unfamiliar bed, and remembered where he was and why he was there. The knocking recommenced, followed by a rolling Northumbrian voice.

'Mr Patterson,' it sang, 'breakfast will be served in fifteen minutes. Mr Patterson, are you awake yet?'

'I'm awake,' Rob replied, recognising the voice and searching for the name that accompanied it, 'Andrew, is that right? Is it you?'

The door opened and the old manservant appeared, deferentially noble. 'Mr Patterson,' he began again, unsure that his monologue had been properly heard or understood the first time, 'breakfast will be served in fifteen minutes. It is Mr Taylor's wish that you be present to meet him and his family.'

'Thank you, Andrew. I'll be down within ten minutes.'

'May I open the curtains, Mr Patterson?' He moved to do so before permission was given, swept the heavy material aside to prove that the day was as bright and sunny as the previous night's sky had promised. Rob blinked and sat up.

'Would you like me to set out your clothes for the day?' continued Andrew. He stalked the room like a predatory heron, longing to open wardrobe doors and drawers to reveal the secrets Rob had brought with him.

'No, thank you,' answered Rob, 'I haven't unpacked yet, and I can manage to dress myself anyway. But if you'd be good enough to tell Mr Taylor I'll be down . . .'

He wasn't sure how to deal with servants, but he knew he didn't want anyone looking through his luggage or his clothing. He decided to adopt the tone and manners that his former master had used with him, though he'd add a little humanity.

'That will be all, thank you,' he said in what he hoped was a dismissive tone.

It appeared to work. Andrew gave a slight nod of the

head, which could have been an abbreviated bow or an acknowledgement that he'd heard the instruction, and left the room. Rob sprang out of bed and hurried over to the dressing table, splashed water over his face and chest and allowed it to dribble down over his stomach, rubbed under his arms and between his legs. He looked around for a piece of towelling or linen and, finding none, sidled over to the nearest curtain. He glanced outside to make sure there was no one to see him and dried himself on the folds of heavy material. Then he shaved as quickly as was prudent, given the age and sharpness of his razor, and dressed himself. He'd spent a large part of the money he'd taken from James Playford (he still didn't think of it as being stolen; it was, he felt, rightly his) on clothes, and he'd chosen them with care. He selected from his travel chest a pair of clean linen drawers and fine knitted hose, light fawn trousers rather than breeches, a white shirt and a silk cravat. He dressed swiftly and tied the cravat high around his neck, topped the outfit with a waistcoat of the same material as the trousers and a deep-blue jacket, cut away at the front but with tails descending at the back almost to his knees. He brushed his hair while admiring himself in the mirror then hurried downstairs, muttering to himself, 'I *am* David Patterson, I *am* David Patterson!'

The door to the dining room was open, he could hear the starling chatter within. He paused, pulled his waistcoat down slightly and marched into the room.

The talking ceased. Four pairs of eyes stared at him. He stood still, two or three steps inside the room, and waited. He expected that Danny would have the presence of mind to introduce him to the family, or at the very least to greet him, but no, the dolt merely sat there, a broad smile on his face, saying nothing. He was evidently cast from the same mould as his father (more compact than his son but with a similarly vacant expression), whose knife and fork were stationary, raised halfway to his mouth. The two women present were caught in the same slip of time which prevented them moving or talking. The mouth of one of them, the younger, was open

wide, though whether this was to expel words or digest food
wasn't clear. It was left to the other woman, identifiable by
her age as Mrs Taylor, to overcome this inertia and intercede
on Rob's behalf, and as soon as she rose to her feet the
tableau unfroze. She pushed back her chair and smiled at
him and he recognised the smile. He'd seen a poor copy of
it in one of the paintings last night, and he'd witnessed its
closer approach to perfection on the lips of the woman who
had danced in the garden. Mrs Taylor tapped her husband on
the shoulder and he too climbed to his feet, closely followed
by their children.

'Samuel,' urged Mrs Taylor, 'will you introduce us?'

'Introduce? Oh, I'm sorry my dear, of course, forgive me.'
He stared at Rob. 'Tall, isn't he?' he said, in what was meant
to be an aside but was heard by all. He quickly covered his
mouth with his hand but realised how childish the gesture
seemed and turned the movement into a stroke of his chin
to cover his embarrassment. 'Mr Patterson?' he enquired.

Rob nodded, and Samuel Taylor mimicked the action.
Then, as if pursued by an angry wasp he'd only just noticed,
he hurried around the table to stand in front of the newcomer.
He eyed him up and down quickly then shook Rob's hand in
a firm and lengthy grip.

'Samuel Taylor. I've been in correspondence with your
father-in-law, Mr Playford. James Playford, that is. Yes?'

Rob nodded again. 'That's right, Mr Taylor sir,' he said,
suddenly unsure of how he should address his host.

'No need for 'sirs' and courtesies around here, Mr Patterson.
I'm Mr Taylor. I seek no other title and will have none uttered
by someone who's a guest in our home. Understood?' He nodded his weathered, white-haired, untidy head to encourage the
correct answer.

'Why, yes Mr Taylor,' Rob said.

'Good. Come then, you must be hungry. Sit yourself
down—'

'Samuel!' It was his wife who interceded, reminding him of
his duties.

'Yes, my dear? Oh, yes, the introductions! Forgive me, I'm not at my best in the morning, Mr Patterson. Allow me to introduce my wife, Rebecca, who is the real head of this household.' She bent her head slightly but kept her eyes on his. He tried to smile at her. 'And my daughter, Mrs Frances Arnison, who is here to help us prepare for the wedding.' There was no smile this time. The Taylors' eldest child seemed to have inherited her looks and manner from her father. Her red, rounded face was framed by sandy hair tied back in a severe knot, and the thin thread of ribbon which performed this act might have had an invisible counterpart holding the corners of her mouth down in an inverted crescent. The only acknowledgement Rob received was a curt raise of the eyebrows. 'You've already met my son, Daniel, the wastrel.' Danny shook Rob's hand briefly, winked at him. 'So please, sit yourself down and eat.' Samuel Taylor ushered Rob into one of two empty chairs adjacent to one another and hurried back to his place.

'We've been *so* looking forward to your coming, Mr Patterson,' said Mrs Taylor. 'I do hope your journey wasn't too tiring yesterday, and please, help yourself to breakfast. We don't stand on ceremony, and we only use servants for our evening meal, isn't that right, Samuel?'

Her husband, now occupied with a bowl of steaming porridge, grunted his reply. Rob looked at the plates of food, boiled eggs and cold smoked fish, thin slices of ham, relishes and preserves, then reached out to carve a slice of bread for himself. He spread it thick with butter and then scooped honey over the top of it.

'The journey wasn't tiring at all, thank you Mrs Taylor. Your son was a most pleasant companion.' He cut the slice of bread in two and began to devour it.

'Somehow the words "pleasant companion" don't sit well with the person I know as my brother,' announced Frances Arnison. Rob put her at around thirty years of age. She wore a ring on her wedding finger, and he wondered idly and maliciously what sort of husband she must have to make her so sour.

'Thank you for the compliment, sister mine,' said Daniel, 'I'd reply in kind but for the presence of a guest and my own politeness.'

'Polite? You, polite? You, dear brother, are normally as polite as a pig at feeding time, which you resemble more each passing day.'

'If I'm a pig, Frances, then you're the sister of a—'

'Children!' It was Mrs Taylor who interrupted, her husband seemed oblivious to the altercation. 'Forgive us, Mr Patterson, although I'm sure that you too will have experienced similar small disagreements with your siblings. It is common enough in all the families I know.'

'Alas, Mrs Taylor,' mumbled Rob through a mouthful of bread which he quickly swallowed, 'I have no family. I'm an orphan. I know nothing of my parents.' He'd decided to simplify his background in order to remove the possibility of him contradicting himself, countering one lie with another, and there was surely nothing simpler than being an orphan. But when he looked at his hosts they appeared to be waiting for him to go on, to provide further information.

'I have reason to believe . . .' he stumbled, then the words came freely, of their own accord, '. . . that my parents were murdered by bandits while on their way to visit a distant cousin's chateau in France.' He was horrified at the implausibility of the tale but couldn't prevent himself gilding the fable further. 'I'm told that I was brought up for a while by my grandmother, a saintly woman, but she died before I reached the age of two, having spent all the family's money on attempting to bring my parents' murderers to justice. I was therefore placed in an orphanage and have had to make my own way in the world since running away from there at the age of twelve.' He reached for a coffeepot and poured himself a cup of the steaming black liquid, aware, though not showing it, that all eyes and ears were on him. He spoke again, determined to tie up the loose ends of his history.

'I taught myself to play music and dance and was invited by one of the leading dancing masters in London to join him as an instructor, but I decided instead to open my own school and chose as a partner Mr Playford.'

'But you are married to Mr Playford's daughter, I believe?' prompted Mrs Taylor.

'Yes, but she is, alas, a frail and sickly lady, unable to travel. She dotes on me, of course, and I do all I can to make each day we spend together a memorable one, as if it may be her last.'

'Oh dear,' said Mrs Taylor, 'how sad.' Her daughter appeared to be swayed to sympathy less easily.

'You have rather an unusual accent, Mr Patterson, not what I would expect from an individual with your background. I've heard it before, or something similar, at the market in Hexham, though I'm not sure who might have been using it at the time.'

'Gentlemen from Newcastle intending to buy sheep and cattle?' suggested Danny.

'No, I think it was more likely their hired stockmen. Abbatoir workers, perhaps?'

'The orphanage,' Rob whispered, 'was that of a religious, charitable order, and no child of need was excluded. I'm not ashamed to state that I spent the early years of my childhood in the company of children from . . .' he shook his head '. . . the lower social classes.'

'There is no shame in that, Mr Patterson,' said Mrs Taylor, glowering at her daughter, 'and as you can see, even the most loving of families cannot guarantee that children will always be polite and well behaved,' she glanced at the clock standing by the door, 'or punctual. Where can Annie have got to?'

As if propelled by her mother's words, Annie Taylor was launched into the room. There was no warning of her approach, no sound of footsteps, but she had obviously been running. Her breast was rising and falling quickly and her cheeks were red. Rob rose quickly to his feet but was motioned down again by Mrs Taylor.

'Annie, you are more than a little late. And we have a guest with us this morning.'

'Yes, Mama, I'm so sorry. And Mr Patterson, I assume you *are* Mr Patterson, please accept my apologies. It was such a beautiful morning and I woke early. I went down to the millpond again to see the kingfishers—'

'You did?' It was Samuel Taylor who spoke, raised from the dead by the mention of kingfishers. 'You saw them again?' Annie nodded, moved to her seat beside Rob. 'Both of them?' She nodded again. Rob offered her a slice of bread. She declined with a motion of her hand and reached instead for the coffeepot.

'I think,' she said in between sips, 'they're nesting in the old stump just downstream of the pond.'

'Really? Oh, I must investigate further. Do you like birds, Mr Patterson?' Rob nodded but was given no chance to add words to the gesture. '*I'm* interested in birds, I keep a chronicle of the bird life of the estate. It *is* unusual that the 'fishers are here, there's normally a pair nests in the sandbanks by the poplars, but I've never known them so close to the mill.'

'My father is particularly fascinated by rooks,' said Danny, his meal finished. 'He spends hours watching them.'

'Not just rooks, my boy, but the *Corvidae* in general. Crows, magpies, jays, jackdaws, I've even seen ravens up on the moors. And I've been in correspondence with a Mr Treherne from Cornwall who regularly attracts choughs to his land. I intend visiting him one day.'

'Well *I* don't like them,' said Annie sulkily. 'Big black birds, they kill young thrushes and skylarks; warblers as well. I much prefer a skylark to a dirty old crow.'

'And what of you, Mr Patterson?' asked Frances too kindly. 'What type of bird is your favourite?'

'I have little knowledge of birds,' Rob answered. It had been easy enough to invent a past that denied a family, but in truth his father had been a keelman and his mother took in washing and bred children – too many children. He could lie about his family, but on the subject of ornithology, about which he knew so little, it was obviously better to tell the truth. 'I know pigeons and starlings,' he went on, 'and crows and some sea birds which come up the Tyne, but I've had little opportunity to investigate them in any detail. Perhaps, Miss Taylor, you might take me to see these kingfishers at some time?'

'Thank you for considering me, Mr Patterson, but I do feel that you might enjoy yourself more if Danny takes you down there. I have so much to think about at the moment, and there's the organisation of the dancing lessons to consider as well. I'm not sure how I'll manage to fit everything in.'

'I saw an interesting bird last night,' said Rob before Danny could confirm his willingness to take him to visit the millpond. 'It was dark outside, and I looked out of the window and saw a pale, white ghost of a bird flying low over the lawn. It was beautiful. It was the most beautiful bird I've ever seen; so graceful, so silent. And when it flew away I felt a sense of loss so keen I thought my heart would stop.' He looked directly at the young girl seated beside him, and she returned his glance with knowing curiosity.

'Barn owl,' announced Samuel Taylor. 'Couldn't be anything else.'

'It had the beauty and grace of a swan,' said Rob.

'It was probably,' announced Annie with confidence, 'some old goose up too late, waddling back to her nest. With birds, as with people, Mr Patterson, it requires careful observation to ensure that what you think you see is actually there. But perhaps we can talk about this further. I think that I could, after all, spare the time to accompany you to the millpond. We can discuss the dancing lessons as well.'

'And I shall certainly be glad to come along,' offered Danny, 'I have little else to do today.'

'And the walk will do Frances good as well,' said Mrs Taylor, to her elder daughter's dismay.

'Mama! I detest walking aimlessly around the village, you know that, and Daniel can act as chaperone. I would far rather remain here.'

'Frances,' her mother pointed out, 'you know how easily Daniel is distracted. It will only need some farmer to come along with news of a fox's earth to dig and Daniel will disappear.'

'More likely a farmer's daughter than a farmer, Mama. But if you say so then I shall brave the elements to carry out my duties.' She wore her martyrdom with pride.

'Good. Perhaps you might take the opportunity to show Mr Patterson around the village. Introduce him to the parson and Dr Allard, if he's about. They will both be attending at some time for instruction.'

'Yes, Mama.'

'Very well, then. I shall leave you to it. Samuel, how will you spend the remainder of the morning?' Rebecca Taylor stood up and her husband joined her, they linked arms as they left the room.

'I thought I might stroll up to the rookery. You're very welcome to accompany me if you wish . . .'

Rob lay on his bed, his shoes, scuffed and covered in dust, drunk on the floor. He was to go down to the ballroom in an hour at five o'clock to begin his first lesson with Annie and Frances, and the enormity of the task ahead of him was beginning to prey on his mind. The strain of pretending to be someone else wasn't great; what was difficult was the need to suppress his own slightly extrovert nature, to behave as he imagined the real David Patterson would behave. And that wasn't the only complication.

The day hadn't proved successful. The three youngest Taylors had escorted him on what he'd hoped might be an intimate stroll but proved to be a campaign march around the village. His attempts to engage Annie in dialogue had been thwarted by her sister's outflanking manoeuvres. Handling a wide-eyed sunshade with the ease of a master swordsman, she managed to ensure that she was between Rob and her sister at all times. The kingfishers had proved to be brilliant jewels but so small and distant that they were, as he tried to explain to Annie, as insignificant as stars when the sun was high in the firmament. His attempt at the flattering compliment, the over-obvious likening her to the sun, was greeted by giggles on Annie's part and by silent derision from Frances. Rob couldn't decide whether her refusal to admonish him was because she was too polite or because she simply lacked sufficient intelligence to coin a suitably barbed riposte.

They visited the parsonage. The church itself was non-descript, a product of roughly hewn local stone and a bare minimum of ancestral Taylor philanthropy warranting neither special attention nor further investigation. The house next door was equally uninspiring, as was the incumbent to whom Rob was introduced, Parson Theodore Westborne, a stooped, gangling man in his mid thirties, dressed in sackcloth and apologies. He spoke at length about his flower garden, a subject which interested no one but him, then invited them to return later for 'a little something to eat, a little something to drink' with him and his wife, Mary, who, when she wasn't looking after her husband and family, Rob was informed, taught the local children rudimentary reading and writing. They were not allowed to depart, however, before the parson grasped Rob by the hand and told him how much he was looking forward to learning some new dances. They left him to converse with his rose bushes.

Rob watched Annie as they walked. She couldn't move without dancing, and when she stopped to talk to someone, the blacksmith, the miller's daughter, her enforced immobility seemed like palpable chains which could only be loosened by skipping on to another liaison. She was nineteen years old, he knew, but she had the sophisticated beauty of one much older. And yet she behaved like a child. The world was nothing but excitement to her, she took delight in the shape of a leaf or the passing dart of a swallow, and her laugh was contagious to all but her sister. Danny, Rob noticed, could only watch her with amazement, filled with pride that she should be so beautiful, so carefree, yet concerned that her lack of fear, her boundless energy, might result in a fall or scrape or sting, that some injury might befall her which he ought to have foreseen. And although he treated Rob as a friend, that friendship was insignificant when compared to his loyalty to his sister. Rob decided that Annie's seduction would have to be circumspect. If Danny should hear of it then he might cause Rob some grievous injury. The thought that he might abandon the attempt to have his way with the girl didn't occur to Rob at all; his self-confidence would allow no other course, and the morality of his plan wasn't even considered.

They stopped again outside a large house sheltered on one side by a wide oak tree, under which an elderly man was sitting in an even older chair, writing in a plain bound notebook.

'Go away,' he announced as they approached him, 'I'm busy.' Rob held back, but the others seemed undeterred by this greeting.

'This is Mr Scrivener,' whispered Daniel. 'He's a poet.'

'I am no poet,' came the angry reply, the quick, clipped voice becoming louder with each word, 'because I am unable to write, and I am unable to write because of constant interruptions!'

'Then we shan't interrupt you for long,' said Annie, and she bent to kiss him. With a grunt of exasperation he threw down the book and the pencil and looked around him. His hair was long and white, his sideburns stretched down over angular cheekbones, and his face was wrinkled and dark, though whether this was due to exposure to the sun or his natural colour Rob couldn't tell. His eyes were green, and he stared straight at Rob.

'A stranger,' he said. 'Our new dancing master?' He held out his hand, and when Rob shook it the grip was firm and warm. 'I'm always pleased to meet another artist, in the broadest sense of the word, of course. Bellingford is, alas, populated with cultural Philistines, the worst of whom are the children of the Taylor family. Is that not so, my darling?' He reached out and stroked Annie under the chin. She smiled broadly.

'Mr Scrivener is the worst-tempered man in the village, everyone is frightened of him. And he *always* tells lies, so if he says anything to you, just believe the opposite and you'll understand him perfectly.' Even Frances smiled at this.

'In that case, my young friends, I am delighted to see you and would welcome the opportunity to spend the rest of the day with you in delightful conversation.'

'We must be away, I'm afraid,' said Frances. 'We must all act as guides to Mr Patterson, in case he is overcome by the perils of the village.'

'Ah, dear Frances, sarcasm becomes you. Be off with you then, we shall no doubt be unfortunate enough to meet again shortly. Goodbye.' He picked up his book and pencil and resumed his scribbling. The four turned away.

'Mr Patterson?'

Rob turned back at the summons. 'Yes, Mr Scrivener?'

The old man didn't look up. 'In all seriousness, I would welcome the opportunity to talk with you further. Perhaps you would call on me one evening, once you have settled in?'

'I'd be pleased to do so, Mr Scrivener.'

'Good, good. You see, I know your father-in-law, we met some years ago. He was a rogue and a scoundrel then and I doubt that he has changed, and I am curious to know more about how the years have toyed with him and his fortunes.' Only then did he look directly at Rob again. 'And I am curious to talk with you, too, Mr Patterson. You're not at all the type of son-in-law I would have expected James to acquire. At your convenience, of course. Goodbye.'

'Goodbye, Mr Scrivener.' The words didn't escape easily from Rob's mouth, they had to negotiate a wildly beating heart and pass a constricted, dry throat. He hadn't expected someone to know Playford! He closed his eyes and breathed deeply. He would overcome the problem; he *had* to overcome the problem.

His mind was occupied for the rest of the journey. He barely spoke to the fat, beaming doctor, ignored completely the giggling attentions of twin farmer's daughters who simpered

and swayed in unison. He answered questions with random
nods or shakes of the head, and his manner was distracted
enough to bring an enquiry from Danny about his health.
He managed to control his feelings then, was even able
to make polite conversation with the parson's wife when
they stopped there again on the way back to the manor.
The 'little something to eat, little something to drink' had
been transcribed by Mary Westborne into a table laden with
food, around which played Katherine, a shy young girl of
seven summers, and Philip, two years younger but twice
as confident. The children proved a welcome distraction
to Rob.

It was mid afternoon when they left, traversed the village
green and skirted the low, squat gaol house and remnants of
ancient wooden stocks. At one corner of the green, four paths
converged. One headed to the manor, another back into the
village, the third down to the river and the mill, and Rob's
feet automatically headed along the fourth. It wasn't that he
was curious to find where it led, rather a general assumption
that, because he'd seen everything else in the village, this last
quarter was certain to be part of the itinerary. It was Frances
who called him back.

'Mr Patterson, the manor lies ahead of us. You are taking
the wrong path.'

'I'm sorry,' he said, 'but I was sure we hadn't yet travelled
this way.'

'We haven't, Mr Patterson. But that path leads nowhere.'

He looked at the ground. The earth was well trodden. Feet
had passed that way regularly, clearly the track wasn't solely
used for the passage of animals. And he could see, beyond a
small copse of trees, smoke rising straight into the still, hot
afternoon air.

'The path leads nowhere?' he asked, puzzled.

'Nowhere of importance,' Frances replied.

'Then what is it at the end of the path that is unimportant?'

'Really, Mr Patterson, I fail to see why you cannot take my

word as truth. I have spent the large part of the morning and most of the afternoon showing you the village, introducing you to our friends and neighbours, and I am now tired. You are to commence your dancing instructions in two hours and I, for one, would welcome the opportunity to rest for a while before expending more energy. If you wish to explore in that direction,' she waved her parasol in the direction of the finger of smoke, 'then you may do so, but you will return having wasted your time.'

She strode on her way, heading home. Annie smiled, shrugged and followed her. Danny too seemed keen to be away.

'She's right,' he said, 'there's nothing there. A few labourers' cottages, hovels really, that's all. You won't get any thanks from anyone you meet there, you'll be lucky to get a word of greeting. And they'll all be out in the fields anyway; there's too much work to be done at this time of year.' He put his arm round his new friend's shoulder. 'Come on, if we head back now there'll be time for a mug or two of good, cool ale, then you can rest. I'll be interested to see how to do this dancing, though I might just watch to start with, see what I can pick up. Save myself for when I can find a partner . . .'

The remaining hour lost itself in a daze of worries. Rob was in a strange place with strange people, unsure of his own abilities, unsure of whether he could go ahead with his plans. He told himself how stupid he'd been to believe that he could deceive so many people in this way. As soon as he had opened his mouth Frances had disliked him; Annie had barely spoken to him; their father had ignored him; their mother seemed able at the very least to tolerate him; Danny was like a puppy around him. He felt that his attempts to teach anyone how to dance were doomed to failure – as soon as he spoke they would laugh at him. And even if he *did* manage to survive the evening, that old man, what was his name, Scrivener, he'd looked at him with those green eyes and straightaway had suspected him.

He heard the clock in the dining room strike five, and

each sonorous, echoing impact of hammer on metal tolled
a warning. He pulled on his shoes and adjusted his clothing,
picked up a sheaf of music and dance instructions and his
flute, then headed for the ballroom and impending doom.

They were waiting for him. Samuel and Rebecca Taylor and
their children had all changed into their evening clothes. Rob
hadn't known who might be there; he'd hoped that, for the
first lesson, it would be only him and Annie and Frances, that
they could discuss the dances they wished to learn, perhaps
try one or two simple steps together. To find the whole
family present was not an insuperable problem, but with
them were Theodore and Mary Westborne, wallflowered
beside the fireplace, and farther down the room Dr Allard
and his wife sat polite and round as salt and pepper pots.
Rob didn't hesitate. He thrust his worries from him and
began to speak in what he hoped was a fair imitation of
James Playford's rounded, rolling tones.

'Good evening, ladies and gentlemen. I'm so pleased to
see you all here.' There was no reply. He headed for the
harpsichord at the far end of the room and left his music
and his flute on it. It was quite hot, even though some of
the windows had already been opened. 'May I open the
doors?' he asked Rebecca Taylor. 'Once we commence
dancing we'll undoubtedly need whatever breeze we can
muster.' She nodded her assent, and he moved down the
room again. There were two pairs of doors and he opened
them all. There was still no conversation behind him. He
turned and marched back.

'Very well, then, let us commence our evening of dancing
by . . .' he smiled at the Westbornes and the Allards, '. . . sitting down. Come, bring your seats, please, gather around.'

'Damn funny way to dance,' said Samuel Taylor to his wife.
She hushed him as the doctor, the parson and their respective
wives took their seats alongside the Taylors.

'Thank you. Now I must confess that I'm in something of
a quandary. I don't know what dances to teach you.'

Even that admission brought no comments, but the looks which passed from each individual to the next needed no interpretation. Any gypsy charlatan travelling the summer fairs could have read the words which hung on eyes and lips and creased foreheads and on puzzled, hunched shoulders. It was left to Rebecca Taylor to act as focus for the group's collective thoughts.

'Forgive me, Mr Patterson, for appearing so ignorant, but I had thought that your instructions were quite clear. You are to teach us English country dances. Is that not what was agreed?'

'Quite so, Mrs Taylor, quite so. But there are dances and there are dances.' Rob hurried onwards. 'Let me explain. There is a beautiful dance by the name of "Newcastle". May I ask if any of you know it?' There was no response. 'Have any of you heard of it?' Again, nothing. Rob continued, pleased that no one had said anything.

'This dance, as I've said, is quite beautiful to watch and to perform. It's from a collection first published in 1650 by a Mr John Playford, a distant relative, no doubt, of my father-in-law. But don't be misled by its age. This dance is no product of a simple past; it is most definitely complex and would tax the most experienced dancer. But it is, nonetheless, a dance of the type you have specified. I hope that we may go on to perform it.' All of this, bar the last sentence, was truth. Rob knew that it was a complicated dance because he'd heard James Playford say as much, he'd heard him shout and scream at a set of dancers who were unable to understand his instructions for the dance. But he'd never seen it danced, and if the assembled company had declared that they did wish to perform it then he would have been unable to assist them in any way.

'You see, before I can teach you a single dance, *I* must know how much *you* know. Otherwise I may choose something too difficult and confuse you, or too easy and bore you. Miss Taylor, the impetus for this comes from you, from some time you spent in Edinburgh, I believe. May I ask the names of the dances you learned while you were there?'

Annie Taylor sucked her bottom lip into her mouth in concentration. 'Why, Mr Patterson,' she said, 'I can barely remember what I was doing last night, let alone two months ago. But let me see. One of them may have been called "The Indian Queen" or suchlike, and another, it was a strange dance, quite difficult, it went by the name "Nonesuch". And then there was one about gathering, a vegetable of some type, probably peas. But definitely a vegetable.'

'Turnips, perhaps. "Gathering Turnips",' suggested her brother.

'Doesn't sound like a dance to me,' muttered Samuel Taylor.

'And the rest of you?' Rob ventured. 'Do any of you know of any dances in this vein?'

'Mr Patterson,' said Samuel Taylor impatiently, 'if we knew the dances then we wouldn't have to employ you to teach us. Now may we progress?'

'Certainly, Mr Taylor.' Rob stood up. 'I believe I've determined the extent of your knowledge, so we'll start, ladies and gentlemen, with the cornerstones of English country dancing; the basic steps and figures which go to make up the dance. Gentlemen, please bring your partner onto the dance floor. There are ten of us and that number will suffice.' He held out his hand to Annie Taylor; she turned away from him and reached instead for her brother and tugged him to his feet. The other couples formed pairs with their marital partners, leaving Rob to bow in the direction of Frances. 'Mrs Arnison?'

She stepped forward, disdainfully offered him her hand, and he led her onto the dance floor to join the others. This was the way James Playford taught. First of all the basics of movement, then the shapes of figures, and only when these had been mastered would he move on to actual dances. Rob hoped that his pupils would not be familiar with the basics. If they were, then he would have an insurmountable problem; he didn't feel confident enough to instruct them in a dance from memory, and was sure that they wouldn't take kindly to him using the instruction book at this early stage. He tried not to let his worries show.

'To begin with, each gentleman should place his partner on his right, and in this position we should join hands in a circle. Good. The gentleman supports his partner's hand, Mr Daniel from below. Now let us circle round to the left, the right foot leads, take your time from me, after four. One, two, three, four!'

They moved off. Samuel Taylor began with a skip and a lurch, uncertain which foot was his right and which his left, his wife pushing him round eagerly. Annie Taylor was, as Rob had expected, graceful and at ease, laughing at her brother's attempts to mimic her poise. Theodore and Mary Westborne moved well together, as though they were happy in each other's company, with many a mutual glance and smile; the doctor and his wife were transformed by the need to cooperate, changed from courteous and happy partners into doleful, glowering gargoyles, pulling and snatching at the other's hands, out of time with the steps and out of sorts with each other. Rob's own partner was stiff and unyielding, as if unwilling to give all of her effort to the exercise.

'Good,' said Rob. 'Most of you seem to have a natural sense of rhythm in walking. Now if we move on to the other steps, the next is very similar but with more of a spring to it, thus . . .' He demonstrated, still walking, but with a more buoyant step.

'Can't tell the difference,' muttered Dr Allard.

'Oh, yes,' said Annie Taylor, 'there is a difference, like this.' She imitated to perfection both steps. 'What are they called, Mr Patterson?'

'I beg your pardon, Miss Taylor?'

'What are they called? The steps? They must have names, otherwise how will you be able to tell us which of them we are to use?'

'I see! Yes.' He thought quickly. Playford had never named the steps in Rob's presence, had merely asked his dancers to copy him in performing them. 'The first step,' he announced authoritatively, 'is most akin to normal walking and is called the walking step. The second is nearer to running and is called, logically enough, the running step. And next after that is the hop, or skipping step—'

'Which must be like this!' cried Annie, step-hopping around the room, right-hop, left-hop, while the others clapped in time. Rob smiled inwardly. They knew nothing. By dint of diligent work he would be able to keep ahead of them.

'Excellent, Miss Annie! And if the rest of you would care to join in, there's no need to dance with a partner here.' He took advantage of the general merriment, the forced concentration, to call the Taylor's daughter by her first name, and no one objected, no one noticed. He smiled again, not inwardly but a broad, beaming grin of confidence. It *would* go well, he was determined of that. Everything was falling neatly and tidily into its predetermined place. He noticed Rebecca Taylor trying to coax her husband into dancing with the rhythm and moved across to assist, pleased with the general industry and movement in the ballroom. Behind him Frances Arnison stood, face immobile. Only Daniel Taylor would have been able to guess at the emotions within. Only he, with the experience of years of her teasing and tormenting him, would have known that she was planning some type of mischief, but he was too busy to notice, too busy learning the complexities of this infernal dancing to pay his elder sister any attention at all. And yet he would have been more than concerned had he seen that round, red-cheeked face twist from its normal thin-lipped mask and move for a brief moment to a smile of smug, satisfied anticipation.

The Fourth Bar of the Musick

Wednesday, 16 June 1830

*In which Rob Tweddle suspects that his musicians
are not worthy of the name, and Frances Arnison
suspects that the dancing master's name is not what
it ought to be.*

Samuel Taylor was holding forth. He had his back to
the fireplace (where the fire had been laid over a week
before but not lit due to the pleasant weather), and his
heels were slightly elevated, resting on the lip of the stone
plinth. As he spoke he rocked forwards and backwards, his
hands clenched behind his back, nestling in the shelter of
his long-tailed coat.

'On the matter of music for the dancing, Mr Patterson,
I feel I must offer you an explanation before you meet our
little band.'

Rob was curious. He'd spent the morning with Rebecca
Taylor and her two daughters poring through his dance
instruction books, searching for dances which might be
suitable for him to teach them and their guests for the
wedding. He found he was able, by means of description and
demonstration, to translate the sometimes obscure instructions (annotated in places in David Patterson's unkempt

hand) into some semblance of the dance. Where this involved showing steps or figures he attempted, and for the most part succeeded, in securing Annie Taylor as his partner. And when he did so he held her closer, whirled her faster and, at the end of the piece, bowed to her more deeply than he did when forced to dance with her mother or her sister. He felt that she was gradually becoming more relaxed in his company.

He mentioned that it would be helpful to meet all the dancers he was to teach, not necessarily together, but in rotas or shifts, and that the musicians he'd been promised would also have to be coached in their tasks. Mrs Taylor explained that everything had been arranged.

'Those guests who must travel for the wedding, from Newcastle and Carlisle, some from York, one or two from even further afield, will receive their instruction from you before the wedding, but they will be assisted by those who live locally who will have learned the dances in the normal course of events, through the regular classes you will give.' She was interrupted by Frances, asking that Rob write down for her the instructions for one of the dances so that she might learn them in her own time. Pleased that she was at last taking an interest he complied readily with her request, while listening at the same time to Rebecca Taylor's continuing discourse.

'As for the music, this is for you to arrange as you see fit. Your musicians will be local people, and my husband has arranged for them to attend this evening for an initial meeting with you so that you may gauge their strengths and weaknesses. I'm sure you will enjoy meeting them, although you may find them, to begin with, rather different to the instrumentalists with whom you generally associate.'

She would not be more forthcoming, and Rob had been forced to wait to find out more, after an early dinner. The whole family was present, and Samuel Taylor continued his peroration.

'We are part of a small community, Mr Patterson, a community of gentlemen and farmers, of hard-working tradespeople. Although music plays a large part in our lives it must of necessity be considered in relation to the need to work, to learn, to eat, to sleep. Do you understand what I'm saying, Mr Patterson?'

Rob didn't, but he couldn't determine how he might say so without offending his host. He made do with a puzzled expression and a deep inhalation, which gave Danny Taylor the opportunity to interrupt.

'Well I've no idea at all what you're talking about, Father, and I'm sure no one else has either. Wouldn't it be easier if you just got to the point?' He was whittling a stick with a sharp knife, with no real purpose but to occupy his hands.

'I would have expected nothing less than a total lack of comprehension from you, my boy, and you have, as usual, not disappointed me. I shall therefore aim my words at you and in doing so be sure that they will be understood by everyone. I was merely attempting to explain that our musicians this evening are not musicians. They play because they wish to, they play when they have a moment spare in their busy lives, and they come along tonight specifically to learn how they may be of assistance in making my daughter's wedding a memorable occasion. They are my friends and the friends of my family, and I trust that you will remember this, Mr Patterson, when you meet them and when you hear them play. Be gentle with them and your kindness will be rewarded with their wish to impress, to learn, and to play well.' He stopped and grinned. It was evident that the speech had been preying on his mind and, now that the burden of speaking was over, he could relax a little. 'Now do you understand?' he asked his son.

'Of course, Father. You're telling David that the musicians can't play very well, but that he's not to be upset at this and mustn't complain about it. I believe that sums it all up.'

'Daniel!' his mother said from a sense of duty, but with a smile on her lips.

'Mr Patterson,' Samuel Taylor continued, 'my son is, for once, almost right. Don't expect too much.'

*   *   *

Rob was introduced to the musicians as they arrived in the
ballroom, where a table had been set up with a large bowl
of punch. First to come in was the parson bearing a violin,
closely followed by one Charles Milburn, a wiry ferret of
a farmer, struggling with the coils of a black and battered
serpent. Rob recognised the doctor and knew that the small
flute he brought with him was a piccolo, but most of the
musicians and some of the instruments were strangers to
him. There was a preponderance of strings (the Woodford
family – father, mother, grinning son and shy daughter all
sharing the same freckled face – brought violin, viola, cello
and bass viol in proportion to their sizes) and brass. The
latter included a cornet borne with pride by Jimmy Gordon,
the blacksmith, who claimed to have brought it home with
him from Waterloo; a valve trumpet and a slide trumpet
in the possession of the Hewitson twins, who confessed
that they knew how to play neither; and a much battered
trombone, unpolished and green, whose owner appeared to
have had too much to drink and who stroked his instrument
and spoke to it in gentle, loving terms. Dick Nattrass, barely
in his teens, face flat as a millstone, brought a side drum that
had belonged to his grandfather and whose skin was split.
He had no sticks to beat it with, he said slowly, but had
heard that the dancing master required musicians and so
had cut some branches on the way in order that he might
join the band.

   Lizzie Lambert, the miller's thin wife, brought the oboe
her father had almost taught her to play twenty years before.
She admitted, pushing strings of hair back from her eyes,
that although she could remember which holes to cover with
which fingers, she wasn't quite sure what the three keys were
for, and anyway, one of them was broken. Her husband,
Gabriel, a bluff caricature of a miller in floured apron and
dusty hair, carried with him a sack from which he lovingly
unwrapped a small harp. Amongst those instruments Rob
was unable to identify was a many-holed cylinder no more
than twelve inches tall; a racket, he was told, which produced

a pleasant, low buzz like a large cat purring; and a reeded hook of pipe, which he was assured was a crumhorn. Add a bassoon and Rebecca Taylor's offer to play the harpsichord, and Rob was faced with an orchestra of twenty or more. He was, to say the least, concerned.

'How did your father find all these musicians?' he asked Danny Taylor quietly.

'He put the word about that he wanted anyone who could play to come along. He said it didn't matter how good or bad they were, that you, as a very able musician, would certainly be able to have them playing together within a week.' He sniggered as he drank yet another glass of punch.

'Is there a problem, Mr Patterson?' It was Frances, pretending to be polite.

'No, not at all, Mrs Arnison.'

'Oh, I'm so pleased. You see, I look around and see all these different people, all these different instruments, so many levels of ability. And it makes me quite dizzy to think how you'll manage. I don't know how I would do it if I were in your place. But then I remember who you are and what you do, your profession, your *calling*, and I have complete faith in you.' She smiled. Her mouth opened slightly and her pink tongue slid from one side of her mouth to the other, like a snake scenting the air before deciding on its prey. 'I had intended retiring early, reading a little, but I feel I would be far better entertained watching you, Mr Patterson. But I distract you from your labours. Please continue. I will be pleased to talk with you further at the conclusion of your task.' She turned on her heels and hurried away to sit beside her sister and mother, but her glances at Rob continued.

'What was that about?' asked Danny.

'I'm not sure.' Rob was worried. Frances Arnison seemed to have taken a dislike to him, which was unusual for a woman. He normally found it easy to relate to them, to talk to them; he enjoyed being with them. But he couldn't even begin to find a way round Frances Arnison, nor could he understand why she looked upon him with such apparent disfavour. The woman was becoming an irritation.

'David?' Danny interrupted his thoughts. 'Would it not be wise to start now? I think everyone has arrived.'

Rob looked up. He counted. There were twenty-seven people sitting in front of him in a wide crescent, each clutching some type of musical instrument, all smiling in eager anticipation, talking and laughing, one or two even singing. Gathered around them were friends and relatives, parents and brothers and sisters, all come to see what was going on. Small children ran and screamed around the room and slid along the polished wooden floor. Behind him sat the Taylors. He stood still but said nothing. He waited.

Silence crept in slowly. Those who first saw he was ready ceased their chatter, nudged their neighbours into similar cooperation. Noisy children were hushed, chased and penned in obedient corners, staring like cautious sheep. From beyond the room, through open windows, could be heard a melancholy curlew. Nearer at hand the cat-warning churr of a startled blackbird bubbled through garden shrubs. Sunlight stood in the ballroom like columns, its warmth palpable, and Rob moved a pace forward to stand in one wide and dusty beam. He felt his strength buttressed by the pressure of light and warmth on him. He held out his arms in supplication.

'Ladies and gentlemen,' he said, then waited. No one was looking anywhere but at him. 'My name is David Patterson.' His voice was not too loud, but it was clear. No one would ever doubt his origins; Newcastle had owned him early in his life and would always do so. But there was a melodic tone to his voice, a singing lilt which linked the words in a regular, hypnotic, almost poetic rhythm. It was the first time he'd ever spoken to such a large number of people, and he found he was enjoying himself.

'I've come here to your village, your community, to help prepare for the celebrations which will accompany the wedding of Miss Annie Taylor.' He turned briefly and smiled at

Annie, a public smile which she had to acknowledge with a similar gesture in return.

'I've been made most welcome by my hosts, Mr and Mrs Taylor,' another smile, another gracious acknowledgement, 'and, I might add, by those of you I've been fortunate enough to meet already. And it's most encouraging to see so many of you wishing to add your own personal contribution to these forthcoming celebrations. Some of you, however, may be disappointed. I need musicians to play for dancing, and since there is little time to instruct you in more than the bare elements of the music, I must rely on your own abilities. Those who are chosen to play for the dancing will have been selected not because they're better than the rest but because they'll need less coaching. And similarly, those who aren't invited to play shouldn't look upon this as a slight, merely as an inadequacy on my part, in that I'm unable to give them the time which would allow them to play in the manner required for accompanying dancing.' He was pleased with himself, pleased with the words he'd chosen and with their mode of delivery, pleased that he seemed able to keep the attention of the disparate audience that he was now addressing. He couldn't resist the urge to go on.

'Playing for dancing is an art which requires dedication and accuracy but is largely without recognition. Dancers won't notice if the music is of excellent quality and perfect pace throughout. They'll be caught up in their own movements, their own excitement. They'll only pay attention if something goes wrong, if the music is too slow or too fast for the steps and the figures, if the music is played incorrectly, discordantly. Musicians who play for dancing will receive only a smattering of applause, the crumbs from the table. Congratulations will go instead to the dancers who have so ably twisted and turned and pattered their feet in time to *your* music. But you'll have the satisfaction of knowing that, without you, there could have been no dance. And no dancers.'

Rob stopped. There was silence, and the brightness of the

evening sunlight meant that he could see little of the faces of those who had, he hoped, been listening to him. Then from behind him he heard a sardonic voice.

'Bravo,' it said without enthusiasm, and he turned to see Frances Arnison staring at him, and as he turned she began a slow, even clapping of her hands that was obviously intended to embarrass him. But the clapping was taken up by others. Its tempo was increased by them. There were murmurs of real approval, 'Well said,' and, 'Hear hear'. It was not rapturous applause – there was no reason for it to have been so – but it showed that he had been able to express himself to those listening, and that they had sympathised with him.

'What I'd like each of you to do,' he said loudly, holding up his hands to bring quiet once again to the room, 'is to play a piece for me. Something of your own choice; a short piece. And then I'd consider it worthwhile if you'd play a few bars of dance music which I've brought along with me, just to see how capable you are. Now then, if we may begin with the strings . . .'

And so began an interesting evening. Rob was being pulled between two opposite poles. He forced himself to remember why he was there, that his aim was to ridicule the Taylors and his former master, James Playford. It would have been too much to hope that all of the musicians were poor enough to make dancing difficult or unpleasant, and sure enough, some of them were able to carry a tune with ease and to read his music quickly and accurately enough to warrant inclusion in his ensemble. For this reason he ought to have excluded them; he did not, ultimately, want capable musicians. But the auditions were being watched by the Taylors, they were being listened to by everyone in the room; it would have been impossible to tell the parson that he wasn't good enough when he was the best violinist there and to include little Harriet Emerson who was barely able to scrape the strings with a bow which had been moulting for over a decade. So Rob compromised. All those who were reasonably good were included. Amongst these were the parson on violin; Mrs Woodford and her daughter on viola and cello; the miller, Gabriel Lambert, whose thick fingers seemed able to pluck tunes with ease from his Irish harp; and Rebecca Taylor's harpsichord. There was also a long-haired youth whose gangling, loose-limbed appearance suggested he might be searching for some hidden corner in which to sleep and gain strength for the coming day, but he was able to conjure beautiful melodies with ease from his bassoon, and when Rob had discarded the players of both the racket and the crumhorn, this youth picked up and examined both instruments and was able, straightaway, to play them. Rob asked the youth his name.

'Harold,' he replied, his voice too deep for his age, 'but everyone calls me Harry. Harry Brown.'

'He lives in the next village,' whispered Danny. 'His father farms, doesn't know what to do with the lad. He shows no interest in hunting. He's hopeless with livestock.'

'I suppose you'd better join us,' said Rob, aware that if he wasn't careful he'd have a group of musicians capable of playing together with ease and sounding good as well. He rejected those who couldn't read music or were unable to play with a modicum of accuracy; to have offered them places would have led to awkward questions being asked by his employers. But there were sufficient others with borderline talents who could be relied upon, he was sure, to provide the little extra imbalance he was seeking. So he chose Dick Nattrass, the young drummer who played loudly and with enthusiasm but whose accuracy of tempo was perhaps a little questionable. The trombonist too added volume, and contrasting tone, and an ability to slide into the right note only a fraction of a second after he was meant to. Rob asked Harry Brown to play the racket instead of the bassoon, with which he was more familiar, and retained Dr Allard with his piccolo, despite his inability to draw breath at the right times. This meant that the doctor began a phrase with the rest of the musicians and kept going, each note becoming more and more strained, his face becoming rounder and redder, until he was forced to draw a loud, off-putting breath and then recommence the sequence, usually beginning to play from the wrong point in the music.

He gathered them round a single copy of the tune 'Nonesuch', a simple enough tune written in a simple enough key (albeit moving from minor to major in this particular arrangement), to be played at a reasonable pace. More importantly, it was a tune which Rob already knew and was able to play on his flute. He took each instrument through the piece with varying degrees of success, and then they all played together. If they'd managed to begin together and end together it would only have made the poverty of the central portion more noticeable.

'That was . . .' began Samuel Taylor, rising from his seat to stand beside Rob, '. . . that was . . .' He appeared to have difficulty in finding a suitable adjective.

'Yes, Mr Taylor?'

'Interesting. Yes, interesting. Not beautiful, not yet, but most definitely interesting. I look forward to hearing more. There is a great deal of—'

'Potential, Mr Taylor?'

'No, that wasn't quite the word I was looking for.'

'Noise, Father. Noise is a good word.' Frances Arnison was alongside her father, eager to make a contribution. 'There was a great deal of noise, so much noise that I feel I must have some respite. I shall be in the library.' She turned away, then turned as quickly back again. 'Oh, Mr Patterson?'

'Yes, Mrs Arnison?'

'I wonder if I might trouble you to call on me, in the library, when you've finished. There is a matter I would discuss with you.'

'Why, certainly Mrs Arnison. May I ask what the matter is?'

'You may ask, Mr Patterson, but you will receive no reply until later. In the library.'

'Do you wish a chaperone to be present, Mrs Arnison?'

There was almost a smile on her face as she replied, '*I* shall need no chaperone. *You*, however, may bring one if you feel the need. Now then, dear Papa, would you mind escorting me?'

She turned again and went on her way, her arm linked with that of her father.

'My sister's up to something,' announced Danny. 'I wish I knew what it was. I've seen her like that before. She's like a terrier; won't let go, just worries and worries. She doesn't seem to like you very much, David.'

'I've noticed.'

'But then she doesn't like me very much either, and I'm her brother. Now are you going to play some more? Because if not I'm going to have another drink. In fact, I shall have a drink whether you're going to play or not. Excuse me.'

He bumbled across the room to the table with the punch-bowl, laughing and joking on the way. Rob looked around, eager to catch the eye of Annie Taylor, but she was seated with her mother at the harpsichord, deep in conversation. He was about to cough in an attempt to gain the attention of his band of musicians when someone tugged at his sleeve. He half turned and found Harry Brown beside him.

'I'm sorry to be presumptuous, Mr Patterson,' he said in his young, grown-up voice, 'but I was wondering if you might be able to use me in some way.'

'And what way would that be, Harry?' Rob noticed that the youth had a slight lisp.

'Well, I know you have to teach dancing, and I know you need music to do that, and I know you play the flute. It must be difficult to play the flute and instruct at the same time, so I thought I might be able to help you by coming along to your lessons, by playing for you.'

'By playing the racket? Or the bassoon? I'm afraid neither is ideal as a solo instrument providing music for dancing.'

'No, Mr Patterson, but I can play a different instrument.'

'And what's that?'

'What would you like?'

Rob was amused. This young man, this large boy, was implying that he could play any musical instrument. 'The fiddle?' Harry Brown nodded. 'Or perhaps the flute? I do enjoy the flute; I'm familiar with it. Can you play the flute, Harry?' Again a nod. 'Or something brass. A good rich sound, though it might be difficult to play a fast jig on a trumpet.'

'I could manage that, Mr Patterson.'

'All of those?'

'Yes.'

'Show me.'

And so he did. Harry Brown played any instrument Rob handed him. He was weakest with the brass, strongest with the strings, but even his flute playing was better than Rob's. He could play the harpsichord, had a few problems with the miller's harp, but was confident that if he was permitted to take it away for a few days he would soon master the basics of playing. The others had gathered around as Harry played.

'Mr Patterson,' said Rebecca Taylor, 'what a stroke of good fortune. You will be able to use young Harry here as your musical assistant, I'm sure his father would allow him to come across each day. Would you like that, Harry?'

Rob didn't like it. The boy was too good, he could even carry the rest of the musicians if he was allowed to play flute or violin. But there was nothing he could do; Rebecca Taylor had all but imposed Harry on him.

'I would like that,' said Harry Brown. 'I'd like the opportunity to learn what I can from Mr Patterson and to play for the dancing. I even have some other tunes which I could play—'

'Oh no, Master Brown, most definitely not.' Rob's voice was emphatic. 'The dances and the tunes go together. They're inseparable; they complement each other. You play what's written down or you don't play at all.'

'Yes, Mr Patterson.'

'In that case you may attend tomorrow afternoon at

two o'clock for the first proper dancing lesson. Can you remember that?'

'Yes, Mr Patterson.'

'Good. Now the rest of us have been kept waiting for long enough. I think we ought to play "Nonesuch" again. Harry, can you write music neatly?'

'Yes, Mr Patterson.'

'Well in that case we need, what, eight fair copies of this tune? And some others, there will be others as well, in time. Could you do that?'

'Yes, Mr Patterson.'

'What a pleasantly affirmative person you are, Harry. Our relationship may yet blossom.' He looked up to see Annie preparing to leave.

'Miss Taylor,' he shouted across the room, 'Miss Annie! We're about to play some tunes again, would you care to stay and listen? It might be possible, if the pace is good and regular, for me to show you one or two individual dance steps.'

'Thank you, Mr Patterson,' she responded, the echoes careening off the walls and ceiling, 'but I think I shall retire early. Perhaps tomorrow?'

'I shall hold you to that, Miss Taylor.' He turned to the band. 'From the top of the page, then. Let us play "Nonesuch", or "À la Mode de France."'

There was still some light when the music ceased and the musicians headed for home, and the strains of flute and violin could still be heard over calm meadows as Theodore Westborne and Harry Brown shared a footpath, a few minutes and a tune. Rob was happy that the evening's instruction was over. It had been difficult to cope with so many instrumentalists. His own knowledge of music was certainly insufficient to cope with the capricious talents of Harry and the stolid dependability of the parson. But they were at odds with each other, those two; the parson studied the text of a tune before attempting to play it exactly as written, while Harry glanced at the score to, as he put it, 'try to understand how it feels' then played it as a theme and variations, each one more complex than the last, as he came to know the tune better. Their preoccupation with each other and the ways in which they played allowed Rob to concentrate on the others without his instructions being questioned; but he wasn't sure how long this would continue, nor was he sure how he'd solve the problem of their musicality. It would wait, however; it would wait until another day. But what wouldn't wait was his meeting with Frances Arnison. He didn't know what she wanted from him, that was the most infuriating fact. He just couldn't read her in the way he could other women. Annie, for example, was a straightforward young girl, a little fickle, adventurous, but he knew her, he could categorise her. He would woo her gently. He would dance with her and thus be able to hold her, and once she was used to that it took little else to move a young lady on to more personal, more private adventures. But Frances . . .?

He left the ballroom and entered the hallway, the darkness had already lingered there for some time and candles had been lit. He thought about finding Danny first, asking him to accompany him in case . . . In case of what? What could Frances Arnison possibly do that would harm him? What could she know about him? And if the worst did happen, if by some means she found out his true identity, then he would simply leave. No one would suffer. He'd committed no crime here, he was a free man and, of course, the nearest constable was miles away, in Hexham. He still hadn't unpacked his chest; he could escape quite easily. There was nothing to worry about.

He knocked on the library door and, without waiting for an answer, went in. Although the room was referred to as a library it was quite small, and two of the four walls were filled with a fireplace and a large window. The two remaining walls were shelved, but not every shelf contained books. There were several bird skulls of various sizes, some wooden boxes, three or four small statues, again of birds, and a similar number of glass cases filled with stuffed animals, from a fox and a badger to a family of field voles. All of them squinted malevolently at him in the light of a dozen candles set in a single clawed stand resting on a large desk. There was a seat behind the desk but it was empty.

'Mrs Arnison?' whispered Rob, hoping he'd been so long she would have given up waiting and retired.

'Mr Patterson,' came the reply from a high-backed seat which sat squat in the shade like a huge, fat toad.

'You wanted to see me?'

'I did. Come round here, please, I hate listening to disembodied voices. You may sit at the desk, I'm sure my father won't mind.'

Rob did as he was told. There was nothing on the desk save a sheaf of papers and a pen and the candlestick, and he moved the latter to one side so that he could better see the woman he'd begun to think of as his adversary. Wax had dripped down onto the desk top. He made as if to remove it.

'Just leave it, Mr Patterson, it will give Father something to complain about when he comes in here to write up his journals. Anyway, there can't be much. I've only had the candles lit for a few minutes. I was watching night fall, which was quite beautiful, and listening to your band of players, which was less so.'

'They aren't used to playing together yet,' Rob defended. 'They'll improve.'

'Yes, I'm sure. It's very noble of you to say so.'

Rob's eyes became more accustomed to the dark. The candlelight picked out Frances Arnison's face against the dark embroidered back of her seat. She was wearing a deep-purple dress buttoned up to the neck, and her hair had been tied back less severely than normal. It fell down over her ears before being pulled over her shoulders by a fierce bone comb. The result was that her face seemed disembodied, ethereal, her wide eyes staring not at Rob but over his shoulder, at her reflection in one of the panes of glass in the window.

'Why did you want to see me?' asked Rob. There was no answer, just the face, and the eyes. 'Mrs Arnison, you wanted to see me. Would you mind telling me why?' The face ceased its attempts at self-hypnosis. Frances Arnison looked at Rob, her head tilted slightly to one side as if she were pondering some insoluble dilemma. Rob found that he'd picked up the quill pen from the desk and was idly tracing whorls on the paper in front of him, but the pen was dry. He put it down again.

'Mr Patterson, you are very friendly with my brother. You call him Danny, an abbreviation I dislike immensely, I might add, and you allow him to call you David. This is understandable. You are close to his age and he, I believe, respects you. It does him good to have someone to respect; respect has been lacking in my brother for too many years. You also call my sister Annie – Miss Annie, to be precise – but I have no doubt that, at some suitable moment, the title will be dropped and you will be able to insist that she calls you by your forename. Do you have any other forenames, Mr Patterson? I have an excess of them. I was christened Frances Helena Susannah.'

'I have no other names, Mrs Arnison.'

'Are you sure, Mr Patterson? You see, in my mind you look very little like a David and even less like a Patterson. When I think of those names I imagine someone considerably smaller, much rounder, more . . . More well bred than you, Mr . . . What shall I call you, since I find the name under which you travel so unacceptable? Would Dancing Master suffice for the moment?'

'It's a description of me, Mrs Arnison, so it would certainly attract my attention if you wished to use that title instead of my name.'

'Very well, Dancing Master. I will admit that I am curious about you. Had I met you without knowing your occupation I would have looked at you and said "clerk". I would have

said "printer's assistant", or any tradesman's assistant for
that matter. I would have said "gentleman's servant". I
would not have said "dancing master". And yet this is
your business, and so you are demonstrating. Yes?'

'Yes, Mrs Arnison.'

'Why do you not call me Frances? You do my brother and
sister the honour of using their first names, why not me?'

'I will call you Frances if you wish.'

'Yes, Dancing Master, I do wish.'

'Then I shall do it.'

'Good. But now you have me at a disadvantage, since I
have no leave to call you by your first name.'

'You have leave to do so, Frances. You may call me
David.'

'Precisely, Dancing Master. But I do not wish to call you
David. I wish to call you by your first name!'

Rob said nothing, but his mind was working. Had she
guessed? Was this supposition on her part, or did she know
the truth? He discarded the latter; she couldn't know his real
identity. But why did she feel he wasn't David Patterson?
What had he given away?

'You may, then, if you wish, call me by a name which
few people use,' he said softly, and she craned forward to
hear more. 'Only those who know me well, who know the
real me, ever call me by this name.'

'Yes?'

'That name is . . . Davie.'

'No, no, no! You toy with me, Dancing Master, and I am
not a woman to be toyed with!'

'I believe that, Frances, I believe that.'

'And don't call me Frances! I am Mrs Arnison to you!'

'But you just said—'

'What I said before is different from what I say now!' She
took a deep breath and leaned back in her seat, closed her
eyes for a few seconds. When she opened them again she
was in control once more.

'Let me tell you something about myself, Dancing Master,

so you might decide for yourself whether or not you have
earned the right to call me by my first name. I am an
unusual woman. I am the daughter of an unusual woman.
My husband is a gentleman farmer who is fond of what I
shall call country pursuits. He enjoys hunting and fishing
and riding. He is like my brother in that. He is fond of his
pack of hounds, he enjoys drinking with his companions.
He will talk for long hours about the crops he raises and
the beasts he tends. He is known throughout the county
for his sheep, and more especially his cows. He dotes on
the animals – he spends more time in their company than
he does with me!' Her voice rose but was controlled again.
'But he is a good man, my husband. I will have nothing said
against him, except when I say it. He is kind and he is gentle
to me, though there are times when I wish he were more . . .'
Her words tailed off into silence

'I beg your pardon?'

'Please do not interrupt me, Dancing Master. My husband,
he is good to me, but we have very little to share. I enjoy
theatrical performances, I enjoy singing, I enjoy the company
of other ladies, I enjoy music, I even enjoy dancing.' Her voice
shrank once more so that Rob was forced to lean forward to
hear her. 'None of these things my husband considers worthy
pursuits for a man of his background, of his station, and even
if he did, there are limited opportunities to enjoy them in a
remote region such as this. And so I visit Hexham when I
can, and Newcastle on special occasions, and I have twice
been to Edinburgh. When I go I try to make new friends, I try
to discover new things. I have read widely, Dancing Master.
The library in my own home makes this one appear a pale
and sickly wretch in comparison. And I write; I correspond
with friends all over the county. We tell each other what we
are doing, we reveal our thoughts and our feelings; we hide
nothing except what manners dictate would be unladylike to
reveal.' She appeared excited now. Her speech had quickened,
her face had become more animated, and her hands which
had previously remained still now fluttered round the arms

of the chair like ghostly moths. 'Some of my friends tell me things they would not tell their husbands,' she added conspiratorially, 'or their lovers.' She sat back.

Rob was, if anything, even more puzzled now. She'd hinted that there was something awry with her marriage without actually saying what it was. She'd implied that she had a wide circle of friends who wrote to her and told her their innermost secrets – surely an unwise thing to do when a letter could be read by any of the many hands needed to deliver it, – but quite what the relevance was of this disclosure he couldn't tell. He decided it would be better if he said nothing, and Frances took her cue from his silence.

'One of my friends lives in Newcastle, in Jesmond. Do you know the area well?'

'I know it,' he answered.

'She is a young woman. She has recently married a man many years her senior who is determined that she shall enjoy a full social and artistic life, even though he himself is too advanced in years to accompany her always. He has paid for her to attend dancing lessons, Dancing Master, and she has told me of her instructor. I have her letter here. She describes the way he teaches. She says he is a small man, though neatly made, with a somewhat piping voice. He has short hair; it curls naturally. He plays the violin as well as teaching dancing. In other words, Dancing Master, he is in his physical appearance quite the opposite of you. And yet he too calls himself Mr David Patterson. Do you have any explanation for this, Dancing Master?'

Rob picked up the pen again. He used it to emphasise his words, his feelings, to amplify the anger he was trying to convey.

'Are you suggesting I may not be telling you the truth? Are you suggesting I'm someone other than who I say I am? Madam, I've no need to explain myself. I've done no wrong. Indeed, my intention is to be of the best possible service to you and to your family. And as for another with the same name, I agree that two dancing masters with the

name of Patterson is stretching coincidence, and I can only
assume that this imposter is trading on my own good name
and credentials in the hope of obtaining business which I
would otherwise have been offered. I have nothing more to
say on this matter, and trust that you will have the good
grace to keep your accusations to yourself and thus avoid
making a fool of yourself and, by association, your family.
Goodnight!'

He rose to his feet and threw down the quill, whose plume
he'd been quietly and methodically shredding, picked up the
bag containing his flute and his dance books and stormed
from the room. He would leave this house; he would leave
now, he wouldn't stay and run the risk of being exposed as
an imposter and a fraud. It would take him, he estimated,
the best part of seven or eight hours to walk to Hexham.
He could be there before the household was awake, before
his absence was discovered.

In the library Frances Arnison moved around the desk
and picked up the broken quill. It was one of her father's
favourites, made from the feather of an osprey. She resolved
to take it away with her, he would assume that he'd lost
it himself. She wasn't disappointed with the events of the
evening. There was yet time to work on the dancing master,
she was sure he had something to hide, and his response
to her questioning had been exactly what she'd expected.
She took out some folded papers from her pocket. The first
was the dance instructions she'd requested, the second a
page torn from the dancing master's manual. The writing
in the margins of the latter was different to that on the
former, but which belonged to the real David Patterson?
There was also her friend's letter, the girl really was too
much. The descriptions went quite beyond what was needed
for identification, although the news that she'd taken this
Patterson person as a lover was quite exciting and, with the
detail she offered, well worth reading again. She would save
that pleasure for her bed.

The piece of paper that had been lying on the desk was

covered with whirls and scribblings which her dancing master had formed with the dry nib. She examined them, held them up to the light, but they were indecipherable and she was about to throw the paper away when she noticed one corner of it was coated with wax. She looked at it again, held it close to the candle, then opened the top drawer of the desk and reached inside to bring out another quill and a bottle of ink. She opened the ink and dipped the pen into it, but instead of writing she allowed the ink to drop from the tip of the pen onto the waxed paper. It ran in all directions and, where there was no wax, soaked into the paper. In the middle of the waxed portion there appeared blue lines and mysterious mazes, a crown and a gibbet with a figure – it looked like a woman – dangling from it. And there was also a scribble of letters, all written over one another. Only one word was recognisable, and as Frances set light to the paper and placed it on a dish to burn out she whispered the word, just once. 'Rob.'

The Fifth Bar of the Musick

Thursday, 17 June 1830

In which Annie Taylor finds herself, at night, alone with a man in his bed chamber, and she discovers that dancing may not necessarily be an innocent pastime.

As Rob climbed the stairs he heard a clock chime midnight; then another, distant behind some closed door, joined in the dolorous celebration. He stopped halfway up the stairs, suddenly tired, both mentally and physically; the effort of sustaining his deception was beginning to tell. He tried to persuade himself that his decision to leave was correct, that he was at risk and would be safer elsewhere. Quite where he wasn't sure. This was the first time he'd been away from Tyneside, and he knew that returning there would bring its own dangers. But he would go, he was decided on that course of action, and he would consider his final destination during the long walk to Hexham. Thus resolved, he was about to recommence the climb to his room when he heard, from above him, the click of a door closing and the sound of feet running down the long corridor towards the stairway. He shrank back to the wall. The candles had all been put out, and only moonlight was entering through the

roof window high above his head, but that was sufficient for
him to see Annie Taylor hurry along the balcony, then slow
to turn down the stairs. She was dressed, as she had been that
first night when he saw her in the garden, in a white cotton
shift, and her hair was loose, it tumbled over her shoulders
and streamed behind her. She wore nothing on her feet.

As she reached the head of the stairs Rob moved forward
and coughed lightly, merely to make his presence known.
The young woman had been looking back, over her shoulder,
and the sound startled her. She turned her head quickly, saw
Rob emerging from the darkness and missed her footing. She
stumbled forward and might have injured herself, but Rob
was there, and she fell neatly into his outstretched arms. It
was a moment he'd longed for but which he hadn't thought
he would experience quite so easily or so early in this fledgling
relationship.

She was obviously naked beneath the shift. Rob could feel
the warmth of her breasts as he held her close, and she'd
bathed in scented water; she smelled of summer meadows
and fresh-cut hay.

'Miss Taylor,' he whispered, holding her slightly away
from him so that he could look at her, but not so far
that the contact between their bodies was broken, 'are you
alright?' She nodded.

'Are you sure? You must have bruised yourself when you
fell. Stubbed your toe, perhaps. Do you feel faint? Perhaps
you'd better sit down.'

He pressed her gently into a sitting position on one of the
stairs and kneeled before her, took her foot in his hand and
stroked it gently.

'Does this hurt?' he asked. She shook her head. He took the
other foot and repeated the operation, pressed a little harder
on the ball of her foot so that she winced. Having secured
that response he tutted to himself, made her straighten her
leg. Her ankle appeared, and her calf, and he moved his
hands over them.

'Mr Patterson,' his patient said softly, 'I do not feel

unwell in any way, thank you, and I'm not sure that
your ministrations, pleasant though they feel, are serving
any purpose.' She took her foot away.

'Miss Taylor,' said Rob, taking her foot back again, 'I'm
no medical expert but I *am* familiar with the strains and
mishaps sometimes caused by dancing, and I'm concerned
that you may have unknowingly injured yourself. Now please
be still.'

'Mr Patterson, this is neither the place nor the time for
such a discussion. We may be disturbed and I would remind
you that I am not suitably dressed . . .'

The sound from downstairs could not have been cued with
any greater accuracy if the meeting had taken place on stage.
For the first time since he arrived at Bellingford, Rob was
thankful for Frances Arnison's presence.

'Quickly,' he said, 'someone's coming. Follow me!' He
pulled Annie to her feet and hauled her after him before she
could object. Up the stairs he led her, down the passageway
and into his room. As soon as he closed the door she began
to speak.

'Mr Patterson, what is the meaning of this? How dare you
drag me into your room in the middle of the night! I warn
you, I shall scream if you so much as—'

'Miss Taylor, I've no intention of doing anything or saying
anything which might in the least way embarrass you. You
may leave immediately if you wish. The noise we heard was
your sister; she'll be making her way up the stairs this instant.
Would you like me to open the door for you?' He reached
for the handle and made as if to turn it, but she was at his
side and her hand was on his wrist.

'No,' she whispered, 'my sister wouldn't understand!' She
let go his wrist only when she felt him relax. 'Very well
then,' she said, 'I shall wait, for a minute or two only,
until we can be certain that she has passed.' They were
close together. Once more Rob was intoxicated by the girl's
perfume. He noticed that the top buttons of her nightgown
were undone. He thought he could see pale flesh in the deep

shadows within shadows, but he could have been mistaken; the room was in comparative darkness. He took his hand away from the door.

'I think we should shed some light on matters,' he announced, and lit a single candle beside his bed. He then closed the curtains and lit more candles, one on his dressing table, another on the desk. As he moved about he saw his guest was shivering, though it wasn't cold. He pulled a folded quilt from the blanket box at the bottom of the bed and handed it, at arm's length, to Annie Taylor. She took it with a nod, wrapped herself inside it. Rob sat down in the only chair in the room.

'Please, feel free,' he said, motioning towards the bed, but Annie shook her head violently. Rob shrugged. 'It was a good job I was there, to catch you,' he said.

'If you hadn't been there I wouldn't have tripped. You frightened me. I didn't expect anyone else to be up.'

'Yes, I imagine so. But given that I wasn't in my bed, it was beneficial for both of us that I was exactly where you found me. Had I been higher up the stairs then you'd have seen me clearly, you'd have turned away from me, and I'd have missed your company.'

'Mr Patterson, do not talk that way!'

'Had I been lower down the stairs then you'd have fallen further. You might have injured yourself quite severely. How is your leg, by the by? Do you wish me to examine it further?'

'I most certainly do not.'

'A pity. Well, I suspect your sister will have passed to her bed by now, and you'd better do the same. But no, I forget, you were leaving your room, not going towards it. Another nocturnal performance in the garden?'

'Yes, if you must know, I was intending walking in the gardens. And I knew that you had seen me the other night, even before your clumsy hints at breakfast that you'd done so, because I could see you. The moonlight was sufficient for me to see you quite clearly.'

'Clearly, Miss Taylor?'

'Yes, Mr Patterson.'

'But the night had been extremely hot. And I seem to remember, before I was disturbed by some noise and looked out of the window, that I'd been sleeping naked.'

'Quite, Mr Patterson.'

'Perhaps one day, then, you will have the opportunity to repay me the compliment.'

'If I do then I trust that you will be more impressed than I was. Now I shall go. My sister will be asleep by now. I need have no worries about disturbing . . .' She stopped; something he had said or done made a connection where none had been a moment before. 'Mr Patterson, I saw no one downstairs, and you saw no one, yet you said with certainty that it was my sister. Why is that?'

Rob held out his hands in innocence. 'Very simply, Miss Taylor, I'd been talking with her in the library. I left her to come to my room, met you, and assumed she was the source of the noise, since no one else was, to my knowledge, still downstairs.'

'You were talking with my sister? That is strange. I was under the impression that she didn't like you at all. Was it some secret assignation?' There was a note of teasing in her voice.

'Miss Taylor, how dare you suggest such a thing!'

'Oh, quite easily, Mr Patterson. I am, after all, a country girl. I'm aware of the ways in which birds and beasts behave to one another. I'm aware that dislike is considered by many as akin to love, and I'm aware of the life my sister leads. If I wish to suggest an assignation then it is because I know these things and I consider it within the bounds of possibility. But if you say that your meeting was to discuss other matters, then I shall believe you.'

'One moment, Miss Taylor. You mentioned "the life your sister leads". What exactly did you mean by this?'

'It is, I'm afraid, one of those hoary old statements which is always accompanied by the caveat, "If you require an explanation, then you have no need to know." And in saying this, I have told you too much already, so I shall take my leave and bid you goodnight. I shall retire, I think. There is no need to wait by the window in the hope that I shall dance for you tonight.'

The realisation had been dawning on Rob throughout their conversation that this young girl was possessed of a wit and self-assurance far beyond her years. Despite her initial fears about his behaviour, and he had remained seated in his chair throughout the conversation lest she consider his movement a threat to her, she was speaking confidently, and there was no doubt in her mind that she had gained the upper hand in their confrontation.

'Goodnight, Mr Patterson,' she said as she headed for the door.

'Goodnight from you, perhaps,' he answered, 'but from me, goodbye.'

She halted. 'I'm sorry, I don't understand.'

'You may dance in your garden if you wish, Miss Taylor. I shan't be here to see you. I'm leaving, immediately, as a direct result of the conversation I had with your sister. She accused me of being an imposter. She's had some communication from a friend who describes a Mr David Patterson who isn't at all like me, and she's decided, from that information, that this paper creation is real and that I, despite being flesh and blood, am false. I'm not willing to remain here while these accusations are being thrown about. I was about to leave when we met, and I'm still resolved to do so.'

Annie Taylor seemed concerned. She stepped away from the door and back into the room. 'Mr Patterson, who did my sister suggest you were, if not . . . if not David Patterson?'

'She made no suggestions of that type at all. She seemed more concerned with who I wasn't rather than who I was.' Rob hurried around, thrusting spare pieces of clothing and his music into his chest. His eyes wandered the room in search of familiar articles but found none.

'How will you transport your luggage?' she asked innocently.

Rob stopped. He hadn't considered that problem, his chest was small but heavy. It contained everything he possessed; his clothes, his other shoes, his money, a chess set he'd won in a game of cards, some drawings of women which he wouldn't dare show to any woman. He couldn't walk all the way to Hexham carrying that.

'I'll borrow the dogcart,' he said, 'and leave it at Hexham. I'm sure Danny won't mind collecting it. Now if you'll excuse me—'

'Mr Patterson, I'd like to say something to you. It may make you change your mind. It may—'

'Nothing will make me change my mind, Miss Annie, nothing at all. Now if you please, you're in my way.'

'I want to say something first.'

'No.'

'I shall not let you go. I refuse to move. I shall . . .' She looked behind her. The key was in the door. She turned it quickly and removed it, clutched it in her hands.

'Please, Mr Patterson, sit down. Let me speak. And if you still wish to go after you've heard my few words, then you may do so. I'll even come with you to drive the dogcart back.'

Rob looked at her, his eyes narrowed. 'Do I have any choice in the matter?' he asked.

'None.'

Rob put down the chest, retreated to the bed and sat down on it. Annie followed him, and stood between him and the door.

'Mr Patterson—'

'David,' said Rob. 'Call me David. That is, unless you too believe that I'm an imposter.'

'No, I believe you are the person you say you are. David.' She glanced down as she spoke, and even in the dim light Rob could see the colour in her cheeks. 'Look at me, David.'

'It's no hardship, Annie.'

'No! Do not speak to me like that! I am taking a great risk simply being here with you. I am engaged to be married. That marriage will take place in a few days' time. If my fiancé were here, if he were to find out—'

'If he were here? I find his absence unusual, to say the least. The man must be mad. If I were him—'

'But you are not! He is kind and considerate. He is a gentleman, and he will attend in due course. He has much to do. He has his farms, his businesses.'

Rob ignored her. 'If I were this man I wouldn't let you out of my sight.'

'Mr Patterson! You go too far. I have no wish to compromise myself further. I am only too aware that I am in a young man's room, unchaperoned, in the middle of the night.'

'And wearing a most becoming nightdress, I might add.'

'Mr Patterson! You will not say things like that! I am, after all, here for your own good.'

'Really? I am pleased.'

Annie looked at Rob, searched his face for a sign of sarcasm but found none. Had she been more experienced in reading men's expressions then she might instead have discovered something more frightening than sarcasm: lasciviousness, a hunger which could be satisfied by a food both rich and rare which he could even then have taken without asking; or which could be offered and whose taste would then be improved a hundredfold. Goods or property Rob would have taken without compunction, but with women he preferred to wait until what he desired was given freely.

'You promised to call me by my first name,' he went on, 'and I'm curious to find out what you have to say to me, what it is that may change my mind about my departure. I'm yours, Annie, to do with as you will. For the next few moments, at least.'

'I shall be brief then . . . David.' It was clear that she found it difficult to be so familiar, but she forced the hurdle and went on. 'I have two things to say. The first is that I do not wish you to go – please try to understand; listen to all that I have to say in case you reach any false conclusions – because you are doing your job so well. No one else will have said this to you; we aren't accustomed to giving praise too readily, but you have adapted to circumstances which are, I will agree, a little difficult. And we would not wish you to leave without completing your work here.'

'We, Annie? We? Can't you be a little more personal in your praise?'

'No, I cannot. I am included in the pronoun and I will go no further.'

'Then I shall have to assume that you, in delivering the words, and creating the words, must have included in them some personal emotions. That will do for me.'

'David, you are twisting what I say! You seem to think that I have some feelings towards you, and it is clear that nothing I can say will dissuade you from that misguided belief. But I will persevere—'

'But Annie, you *do* have some feelings for me.'

'I do not!'

'You do. They may not be the emotions I seek and you deny, but they are emotions. Look at you. Aren't you angry? Is anger not an emotion? Don't you feel frustrated that I appear not to be listening to you? The concern you expressed earlier may have been centred on the village and the feelings of its inhabitants, but you've moved on from there, from the general to the particular, from the villagers to you, and to you alone. You can't hide your emotions, Annie.'

'You're doing it again! You're not content with twisting my words, now you're playing with my feelings! I don't know why I'm trying to persuade you to stay. I ought to let you go. I should be glad of the chance to be rid of you!'

In her anger Annie had moved towards Rob, she'd begun to gesticulate, her eyes had grown wide. Her voice had become louder, though still a whisper, and she spat the harsh sibilance at him across the room. Rob's voice, in contrast, remained low and steady, and his evenness of tone and temper seemed to animate his sparring partner to wilder gestures.

'But *you* locked the door,' he said, 'and *you* have the key. And you've told me only one reason why I should stay, though you promised me two.'

'That was before you started behaving in such a silly and annoying manner. I really do think you're doing this just to make me angry, and I'm afraid you're succeeding. I can't think why I should say anything else to you at all!'

She crossed her arms and, for a moment, appeared the spoilt child Rob knew she wasn't, petulant and sulking. She was trying to help him, she really did want him to stay, and he could only reward her with innuendo and cynicism. It wasn't surprising she was tiring of the way he was playing with her, and Rob himself was becoming unsure of his own motives. What had started as a game, as a means to the end of securing his revenge, was becoming more serious. He found he really did admire the young woman standing resolute before him. She was, as she'd said earlier, risking her reputation in an attempt to persuade him to stay. But his ambivalence (he couldn't yet admit that it might be guilt, or that admiration might be more akin to affection) was balanced by her sister's suspicion that he wasn't the real David Patterson. If he were to be unmasked then he could be imprisoned for deception and fraud, and theft if James Playford was involved. But there was also the matter of what Annie had just told him, that his efforts were well appreciated, that he was looked upon as a teacher of dancing and music, and a good one at that. So what if Frances Arnison did make her accusations public? He could demonstrate that he was a dancing master, hadn't he shown people how to dance? Were the musicians guided by him or not? The other David Patterson must therefore be the imposter. Aware that this logic might be flawed, he was prepared to listen to Annie's other reason for him staying. If he did decide not to leave then he wished to be fully armoured against any other missiles Frances Arnison might throw at him. And then there was the matter of Scrivener to overcome – Scrivener, who had met James Playford and wished to talk about him. He looked at Annie. She was still standing before him, waiting for his response, her bare foot tapping lightly on the carpeted floor. Her eyebrows were buried in a frown so deep it was amusing, and Rob found himself, despite his worries, despite his misgivings, unable to prevent himself smiling.

'You see!' crowed Annie triumphantly, 'you can't take anything seriously at all.' She stamped her foot. 'I will not be laughed at, by you or anyone else! Go – I'll be well rid of you!' She spun round and unlocked the door, but Rob rose swiftly to his feet and was alongside her before she could twist the handle to open it. He put out his hand and leaned his weight against the flaking varnished panels. Annie looked at him, her eyes wide, the disbelief that he should prevent her from leaving ready to be replaced with terror if he should do anything further. She took a deep breath, as if she were about to scream, and he immediately backed away.

'I'm sorry,' he said quickly, his words tripping over one another in their urgency. 'I didn't mean to frighten you. Please, don't go. I want to apologise. I know I've been rude to you; I know I've abused the hospitality you and your family have offered me.' He tried to appear contrite. He linked his fingers in an attitude of prayer. 'You were right. I was making light of your emotions. It was wrong of me, and I apologise. But it was done from no sense of mischief, but from . . .' He struggled for words which would convey an aspect of what he saw as the truth but which wouldn't offend her. 'It was done from a sense of appreciation that between us there is the potential for a real . . . a real friendship. And if I chose the wrong words in an attempt to explain this, if my manner appeared too flippant, then I must claim ignorance and a lack of vocabulary rather than intent to deceive or embarrass. And, once again, I apologise.'

It was now his turn to wait. Annie's thoughts teased her face into motion. Her eyes searched the farthest dark corners for inspiration, her tongue played across her lips, her fingers stroked her nose.

'I accept your apology,' she said, 'though no one would

accuse you of a lack of vocabulary. But I must go; I have lingered too long. My sister is a light sleeper and sometimes visits my room in the night. I may have been missed.'

'And that is more than I shall be if I leave, Miss Annie. If you have anything else to say that will aid me in my decision then please, I beg you, don't keep it secret. Your words of kindness have swayed me, I'll admit, but I'm still ill at ease and confused. Have pity on me.'

Annie Taylor shook her head. 'You should have been a teacher of the dramatic arts, Mr Patterson, you surely have skills in that field. No, do not protest! I may believe that I can see through your sophistry, but my viewpoint is still clouded by my own emotions, and beyond the veil of your words there are only hazy, distant clouds. So I will tell you what I intended saying, and then I will leave, and you will mention our meeting to no one. It did not occur, and what I have said to you and will say to you cannot, therefore, have been said at all. Am I understood?'

'My ears are deaf. My voice has disappeared.'

'Then let both senses return by tomorrow's lesson.' Far away in the house a single chime resounded. 'It is late; the lesson is today's. I shall speak quickly. The second thing I wished to tell you concerned my sister. She is not, I believe, like other women. She feels frustrated in so many things. She is jealous, I believe, of me and the way I look, and had she been born male then she would have been far more capable than my brother of working on the land, and this also galls her. But she is plain, and she is a woman, and she is married to a man she does not love, though he cares for her in his own way. She corresponds with friends, acquaintances, sometimes with friends of friends whom she has never met, in an attempt to bring something extra into her life. She is a sad woman.'

'I know enough of her to agree with that sentiment.'

'But you do not know her well enough.'

'I certainly have no wish to know her better.'

'Then that too is sad. Despite her jealousy of me, which she has recognised and acknowledged, she is a true and faithful friend.'

'And are you seeking to have me sympathise with her?'

'No, merely attempting to explain why she is as she is. At thirty years old she already appears to be an old maid. You see, she has been married for eight years, Mr Patterson, and she has no children. She has been unable to conceive.'

'Miss Annie, is this a matter that a young lady should speak of? I feel uneasy hearing you talk of such matters.'

'Really, Mr Patterson? I am, as I mentioned before, country bred, and quite familiar with the details of, let us say, stockbreeding. I have watched ram with ewe, stallion with mare; I have assisted in the birth of foal and lamb, I feel no shame in talking of such matters. Why should I balk at telling you that my sister has no children? I do not know whether the fault is hers or her husband's, but I have no doubt that they will, earlier in their marriage at least, have attempted congress.' She watched as Rob's face began to turn pink. 'I have no wish to embarrass you, but I mention this as some explanation of the way Frances behaves towards men. The examples she has around her – my father and my brother, her husband – are hardly likely to encourage her in developing an affinity with other males. And consider this also: you are everything she is not. You have power over others, you are musical, you can dance, you have a way with words, you are young, you are attractive – though I would not normally say so in case it should bring on the ridiculous posturings which dominated our earlier conversation. You are mobile; you meet many different people in the course of your work and your travels. Frances is, I am afraid, jealous of you, and when my sister is jealous she strikes out. The only means she has of striking out at you is by accusing you of some misdemeanour, and if none exists it would be within her abilities to fabricate one. She means no harm to you. She is unable to help herself, and generally such an accusation is met by immediate withdrawal if she is challenged. You may count on my support if she decides to make this particular allegation public. I do not wish to discuss the matter any further, I mention it only in the hope that you will not be pushed by my sister's actions into any precipitate move. I shall now retire. Goodnight, Mr Patterson.'

'Thank you, Annie. And goodnight to you, also.'

She opened the door slowly, peered out into the darkness beyond. The candle flames sputtered and danced in the slight draught.

'Goodnight, David,' she whispered, and was gone.

The day would be hot again. Rob woke late and dressed slowly. The fact that he was still there, still at the manor, still in Bellingford, was due both to Annie Taylor's powers of persuasion and to his own immoderate self-confidence. He was convinced that Frances would not attempt to expose him, that if she did then she would be thwarted by lack of proof, and that his ability to persuade everyone that he was truly a dancing master would win through regardless. Thus armed and armoured he spent the morning strolling in the gardens, hoping, without fulfilment, to meet Annie. Having exhausted the entertainment value of lawns and clipped hedges, he headed for the village. He was unused to solitude and felt a need to be in a crowd, to experience noise and bustle, to come across someone he'd never met before. Yet he was prepared to acknowledge that the only crowd he might encounter would be a flock of sheep, and the loudest noise would be the bellowing of a lovesick bull, and that he'd already met everyone in the village at some time during the last few days. Still, he continued his walk in search of some form of novelty.

The village was as empty as when he last visited it. The same pencil line of smoke showed that the blacksmith's forge was at work, skeins of wool hung dyed and drying in the sunlight, cottage doors were open wide to encourage the slightest breeze into dark interiors. There were people about, mostly youths and children, and they tipped their hats or performed awkward curtsies when they saw him, but none would join in conversation. He soon found himself at the meeting of paths where one track wandered away from the village towards the distant coppice, showing no sign, on this hot morning, of the habitation he'd witnessed two nights before. He was curious. The warning that he shouldn't stray in that direction was enough to encourage him to do precisely that, to go there, to find out why he, or the hidden cottages, should be in quarantine. It was no later than noon and he didn't have to return until two o'clock, and his feet seemed eager to exercise themselves along the ruts and folds of the earthy track. But no sooner had he made the decision than he was thwarted.

'Mr Patterson!' It was a shout, a man's voice. Rob looked around, but could see no one. 'Up here, sir, up here!'

Rob raised his eyes in the direction of the voice and saw, almost hanging out of the gable window of a cottage on the far side of the green, Emanuel Scrivener waving at him. At that distance it was only the poet's white hair that identified him, although his voice carried with the ease of one used to declaiming. Rob was only too aware that the poet had expressed a wish to talk with him about his 'father-in-law', James Playford, and he wondered if he might pretend that he hadn't seen him.

'Come on over, Mr Patterson,' the voice boomed, and Rob knew that escape was impossible. He made his way across to the cottage. 'Be down in five minutes,' Scrivener continued, 'do you mind waiting?' He withdrew his head, then popped it out again. 'There's no need to come inside. If you don't mind.'

Rob didn't mind. He needed time to compose himself, to think of how he would answer Emanuel Scrivener's questions. He sat down on the warm grass and closed his eyes in an attempt to concentrate, but was overwhelmed by the persistent droning of urgent bees, the warbling of invisible birds, the summer countryside sounds which he'd heard others describe with such passion but which were, to him, insidious interlopers. They were in no way as soothing as the rumble of iron-shod wheels on cobbles and the raucous cries of peddlars and rapacious dockside gulls. He smelled flowers and wanted smoke and old fish heads, he felt slender knife grass beneath his hands and longed to sit on an uneven, low stone wall. He was aware, even with his eyes closed, of the overpowering green heat of the countryside. He imagined instead the cool slate-grey of the river and the town and the clouds, and the home which wasn't home when he was there but now he was away had revealed a powerful possession of his spirit which he'd never realised could be so strong.

'Pleasant to daydream a little, eh Mr Patterson?'

Rob opened his eyes. His thoughts had been kidnapped. He had no excuses ready, no explanations at hand. The poet was standing before him, dressed simply in a loose white shirt (open at the neck to reveal a chest thick with white hairs), pale breeches and hose, and a pair of scuffed and scruffy black shoes. He seemed indifferent to his inelegant attire.

'Yes, Mr Scrivener,' Rob answered. 'I don't normally have much time for relaxation.' Perhaps, he thought, Scrivener would choose not to pursue the questions he, Rob, most feared.

'But are relaxation and daydreaming the same thing, Mr Patterson? For me daydreaming is not relaxation. Daydreaming, or free thinking as some would call it, is part of my work. I must let my fancy roam free to bring me inspiration for my poems, for my pamphlets, for my novels.' His words fell from his lips with great speed and were sent on their way with amplified gestures of the arms and hands. 'I usually find that my thoughts, given free rein, always return to some item which has been taxing my mind, a rhyme, perhaps, or some unresolved element of plot. Does this not happen with you?'

'No,' answered Rob, thankful that they were pursuing matters unrelated to his old master, 'not that I'm aware of. Although sometimes I do try to work on the figures of dances, to imagine how they would look if they were danced in a different way.'

'Then you prove my point, dear boy! Come, I shall

accompany you to the hall, I wish to speak to Mr Taylor before this afternoon's lessons commence. It is some time since I had the opportunity to converse with someone whose responses I did not know before he had begun to think of them. Living in such a small community can be so ... so insular!'

'I can understand that, Mr Scrivener, already I find myself missing the town.'

'One becomes used to it after a while, dear boy, and the advantages of country living, certainly in my profession, far outweigh the inconveniences. For example, when I lived in town I had a social life which largely prevented me from writing at all. It took me three years to write my first novel – three years. And once that had been published, with a certain success, then it took even longer to write the second. I never did finish the third, and I was always taking myself off to new places in an attempt to attract inspiration, at home, abroad, but only when I came to spend a summer here did I realise that serenity can provide imagination with its own impetus. I found that, when there were no distractions, I could be more productive. I started and finished a new novel inside four months! I found time to write poetry, good poetry as well, mind you. And now I would live nowhere else.'

'I'm pleased you seem to have found your spiritual home, Mr Scrivener.'

'Oh, not only spiritual, dear boy, not only spiritual. One's physical needs are catered for also. The local people are kind and generous, and so very close to nature. There are times when I believe a man could not ask for more.'

Rob was puzzled. 'Forgive me if I appear stupid, Mr Scrivener, but what do you mean, exactly, by "physical needs"?'

The older man smiled. Rob realised for the first time what a large head he had, though there was little excess flesh on him. It was as though his body had been shrunk, or someone had removed the correct head and replaced it with one belonging to a giant.

'The needs which a man cannot deny, Mr Patterson. I

shall tell you, for I know that a man such as yourself, whom I know to be married, may require the service I speak of when forced by circumstances to be away from his wife. I myself have never married and therefore make frequent use of such services.' He drew closer to Rob, put his arm round his shoulder and began to talk more softly, more slowly. 'For such a service there is often a need, of course, to make a payment. I am fortunate in that my needs are catered for by a variety of sources. When I saw you I was paying a visit to a close friend, a widow of some seven years standing, with whom I share conversation and more intimate pastimes. There are others who, in need of extra income, are prepared to exchange their favours, or the favours of their daughters, wives even, for cash.'

'I see!' said Rob, aware at last of the reason for the poet's circumlocutions. 'You're talking about prostitutes.'

The poet stopped walking, and in doing so brought Rob to a halt, and looked around guiltily. 'I prefer not to use that word, sir,' he said, holding his finger up to his lips.

'Very well then, let us say instead whores, or strumpets, ladies of the night. Call them what you will, the words mean the same.'

'I beg to differ, young man, and I consider myself something of an expert on the subject of words and their meanings. These people, these women, are no common bawds or courtesans, at least not those who live in the village itself. There are others ... But I should not talk of *them*. These village women, only one or two of them you understand, they help men such as me because they want to. If they have a clientele then it is a limited one, as you can imagine. They provide a service to the community, just as you are doing. I count them as my friends. And just as you would take offence if your friends were referred to as harlots, so should I, were it not for the fact that you are unfamiliar with our ways. But now that I have made you familiar, I would consider it an insult if you continued to use phrases similar to those you have previously offered.'

'I understand,' said Rob, not sure where the dividing line between prostitution and friendship should be placed in this instance, but not wishing to cause further offence. Besides, he told himself, if his advances towards Annie Taylor continued to be repulsed then he might have some need of the poet's 'friends' before the end of the fortnight. 'And I thank you,' he added, 'for your consideration that I too may wish to make use of this service. If I do so I shall not hesitate to contact you. Now, should we continue our walk?'

Rob was treated along the way to examples of the poet's work, and when he ceased his verse his explanations of the true meaning he was attempting to convey were only marginally more interesting than the lines themselves. Emanuel Scrivener, it appeared, made his money from penny novels, high melodrama and moral tales which allowed him the luxury of writing bad poetry. That no one wished to publish his verse didn't deter him; he merely published it himself and absorbed the inevitable losses. Rob's interest in the novels, which seemed far more exciting than the pastoral poetry, was discouraged.

'They are poor things,' Scrivener admitted, 'in which good is always rewarded in the last chapter, evil is punished, and sinners are made to repent. Those who fall from the path of righteousness are allowed to experience a certain temporal enjoyment, but this is more than balanced by the woes piled upon their shoulders by the long-term results of their actions. Life is never that easy, as I have argued repeatedly with our good pastor, Mr Westborne, but he will have none of that, and the worthy reading public seem to agree with him. They require some assurance that villains, even though they become rich and powerful, will receive their comeuppance. The worthy reverend promises this in an afterlife; I merely bring the day of their reckoning forward a little. They are made to suffer while they are still on earth. But I deal with this in one of my poems. Allow me to show you how the . . .'

The words passed by like grains of airborne pollen. Rob knew that they were there; he could sense them, but they meant nothing to him. He was pleased only that the poet's preoccupation with his own writing left him no time to ask Rob about James Playford. When they approached the manor he made an excuse that he had work to do and thus escaped, though he was aware that the day of reckoning had probably only been deferred. He calmed himself and, with an hour still to spare, spent the time copying out music for his band of musicians, taking care to insert the occasional wrong note. He suspected that many of them would play by ear anyway, and others would play the wrong note incorrectly, transposing it to the correct note by their accidental errors. He intended taking the musicians for instruction first, then the dancers, and then bringing both together later in the evening. He knew the dances he wished to try, a variety of squares, contras and circles. And the music wasn't too difficult. He had to admit that he was looking forward to seeing how they all managed.

He was gathering together his materials, just before two o'clock, when there was a knock on the door. He opened it to reveal Danny Taylor, dressed in unusually fine clothing. His trousers were unstained by mud, his waistcoat buttons were all fastened, his cravat was bound high and tight around his neck, but the whole was slightly unfashionable and sat uncomfortably on him. Perspiration jewelled his forehead; his face was red, and he appeared anxious.

'May I come in? he requested. Rob nodded, curious to find out why he appeared so troubled.

'You seem uneasy,' he suggested. 'In fact, you look drawn tight as a bowstring, Danny. What's the matter?'

'David, I feel ill. There is a young lady. I don't think I've mentioned her to you, not specifically, but in passing, on the general matter of young ladies, I think I may have said something about her, though you will not have realised that it was her I was referring to.' He stopped, unsure whether he'd finished his sentence or not.

'Go on. There's a young lady, you intimated as much when we last spoke.'

'Yes. She is here, to stay for a few days, to join in the dancing. Her name is Stephenson, Miss Charlotte Stephenson. She is a friend of my sister.' Again he stopped.

'Yes?' Rob prompted. 'Is she the reason you're trussed up in all your finery?'

'No! I . . . That is, yes. Yes it is.'

'So you have some feelings towards her, perhaps some amorous intent, yes? There's no need for shyness with me, Danny, I can read you quite well, despite not having known you for long. Tell me, does this young lady know of your feelings towards her?'

'I've never properly expressed my feelings, David, I wouldn't know how to begin. But she knows, I'm certain she knows. I can't hide the way I feel.'

'And what of her? Has she expressed any interest in you beyond that of friendship?'

'I think so. But I can't be certain.'

'And you want me to find out for you?'

'No! Good Lord, no, I couldn't ask you to do that. How would you do that anyway? You don't know her; you've never met her.'

'Danny, dancing partners express far more in their dancing than in the words they use. I shall simply watch her. And I shall instruct her, and I shall have the opportunity to dance with her, and I shall be on talking terms with her without the need for formal introductions. Dancing breaks down many social barriers, that's one reason the Puritans sought to have it outlawed, did you know that? I'll find out for you, if you wish me to do so.'

'Oh yes, I would welcome that, thank you. But that isn't the reason I came to see you. It was merely to ask that, when it came to selecting partners, you ask her to partner me. That was all.'

'I shall do that as well, my friend. But I'd suggest you go away and change quickly into clothes that are a little less restricting. It'll be warm this afternoon, and I'm sure your lady friend will have no wish to dance with someone who sweats all over her dancing gown. Do you agree?'

'Yes, I shall do as you say. And thank you once again.'

'You're welcome, Danny. But tell me one more thing. Is she a handsome girl?'

'She is, without a doubt, the most beautiful woman I have ever met.' He turned and left.

'If that's love,' said Rob to himself, 'then I'm glad that, at present, I appear to be immune to the illness.' And he put his flute into his bag, looking forward to seeing Annie again, unaware that the symptoms of the disease were already showing in his smile and in the eagerness with which he hurried down the stairs.

Annie Taylor was walking in the twilit garden alone. She'd enjoyed the dancing that afternoon, she'd enjoyed listening to the music, she'd even, though she would admit it to no one, enjoyed the company of David Patterson. He'd infuriated her the night before, but during the day he'd been warm and polite, gentlemanly even, and she found her mind occupied by thoughts of him. Perhaps that was why, as she strolled the narrow paths between well-clipped hedges, she wore a frown. She should have thoughts only of her fiancé, she told herself. No other man should intrude upon her anticipation of the next few days, her last days as a single woman. She forced herself to concentrate on other matters. She was pleased that her sister didn't appear to have said anything further to upset David Patterson . . . No! There he was again, why did his name keep returning to her? She needed someone to talk to, someone to distract her. Charlotte had come to stay. Charlotte should have been walking with her, but instead she chose to spend time with her brother as he gambled at cards. Perhaps if she sought Charlotte out she would shun the close atmosphere of the drawing room and walk with her. Perhaps Charlotte was at this very minute looking for her, bored; her span of attention wasn't huge.

Annie had made up her mind to return when she was halted by someone calling her name. She turned.

'I've been looking for you, Annie,' said Rob.

'Mr Patterson, I thought—'

'David, remember. You said you'd call me David.'

'No, Mr Patterson, *you* said I should call you by your first name. That is a different matter altogether.' He seemed put out that she'd been so strict with him. His face clouded like that of a faithful lapdog banished from a comfortable seat.

'I'm sorry,' he said, 'I'd no wish to offend you. In fact, that's why I sought you out, to apologise for my behaviour last night.'

'What behaviour was that, Mr Patterson? I cannot speak for you, but I retired early and slept late. I'm not sure I wish to know of your nocturnal adventures.'

'Yes,' he said sadly, unable to complete his confession and demand his penance, 'I see. I understand, that is, what you're saying. Thank you. In that case I'll go. I have music to arrange, dances to consider. Goodnight, Miss Taylor.' He turned to leave.

'One moment, Mr Patterson.' The words pulled him swiftly back to face her. 'I would talk to you, on the subject of dancing, and of music.'

'Yes, Miss Taylor?' His shoulders were bowed slightly, his attitude one of subservience that was laughable in such a tall and, so far as she could see, naturally self-confident man. She smiled at him; he smiled back.

'Very well,' she relented, 'you may call me Annie, so long as no one else is about to hear. And I shall call you David, given the same circumstances. For with that degree of familiarity it may be easier for me to talk to you. Please, will you walk with me?'

'I shall be delighted, milady.' He bowed, deep as a dandy courtier, with much flourishing of fingertips and generous hand gestures. She followed with an equally low curtsy, head down as she descended, eyelashes fluttering as she rose.

'Tis my pleasure, sirrah.' She held out her hand and he

supported it gracefully, but they could manage to play-act their way for only two steps before each was attacked by giggles brought about by the ridiculous and haughty demeanour of the other.

'I think that neither of us could be the courtier,' laughed Rob.

'Methinks, good sirrah, thou art verily mistaken,' continued Annie, her face alternating between disdainful superiority and undisguised mirth. 'I am perfectly able . . . perfectly able to play the part of the . . . of the disdainful lady . . . No, I cannot!' It was her turn to double up, and the sight made him laugh more, which redoubled her hilarity. Their breath came in gasps, their faces became red, their eyes watered. They both had to sit down on a grassy bank to recover their collective composure.

'Oh, dear me,' said Annie, shaking her head, breathing deeply. 'I haven't laughed so much since I was a child!'

'I think I've never laughed so much at all,' countered Rob.

'Really? That is sad; that is very sad.'

'No, I think not, Annie. Not all lives can be as happy as one another. Some are born with sadness as a companion and continue thus through the years until they sink together to the earth. I myself am finding happiness more often in so many things. But particularly when I find myself in your company, Annie.'

'Mr Patterson, such talk. I have told you before—'

'David. You promised. David.'

'The name does not alter the warning. I told you last night—'

'But last night you went to bed early and slept late. You told me so yourself.'

'Mr Patterson! David, then! You are impossible!' She rose quickly to her feet and flounced away, but he was faster than her, he caught up with her crossing a small lawn hedged on all sides, in its midst a lichen-stained statue, a semi-naked Greek or Roman goddess, only a scalloped seashell protecting her modesty.

'I'm sorry,' he said, 'you must forgive me, these words aren't mine, it's as if someone else were talking.' He barred her way and she glared at him. 'That must be it! My mind is being taken over by someone else, someone . . . Let us call him by another name. Let us call him . . . I know, Rob! This Rob says things through my mouth, he expresses his own emotions. You must admit this is possible, Annie! Look at me, I'm happily married. You're to be in that same worthy state within ten days, how could it be that I would woo you?' She made as if to duck under his outstretched arm but he lowered it, and her effort was half-hearted anyway; she was intrigued by what he was saying.

'I, David, who am at present in control, could not bring myself to . . . to indulge in such sweet-talk, such nonsense. Why I don't find you attractive at all. In fact, to my mind you're quite plain, and your conversation lacks meaning and depth. You're too short for a man of my height and too flippant for one so serious. It's only when I'm taken prisoner by that demon, that Rob, that his lascivious nature takes control and he offends you. He presumes familiarity, he attempts to seduce you with his false love and sweet words. And I, alas, can't help you when he assumes that power.'

Annie stood back, not sure of herself, watching Rob.

'You're insane,' she said, 'there's something wrong with your mind. I don't know what it is but it frightens me. I'm—'

'No, please don't go. I can feel him coming back. Quickly, you mentioned dancing and music. Keep hold of my mind, talk to me of those matters. What was it you wished to say?'

'Just that . . . Just that I was . . . Mr Patterson, this is silly!'

'David! Now tell me!'

'It was just that there was something wrong. With the dancing.'

He let go of her hands and stood up straight. The

mania left him at once. 'Something wrong? With the dancing?'

'I knew it, I knew you were play-acting!'

'I was nothing of the sort. It's just that I've been brought
back entirely in control of my senses by your statement. Tell
me, please, what's wrong with the dancing?'

'Nothing, not with the dancing itself. It was the dances,
and the music. They just weren't ... They weren't as I
wanted them to be. They weren't exciting. Oh, I know
everyone's learning them at the moment, I know it's all
new, but they just seemed so staid and old-fashioned. It
was as if you were deliberately trying to make them dull,
though I know you wouldn't do that.'

'And the music? You mentioned the music as well.'

'The same. Dull. Boring, even. Certainly uninspiring.'

'Oh.'

'I thought you'd want to know.'

'Yes. And you're not just saying this because of what I
mentioned before, about you being plain and shallow and
... and whatever else it was I said?'

'David, how could you suggest such a thing? Besides, I
mentioned to you that I had something to tell you about
the dances long before you began insulting me.'

'But you could have changed your mind. You might have
been about to congratulate me on my choices, but then been
upset by my—'

'Yes? Your honesty? Your forthright opinions? Your silly
play-acting, perhaps, or your rudeness? No, how could I let
them affect me? David.' She spat out his name as if the taste
of it were bad, as if she wanted to hurry its passage through
her mouth.

'Then I shall change everything,' he said, 'starting now!
If you want excitement then you shall have it. Can you
waltz?'

'I beg your pardon?'

'Can you waltz? It's all the fashion on the continent, has
been so in London society for years now, but only recently

has it been considered suitable for the distant, somewhat backward regions of the country, such as this. Do you know the dance?'

'I've heard of it. I heard that some poet described it as lewd, and I believe I've seen it danced in taverns when the coach in which I was travelling stopped, but I've never danced it.'

'Then you shall. The music is in three beats to the bar. The emphasis is on the first beat, like this: ONE-two-three, ONE-two-three, yes? Now come here. Stand closer, put your right hand in my left. I place my right arm on your hip, just so—'

'Mr Patterson! You have gone too far!'

'Miss Taylor, I have not gone far enough! I tire of your presumptions, your incessant whingeing, your tireless and tiring attempts to read into my actions an assault on your good name and nature. You stated, a moment ago, that you wished to learn a dance more exciting, more adventurous, did you not? This is just such a dance, and yet I hear nothing but complaints. I'm afraid I can stand no more. I bid you goodnight, Miss Taylor.'

'No!'

They stood still for a moment, he half-turned and ready to leave, she with her hands held out, almost in supplication. It was getting darker, candles had been lit in the house though the curtains had not been drawn, and the windows had been opened. Laughter, filtered through leaves and blossoms, augmented by a high-branched song thrush, tempted them into slow movement again.

'I'm sorry,' said Annie.

'Then I accept your apology, and in turn apologise myself,' countered Rob, 'but I feel it would be better if I left you.' He waited for her reply. Would it be the one he expected, had he read his prey correctly?

'I would wish you to stay,' she said softly, 'and teach me to waltz. If you still wish to do so.'

Rob kept his face from her, afraid she might see the triumph written there. He swallowed, composed himself, and turned.

'If you're sure . . .' he began.

'I'm certain,' she answered.

'Then we stand like this.' He moved closer to her, placed his right hand on her hip. She closed her eyes. He settled her left hand on his arm, took her right hand in his left. 'It is, so far, without pain?' he asked.

She nodded her reply.

'Then open your eyes. Remember the rhythm? Three beats. You step with that rhythm. LEFT-right-left, RIGHT-left-right, while I do the opposite. Try it, on the spot, to the tune.' He began to whistle an air she'd heard before, a tune in a plaintive minor key. He nodded his head on the first beat of each bar. He swayed from side to side, and she swayed with him, gently pushed and pulled by his insistent hands.

'Good,' he whispered, 'now we try moving. With me.' His sway became a shuffle, each foot in turn lifted slightly from the ground, and she copied him.

'No, don't look down, don't look at your feet, they won't fall off. Look at me, you follow a dance by seeing it in your partner's eyes. The eyes give the first hint of movement, the rest of the body follows. Now follow me.'

The shuffle turned into a definite movement as he stepped backwards and she followed. Then he moved forward, and she moved with him. Hesitant at first, she became used to the step and the timing. They began to dance as a couple rather than as two individuals.

'I knew you'd manage it,' he said, 'you're a natural dancer. Now we turn, left or right, it doesn't matter, like this. Take the lead from me.' He turned out to the right with his right foot and she copied him with her left, mirroring his style and his movements. They completed a circuit of the lawn and halted. He looked down at her. She no longer appeared troubled to be in such close proximity to him, her eyes were wide with excitement, her breasts rising and falling as she took deep breaths.

'I enjoyed that,' she said, though the words were unnecessary.

'That's only the beginning,' said Rob. 'Imagine a room full of people dancing like that, all turning at the same time, and the music emphasising the beat. You can dance it much more expansively than we did. But it's getting dark. We need more room. Come on!'

He pulled her after him towards the house, but they avoided the area overlooked by the dining room and the drawing room (which the Taylor family and friends were still occupying), and instead went to the west side of the house where the setting sun had coloured the sky white and blue and green, where pipistrelles sounded for moths over the wide flat lawn. Rob halted in the middle of the short, summer-browned grass and detached himself from Annie. He bowed deeply.

'Mistress Taylor, may I have the pleasure of this dance?'

Annie curtseyed and replied politely, 'Master Patterson, I should be delighted.'

He took her hand again, placed his hand on her waist, and began to sing the same tune he had sung before. He nodded the first of the three beats in each bar, four times to show the passage of four bars, then signalled to Annie with a smile that they should start to dance. And so they waltzed, and this time they danced faster. Annie laughed aloud as they twirled and span, and she held on to Rob tighter with each turn, and he whirled faster again so that she would move closer to him. His hand was forced to move from her waist to the small of her back; her own hands moved higher and higher up his arms. Their bodies were pressed close together. Rob sang the tune three times, and then again, until he was forced to concentrate on dancing and they circled the garden in silence, the melody resounding in their minds. And then they slowed. And they stopped. But they remained in each other's arms.

Each could feel the beating of the other's heart, the shock of new emotions. Annie was intoxicated by this new dance and by the sense of intimate closeness between her and her partner, and Rob was exhilarated by a sense of triumph, that he'd achieved one of his aims, one of his desires. The couple were looking at each other, looking into each other's eyes. Their heads drew closer, closer still, and their lips met in an inevitable kiss.

From her bedroom window Frances Arnison stared at them, her face unreadable. She saw their lips part briefly, then they kissed again, but more fiercely this time, and when Rob drew back slightly it was Annie whose hand reached to hold him at the back of his neck, who pulled his head down to her once more. Frances watched impassively as Rob's hand, his right hand, detached itself from Annie's waist and slid up the front of her dress to halt at her breast. She showed no sign of wishing to interrupt, to fulfil her role as chaperone, even when it became clear that her sister would not move the hand away, even when the strength with which she pressed herself against her companion showed that she was enjoying the hand's attention.

Then Frances noticed Rob's other hand move. It reached up below Annie's arm to rest on her shoulder, then slid down that arm to take her hand in his. He moved her hand to his waist, then forward onto his stomach, and then down onto the tight flap of his trousers. There it rested for a brief moment like a pale fan, frail and helpless. Then, in one movement, the two bodies separated, pushed apart by Annie Taylor. Her hand balled into a fist and retreated, was brought forward again far more swiftly to the same position it had occupied a fraction of a second previously. The punch in the groin felled Rob. He doubled up and collapsed to his knees, but that wasn't enough for Annie. Had her skirts been less voluminous she would have kicked him, that much was evident from her anger. Instead she slapped Rob with the flat of her hand, and that blow knocked him to the ground, where he lay, coiled and writhing like a salted slug, as Annie ran into the house.

Only then did Frances permit herself the luxury of a

smile. David Patterson, or whoever he really was – she wasn't convinced by his protestations of the previous night – had performed well for his audience of one. She applauded gently and turned back into the darkness of her room.

The Sixth Bar of the Musick

Friday, 18 June 1830

In which Rob shares a bed, though the bed is not his own, and sleep is not uppermost on the other occupant's mind.

Again Rob rose late. He was amazed at the resilience of the human body. He'd thought the previous night that he would never be able to walk again, at least not with his usual gait, and he imagined that his face would be bruised to blue and red by the morning. Once again he'd considered leaving, but found that he barely had the strength to limp, miraculously unseen, to his room, let alone travel the road and the miles to Hexham. But the morning found him rested. The ache in his groin had subsided, and his face looked no worse, after his shave, than it normally did. He dressed slowly, trying to predict what the morning might bring. Annie couldn't have told her father about the previous night's incident, the fact that Rob was still there, that his arms and legs remained attached to his body, was evidence of her secrecy. But would she remain silent? Would she be tempted to tell someone, if not her father then her brother? That, Rob decided, would be a worse alternative. Danny Taylor was fiercely protective towards his younger

sister, his punishment might be more permanent than mere
physical injury. Argument that he hadn't gone too far, that
it was a mistake brought on by alcohol or her beauty or the
mysteries of the dance, was unlikely to warrant forgiveness.
There were therefore two alternatives. He could, somehow,
secure Annie Taylor's silence; or he could flee. It was while
he was considering how to leave without being seen that
he saw the envelope nestling on the floor just inside the
door. The name 'David Patterson' was inscribed on it in a
florid hand.

Rob picked it up, turned it over. It was sealed with wax,
but there was no monogram. He broke the seal, took out
the single sheet of paper and began to read.

Dear Mr Patterson

*Your behaviour last night was inexcusable. If I were to
tell my father or my brother what happened, then your
life would be in danger. I have told no one, and I shall tell
no one. This is not because of some misplaced affection –
though I cannot deny that, under different circumstances,
I might have found your company welcome – neither is
it because of pity for your shortcomings. It is because,
at this stage in proceedings, it would prove impossible to
find another dancing master to take your place. I trust
that with this information you will continue to provide
the service which you are contracted to supply, and with
which I have no quarrel. But I have no wish to dance with
you further, either alone or in the company of others. I
should be grateful if you would address me from now on
as Miss Taylor, and the time and conversations you share
with me should be as little and as infrequent as politeness
dictates. Failure to comply with these requests in all areas
will force me to report the events of last night to my father
and my brother, and to your wife.*

There was no signature, save a large *A* at the bottom of the
page. Rob sat down on the bed and read the letter through

again. He realised he had little choice in the matter. As well as the threat of exposure if he didn't behave himself, the same threat was implied if he attempted to escape. For a moment the previous night he had felt exhilarated with the power he seemed to possess, power over the Taylors and power over Annie. But if the latter was gone, and that was certain, then the former was still there. He had power over the Taylors because he was their dancing master; the success of Annie's wedding was still in his control. Annie had asked for excitement and had got it but hadn't enjoyed the practicalities that went along with it. She'd spurned him, so he'd make sure there was no more excitement of any type. The dances would be so lacking in stimulation that the musicians would fall asleep mid-tune and the dancers would pray for the evening to end. And he'd think of something else. He'd find some means of exacting his revenge on Annie Taylor. He crumpled up the piece of paper and threw it into the fireplace where it fell amongst the twigs and logs set there for the next cold spell.

The afternoon was spent dancing. Annie was distant but not overbearingly so. In those dances where he was forced, during changes of partner, to take her hand, she expressed no overt discomfort at being close to him. But she made a point of not talking to him and ensured that she was always partnered by her father or brother, or Parson Westborne or Dr Allard. When Danny was forced to dance with his sister he gazed soulfully at Charlotte Stephenson, and it was she who seemed inevitably to be Rob's partner. She'd come to stay with the Taylors and was pleasant enough to Rob, she smiled when he tried to be humorous, and she could dance well enough. He did consider that it might be worth paying her some attention. She was pretty in a small way, and to bed her would have been some compensation for his failure to have his way with Annie. But she was as besotted with Danny as he was with her, and though her feet no doubt welcomed the respite when Danny and his sister danced together – Danny was as good at dancing, Rob reflected,

as he, Rob, seemed to be at seduction – as soon as the dance
was over Charlotte would hurry across to sit by his side. They
were an unusual couple, Rob decided, she so small and he so
overwhelmingly bulky in comparison, but they did, at least,
appear to be happy.

That was more than could be said for Frances Arnison. The
scowl on her face reminded Rob of some scurrilous drawings
he'd once seen of an old dame squatting in a privy, obviously
in some discomfort, her eyes pinched and her mouth high
up below her nose. He wondered if her burden might be
relieved by a copious quantity of fresh fruit, or perhaps a
dose of syrup of figs. She'd been staring at Rob whenever
he looked at her, which was inevitably by accident, when he
was circling the room to see the set from different angles or
asking Rebecca Taylor's opinion of a dance. The matriarch
attended all the dancing sessions and the music practices,
nodding her approval when a figure caught her attention
and providing a steady enough backbone of sound on the
harpsichord. Rob tried to include her in the dances but she
demurred. These stately dances were too fine for her, she
insisted; she was brought up on simpler fare. Her elder
daughter attempted the dances sometimes, but she was as
inelegant as her brother and knew herself to be so, and
her contribution of late had been little more than a show
of distaste when Rob announced a particular dance, which
she would dismiss as being too slow or too fast, too difficult
or too easy, too long or too short. Nothing pleased her.

Such an attitude would have been discouraging if it
had been any dancer, any student expressing it. When
that dancer was Frances Arnison it raised the spectre of
disapproval amongst all of the others, and Rob's decision
to dance Parson's Farewell, for example, or Jack's Maggot
would be met with glances from his pupils in the direction
of Mrs Arnison. Her grimace of displeasure would set the
tone for their own enjoyment of the dance. Only Danny
and Charlotte, caught in each other's spell, were immune
to this conspiracy. Annie, whose buoyant enthusiasm might

have swayed the others, seemed disinclined to offer Rob any material assistance.

Rob left the dancing session thoroughly discouraged. For the first time since his introduction to the family and their friends, musicians and dancers both, he felt that matters were slipping away from him. What had been progressing well was suddenly awry, and he pleaded fatigue in order to avoid dining with the Taylors. Instead he took to his room with a tray to rest and to think. He should, he told himself, be pleased. The general discomfort with his choice of dances and their method of execution was surely a reflection of his desire to teach only figures and steps which were uninteresting, which would make the wedding ball an anticlimax. This dissatisfaction was a sign that he was succeeding. The dancers, at first keen to learn something new, were slowly becoming aware that the new clothes they had been sold were old fashions from some distant past. Rob knew now that he'd underestimated them, that they'd made this discovery too early. By the middle of next week it would have been too late; that was when the wedding guests would start to arrive, that was when the dancers he'd been teaching would be used to pass on their skills to the newcomers. But there was discontent now, and that meant he might have to teach some new dances; it meant he had time to teach them. There was, however, something else troubling him.

He was, he realised, becoming used to having others defer to him. He'd become aware that he could do the task in hand properly, that he could, if he wished, teach good dances and have them performed properly by dancers who'd been well instructed by him. He found himself enjoying the responsibility and the power of his post, but what was worse, what was far worse, was that he found himself wanting to do the job properly. He wanted, from a sense of personal pride, to have the wedding guests perform dances skilfully. Good dances at that; dances which lifted the heart and brought smiles to dour faces. Yes, even to Frances Arnison's face. It was a worry to find that his original pilgrimage to the altar of revenge might be superseded by this unholy desire to do things right. He castigated himself for thinking in this way, but it did little good. He was confused.

His confusion was to deepen as the evening progressed. He went down to the ballroom at eight o'clock to meet with his musicians only to find that of his chosen band only Theodore Westborne, Dr Allard and Harry Brown were present. He was told that the others were too busy to come, that work demanded their presence elsewhere. Then Parson Westborne took out his violin and informed Rob that he'd broken a string and didn't have a spare with him, and Dr Allard announced that he could only stay for twenty minutes anyway, he had a patient to see. It was agreed there was little point in continuing, and Rob announced that there would be a practice instead the following afternoon. The two men left in a hurry, promising to spread the word, leaving only Rob and Harry Brown.

'That wasn't very successful,' Rob admitted Harry nodded.

'I'm surprised. I didn't think there'd be so many people away all at the same time. Especially when they knew in advance.' Harry nodded again, picked up the case containing his bassoon and the racket he'd borrowed.

'I'll be off, then,' he said, heading for the door.

'Till tomorrow,' Rob threw after him. The call stopped the young man. He shook his head and returned.

'Mr Patterson?'

'Yes, Harry? Is something the matter?'

'Yes. The thing is, I don't know if I should tell you.' Harry's voice was low. He blinked from behind spectacles as he talked, his long hair swept forward to hide a face recovering from puberty.

'Why not, Harry? That is, if it's something that would get you into trouble, then don't tell me. But if you think it's something I should know—'

The words came out in a rush; no further prompting was necessary.

'I've enjoyed playing with you, Mr Patterson. I've enjoyed the tunes, whatever they were, it's what I like doing, playing. And I know I can play them well, I just know that, I can play them better than the rest of them. I'm not trying to show off or anything. It's just that, well, I'm not much good at anything except music and I know; I know I can play well.'

'Yes,' acknowledged Rob, 'you're good. I've noticed that.'

'And the tunes you've picked, they're good tunes, they're challenging tunes. I like them. But you could have picked easier ones. I've looked in your music book and there are lots of easier tunes, but you've picked ones that are quite difficult. And that's the problem.'

'What? That the tunes are too difficult for you?'

'Not for me, Mr Patterson, not for me. For the rest of them. That's why they've been dropping out, one or two at a time; that's why they've not come. They could've managed some of the easier tunes, but not these. So they just stopped coming.'

'Why the hell didn't they tell me?'

'I don't know, Mr Patterson. I think they did. Mr Lambert, Gabriel, he did. He said he couldn't get his fingers round the strings fast enough, and it was a key he couldn't play in, not on his harp. And you said to just try, to miss out the notes he couldn't play.'

Rob remembered now. The miller had mentioned that he was having difficulty.

'And Dick Nattrass, the drummer, he's just a young lad but he could practise simple rhythms. I've taken him through one or two meself. But you tried to teach him some that were complicated, more than he could manage. So he stopped coming as well.'

'I see. And do you think if I chose some new tunes, easier tunes, they might all come back?'

'I can't say for sure, Mr Patterson, I can't say. Me, I'll play anything, anywhere, I don't mind what. But the rest of them, they're not like that. Do you understand?'

'Yes, I understand. Well, all I can say is thank you, Harry. I'll see what I can do. Will you be here tomorrow?'

Harry nodded, and Rob patted him on the back. 'See you then,' he said, and watched as the young man headed once again for the door. Then, as before, he stopped on the threshold.

'I do know where you might be able to get some different musicians, a bit wilder, but still very good . . .' But when he turned it was too late. Rob had already gone.

'There's nothing else,' Rob told himself as he mounted the staircase, 'could go wrong today. Nothing could happen to make the day any worse. Nothing at all.' He stepped onto the landing and stared at a dark, cracked portrait of some distant female Taylor ancestor. 'And not even you,' he addressed the frail dowager, 'can possibly feel more uneasy than I do at the prospect of tomorrow. I shall simply go to bed and consider how I might deal with the matter.' He bowed. 'Goodnight, madam.'

He opened the door to his room. It was full of a soporific warmth which rolled forward to greet him with a smell of comforting, all-enclosing security, a welcoming scent of dry flowers and dusty curtains, of old wood and clean linen. He stretched as he strode over the threshold and so almost missed seeing the scrap of folded paper lying on the floor. When he did notice it he ignored it at first, put his bag down on the bed then came back to examine it carefully as it lay there, in case it should be poisonous; he was wary of unsolicited letters. He turned it over with his foot, but there was no discernible mark on it which might identify its origins. He bent down to pick it up and gingerly unfolded it. The writing was slanted heavily to the right; reading it was difficult. But there was only one sentence, seventeen words. Rob mouthed them, counted them, then read them aloud as if he couldn't believe what they said.

Mr Patterson,
I would like you to teach me to waltz, tonight, in
my room.
Frances Arnison.

He shook his head. There might be hidden meanings
behind those simple words, but he was aware that he might
be reading implications into what could be a straightforward
statement. Frances Arnison might genuinely wish to learn
how to waltz; she might be afraid of showing her ungainliness
to others and therefore desire to be taught in private. To an
innocent the note could be read in no other way, and for him
to decline the invitation would make him seem rude. But if
Annie had spoken to her, had told her of his fumblings and
pawings the previous night, then this might be her opportunity for revenge against him. It would certainly explain
her sulks and lemon-faced grimaces during the day, and she
might feel it her duty to expose him. She already suspected
that he was an imposter. And yet the note was, from the
outside, innocent, he dare not turn down the invitation. He
considered the dilemma. He needed a chaperone, a third
party whose presence would protect everyone present. But
who could he invite? Danny and Charlotte would be away
together; Annie would refuse any request from him. There
was no one else. He knew he had no choice. He made up
his mind, hurried round the room packing away his clothes;
if flight was necessary then he'd be prepared. He adjusted
his cravat, swallowed, and left his room, heading for that
of Frances Arnison.

It was not yet late enough for candles to be lit, but the
walls were dark with years and smoke, and they echoed his
feelings of impending doom. He stopped in front of the door
and knocked, quietly, hoping she wouldn't be within, hoping
that if she was in then she wouldn't hear this tiny rapping.
But both hopes proved false. He heard her voice, definitely
her voice, bidding him enter. He did as he was told.

He couldn't see very well; the curtains had been closed. It

was hot. A fire was burning in the grate, and this was the only source of light, a flickering dance of orange shadows on ceiling and walls. Rob could feel the sweat beading on his forehead already. Frances Arnison was sitting in a chair by the fire, wrapped in a deep-red gown which covered her from neck to ankles. Her feet were bare.

'Mr Patterson, thank you for coming,' she said in a manner that was almost gracious. Rob nodded his response, not quite sure yet what was expected of him.

'You may approach. Please, take a seat.' She held out her hand, but the well-upholstered, heavy chair was too close to the fire. Rob had to drag it away a yard or so before he sat down.

'You're right,' his hostess said, staring into the fire, 'it is too hot in here. It's not that I'm cold, far from it, but I enjoy watching the flames. I read them; I see shapes in them, the figures of men and women. They dance together in the flames. Oh, Mr Patterson, you won't believe the dances I've seen.' She looked straight at him. 'Dances straight from the pathway to hell. You did know, didn't you? I'm sure Daniel told me you'd mentioned it to him. The Puritans thought dancing was an original sin, far too sensual for God-fearing people. Dancers would be able to caper easily down that broad and well-paved road that leads straight to hell. Do you believe that, Mr Patterson?'

'I'm not sure,' blustered Rob. 'I've never really thought about it in that way.'

'I have. I don't believe it at all. Certainly not with normal dancing. But some dances . . .'

'Yes?'

'Some dances, Mr Patterson, are perhaps worse than others. Some dances might actually corrupt the morals of young people, don't you think?'

'I can't—'

'—say I've really thought about it in that way. Really, Mr Patterson, you haven't done much thinking at all, have you? Perhaps you're more a man of actions, eh? Perhaps it's the physical movement of dancing that attracted you to it in the first place. You see, Mr Patterson . . . Dear me, that name is a mouthful. Do you have no other I can use?'

'We've already discussed my name, Mrs Arnison. If you wish to call me David—'

'Oh, let's not play games. If you won't be honest with me then I'd rather call you by your last name, at least it adds an air of mystery to our adventures.'

'Adventures, Mrs Arnison?'

'Adventures, Mr Patterson. Our voyage of discovery. I suspect you aren't the real David Patterson, I have my friend's letter to suggest this. I also have examples of your handwriting, and it is entirely unlike that in your dance book. And before you mention any excuse, I know that you will say that the writing is that of your father-in-law, or at least the man who would be your father-in-law if you were the real David Patterson. And your scribblings when I spoke to you in the library – there was no ink in your quill but you left your mark. You left a name, and it wasn't David. Shall I tell you what it was?'

'It means little to me,' said Rob, but he could remember adding columns of figures for Playford, his pen in his hand, and on completion of the task his scribbling sheet would be filled with the ornate, ornamented curls of his name in black ink. His real name.

'If it means so little then I shall not mention it. Such evidence is, I know, circumstantial. Each piece on its own has little weight, but put them together and each links with the other to form a chain, and that chain is what I shall use to bind your will to my purpose, Dancing Master. But first, the business in hand. You read my note; you came here. I wish to learn to waltz.'

Rob rose to his feet and bowed deeply. Whatever this woman's motives, whatever her wishes to bring him harm, he could at least do this for her; he could teach her how to waltz. And he would do so with as much speed as was decent, and then escape to his room, and then leave Bellingford.

Nothing would now make him stay, he was resolved in that. He covered his fear, his confusion, with bravura.

'I shall be pleased to teach you to waltz, Mrs Arnison. But it really is unpleasantly hot in here, if I might draw the curtains and open the windows I'm sure we would find the atmosphere more suitable for dancing.'

'Dancing? Who mentioned dancing, Sir Dancing Master?' The question in her voice seemed real.

'But you said—'

'I said I wanted to learn to waltz. To be more specific, I said I wanted you to teach me to waltz.'

'But the waltz is a dance. Surely you were aware—'

'Dancing Master, you are so unbelievably naïve.' She stood up. Rob noticed that she had unpinned her hair, it was hanging loose over her shoulders like autumn cut straw and red-brown leaves, it made her face less round than it normally appeared. 'I wish you to teach me to waltz,' she continued, taking a step closer, 'in the same way you attempted to teach my sister to waltz last night on the lawn. On the lawn which lies, I might add, just below my window. You need have no fear, Mr Patterson. I shall cause you no injury as my sister did.' She stepped closer again, and again, until she was standing only inches away from Rob. He felt unable to escape, he couldn't resist as she reached out and took his hand.

'I believe that the first move is something like this,' she whispered. Her fingers were tight around his wrist. Somehow, without him noticing, she had undone the cord which fastened her gown around her waist, and she forced his hand through the folds of material on to the warm, damp flesh of her breast. He felt her nipple stir into life under his palm, and she inhaled deeply. She had her back to the fire, so Rob could see nothing of her body inside the shadows of her gown, but he could smell an earthy perfume, a natural fragrance, the product of the heat of the room and of her desire; and he could feel her other hand snaking down his chest, over the waistband of his trousers and further still, mimicking his own choreography of the previous night. It was his turn to breathe in sharply as her fingers raked the front of his trousers.

'It feels to me as if you're ready to dance,' Frances Arnison murmured. 'Should we repair to the ballroom?' She pushed Rob back towards the bed but he resisted, stepped away from her, put out his arms to hold her at that distance.

'I don't understand,' he said, 'I thought you didn't like me.'

'I don't like you,' she answered. 'There is little in you I can find to approve of at all, let alone "like". It's a verb I find is used most often with foods anyway, "Do you like pickled cauliflower?" and such. I prefer not to use it for people. But if I did, then I certainly wouldn't like you.'

Rob was taken aback. 'Then why this false intimacy? Why this attempt to ... yes, to humiliate me? Why are you doing this?'

'Oh, I'm not trying to humiliate you, though that may come as the night progresses. I'm blackmailing you, because unless you do as I say I shall summon witnesses who will see me in this state of undress. They will undoubtedly believe me when I say that you attempted to rape me. You may produce the note I left you and I will agree that I did, indeed, write it, but it was an attempt to get you to come to my room so that I could expose you ...' she giggled at the choice of the word '... as an imposter, so that I could confront you with my evidence. You see, Dancing Master, I've thought of everything. I intend, to a certain extent, using you, and not only tonight. Don't think of leaving Bellingford before I finish with you; you won't get far. My husband and my father and my brother will seek you out and hang you from the nearest tree without even asking you any questions. Your guilt will have been proved by your leaving, you see. But don't be worried about being used, what does that matter anyway? You're a young man, a healthy man with normal desires, I've seen that much in the way you've behaved towards my sister. Would you normally turn down an offer such as this?'

'Yes! That is, no, but the circumstances are different. I don't know, that is, I might not be able to—'

'You were prepared to dance with my sister. Why will you not dance with me? Is my body so repellent?' She took off the gown and let it fall to the floor; she was entirely naked beneath.

Rob had seen women naked before. One or two had even stood for him like this one, submitting themselves for inspection, for approval even. But this time he had no choice in his actions; Frances Arnison had left him with no doubt of that. He would do exactly as she said. And she was waiting for him to answer her. He glanced at her, trying not to stare at her nudity. She was shorter than her sister, with small, slack breasts and wide hips. The tops of her legs were fat, as was her stomach. Her body hair was thick and dark red between her legs; a faint line ran up to her navel, and dark strands were visible in her armpits. Her arms and legs held a faint sheen of almost blonde hair. Rob had made love to women who were far less pretty than this. He'd paid them compliments which both he and they knew were lies, and they'd laughed together. But now no such words would come to him.

'No,' he answered finally, honestly, 'your body isn't repellent.'

She snorted, placed her hands on her hips. 'I recall a proverb of some sort,' she said, 'about damning with faint praise. Can you think of nothing more gallant? Can you make no comparison with beautiful hills and rolling dales, with verdant pastures and lush meadows? Have you no voice, no imagination?'

'I have a voice,' Rob said softly, 'and I will say this. You are a woman of rare and unusual beauty, Mrs Arnison. I consider—'

'Be quiet! For God's sake, be quiet, I'll hear none of your lies! You don't find me beautiful, nor does anyone else. You didn't come here of your own free will, and you remain only because I threaten you. I have no natural charm like my sister,

I lack my mother's elegance, I don't even possess my father's even temperament. You hate me as much as I hate you, is that not the truth?'

'No, it is not! I can't hate you because I know nothing about you. You remain closed to me, even though you're standing naked in front of me. I feel . . . I feel only sympathy. And curiosity to know how you came to be this way.'

Frances was angered by Rob's words. She picked up her gown and threw herself into it, then grabbed him by the arm.

'I don't want your sympathy! I don't want your soft consolations whispering in my ear. I don't need your lies and endearments. There's only one thing I want from you, and I'll tell you what that is now, and you'll do just as I want.' She pulled him across to the bed then pushed him from her as she climbed on to it and lay on her side like a Roman *domina*, staring at him.

'You will undress for me, now. You will say nothing while you do so, but I shall grant you one wish. I shall satisfy your curiosity. I will explain why you are here. Now commence.' Rob did as he was told, starting with his boots and his hose, then moving to his cravat and working his way downwards. Each item of clothing he removed he laid neatly on a chair at the side of the bed, aware that Frances's eyes were on him. He found that he couldn't return her bold stare; instead he concentrated on her voice, her words.

'I was married when I was sixteen. I was a virgin. I am now thirty-one years old. During that time my husband and I – you will meet him in due course, though I doubt you'll be able to make *him* dance – we enjoyed all that married life brought us, including the physical union of our bodies. But there were no children. This didn't worry us at first; we were young, we had our work building up the farm, life together was new and interesting. But then I began to feel something was missing. I found myself looking at other women's children and coveting them, I longed for my own child. At first my husband didn't understand this need, and when he did, when he began to share it, there was little we were able to do. No amount of trying would bring results. I consulted doctors and fortune-tellers, old gypsy women and healers. We drank herbal draughts and ate foul-smelling broths and anointed ourselves with pastes and creams, but each month my menses came, and my hopes dissolved in the blood.

'We decided that the problem must lie with one of the two of us. We felt that we had to find out which it was. A year ago I gave my husband permission to lie with another woman, a widow who had mothered children previously. She was unattractive, I would add. The congress was to be used only as a means of experiment. Had there been a child then I would have raised it as my own, knowing I would never be able to experience childbirth, that my body was in some way cursed. But there was no child.

'My husband is a kind and generous man. He then gave me the freedom I had given him. I was to seek another partner for the sole purpose of implanting his seed in my womb. But there were conditions; the man was not to be a friend or a neighbour, or someone who would ever speak the truth elsewhere, and my husband wished to know none of the details of the coitus. This person must therefore be a stranger, young and healthy, here for a few days and then gone. You are the first to satisfy all these conditions. I have chosen you to be the father of my child.'

Rob finished undressing and it was his turn to be inspected. His partner evidently liked the goods on offer. During her monologue her hand had pushed aside the folds of her gown and was gently moving to and fro in the forest of red hair between her legs. The sight brought an immediate and undisguisable reaction from Rob.

'I'm honoured to be chosen,' he said.

'So I see,' answered Frances. 'Now come to me.' Her voice was, for the first time, soft. As Rob moved to the bed she extricated herself from her gown and rolled on to her back, her legs wide apart. She motioned him into place, kneeling before her.

'I don't wish you to kiss me,' she said, 'nor to indulge in any display of affection. That is not the purpose of this congress. You will allow me to take control.'

Not waiting for a response she reached forward to take him. Her hands were rough-skinned, their grasp urgent. She pulled at him and he fell on to her. He took his weight on his elbows, and then she was guiding him inside her, slowly, softly. He looked at her; she had her eyes closed. He felt her hand move round to rest on the small of his back where it pressed hard, and he went with the pressure, pushing until he felt the roughness of her hair against his stomach and the tops of his legs. Then she took her hand away.

'You may do as you wish now,' she said, 'but don't expect me to react. I am nothing more than a repository. Please go ahead.'

Rob hadn't been with a woman since . . . He struggled to remember. There was the keelman's daughter, but she'd thought he was a serious suitor and that most definitely wasn't the case. Then there was that drunk doxy, so insensible she'd forgotten to charge him. He moved slightly, and all thoughts of other women disappeared, whenever it had been it had been too long. He had to concentrate on the moment, on now, on the need to move faster and harder, on the delicious warm sensation creeping from his groin, rapidly ascending his spine, circling his head and then bursting from him in an explosion of light and sound.

He fell forward on to warm, compliant flesh; he couldn't remember whose it was. He could feel the dull thud of his heart and the sweat on his forehead and back, under his arms, and the stickiness in his groin that was far sweeter than perspiration. He felt tired, suddenly and irrevocably tired, and the last thing he remembered as he fell asleep was being rolled over, and a voice whispering in his ear.

'It's a good job I didn't blink, Dancing Master. I might have missed it.'

*   *   *

He wasn't sure of the time when he woke, the fire had gone out but it was still too hot in the room, still dark. He was lying on his side, his left arm draped over the sleeping body at his side, his right arm beneath it. He was confused at first. He couldn't recall where he was, but then his memory of the night returned. With it came a strange despair, not that he'd behaved in a certain way but that he'd had no choice in the matter, that he'd been forced into having intercourse with Frances Arnison because she wanted him and not because he wanted her. The motives behind her desire were sad, he acknowledged, but still he felt used. It would have been better, he decided, if she'd at least shown some emotion, but she'd lain still, not moving, hands by her sides, eyes closed throughout. And then there was that disparaging remark she made as they separated. Surely she must have felt something.

The sheet covering them both was rucked and twisted around their bodies, and in an attempt to allow the passage of some cool air Rob lifted the sheet a little. He inhaled the scent of two bodies, the smell of intercourse, the smell of rutting. It aroused him, that and the warm backside pressed against him, and his natural desire was reinforced by a conscious decision to do what *he* wanted rather than what he'd been told to do. He moved closer, felt her night-scented skin hot against his chest. One hand, still trapped beneath her, began to tease her nipples, softly to begin with; the other dived deep between her legs, peeled her open, felt the moisture there. His fingers went to work, stroking rhythmically, while his thumb sought a small pearl of muscle and circled it slowly, felt it grow, caressed it gently, firmly.

Frances Arnison lay still, feigning sleep, trying to ignore the sensations coaxing her body into movement. She wanted to push against Rob's hands, to instruct him, to tell him to pinch harder *there*, to be more gentle *here*. But he thought her, for the moment at least, still unconscious, and she wanted him to believe that that was so. While he was manipulating her physically she was doing the same with him mentally. How sweet it was to have a man believe he was in charge when he was doing exactly as she wanted him to do. If she'd said to him directly, 'I want you to make love to me, but I want you to ensure that I am satisfied before you,' he might have laughed at her; he might have ignored her; he might even have agreed to try to do as she requested but then lost his will in the act itself. But not now. Now he was determined that she should experience the height of her excitement, and though she would hold back and hold back, she knew the moment would come.

Now his hand was cupped over her mound as he eased forward and smoothly entered her from behind, and then he was at work again, fingers stroking and pinching her, his breath heavy in her ear. She heard an animal groan and realised it had come from her own throat, and she was moving in time with him, pressing back against him as he surged forward, her fingers fluttering against the palms of her hands.

'Bitch!' she heard him say, 'Whore!', and his words drove her on. She felt his tongue and his teeth at her neck, and it was too much, the waves had been getting larger, she could see this one coming, it was taller than the rest, more powerful, it would engulf her completely. She welcomed it, she wanted to drown in it, she felt it possess her body and draw her life from her, roll her over and over, on and on . . . And then it was past, there was only the warmth and the sweet tiredness, the pleasant ache of satiation. She sighed softly to herself.

'Oh no, Mrs Arnison, not yet. You're not finished yet!' Rob's voice was harsh, in one movement he pulled her up and on to her knees, still hard inside her. One long arm snaked under her belly to pull and pinch her nipples, the other was tugging fiercely at the hair between her legs. He thrust into her, retreated, then forced himself forward again. She heard the slap of his thighs against her backside, flesh on flesh, and his hand was on her shoulder, pulling her body back so that she was impaled more deeply on him. She moaned her protestation but this only encouraged him further. He began to move faster, and she could do nothing but go with him. It was too much, she could feel moisture dripping down her arms and legs; her hair was matted with sweat, but still he went on. This time it would be no wave, this time she would explode, she felt the fuse within her, she heaved at him, her hand went between her legs to speed the progress of the flame, she joined in his animal grunts of passion, and they screamed together as the eruption tore through them.

They descended on to the wet bed together. No sheets covered them. Their breathing slowly calmed and became sleep. At some time in the night they separated, turned their backs on each other, and remained perched on the very edges of the bed, as far away from each other as possible.

The Seventh Bar of the Musick

Saturday, 19 June 1830

*In which Rob explores new territory but ends the
day as he began it, on familiar ground.*

The world, Rob decided, was an unusual place. He'd just
taken, in the space of three hours, a dance lesson and
a band practice. The first had gone well in comparison to
his previous effort, and he was aware that this was largely
due to Frances Arnison's change of attitude. She still refused
to smile at him or with him, but at least she'd ceased her
overt criticism of his choice of dances, and that in itself was
enough to lighten the mood of the other dancers Only as she
was leaving did she acknowledge him, asking him to ensure
that the lesson of the previous evening might be repeated at,
say ten o'clock. The statement required no response.

If the dancing was making progress then the music was
moving backwards. Although his musicians had all appeared,
none save Harry Brown showed any enthusiasm for the
task, and it was clear that none of them had practised. In
desperation Rob sought out some easier tunes and gathered
the instrumentalists around the single copy to play. They
coped, but without heart; they were ready to stop at the
first opportunity. The session ended with Rob's promise

that by Monday (there would be no music or dancing on
the Sabbath) he would have written out some newer, easier
tunes in full, but there were few smiling faces. He decided
he would canvass some individual support, but that was the
moment Rebecca Taylor chose to confide in him that all did
not appear to be going well.

'I am concerned,' she told him, 'that we will not be ready
for the wedding. Without music we cannot dance, and I
have little confidence in the ability or eagerness of my fellow
musicians. And Annie has confided in me – she felt unable
to approach you directly, she said – that the dances lack
the life and energy she anticipated. This is not intended as
criticism, I assure you of that, Mr Patterson. Samuel and I
are both aware of the difficulties you must be facing. You've
been left to your own devices in choosing music and dances.
None of us has been of any help at all, and for Annie to
be so discriminating at this late stage is disappointing. But
I felt I ought to tell you. You do understand, don't you?'

'Yes,' Rob had answered, fully aware that the question
was a statement. And when Mrs Taylor had left there
was no one else there save Harry Brown. The young-
ster asked to speak to him, so they sat together on the
lawn.

'I tried to tell you the other night, Mr Patterson, about
the problems with the music. I've been doing some thinking,
and I know where you might be able to find some more
musicians, good musicians as well.'

Rob had been lying down, but the news made him sit up
quickly.

'Where are they?' he asked, 'are they local? They can't
be, otherwise they'd be here already. Where do they live,
Harry?'

'Oh, they're local alright. I've played with them in the
tavern across in the next valley. They could play for your
dancing, no problem.'

'Then where are they? Where can I find them?'

'They can't read music, most of them, but they can pick

up a tune quickly. Listen to it once, try it through once, then they're away.'

'Where, Harry, just tell me where?'

'And then there's the problem of getting them to play, they might not want to. Even if they did, there's no telling whether or not they'd be wanted. It's difficult.'

'Harry, unless you tell me where I can find these people I might just make you swallow your bassoon whole.'

Harry blinked innocently, unsure why such a threat should be made when he was merely trying to help.

'I don't think I'd like that, Mr Patterson, quite apart from the damage you might cause to the instrument—'

'Harry!'

'Alright, Mr Patterson, alright! They live right here, in Bellingford.'

'Here? But I thought I'd met everyone who could play anything, Mr Taylor told me that earlier in the week. Surely he can't have missed any out.'

'They don't actually live in the village itself, Mr Patterson. You go through the village, then you take the path that leads out past the marsh and along the riverbank—'

'I know it!'

'Well, just go along there and you'll find some cottages, about a dozen. Just ask there. Tell them Harry sent you. Describe me to them as well; I'm not sure if they'll know my name. I'm not promising anything, mind you, but it might be useful.' His speech turned into a yell as Rob climbed to his feet and strode away, leaving a bemused Harry Brown with only his bassoon for company.

It was a pleasant walk into the village. Rob was greeted along the way by individuals whose names he'd forgotten, children yelled to him as he passed, scattered in mock horror as he pretended to chase them. He felt almost at home, and he contrasted that feeling with the longing to be back in Newcastle he'd experienced only a few days ago. Why, he wondered, should he feel this way? Had the night spent with Frances Arnison anything to do with it? Or was it

just that he felt he was now doing something positive. He
stopped suddenly. Surely that was wrong. He'd been told by
his employer that his music and dances were too staid, too
boring, too old-fashioned, and here he was making an effort
to improve matters. That wasn't what he'd set out to do when
he came to Bellingford. He was here to do a *bad* job; he was
here to make his employers *unhappy*; he was here for revenge.
He began walking again, more slowly this time. It would do
no harm to continue his search. After all, if these strangers
were as good as Harry had led him to believe then he ought
to see them, if only to make sure they were excluded from
his arrangements. And he would satisfy his curiosity at the
same time. His stride increased in length again.

'Ho! Mr Patterson, hello there! We meet again!' Rob
cursed, it was the intrusive, effusive poet hailing him from
the far bank of the river. He waved back, thankful that
the width of the stream made conversation difficult. But
Emanuel Scrivener was not to be put off by a mere detail
such as that. Without hesitation, without removing his shoes
even, he stepped down from the bank and into the water and
waded across to the other side. The darkness on his pale
trousers showed as he emerged that the deepest point was
no more than three feet.

Rob's face must have shown his incredulity. Scrivener
merely smiled.

'Clothes dry easily,' he explained, 'skin's waterproof. And
we didn't really finish our conversation last time we spoke.
Where are you off to now?'

'Exploring,' answered Rob noncommittally.

'General or specific?' countered the poet.

'I'm sorry? I'm afraid I don't understand.'

'General exploring, my dear boy, is largely aimless, fired
by curiosity. It doesn't matter where you go; the purpose is
to go somewhere new. Specific exploring, however, is quite
different, that implies a search for something you know you
want, even though you may never have been to the place
where you hope to find it. So which is it with you?'

'Specific,' answered Rob, 'though I can't tell you where I'm going nor what I'm looking for.'

Emanuel Scrivener nodded deeply. 'I understand,' he said. 'Matters like this are sometimes best kept private. But if I may recommend a certain young lady of your own age. Her husband is a thatcher and spends a large part of his time away. I believe he is not at home at present, and I know his wife might welcome—'

'No, Mr Scrivener, please, you mistake my purpose,' Rob protested, then realised it might be better to let the poet think that he was indeed intending meeting a woman; it might prevent further awkward questions.

'That is,' Rob continued, 'I've already arranged my liaison. I thank you for your kind thoughts, but—'

'No matter, dear boy, no matter. It is indeed pleasant to find you so settled in our community. You remind me so much of your father-in-law. He was always up to such tricks when I knew him. This was, what, thirty years ago, long before he married. He did marry, I take it? His daughter is the legitimate child of a marriage in law, in the eyes of the state and . . .?'

'So far as I'm aware, Mr Scrivener. But this is a side of my father-in-law I know little about. Please tell me more.' Rob's initial horror that the subject of James Playford had been raised subsided quickly, a friendship some thirty years old was unlikely to prove any danger to him. And it seemed that Playford, like Scrivener, had been something of a hedonist in his youth.

'You mean he hasn't confided in you? My word, I'm not sure whether I should go on or not. And what should I tell? But it's clear you're tarred with the same brush as him, so no harm will come of it, and the tales themselves are certainly worth repeating. I would suggest we meet later this week and drink together, we can talk of times past. I've some good claret I've been saving for just such an occasion. And you, my dear boy, will be in a better frame of mind for listening when the urgency of your needs has been assuaged.

Until, let us say, Tuesday evening then? Come for dinner. Seven in the evening?'

'I'll be there, Mr Scrivener.'

'Emanuel,' the poet called as he waded back to the opposite bank, 'call me Emanuel.'

It was a pleasant evening, and the path Rob followed was easy underfoot. After leaving the village green it separated a small farm from its barn and outhouses, then dipped down again to court the river for a quarter of a mile. Despite the recent dry weather the ground was wet, and it was clear that in any other season the small expanse of marsh, droning with scarlet and blue dragonflies, would engulf the path and the field beyond making passage uncomfortable. Although it was now possible to find a dry path, the subsiding waters had left behind beds of rotten vegetable matter, and the smell was choking. Clouds of insects pursued Rob as he negotiated the muddy puddles.

Beyond the marsh the path snaked through a copse of young birches decked with green leaves hiding small, darting blue birds with barrel chests and loud calls, blurs of movement at the very edge of his vision. The pale trees filtered out what little breeze there was, and it became oppressively hot. The leaves were too small and too high to halt the evening sun's assault. Rob's shirt stuck to his back and he was forced to take off his jacket and his cravat. The first evidence that he might be near habitation was a distant caterwaul of children playing, a sound which seemed to circle around him as he followed the eccentric twists and turns of the path. Gradually the birches gave way to stunted bog oaks dressed in green-velvet moss, and then he was in the open, looking across a long-grassed field to a huddle of a dozen or so small cottages. The path skirted the long grass, and as Rob approached the cottages he could see that, although no two were alike, they were of the same breed. They had a unity of purpose which demanded he consider them, together, as a hamlet separate in both character and location from the

village of Bellingford. The walls, foursquare, were uneven.
The stone used to build them had been augmented with straw
and clay and finished with whitewash, but many years had
passed since the most recent application. Most of the roofs
were thatched with dark straw, or perhaps rushes; two of the
buildings, surrounded by the others, had canopies of green
grass speckled with clover and daisies and dandelions. Only
some of the cottages had chimneys, and though Rob couldn't
see every side of every building, some of them appeared not
to have windows.

The yelling of children grew louder, mixed with rough,
persistent barking, and Rob halted; although the barking
wasn't deep (a sign, he hoped, that the dog wasn't large)
he'd been bettered too often by small, yapping terriers and
was wary of allowing any such beast access to his ankles.

The children who appeared before him were dirty, their
clothes were ragged, and none wore shoes. The eldest could
have been no more than eight or nine years old, a gangling boy brandishing a length of branch which might
have been a sword or a whip. He was looking over his
shoulder, being chased by at least half a dozen others,
all smaller than him. The youngest was a wide-eyed baby
hung on the hip of a girl whose short, dark hair grew
from her head like hedgehog spines. It was the girl who
saw him first. Merely by halting she caused the others
to cease their pursuit, although the pursued continued his
gallop towards Rob for a few seconds longer until she
yelled a warning to him. His eyes were wide. He stared
at Rob then began a slow retreat into the safe fellowship
of his companions. Rob held out his hands, took a step
forward.

'Hello,' he said. 'My name's David Patterson. Are your
parents . . .?'

Whether it was the movement or the voice which frightened
them, or perhaps just his presence, his being a stranger,
Rob wasn't sure. But they turned in perfect formation and
scampered back the way they'd come, into the village, the

dog (a terrier, Rob noticed, white and scud-tailed) leading them on their way.

Rob followed the children slowly, leisurely, aware that he was being watched but unable to see his watchers. He walked past the first of the cottages and saw chickens grubbing in the dirt; from one of the buildings came the snuffle of a pig. Penned within a wooden prison was a sullen, hissing goose, while a pair of mallards hung by their necks under the eaves and buzzed with the attention of flies. There were broken shards of pots and the ashes of fires enclosed in rings of river-rounded stones, piles of sticks and logs and turves; here the head of a mallet, there the shank of a broom. Some of the windows still held glass, others were nothing more than wooden frames, their shutters tied back like books. Beside one open door (Rob peered around it but there was only darkness within) sat a water butt, and Rob dipped his hand in, splashed the cool liquid onto his head and down his back.

'Hello,' he shouted, 'anyone at home?' There was no reply save the excited crowing of a vain cock perched on a low roof, and that call was soon stifled by the heat and stillness. Rob kept walking. There was no natural centre to the hamlet, it seemed just an arbitrary collection of buildings, each supporting the fragile flank of the next like massive oxen under threat of attack from bear or wolf. He heard a shuffle of dusty feet behind him and whirled around to find only a startled goat emerging from one of the cottages. What he thought was a giggle, quickly silenced, was repeated; its owner proved to be a nervous pigeon which erupted from the ground as he rounded a corner, its wings beating applause at its escape.

A circuit of the hamlet showed signs of occupation, but no inhabitants; even the children had been spirited away. There was a wooden bench outside someone's door. Rob sat down on it, laid his jacket to one side, and reached into the pocket. He drew out a metal pipe, tapered at one end, a wooden fipple forced into the other to form a mouthpiece.

It had a rectangular hole near the mouthpiece to make a sound and six smaller circular holes for three fingers from each hand. He raised it to his lips and began to play.

The tune was a slow air; it slipped like smoke around the cottages, sad as autumn, plaintive as a last goodbye. Rob's fingers slid over the holes. There was sometimes no end to one note, no beginning to the next, but a graduated rise or fall in tone which would have seemed impossible to one unfamiliar with the instrument. Any of the musicians or dancers at the manor who had seen and heard his workmanlike efforts with the flute would have been amazed at the breadth of feeling which could be produced from such a simple instrument.

A shock of hair appeared around the corner of the building; it was the girl. Rob could see her through half-closed eyes, but he ignored her and kept on playing. Her body followed her head until she stood in full view, this time without the baby, and slowly, one small step following another, drew closer. Her dress had once belonged to someone older and taller than her. It still possessed a vestige of its rich, red colour, and some of the ribbons that had decorated it remained attached. As she walked she pulled the dress back up onto one bare, brown shoulder, and it immediately began its slow descent from the other.

Other children appeared; the boy with the stick holding the hands of two urchins who could have been twins and were clearly his siblings, but whose sex was indeterminable either through looks or clothing. Two of the youngest were naked from the waist downwards, their top halves barely covered by short vests, and the clothes of all of them were tattered and torn, too small or too large. One boy crept closer than the rest but was quickly cuffed by the spikey-haired girl. He went back to his place rubbing his ear but made no sound of complaint. Rob reached the end of his tune, slowed to a last long, low note, then stopped. All movement ceased as that note died away, except for the girl. She nodded her head at him, the signal for him to start again. This time he chose a reel, a complex creature with a good, bounding rhythm, full of trills and grace notes. He kept his eyes open this time, fully open, and he saw the girl nod her approval and begin to tap her foot on the ground. It was a horribly dirty foot, the nails were cracked and lined with black, but it kept good time, and it was soon joined by other feet, and then hands clapped along in time, and then the girl grabbed a partner, a child a good foot shorter than her, and began to polka round the dusty patch of ground. Other couples joined them, and those too young to dance (or too infirm – one boy dragged a furrow behind him with his twisted leg) beat their support on barrels or pans, or yelled their happiness into the summer air.

Rob changed tunes and played faster, and the dancers joined him, always alongside, never ahead of or behind the beat. He was amazed to see four couples form themselves into a square and start some set dance he didn't recognise, a mixture of swinging and bowing and arching, danced throughout to some skipping step that was more than a skip; it had a heavy beat to it which crossed the rhythm but still kept in time. The effect was mesmerising, almost primitive. Rob could feel the earthy pace of the children's stepping through the ground, through the soles of his feet, in the bones of his body. He was finding it difficult to play now; the tune was an awkward one. There were few opportunities to draw breath, and as if sympathetic to his plight the girl nodded to him as he approached the end of an eight-bar section, and he stopped with an arpeggio of chord. The children ceased their dancing, gave polite bows or curtsies, and then stood still, staring at him, breathing heavily, while he returned the favour.

'You're good dancers,' he said eventually, and was rewarded with a set of smiles. He tried to look at each child in turn. Some stared back at him, others glanced away; one spat on the ground, another wiped her running nose on her forearm. There was much shuffling of feet, and the dust climbed slowly into the air as if the ground was smoking with the heat of dancing.

'You're good on the whistle, mister.' It was the girl who spoke, and her voice was rich with the countryside, not unlike that of Andrew, the manservant at the manor, and the way she pronounced 'mister' held a touch of the flat *a* of 'master'. But there was no deference in her manner. 'Aye,' she went on, 'you're good. But why're you here? Nobody comes here unless they want somethin'. And who are you, anyway?'

Rob grinned at her in genuine amusement. She was standing opposite him, her hands on her hips, head on one side, taking charge of the situation as would a man three or four times her age.

'My apologies, mistress, my name is Patterson, David Patterson. And you are . . .?'

'Me? You want to know me name?' She looked around her for the giggle of support which duly came, then curtseyed deeply. 'You can call me Mistress Fiona,' she said grandly.

'Why, thank you Mistress Fiona, I'm honoured to meet you. And please, call me by my first name. Call me David.'

'Well then, I'll do that. David.' There was another chorus of laughs which she silenced by lifting up her hands. Rob noticed that they were as dirty as her feet.

'But I asked you another question, David, aye, I did that. I asked who you were, but I also asked why you were here. And you haven't yet answered that, have you?' The others echoed their consent that the interrogation should continue; some of them sat down on the hard earth to wait for his answer, and the terrier which had only just reappeared showed its dissatisfaction by raising its leg against the upright of the bench on which Rob was sitting. He willed it away. It rolled over onto its back while one of the children scratched its fat, round stomach.

'As I said, my name's David Patterson. I'm a teacher, from Newcastle. Do you know where Newcastle is?'

Most of the children shook their heads, but Fiona wasn't one of them.

'It's a big place,' she said, 'bigger 'n Bellin'ford, bigger 'n

Hexham, even. That's what me granda says, and he's been there. He's been there three times.'

'Me da's been there more 'n that,' countered the tall boy, 'me da says there's a big river there. He says the water from oor stream gans all the way doon into that river and then into the sea, and there's big ships sail up the river from the sea.'

'You're right, Mister . . .?' said Rob. The boy stepped back, surprised that Rob should ask his name, amazed to be addressed as 'mister'.

'Don't pay no notice to him, David,' interrupted Fiona. 'He tells lies, and his da tells worse lies. And his name's Arthur.'

'But he's right, Mistress Fiona, Mister Arthur's speaking the truth. There are big ships, they call to deliver all sorts of things, grain and flour, bolts of material to make dresses, wine, pig iron, and they take away coal and timber.'

'Aye, p'raps they do, but they don't come this far upstream,' she finished conclusively, then went on in case there should be any further attack on the authority of her statements, 'and you still haven't told us why you're here. What type of teacher are you?'

'I'm not the type of teacher you might know, like Mrs Westborne. She teaches you how to read and write, how to add up.'

'You mean the pastor's wife?' said Arthur. Rob nodded. 'She don't teach us nothin'. She teaches the young uns from the village, not the likes o' us. Fiona's granda, sometimes he teaches us letters and countin', when he's well enough. But not Mrs Westborne.'

'Oh,' said Rob, puzzled, 'I'm sorry. Why doesn't . . .' He stopped, curious that these children should be excluded from the admittedly arbitrary education supplied by Mrs Westborne, but aware that the children themselves were not those from whom he ought to seek explanations. He decided to stick to the matter in hand.

'I teach dancing and, to a certain extent, music. But mostly dancing. I've been hired by Mr and Mrs Taylor. It's their daughter's wedding in a week's time, and they want me to teach them and their guests how to do some dances.'

'You mean they can't dance already?' Fiona's voice was incredulous.

'Well, they can dance a little. Some of them, that is, though not half as well as I've just seen you dance. But they want to learn some new dances, some different dances, and that's why I'm here.'

'No, Mr Patterson, that's why you came to Bellin'ford. But that still doesn't answer me granddaughter's question. You still haven't said why you're here, on this spot, visitin' us.'

The voice belonged to an old man. With the aid of a gnarled and twisted stick, he limped round the corner of the nearest cottage. His voice was deep and slow and his words carefully pronounced, as if he was speaking a language unusual to his lips and his mind and he wanted to make sure the words he chose were the correct ones. He was dressed only marginally better than the children. His clothes were patched and shabby, though he did have on a pair of scuffed old boots. His floppy moleskin hat was pulled down to hide his eyes, and instead of a jacket he wore a long, ragged smock, completely open at the front, all of its buttons missing. From his shoulder there dangled a sack, and he threw this to the ground.

'Rabbits,' he announced. 'Fiona, you take 'em away, gut 'em, skin 'em. We'll have 'em in the pot tomorrow.'

'Aye, I'll do that, Granda.' She made no move.

'Now, then.'

'But Granda, I want to listen to what David has to say. He plays the whistle good, better'n I've heard anybody play before. And we danced for 'im.'

'Aye, lass, I know, I heard and I saw. But now *I* want to talk, and to listen, and I don't want to be cluttered up with you kids, so be away with you.'

'But Granda—'

'You heard what I said. Now go on, the lot of you. Go

and play.' The crowd scattered immediately, all except for Fiona.

'Am I to play too, Granda?'

'Didn't I say so?' the old man asked.

'Well, yes, but I thought if I stayed around here I could listen . . .'

'Go and play!'

'Alright then, I'll go and play . . .' She skipped away, shouting over her shoulder, '. . . but I hope David'll play some more for us to dance.' She ran round the corner, but her voice could still be heard. 'And I'll do the rabbits later!' The old man looked down at the sack and shook his head as if to signify that he'd been outwitted again, but Rob suspected he'd allowed his granddaughter to win this battle.

'Now then, Mr Patterson, I'll admit I'd like to hear you explain why you're here. But I heard what you said before, to me granddaughter, so there's no need to go back over that ground. Speak away then, lad, I'm listenin'.'

The old man's eyes were deep blue, and seemed out of place in such an old face. His hair, at least that which straggled from below the hat, was white, and the stubble on his chin was coarse and grey. His face was thin and lined, brown as an autumn-ploughed field; his cheeks were concave, and when he opened his mouth to speak Rob could see that most of his teeth were missing.

'I'm sorry,' Rob said, 'you have me at a disadvantage. You know my name but I don't know yours.' The old man inhaled, nodded, considering whether the information Rob sought might be safely divulged.

'Jacob,' he said eventually, slowly. 'Jacob Lee.'

'Well, Mr Lee, you've told me you heard what I said. There's little more I can offer, other than my own curiosity to see what was at the end of a mysterious path that no one seemed to want me to tread.'

'Curiosity? That's all?' Jacob Lee lowered himself to the end of the bench furthest from Rob.

'Yes, that's all.' Rob decided not to say anything about

Harry Brown and his need for musicians, not yet. He too wanted to find out more. But he wasn't sure if this old man was the one to supply the information he needed.

'Well in that case I won't keep you any longer, Mr Patterson. Goodbye.'

'Goodbye? But I've only just arrived here, and—'

'You've seen all there is to see, Mr Patterson. There's nothin' else. Surely your curiosity's been satisfied.'

'No, not entirely. I mean, where's everyone else? There's only you and the children, and they're all so young. Are there no older ones? And where are the adults?'

'Your curiosity's obviously a very large animal, Mr Patterson. It needs a lot of feedin'. I could say your questions are impolite, pryin' even, that it's not your business to know anythin' about this place and the people who live here. Or I could answer them, not really knowin' why you're askin' them in the first place. But the best response would be for you to tell me why you want to know, why you *need* to know these things. Don't you agree? And if your need's great enough, if it's good enough, then I'll tell you.'

Rob could think of no plausible lie which might persuade Jacob Lee to answer his questions, and anyway, the real questions he had to ask hadn't yet been broached. He decided to tell the truth.

'Alright then. I'm trying to teach dancing at the manor, you know that much, but I'm having difficulty with the music. The people I have are ... they're too staid, or incapable of playing, or they play too slavishly, and the dancers feel this and they lose their sense of enjoyment. There's a young man called Harry Brown, he's the only one who can really play. He said he'd heard some men from the village, from here, and they were good. I thought I'd come along and talk to them, listen to them, and if they could play well enough, if they could play the way I wanted, I'd ask them to join us. That's it. That's why I'm here.'

Jacob Lee was laughing. He was making little noise, nothing more than a regular hissing of expelled air through his nose and then a long, sibilant inhalation through his mouth, but Rob could tell by the way he moved backwards and forwards and by the way his body was shaking that he was laughing. It was annoying. He couldn't recall having said anything that could be misinterpreted, that could be considered funny.

'Are you alright, Mr Lee?' he asked, the possibility occurred to him that the old man might be having a fit. He was rewarded with a nod, hands outstretched to signify that all was well.

'I'm sorry, Mr Patterson. I shouldn't behave like this. You're a stranger here; you don't understand. But I'll try to explain. Please, come inside, lad. I've a little small beer, if you'd like to try it. Not the best I've brewed, but it keeps me satisfied.' He rose to his feet and led the way into the darkness of the cottage, pointed Rob into a wooden seat with a high back. He then bumbled about in the shadows, humming to himself and occasionally indulging in a little gentle laughter.

It took Rob's eyes some time to become accustomed to the gloom. The only light entering the single room was from the doorway and the small window and a few holes in the thatch, but even when he could see he found there was little to look at. The furniture was sparse; a narrow cot and a small table, a crude wooden chest, a pair of three-legged stools. From the rafters there were hung blackened, misshapen pots and pans, and metal spoons on curved hooks, and a lazy fire smoked in a stone grate. The floor was made of uneven sandstone flags, some of them cracked, and beside the cot was a mat woven from numerous small pieces of cloth. In its time it might have been colourful; now it appeared older and greyer than anything else in the building. Up on the rafters a dove cooed, and hens jostled for the most favourable position, which could be judged by the white stains on the sandstone beneath. There was a smell of damp and squalor.

'There we are, Mr Patterson,' said Jacob Lee, passing him a battered pewter tankard filled to the brim with a dark liquid. 'Your health.'

'And yours,' Rob rejoined, raising the tankard warily to his lips. He need not have worried; it was as good an ale as he'd tasted in many a tavern, and better than most. He smiled his appreciation and took a deeper draught. Jacob Lee hooked a stool with his stick and dragged it closer to Rob's seat, sat down carefully, placed his own pot of beer on the table at his side.

'Now then, I owe you some answers, I believe. Where should I start? Oh yes, I know. Where is everyone? Where are the older children, the men and women? The answer's easy, straightforward. They're at work.'

'At work? All of them?' Rob looked out of the window, the shadows were long and framed with red. 'But it's late.'

'Aye, it's late, lad, but it's not yet dark, that's why there's no one about. Some of them won't be home at all. The shepherds, they stay out on the moors for the whole of the summer; they only come down when their beasts move inby. And if you'd come earlier you'd have seen no one at all. The young uns, they'd have been out helping their mams and dads; it's first hay, you see. Or they'd have been in the fields, scaring birds. They work as well, you see.'

'Even the babies?'

'No. The newborn, they can't be separated from their mams, they'll suckle while their mams work. It's the way it is.' He snorted, drained his tankard and encouraged Rob to do the same; he filled them both from a barrel beside the fireplace.

'I was goin' to say it's always been like that, but that's not true. I can remember the days when we worked for oorsels as well, when each man kept a pig or a cow, even a few sheep on the common land, and we'd meat and bread and vegetables to eat. Aye, I know the land wasn't good, but it was enough. We could live on what we raised, and the pay we got let us have extras. We could buy good hops and sugar. Oor women could go into market once or twice a year and bring back material for dresses and trousers and the like. We'd blankets to keep us warm in winter. I know it's possible to remember the past and say how glorious it was, but it's not just memory; I can feel the difference, Mr Patterson. I can feel it here.' He put his hand flat on his stomach and patted it gently. 'And what's worse, I can see me bairns and me grandbairns have that same hunger. Those that's still alive, that is.'

'But why? If it used to be good, what's made it change?'

'Why, lad, if I knew I might be able to do somethin' about it. I know part of it. The land we had, the common land, it's been taken away from us. It's been fenced in, enclosed. We can't keep oor own beasts any more; there's nowhere for them to feed. We just have chickens and a scrawny pig or two. We used to have a pig each, and piglets; now we've two old sows between the lot of us. And they say that, during the wars, when Napoleon was out and about, they needed provisions, they needed grain, the farmers made lots of money and they could afford good wages. But now there's nothin' but hardship. Wages are down for those in work, and those who don't work go to the poorhouse. And once you get in there you don't get out again. You can see why Captain Swing's been seen in Yorkshire, and he's comin' north, they say; he's comin' north.'

'Captain Swing? Who's he?'

'Don't you read the newspapers, lad? Even here they're talkin' about him. He leads the agricultural workers, the labourers. He breaks up machinery, he fires barns, he threatens farmers who don't pay the going rate. He organises the men. He's nowhere and everywhere. They hunt for him, the constables, the militia, the army, the hired bullies, but they can't find him. He doesn't exist, you see, but he's still the focus. He's the one who'll win the day for us, you wait and see.'

It was Rob's turn to drain his mug. Unthinkingly he placed it close to his host's outstretched hand and found it returned to him, full again. It was getting darker in the room, but he was sure the walls were closing in slightly, the floor tilting slowly towards the door.

'So that answers your first question, about where everybody is. Except me, that is. I'm too old to work properly. I can't walk far, so they leave me here to watch the young uns, to keep an eye on things, to catch a few rabbits when I can. 'S all I'm good for now.' He stared morosely into his beer, hunch-shouldered and pinch-nosed, a gargoyle come to earth. 'Your friend, this Harry Brown, what did he say about the music?' The old man didn't even raise his head to speak.

'He said I might find some musicians here. He said they'd be good.'

'He lied then. They're not good.' He looked up, fixed Rob with his blue eyes. 'They're better'n good, they're the best. They can make an angel weep. They can make the devil pray to God. They can make bodies come out of the ground and dance. They can make the sun shine and the wind blow and the rain fall. They can make a woman fall in love with a man, then a minute later they'll tell her to take out a knife and plunge it into his heart, and she will, she'll do it; she'll do it because the music tells her to. They play music with a life of its own, music that breathes and moves, music that loves and hates, music that can be jealous and angry, happy, sad, lustful, gentle, soft; music that's more real than most people. And you know the best thing of all, Mr Patterson?' His voice changed. The poetry ceased; there were only bare, harsh words. 'They won't play for you. They won't play for the Taylors. They won't play for anyone except themselves. So it's no good you waiting here for them to come back, the answer'll be no. Now drink up.'

'But why, Mr Lee, why? Why won't they play at Annie Taylor's wedding?' Rob attacked his mug with a desperate thirst. He could feel himself sweating in the near darkness. The old man lit a candle and placed it on the table next to the window. For a brief moment the evening entered the room with its sounds of swifts and children. A moth courted the dancing candle flame. The old man leaned closer, cloaked Rob with his beery breath.

'They won't play, Mr Patterson, because they don't exist.

You see, lad, the Taylors and their like, it's not that they ignore us. It's that we're of no value to them. Their beasts are worth more, they take better care of *them* than they do of *us*. If one of us is ill, if one of us dies, another can be found easily enough. Oh, we have oor uses. The work we do needs a certain amount of skill, they can buy oor women and we're thankful for the money because we know, if we argued, they'd take what they wanted without paying. But they want us out the way. They don't want to see us, they don't want to touch us, they don't want to smell us.' He stood up suddenly and groped for his stick, stumbled for the doorway.

'Come on you kids!' he yelled into the night, 'It's dark. Get yourselves to bed!' He lurched away and Rob rose unsteadily to his feet, swayed after him. He heard the sound of liquid falling on grass, joined the old man in his own relief.

'You haven't asked the Taylors anyway, I know that. How do I know? Because you're here, asking me. If you'd asked them you wouldn't be here asking me, because they'd have told you not to come. So it's all pointless.' He stared up at the sky darkening to black, whispered the same message to the first stars. 'It's all pointless.'

'Is it really that bad?' slurred Rob.

'It's Sunday tomorrow. You'll be at church. You'll see what it's like, Mr Patterson, you'll see. But I've got to get the kids to bed, and you'd better be goin'. I trust you won't be ignorin' me tomorrow, but I wouldn't wager any money on it.' He giggled, a strange sound which turned rapidly into a cough. Rob slapped him on the back; the old man spat and breathed in deeply. 'Not that I've money to wager. Go on, lad, on your way. Say a prayer for me tomorrow.'

He limped away, and Rob would have followed but for the small terrier which bared its teeth at him as he stepped forward. Instead he turned around and spiralled his way through the long grass until he met his path through the copse of trees. He turned once, but there were no lights showing from the cottages; they lay still as battle-fresh corpses.

* * *

The journey back to the manor took a week of nights, a month of hours, a year of stumbling, muddy footsteps. Branches whipped into his face, roots conspired to trip him, brackish puddles darted beneath him each time he fell. He saw the sky as he'd never seen it before, rich with a belt of silver which twisted away from him each time he raised his eyes. He couldn't do that too often. The dizziness overwhelmed him and laid him out faster than a cudgel blow; but the stars were an addiction. He negotiated the area of boggy ground with difficulty, found the path beyond and lay down on a grassy bank at its side to rest, to gather his strength for the last part of the journey, to stare at the sky without danger of falling over. He fell asleep. He was sure it must have been sleep that took him momentarily, because a procession passed him by, a train of soft, luminous figures led by a transparent king and his diaphanous winged queen, escorted by lines of noblemen and -women with haughty stares and strange, wide almond eyes. Their entourage, a panoply of fairy dancers and musicians escorted by goblins riding giant shrews, capered past him wearing animal masks and little else, and behind them came a garrulous jumble of porters and servants bearing rich fruits and viands, carrying flags which cavorted high above their heads, and the tumult of their passing filled his ears though he understood not a single word. And then, last of all, came a disjointed figure dressed in rags, all arms and legs, rounding up the slowest and chivvying them on their way, sniffing the air through wide nostrils, running low, close to the ground. The procession had ignored Rob's presence. He'd kept still; only his eyes had moved as wonder followed wonder and disappeared across the marsh. But this figure seemed to be taking some interest in the surroundings, and Rob found himself retreating up the bank, searching for a hollow or some long grass in which to hide, fearful for some unknown reason that he might be discovered. He realised, too late, that he should have remained still. Two eyes found him, and their gaze ceased his movement. They were green eyes, the eyes of a cat, and their owner approached with a feline grace and purposeful curiosity. But the tread wasn't that of a cat, or of any other beast, but of a human. And as the figure drew closer, and closer still, Rob could see that it was a woman. She could have been half animal. Her skin was darkened by sun and soil, her hands were like claws, her hair was long, weather-bleached, woven with moss and twigs, and as she approached him her tongue licked her lips like that of a snake tasting the air, or of a wolf nearing its prey. He kept still, though tensing his body for flight, and she reached the bottom of the bank, clinging close to the ground. Then she was rearing over him, and he closed his eyes, waited for some blow, the strike of talons, the tearing of sharp teeth. But there was nothing. And when he opened his eyes she was gone, and the sky in the northeast was tinged with the pale warning of dawn.

Suddenly sober he hurried back to the manor, took off his shoes and slid upstairs to his room. He closed the door behind him with relief.

'I was wondering when you'd come in,' said the voice of Frances Arnison. She stalked naked from his bed. The curtains were all open, she could see him clearly in the light.

'You smell of beer and mud and sweat,' she said, pulling at his shirt buttons, 'but I don't want to know what you've been doing.' She rapidly undid his trousers and tugged them to the ground, did the same with his cotton breeches. 'I don't want to know who you've been with, either.' She pulled him towards the bed, tugging the shirt from his back as she did so, then gave him a push so he fell face down onto the mattress. 'And I don't want to know where you've been,' she finished, dragging his trousers, breeches and stockings from his feet in one urgent move. Somehow she managed to turn him and climb on top of him in one move.

'In fact, Dancing Master, I don't want you to say a single word.'

The Eighth Bar of the Musick

Sunday, 20 June 1830

In which Rob goes to church, and the sermon is explained to him by one who has listened.

The church was cool and dark. Rob had been permitted to sit with the Taylors. Their pews had small doors at the aisle and space for long legs, and spirals of dark oak had been fitted to the pews to support wooden fasciae, a framework for a canopy, had one been requested. The church windows were mercifully small and filled with clear leaded glass; what bright shafts of sunlight did enter were directed at the oak table, which served as an altar, and at the pulpit leaning against the far wall. There stood Parson Theodore Westborne in his Sunday black, perspiring in the heat, arms waving as he sought to fill his parishioners with the spirit of the Lord, to warn them of the eternal torment waiting for them if they left that narrow, difficult path which led to heaven. Rob heard little of what was said. The demons were already at work inside his head, digging their poisonous, barbed pitchforks into his brain, stamping and carousing through his mind. They were laughing and jeering at him; he could see them when he closed his eyes. He was hunched beside Danny Taylor, his head in his hands, fingers probing at his temples in an attempt to soothe the pain. He hoped the others would assume his position was one of devout prayer.

'When Moses came down from the mountain he brought with him from God the commandments. You know these commandments, these ten commandments, they are written on the wall behind the altar. I have spoken of them often, they provide us with spiritual and moral guidance to which we should all pay heed.'

Speak quietly, said Rob to himself in silent prayer. *Please, speak quietly.*

'We may all find, in the commandments, instructions which are relevant to the lives we lead. At times I have selected one or other of the commandments as the subject for a sermon and tried to draw attention to the way in which the Lord's words can be read, and understood, and acted upon in these modern times. And so, today, I choose one commandment in particular. I would ask you not to presume that this is more important than the others, because this is not so, and to reinforce that statement I will repeat the other nine commandments and I hope that you will consider them all, think how you yourself may build your life around them.'

Rob felt sick, he breathed in deeply. His mouth was sour with the taste of the beer he'd been given by Jacob Lee, it had been far more potent than he could ever have imagined. But he couldn't be sick, not in church, not in the middle of the sermon. The parson's voice thundered on, giving a list of items which Rob was sure he must have transgressed regularly, and recently. After delivering each rock-hewn regulation Theodore Westborne paused, and his gaze travelled the congregation searching for some flicker of guilt which he could memorise and store in the catalogue of his suspicions, to be retrieved in private moments and savoured. He collected sins, delighted in the wickedness of others, rejoiced in the investigation, dissection and inevitable confession of these wrongdoings which would result in the salvation of the sinner. He ignored the vicarious pleasure he derived from the proceedings.

'"Thou shalt have no other gods before me; Thou shalt not make unto thee any graven image, nor bow down thyself to them, nor worship them; Thou shalt not take the name of the Lord thy God in vain; Remember the sabbath day, keep it holy; Honour thy father and thy mother; Thou shalt not kill; Thou shalt not commit adultery."' At this Rob found the strength to look up, to seek out the bonneted head of Frances Arnison. She was away to his left in the pew in front, but her head remained still; she didn't move. He hadn't had time to wash properly that morning, he could still feel the sting of a hurried shave, and the warm earthy smell of excess hung about him.

'"Thou shalt not steal,"' the parson went on. '"Thou shalt not bear false witness against thy neighbour." And the commandment I've left out, the one I wish to discuss today? You're aware of it, of course you are, but I'll repeat it, because it is of such importance to us all. "Thou shalt not covet thy neighbour's house, nor his wife, nor his manservant, nor his maidservant, nor his ox, nor his ass, nor any thing that is thy neighbour's." That is what I must share with you today. What does it mean, this word "covet"? And why do I consider it of such importance? I shall tell you.'

Rob looked up again. The preacher was conducting the congregation, reaching out to them with arms wide, bringing his hands close together, fingertips dancing, he was swaying and rolling with the rhythm of his words.

'To covet is to wish to possess something, to long for something, to crave something, especially when that something is the property of another. It carries only the sense of wishing to own a thing, without that which must always accompany ownership; the earning of that particular thing. It is a word which has allies, other words with similar meanings, such as "desire" and "envy"; small words, ugly words; words which should not belong in our vocabulary. It is sinful to covet another's possessions.

'Of course, the Bible is not being prescriptive in its pronouncement. It is not saying that it is wrong only to covet your neighbour's house and wife, his manservant and maidservant, his ox and his ass. It is not saying that it is therefore permissible to covet his land and his daughter, his cooks and his footmen, his sheep and his cattle. The Bible says that it is wrong to desire anything which belongs to another!' His voice rose in a crescendo, and Rob narrowed his eyes. How was it possible, he pondered, for the human voice to affect the eyesight like this?

'This message has meaning for us all. We know that it is wrong to take that which does not belong to us, whether it be a knife or a cup, food or clothing; game, perhaps, or wool, or straw, or hay, or wood, whether it be cut specifically or a storm fall; *anything* which belongs to another. No one can doubt that this is wrong. It is the law of the land, the law of the Bible, and the law of God. But the Bible goes further. It states that it is wrong *merely to think* about owning something which does not belong to you. "Thou shalt not covet thy neighbour's property." And this is something we should all remember.

'My friends, we should all remember that we have been placed upon this earth for a purpose, and that purpose, that ultimate purpose, is to glorify the name of God our creator. God in his wisdom has chosen to give us our positions in life, he has chosen the tasks we must carry out. It is God's will that we be placed in a hierarchy, because only in such a hierarchy may we live in peace and harmony. There are men at various stations in life who have been given the responsibilities of those stations, who must bear the burden of their responsibilities. It is not our lot in life to question that hierarchy, to attempt to alter the balance of things, to move beyond our predetermined position. In short, we must not covet that which is not ours but must trust in our betters, our superiors, and in the Lord our God to care for us in the manner they determine as being most appropriate for the good of the people as a whole. Not one of us is indispensable. Any man, no matter how much of an individual he may consider himself, may be replaced. We must be content within ourselves, happy that we all have our part to play in God's great plan, certain that we are all beneficiaries of God's wondrous love. And now let us pray.'

There was a shuffling of knees on hassocks as the congregation descended from their seats.

'Dear Father, Lord our God, we pray that You reward us who know of Thy eternal love, who obey Thy commandments, who trust in Thy word and in the words of Thy servants. We ask for forgiveness of our transgressions, Almighty Father, who knows our every thought and deed.' There was a brief pause, then a few words were added, almost as an afterthought. 'And we offer our prayers for the recovery of Thy beloved son, our King George, that he may reign on Thy behalf and in Thy name. Amen.'

The congregation muttered its response as its shepherd stepped down from the pulpit to the communion rail. He looked up and nodded. Samuel Taylor rose to his feet and undid the latch holding the door of his pew closed, stepped into the aisle and took three steps forward to the communion rail where he partook of his wine and bread. He was followed by his wife and daughters, and then Rob was bustled out by Danny with Charlotte Stephenson in close attendance. As Rob returned to his place he saw the doctor and his wife step forward, and Emanuel Scrivener behind them gave him a wink as he passed by. Then came Mrs Westborne and her brood, decked in their best clothes, the children looking nothing less than miniature versions of their parents. Rob noticed as he turned to sit down that the church was full, and right at the back, standing because there was a lack of seats, he spied Jacob Lee. He smiled briefly, was sure the old man had seen him, but there was no answering gesture.

Next up were the farmers. Rob had met them all, it was clear that the determining factor in which family had priority was the acreage of land each controlled. They took their turns at bobbing, sipping and swallowing, then came the tradesmen, the wheelwright and the blacksmith, mason and miller, nodding at each other and at those who had passed before them, all deferring gently to the Taylor family in their pew. There was a gentle hubbub of subdued conversation throughout. Rob could see that the celebration had as much social as religious significance, but that murmur of sound died as the last group of worshippers stepped forward: the agricultural labourers. They moved as a body, not as individuals, Jacob Lee in the front row. Most of the men wore clean white smocks over what were probably working clothes. The women were dressed in simple skirts and blouses. Most wore shawls around their shoulders, a few were carrying hats or had garlanded their hair with flowers. Although they approached the rail with heads high, on their return they looked down, seeking the eyes of no one else, and Rob saw that no one was looking at them, no one was acknowledging their presence.

Rob looked out for the children he'd met the previous night but there were none under the age of fourteen. Their eyes were tired, their faces were tired, their bodies were tired, not just with the fatigue of hard, continuous labour, but with a spiritual tiredness which the church and its parson could do nothing to dispel. They resumed their places at the rear of the building, and Rob was lost in his own thoughts for the rest of the sermon. He mouthed empty words during the singing of a hymn he didn't recognise, mumbled responses too late, didn't hear prayers at all.

'My friends,' the parson proclaimed at the close of his dissertations, 'the weather has proved particularly clement during the month and, as we approach the longest day and the shortest night, we should continue to pray for a good harvest in order that we may all enjoy a secure winter. I urge you to go to your beds early and rest. Conserve your strength for the hard work which lies ahead. May the Lord be with you.'

He stepped down and led the way to the door. The

church emptied from the front in the same order as communion.

'What was that about going to bed early?' Rob asked Danny, holding him back from accompanying his partner down the aisle. 'It sounded strange advice for a parson to be giving at this time of year, I'd have thought people would be needed to work in the fields as late as possible.'

'You'll see,' Danny replied, eager to catch up with Charlotte, 'you'll see. But I'd do as he recommends, tonight at least, because tomorrow you'll be up early. I'll wake you myself before dawn.'

'Before dawn? But why?'

'To watch the sun rise, of course.'

'But I've seen the sun rise before, I know what it looks like. Why should I want to see it again?'

'David, it's not that the sun rises, it's *where* it rises and *how* it rises that will matter. We'll all be there, the whole family, and quite a few others as well. Even Parson Westborne, though he doesn't approve, but if the weather stays fine it'll be a wonderful sight, believe me.'

'Do I have any choice?'

'No, not really. You'll thank me for it, I promise you.'

'Yes, I'm sure. But the way I feel at the moment I think I'd better go straight to bed as soon as I can.'

'Yes, I would. Your breath smells like a brewery, and you were groaning during the sermon.'

'Was I?'

'Yes. Not too loudly, only Charlotte and I could hear you, but it was beginning to make us laugh. You must have had quite a night last night. What were you up to?'

They found themselves close to the door and Rob raised his finger to his lips. 'I'll tell you later,' he whispered as they approached the parson, shook his hand and went out into the bright sunlight. Rob felt hot, and his discomfort increased as he saw Frances move towards him. It was difficult to reconcile her cold daytime behaviour with the passion she displayed in her bedroom. If she was about to arrange another assignation then he'd have to protest his fatigue; he wouldn't survive to the end of the week if she continued to treat him this way.

'Mr Patterson,' she called. She'd seen him turn away from her and didn't want him to disappear. 'Mr Patterson, I wish to speak to you.'

'Mrs Arnison,' he replied, trying to put on his best smile, 'how are you?'

'Very well, thank you. I trust you are the same.'

'A little tired, perhaps. I didn't retire until very late last night.'

'Really? And what arduous task kept you from your bed?'

Rob looked around, there were many people within hearing distance. She was teasing him, eager to see him in discomfort. Rob could think of nothing to say, he stuttered and his mind raced, he noticed Mrs Taylor coming to stand beside her daughter.

'I, uh, that is . . . I was involved in copying out some music. Yes, that's it, transcribing it for different instruments, arranging it, melody and counter melody. It was very interesting,' he continued, warming to the deception, 'exploring new areas, teasing new sounds from old instruments, peeling back the layers of a tune to reveal the warmth within, penetrating its depths, making it resound in a new and different way.'

'And tell me, Mr Patterson,' Frances asked, 'did you find this work satisfying? Was it rewarding for you? Is it the type of work you would care to repeat?'

'It was satisfying, Mrs Arnison, very much so, but it demands much attention. I feel quite fatigued. But I don't mind the task at all; providing I were to be rested I could, I feel sure, rise to the occasion again if the need arose.'

'But was the result satisfying as well? Were your efforts rewarded? Was the final tune as joyous as you lead us to believe? And the old instruments you mentioned, were they up to the task? I feel myself that you are the type of man who would rather work with a younger, more modern instrument, a flute, for example.'

Rob found himself enjoying this game of words, and Frances Arnison seemed willing to join the conversation with similar relish.

'I feel sure the result was satisfying, and the tune itself seemed to me, as I played it, as it reached its final throes of abandon, to be the most joyous I've heard for some time. And as for the age of the instrument, I'll admit that a modern flute requires a different fingering technique to one that is a little older. The more elderly instrument demands that the lips be placed very carefully on the mouthpiece, that the tongue be used to provide a more percussive trill. And of course the older instrument has usually been played by others, has sometimes even been subject to ill-use, and may not appear quite as beautiful as one newly manufactured. But the connoisseur would, I'm sure, prefer the older. He would admire its more mellow tone and response. He would enjoy the way musician and instrument became one, until the ultimate goal was achieved. Do you agree with me, Mrs Arnison?'

'I do, Mr Patterson, I most certainly do.'

'And I,' interrupted Mrs Taylor, 'am very pleased to see that the two of you are able to enjoy a pleasant conversation with each other, and to find that you can even agree upon something. That is very good indeed. But have you told Mr Patterson your good news yet, Frances?'

'Not yet, mother. I was about to do so.'

'Well go on then, there are other people we must talk to.'

'Yes, Mother. My husband will be joining us today, Mr Patterson, I expect him to arrive this afternoon. You will therefore have one extra in your dancing classes.'

'Thank you for letting me know, Mrs Arnison.'

'You're welcome, Mr Patterson. But please, I trust I will continue to enjoy instruction from you. I feel sure our liaison in that area will continue to be to our mutual advantage.

I would not wish to see it end abruptly; that would be a matter of great annoyance.'

'I understand perfectly and shall ensure that I am ready for you at any time you feel your husband is overtaxed by the demands this new art places upon him.'

Frances bowed her reply and, as she did so, dropped a small posy of flowers. Rob bent to pick them up at the same time as their owner.

'I'll come to your room,' she whispered as she rose, 'when I can.' Rob nodded his consent, then the two women were away, speaking to everyone else in turn, bestowing their favours on their fawning friends and tenants. The other Taylors were similarly engaged. Annie in particular seemed desperate to speak to as many people as possible, and the subject of her conversation (at least those snippets that Rob managed to overhear) was her forthcoming wedding. Peals of raucous laughter followed her progression around the graveyard, and it was while looking in the direction of the loudest of these, a metronomic braying which would have been more at home coming from an ass than from a farmer's red-faced son, that Rob noticed a crowd of people leaving the church from the vestry door. He looked more closely. It was the labourers, Jacob Lee amongst them, and he hurried over. The old man saw him coming and detached himself from the others.

'Mr Patterson,' he said gruffly.

'Mr Lee,' Rob responded. Then there seemed little else to say.

'I'm pleased you found your way back last night,' Jacob said, 'now if you'll excuse me . . .'

He turned to leave but Rob put out his arm, took hold of the other man's sleeve. Jacob turned back, slowly, but he didn't look at Rob, he stared at the hand holding on to him, as if it were an insect he was on the point of squashing. Rob took his hand away and the old man relaxed.

'Thank you for your hospitality last night,' Rob said. 'I'd

hoped you might be here so I could ask you to reconsider, about the music. About me hearing the music, that is.'

'Oh, I could have told you we'd be here, we're always here; every Sunday we're here. Didn't you listen to what the parson said, lad, didn't you listen to the sermon? That was meant for us, that was, for nobody but us. "Don't get ideas above your station", that's what he was sayin'. "Don't think about tryin' to get food for your bairns, or teachin', or shoes", that's what he said. And other people might have been listenin', but the message was for us.'

'Why do you think that?' Rob asked, hearing the anger in his voice, seeing the sideways glances at the groups of people scattered around the church lawns.

'I don't think that, Mr Patterson, I know that. They're frightened, that's why, they don't show it, but they're frightened. They know Captain Swing's about, they don't want their threshin' machines smashed, they don't want their barns burned down. They want things to stay as they are, they want us to live like animals in byres, they want to see us kept in our place by hunger and disease. They want to see us crowded ten in a room so they can control us more easily. They want to send oor bairns to the fields to work as soon as they can crawl. They want to keep us as their slaves.'

'Don't you think that's an exaggeration, Mr Lee? Don't you think—'

'No I bloody don't! Look at them there, chattin' away to each other. To each other, mind you! They let us use their church, yes, they do that, so they can preach the messages they want. But they make us take communion after them, just to show that, even in the eyes of the Lord, we aren't equal. And we come in and go out through a different door, just so's they don't have to mix with us. They give as little as they can, take as much as they can, that's all there is to it.'

'Why are you talking to me like this, then? Aren't you frightened that I'll tell them what you said? Why, I could go over to Mr Taylor now and say very nearly the exact words, then what would you do?'

The old man shook his head and laughed.

'I don't think you'd do that, Mr Patterson. I'm not sayin' that because I've got a hold on you, because I haven't. I'm sayin' that because I think I can read a man, and I can read you, and I don't believe you'd do that. You're a mess of contradictions, mind you, I could be mistaken. But I'm not wrong very often.' He took off his hat and scratched his head. 'And anyway, you wouldn't be telling them anythin' they didn't already know, one way or another. They know somethin's wrong, they just can't bring themselves to admit it's their doin' and they're goin' to have to sort things out eventually. Sooner rather than later.'

'I shan't say anything, then.'

'I didn't think you would. But you'd best get back to your friends. They won't take kindly to us talking together.'

'But you still haven't said, about the music. I'd like to hear it played.'

The old man looked at Rob, as if measuring him for some task. 'Will you be watchin' the sun rise in the morning?' he asked. Rob nodded. 'I know where you'll be goin', then. Go back there at dusk tomorrow night. I'll be there. There'll be music, there'll be dancin'. You might learn something. Now I'd best be away. Goodbye Mr Patterson.'

'Goodbye, Mr Lee,' Rob answered. He watched him join his fellow workers and they drifted away, unseen. Rob returned to a group of people surrounding Danny, stretching his arms as he did so.

'I think,' he said, 'I need to retire early. I've a feeling tomorrow will be a busy day.'

The Ninth Bar of the Musick

Monday, 21 June 1830.

*In which Rob sees the sun rise and the moon rise,
and meets the woman of his dream.*

'David, wake up. Come on, we've a long walk and a
steep climb ahead of us.'

Rob opened his eyes. The eager, candle-lit face of Danny
Taylor loomed before him like the full moon.

'Go away,' he said, 'whatever time it is, it's too early.'
He looked across at the curtains, there was no frame of
daylight around them. 'It's still dark,' he whined, 'leave me
alone, let me sleep.' He groped at the sheets and pulled them
over his head, but they were tugged back down again by his
tormentor.

'You can sleep when we return, David, we all do, we'll be
back before six, I promise. And it'll be worthwhile, believe
me. If it wasn't do you think I'd be going out this early?'

'Is Charlotte going?' Rob asked pointedly.

'What? What do you mean by that?'

'Good God, Danny, people do all sorts of stupid things
when they're young and in love, and you're both of those,
and I believe Charlotte loves you too. It's not surprising the
two of you don't mind charging about in the middle of the

night, but I do mind, and I've no intention of joining you. Now be a good lad and close the door behind you when you go out.'

'David!' Danny's voice was sharp, imperative.

'No!'

'You're a guest in this house, David, and my parents have invited you to go with us this morning. You have my word that there will be a spectacle worth seeing. My sisters have specifically asked that you attend, and I—'

'Your sisters? Both of them?'

'Yes.'

'Why? Why should they want me to attend?'

'I don't know! At least, I don't know why Frances wants you to come, but she did urge me to come and wake you. And Charlotte told me what Annie said. *She* didn't see why you should be able to lie in luxury when the rest of us were out tramping the moors. And I'd like you to come because . . . because I think you'll enjoy it, once you get going.'

'I'm willing to wager you'd be wrong, Danny.'

'Good! That means you have to come, otherwise you'd be unable to show you were miserable. I'll see you downstairs in ten minutes. Yes?'

Rob threw back the sheets and yawned, scratched himself inelegantly and stretched. His clothes were laid out on the back of a chair. He headed unwillingly towards them.

'I'll be there,' he said. 'But don't expect me to be merry and smiling, I don't feel—'

'David!'

Rob stopped, only halfway across the room, completely naked. 'Yes?' he said.

'Your back! It's covered in marks, it looks as if someone's been whipping you. What happened?'

Rob looked back over his shoulder but could see little. He reached round with his fingers and could feel raised welts of flesh he'd known were there, but which had caused him little discomfort. He knew the cause; Frances Arnison had sharp nails. But he couldn't admit that to Danny. He couldn't say his sister had ripped at his back while they were making love, nor could he point out that Frances herself would be wearing high-necked dresses for a few days until the bruises caused by his teeth diminished slightly. And she'd said that her husband would be arriving during the day, how would she hide the marks from him? Still, that was her problem, just as dealing with Danny's question was his.

'It's your sister's fault,' said Rob as he reached for his shirt.

'Annie's?'

'No, the blame lies with Frances.'

'With Frances? How did she do that to you?'

'She told me of a pleasant walk and I took her at her word. I followed her instructions, though I'll admit that I may have taken the wrong path somewhere.' He pulled on his pants, and then his trousers. 'It was very hot and humid, there was no one about. I took off my shirt, but just as I was pulling it over my head I slipped. I fell down a steep slope and the scratches on my back are the result of contact with stones, or thorns, I'm not sure which. It doesn't hurt.'

'Oh, good.'

Rob searched for his stockings. 'Look, I'm nearly ready. You tell the others I'll be down shortly. I hope the journey won't be too rough, I've only two pairs of shoes, and one of those is for dancing.' Danny did as he was told and Rob was left alone, wondering where they might be going, determined, despite his apparent reluctance to get up, to mark the path well. He knew he'd have to tread it alone later that night. He fully intended meeting Jacob Lee and his companions, he wanted to know more about their music and their dancing. He put on his waistcoat and jacket, wrapped a silk scarf around his neck. Danny had mentioned a climb; it might be cold. Suitably attired he descended to the dining room.

There was hot, sweet tea and a bustle of noise. All of the Taylors were there. Charlotte Stephenson was giggling in a corner between Annie and her brother. Dr Allard and the parson were conversing earnestly on a subject which appeared to demand resolute, unsmiling faces and much nodding of heads.

'Mr Patterson,' said Frances Arnison, approaching him with a smile, 'I looked for you yesterday evening but I was told you retired early, I trust you were not unwell?'

'No, Mrs Arnison, merely tired. And I was aware I'd be woken early this morning.'

'Oh, you should have taken the same course of action as the rest of us, none of us have yet seen our beds. We have sat and talked and played cards. Mother entertained us with songs and music. We've seen the passing of no small number of bottles of wine. You've been missed, your talents would have allowed the hours to pass more swiftly.'

'My apologies are due then, Mrs Arnison, for I would have spent the time with you had I known. But your brother told me—'

'My brother has the brains of an ass. You should never pay any attention to a word he says. If you require information, advice, opinion, then come to see me. At *any* time.'

'I shall bear that in mind, Mrs Arnison, though I'm sure your husband wouldn't wish to be disturbed at some ridiculous hour—'

'My husband is even now in bed, Mr Patterson, having drunk too much too early, and even your band of musicians playing beneath his eiderdown would not disturb him. And as for disturbing him when he is sober, I feel sure he would welcome any diversion which would take me from his presence.'

Rob was surprised at Frances Arnison's forthright words, but when he looked at her properly (he was in the habit of avoiding her direct gaze) he saw her cheeks were flushed, her eyes wide. She'd obviously been sharing the wine which had driven her husband early to his dreams. She was standing close to him, closer than would be considered normal in an unrelated couple, and he could smell alcohol on her breath. He looked around, but no one seemed to be paying them any attention. It was then he realised that all the conversations were slightly too loud, that the gestures of those talking were exaggerated, grandiose even, and that the whole company – save him – had indeed spent the night and the early hours of the morning in some celebration. He felt sure Frances was about to proposition him, to take him by the hand and lead him to the nearest couch, and he found himself backing away from her. She smiled and followed him, unworried at the thought of the pursuit, but they were brought to a halt by Samuel Taylor's voice, strident and brassy as a trumpet, staccato as a hand clap, each word uttered in isolation as if he mistrusted their need to form phrases or sentences.

'Ladies and gentlemen! Friends, family! It is time to go!'

He picked up his walking stick, banged it on the ground once, then marched across the room and out of the door in an uneven waltz with his wife hurrying to catch him up. The rest followed at a more leisurely pace, and Rob found himself partnered by Annie Taylor as they left the house by the rear exit. There was little opportunity to talk. They were handed fiery brands by servants waiting at the door, and the hiss of their flames crept like snakes, secret as shadows in the dark courtyard. Samuel Taylor was still in the lead. His brand bobbed and weaved as they passed under the archway and on to the track beyond, into the distant night. The sky was beginning to lighten in the northeast, and Venus hung fat and low over the horizon. Stars bent and twisted overhead in a glorious belt which even the flickering torch couldn't dim, and the smell of tallow couldn't obscure the scent of hidden flowers and green fecundity.

Annie appeared nervous. She glanced around as they walked, she wouldn't catch Rob's eye, just as he avoided her sister's stare. His attempts at conversation met with monosyllabic replies, and it was clear to Rob that she didn't wish to remain in his company.

'Please,' he said, 'feel under no obligation to stay with me. I can't get lost, not with all these torches ahead.'

This time she looked at him. 'I beg your pardon?' she said with what sounded like genuine incomprehension.

'There's no need to walk with me. I can see that it causes you discomfort to be in my presence, there's no need to pretend politeness. Please stride out, walk with the Doctor or Miss Stephenson. I won't mind.'

She shook her head. 'Mr Patterson, you misread my emotions yet again, though I should expect nothing else from you, I suppose. You honour yourself to believe that I care one way or another about your presence. The truth is that my mind was on other matters entirely, I'd barely noticed you walking alongside me. Your supposition that I should be thinking of you explains a great deal about the way you see yourself. But you are mistaken, I was thinking only of our destination, and of the fact that when we get there my fiancé will be waiting for me. He will have travelled a great distance. I may even be able to see the light of his journey on the moorlands around us, *that* is why I may have appeared distracted, because I was looking for *him*. But I think I will walk ahead, if you don't mind. I do, after all, find the present company distasteful. Goodbye, Mr Patterson.'

She hurried away, her dark hair haloed by her torch, until only the light itself could be seen, the figure itself lost in the darkness of the moor. Rob shook his head, unable to understand how his words could have been twisted so easily, thrown back at him in a form so different from the way he'd first seen them. And why? Because Annie was on her way to met her fiancé. He realised that he'd heard her speak of him only once before, that night when chance had brought her unwillingly to his room. And he was suddenly aware that he didn't even know the poor man's name. He smiled to himself. Poor man. Was he a poor man because he was due to marry Annie? A few days ago Rob might have envied him, after all, hadn't he dreamed of bedding Annie himself? Hadn't he tried to make his dreams reality? And instead he found himself subject to the demands of the sister, the sister who seemed to relish the dangers of discovery, the sister who even now was probably planning some way of luring him to her bedroom and having her way with him while her husband snored beside them. He tried to tell himself that Annie was right to think of him as self-centred and that his own arguments against this were merely justification of his injured pride, but he found it difficult to believe that he was as bad as Annie argued. He put to one side his original motivation for coming to Bellingford. It was becoming too complicated, too taxing to think of revenge while he was in this state of confusion. And besides, there were other things to occupy his mind, such as keeping upright on the path, avoiding tussocks of sharp grass and fragrant nests of heather, and wondering why the others, despite having had no sleep and too much to drink, managed to keep up their pace.

From the front of the group there came the words of a song. Rob wasn't sure who was singing, it was a man's voice, a reasonable tenor, the words clearly enunciated and the notes accurate, as if the singer was speaking a sermon. The parson, Rob thought to himself, using his hymning voice, but it was no hymn, this. He hadn't heard the words before, he speeded up a little so that he might catch them.

> *Hark, hark, I hear lang Will's clear voice*
> *Sound through the Keilder glen,*
> *Where the raven flaps his glossy wing,*
> *And the fell-fox has his den.*
> *The shepherd-lads, they're gatherin' up*
> *Where many a good ewe'll gra',*
> *Wee wiry terriers, game and keen,*
> *And foxhounds fleet and true.*

It was a hunting song. Rob hadn't heard it before, it was in a slow minor key, and it seemed to hold within it a sense of time and place which made it right to be sung on this midsummer morning as they climbed the heights of this unknown hill. The single voice was joined in a chorus by others in close harmony, and Rob had to halt. He strained to catch the nuances of tone and words and notes as the melodies drifted lazily and easily around him.

> *Hark away,*
> *Hark away,*
> *Ower the bonny hills o' Keilder, hark away.*

There were other verses too, full of references to places
Rob had never visited, people he'd never heard of or met,
he didn't know if they were still alive. The song might be
old as the ages or some local bard's winter writings. But at
the end of every verse the chorus filled the moor, and the
harmonies grew more close, more complex, gilded with grace
notes and trills which encouraged other singers to elaborate
their own parts.

'The songs of angels, eh, Mr Patterson?' Rob looked
around, surprised. He'd thought he was at the rear of the
column. It was Emanuel Scrivener and he carried no torch,
that was why his approach had been unseen.

'It's beautiful,' Rob acknowledged, 'it drives all other
thoughts away. I just want to listen.'

'Bewitching, I think, that's the word you're looking for.
And appropriate too, for this night, the shortest night. We
start the slide back down into darkness now. Winter's on
the way. It's a time to celebrate darkness, even as our world
becomes dominated by light.'

'I'm sorry, Mr Scrivener, I don't understand.'

'You will, Mr Patterson, if you hurry on ahead. See,
look up!'

Rob did as he was told. The sky was changing colour,
from dark blue to pale, then through to a delicate filigree
white, and the torches ahead of Rob were going out. He
strained to see the figures beneath, but there was nothing
there to see.

'They've disappeared,' he said, 'there must be a cave.'

'No, no cave. Come on, follow me. You'll see.'

Emanuel Scrivener took the lead without the torch, and
Rob realised that the grey-green and grey-purple of dew-laden
grass and heather, of sphagnum and bracken, was now
visible. He waved his own brand about his head in an

attempt to extinguish it but met with no success. Plunging the flame into the wet grass, he finally managed to put it out. He ran on, slipped and fell, and climbed again to his feet to see his companion waiting for him a few yards ahead at the top of a small knoll. He could see now why he'd thought that those ahead of him had entered a cave. Hills continued to rise to both sides and in the distance, but Emanuel Scrivener was standing at the edge of a plateau. When the Taylors and their friends had crossed onto the plateau it had appeared to Rob, from his viewpoint below them, that they'd vanished. Now he could see them, insubstantial shadows, some of them still bearing their lighted brands.

This artificial light wasn't needed. Directly ahead of them was a break in the rolling hills surrounding them, a V-shaped notch like the distant muzzle sight of a gun, pale with the light of the sun which would shortly rise. And silhouetted against the sky were a dozen or more stone monoliths, pointed like thick fingers at the dissolving stars.

'Sweet Lord,' whispered Rob.

'Nothing to do with Him, I fear,' commented Scrivener. 'These stones have nothing to do with Him, nor with his son, nor with any religion that we know of. They're relics of a far older age.'

One by one the torches were being extinguished ahead of them. 'Come, we must be quick! Run!' said Scrivener, and Rob did as he was told. His feet seemed able to pick a path of their own now, there was no need to look down, no fear of falling. As he ran he saw other stones lying flat on the ground, yet others split in two, all forming an imperfect circle. He slowed down. His companions were standing silent in the middle of the circle, close by a broad, wide stone, weathered by the years, almost flat. They were all staring at the pass through the ring of hills, flanked by the two tallest stones.

'It looks as if . . .' Rob began, but was hushed into silence by those around him. Far away a curlew mourned, then was silent.

The sun thrust its way into the sky, angry that it had

been forced to obey those who had summoned it, puny
men who gathered in the circle of stones and bid it rise
to their command. It reached between the stones and its
heat seared the ground and banished grey, its light stretched
molten fingers through the air and clawed at the watchers'
eyes, they could feel its power on their skin and through their
flesh and in their bones. The stones themselves seemed to cry
out in pain. Rob closed his eyes but still he could see the sun.
He held his hands in front of his face but his head was still
filled with light, and he knew it was searching for him, it
had risen on this day only to seek him out. It wanted to be
part of him, it wanted him to join in its glory, it wanted him
to acknowledge its power. It needed no worship, no praise;
it sought only his approval. It wanted him to concede that
it was majestic and awful and wondrous and inexplicable.

And then the voice began to sing again.

The words were unclear at first, the melody familiar, and
Rob remembered the harmonies of an hour before. The
memory soothed him, cooled him, he was able to listen
and hear more clearly. But this was no hunting song now, no
story of hounds and fells and wise men, it had no part in this
land. It was a tune Rob knew but didn't know, with strange
words. He could hear them, he could understand them, but
they belonged elsewhere. They belonged in a world that men
had fashioned from stone, not here where stones raised by
men had been left to take on whatever life they wanted,
whatever life they needed.

It was a hymn, and it was wrong, and the notes broke on
the moorland, and no one would join in.

> *All people that on earth do dwell,*
> *Sing to the Lord with cheerful voice;*
> *Him serve with mirth, his praise forth tell,*
> *Come ye before him and rejoice.*

It was the parson who'd begun the singing, and his voice
faltered. 'Come, my friends!' he bellowed, 'you know the

tune. "Old Hundredth", we've sung it many a time in the church!'

He began again, and this time other voices joined in, meekly, without love. There were no counter-melodies. There was no second verse. And yet in those few words the magic was driven away. Rob opened his eyes. The sun had crested the stones and was now just the sun, no longer the life bringer, the creator of seasons. The stones squatted over their thin, drawn out, moss-creeping shadows, the fire of their genesis, briefly rekindled by the dawn, lost once again. Rob too felt lost, not only because of the awe and majesty of his experience, but because the people around him didn't seem to have been affected at all. They were moving around now, talking to one another, breathing columns of damp steamy air, laughing and joking. Only he stood alone. Annie saw him, glanced away, then looked back at him. She separated herself from conversation with Dr Allard and her mother and came towards him, said nothing to begin with, just stood by his side. Unmoving as the stones themselves they stared at the moorland, segmented by grey walls, dotted with crazed circular sheepfolds. The stillness was broken suddenly by a harsh black raven cry cracking the sky.

'We come here every midsummer morning,' Annie admitted, 'even when we were babies, we'd be carried up. It's not a celebration. I used to think it was, but it's not. It's more like ... it's defiance, that's what it is.' It was clear she was finding it difficult to explain what she wanted to say.

'When I was fourteen I came on ahead, and I didn't notice the rest weren't keeping up with me. Some distant aunt was staying with us, she'd hurt her foot and the others had to help her back down to the house, and they didn't see me go on ahead. I watched the sun rise alone, it was the first time, the only time. I felt ... I think I felt the way you do now. Frightened, wondrous, I can't imagine all the words. But the next year there was nothing, because everyone else was here as well. They come to watch, to see the sun rise through the standing stones, to sing a hymn to show that their world, their God, is as it ought to be. But that one time I came here alone and I was part of it. I was the sun and the earth and the air, I was the hard rock and the soft light, I was the mist and the marsh. Just once.'

She shrugged and wiped her eyes.

'The sun's too bright,' she explained, 'it makes my eyes water.' She snorted, a single forced laugh. 'Anyway, you looked the way I felt five years ago, but more so. Just think, the rest of them have never experienced it. We're fortunate.'

Rob nodded. People were beginning to move, to head off to the edge of the plateau and down the hill, and Rob identified them all.

'I'm sorry as well,' Annie continued, 'about what I said before. It was very rude of me.'

'There's no need,' Rob answered, 'I deserved it. But you said your fiancé was due to meet you here. There's no one I don't recognise. Shouldn't we wait? He could have fallen, hurt himself perhaps. Should we go look for him?'

Annie forced a smile. 'No, there's no need for that. Something will have happened which needed his attention, he's a very busy man. No doubt he'll join us later, or send word to the house. He knows these moorlands well.' She paused, lost for a few moments in her own thoughts, then beamed up at him. 'He is a good man, my fiancé. He's a man of this land. His feet are rooted in its soil. He was born here, brought up here. I've known him since we were children. He used to tease me, pull my hair, throw water at me.' She smiled to herself. 'I think he loves me, and I have . . . I have a very deep affection for him. He will keep me well. His estates are large, far more fertile than these bare rocks and damp moors. Our thoughts coincide on many matters, and where they do not – he is no great lover of music, or dancing, or of reading and poetry and singing – then I shall win him over. It will be a good match.'

It sounded to Rob as if she was trying to persuade herself that what she said was the truth. He could have interrupted her to ask questions, he could have tried to find out more about this stranger who was to be Annie's husband, but it would have been too rude of him. The words he was hearing were her thoughts spoken aloud, meant for her to hear, not him.

'He's handsome as well. He has beautiful auburn hair, and though he has an eye for the girls – yes, he'll admit that – he's sworn to be true to me. And I to him. I think we'll be happy together.' She shook her head, as if to dispel unlooked-for thoughts and emotions. 'We ought to move along now, or there'll be no breakfast for us! I'd race you down the hill, but I've not had any sleep yet while you retired early. Should we content ourselves with overtaking the others at a brisk walk?'

'I'd like that. I could manage a brisk walk.'

'And would you take my arm, David?'

'It would give me great pleasure, Annie.'

They breakfasted well on ham and eggs, thick-cut bread spread lavishly with butter, kedgeree with mushrooms. Then, their conversations punctuated with yawns, the majority retired to their rooms to chase sleep. Rob agreed with them that all attempts at teaching dancing that day should be abandoned; there would be little chance of assembling everyone at a given time. The next day would suffice. It would also give him the opportunity to look again at the dances he'd chosen, to reconsider the music, to pull together the various strands in a material of his own choosing. His problem lay in the cloth; he'd intended a coarse mixture, a sackcloth, rough to the touch and unpleasant to the sight, but the fabric he was weaving at the moment was better than that. It was smoother, but it was thin, and there were many holes; it was unsatisfactory. He had to decide how to proceed, whether to repair this fabric or begin a new one. And if a new one was chosen, was it to be of sacking or silk?

His considerations were allowed to become no more than

that. As he mounted the stairs to his room he heard footsteps behind him and turned to nod at Frances Arnison. But she did not head for her own room where her husband was sleeping, instead – after making sure that no one was present to see her do so – she followed Rob into his chamber.

'Harry is asleep and snoring,' she explained. 'I've left a note to explain that I was unable to bear the noise and have sought another room within the house. He won't come looking for me; he'll spend his time wandering the farm, examining the cattle. We need fear no disturbance.'

'Frances, this is too dangerous!'

'There is no danger at all.' She began to unbutton her dress at the front, paused only once to stare at him. The meaning of her look was clear, and Rob sat down on a chair to untie his shoelaces.

'There *is* a danger,' he muttered, 'if only because the way you look at me, the way you talk to me, the way you *treat* me has changed. It will be noticed. I've no doubt that it has already been noticed.'

'If that is so then no one will say anything, and no one will do anything. They may suspect something, but they will not suspect that we share a bed.' She shrugged her dress to the ground and began the same unbuttoning process with the shift she wore beneath.

'And if one of us should say something?' Frances looked hard at Rob as he removed his stockings. 'By mistake, of course,' he added, 'I wouldn't suggest that either of us would do such a thing deliberately.'

'We must take care, then, that we do not make such a mistake, David. Or is it Rob?'

Rob was standing, undoing the buttons holding up the flaps of his trousers. He stopped, and the flap fell forward like a flag signalling his surrender.

'You see, Rob, you should take care. In idle moments your brain has little control over your hands. They scribble the most inappropriate words on scraps of paper. I mention this only to show that I know more about you than you imagine, and certainly more than I am willing to say. Your compliance is therefore requested.'

'Which means?'

'Which means that you are my creature, to do with as I ask, as I demand, between now and the weekend when you depart. Am I understood?'

'Yes.' Rob's voice was sullen.

'Then finish undressing and get into bed. I am very tired, but I feel the need of something to produce that final state of lethargy which guarantees sleep. And you will be the means of achieving that pleasant state, Master Rob.'

He took off his shirt and under-trousers and stood naked before her, unaroused and determined that she should see that that was the case. If such a sign discouraged her then she refused to let it show. Instead she motioned him to the bed and completed her own *déshabillement*. Once naked, she reached behind her to undo the knot holding her hair up, and let it fall over her shoulders. She shook it gracefully, ran her hands down her body, and Rob felt himself react involuntarily. She smiled at him as she walked forward.

'Men can be read like books,' she said, 'and they react like animals. So predictable.'

She sat down beside him and reached out her hand.

Rob heard the clock chime, six, seven, eight, then nine. Not nine in the morning, but nine in the evening. He'd been in bed with Frances Arnison for almost twelve hours. They'd made love and slept, and then she'd woken him with her demands again, and so the cycle had repeated itself. She was asleep now, her backside pushed against him. He could feel the warm, damp skin of her and smell the spent passion. And then he remembered. Jacob Lee had said that he should return that night to the same place where he'd spent the morning. It wasn't yet too late, but he didn't relish making the trip on his own in the darkness. He peeled himself away from Frances. She turned onto her back and clutched at the sheets but didn't wake up. He padded over to the bowl of water and jug, splashed his face and under his arms, between his legs, determined to remove the night scent from his body. He dressed quickly, pushed his whistle into his back pocket, opened the door softly, stepped outside, and closed the door equally softly behind him. He then turned to find himself looking down on a short, wide man with spectacles, his flared lapels as wide as his eyes. The man looked at him carefully.

'I don't know you,' he said.

'Nor I you,' Rob replied. The man was indeed broad, but not fat. His width was not at his waist but at his shoulders and his arms, and his neck seemed to have been borrowed from an ox. His hair was thin and pale, neatly trimmed, his sideboards running down the side of his face to halt abruptly as they met the right angles of his jaw.

'I speak as I find, sir. I don't know you, yet I should know everyone in this house. You could be a new servant, you have that look about you. Or you could be a guest. If you're the former then I have a question for you ...' He stopped, frowned, as if defeated by his own logic. 'And if you're the latter, then I have the same question for you, but with apologies for suggesting that you might be a servant. Now speak, sir, which might you be?' His voice was like gravel worn smooth by water and years, a local voice, low and peaty.

'I am neither, sir, yet both,' Rob said, and bowed slightly. The man considered this response carefully.

'Neither yet both? I must confess to puzzlement in this, and I must also state that, since I'm well known for possessing no sense of humour whatsoever, and since I dislike riddles, it may be best for us both if you just tell me who you are.'

'It would be easier than guessing.'

'It would.'

'But then you would be at an advantage, since I wouldn't know who *you* are.'

The man frowned his exasperation. 'You certainly don't use words like a servant, though your accent is of the labouring classes. But you won't admit to being a guest. I ask whether you are a sheep or a goat, and you state that you are both, but neither. You must be one or the other. You cannot be both.'

'This talk of sheep and goats confuses *me*, sir, I'd thought we were discussing the matter of my being a guest or a servant. If we talk of beasts then I may be an entirely different creature. I may be a fox.'

'I hunt foxes,' the man grinned.

'But they're clever, and sometimes they escape,' Rob rejoined.

'I get them in the end. Believe me, I get them in the end.'

The two stared at each other, neither willing to give way.

'Perhaps if you asked me the question,' Rob suggested, 'the question you were going to ask regardless of my position? Then I could answer, if I know the answer, and I could go on my way.'

'No, that wouldn't do. The question itself would give you information about me. But wait, I see a certain logic taking form. You wouldn't speak to me in this way if you were a servant, not a common servant. And yet you won't deny that you are a servant. So I may deduce from this, since you're emerging from one of the best bed chambers in the house and have the air of a gentleman about you, that you're the dancing master engaged for the wedding by Samuel Taylor. Mr Patterson? Am I right?'

'You're as right as I am, sir, in believing that, since you know the house well, and yet I haven't met you in the week I've spent here, you must be a relative of the family newly arrived. And since I was informed that Mrs Arnison's husband was due late on Saturday, and I have been otherwise engaged for most of the time since, then I think that you may indeed be Mr Arnison.'

'So we now know the other's identity?'

'That would appear to be the case.'

'Yet neither has introduced himself to the other.'

'A strange occurrence, but true. Now if you'll excuse me ...' Rob made as if to pass by, but Harry Arnison moved to block his way.

'Mr Patterson, that is the longest conversation I've had with anyone for years, since my father died, I believe. Not counting talking about beasts, that is. I'd like to take a drink with you some time, I'm curious to know more about you. I'm partial to a glass of claret, I don't suppose you have any hidden away in your room. There's no one else about and I'm damned if I can find—'

'No! No, I've nothing of that sort in my room at all.' That much, at least, was the truth. 'Is that the question you wanted to ask?'

'The what? Oh, the question! No, not at all. I was searching for my wife, she left me to sleep and I haven't seen her all day. I was about to ask if you'd seen her.'

'Mrs Arnison?' Rob swallowed.

'I'd hardly have a wife by any other name, would I?'

'No, I haven't seen her since early this morning. Perhaps she's taken herself off for a walk.'

'I think not, she dislikes walking for walking's sake.' There was a sound from below, they both looked down over the balustrade to see Andrew emerging from the study with a tray containing a bottle and two glasses. Harry Arnison was away like a weasel. 'If you see her,' he said, pattering down the staircase, 'Frances that is, tell her I was looking for her.'

'I will,' whispered Rob to himself. 'I will.'

The climb was easier in daylight. The sun was low, but still warm and friendly on his back. Bees droned fat in the heather; larks were still sky borne. He could see no one else trudging the path up to the stones, only sheep spread evenly over the moors like cotton grass. The ridges of the distant hills were sharp against the sky, the slopes below them a quilt of browns and greens and purple-reds, sometimes flecked with silver where a quartz stone raised its head to catch the sun's

rays. Strands of high cloud streaked the darkening, deepening
blue, but there was no breeze, and the air was heavy with
the drunk fever of pollen.

It didn't take Rob long to reach the plateau. He found it
necessary to stop only twice, and he disguised his fatigue with
backward glances at the village and the country beyond. It
was beautiful, and he felt none of the longing for the city
streets which had dogged him only a few days ago. His
stomach told him it was a long time since he'd eaten, and he
hoped that, whatever was to happen that night, food would
play its part. He climbed the last few feet, expecting to see . . .
He wasn't sure what to expect; he'd hoped someone would
be there, but the scene was no different from that which
he'd left behind earlier the same day.

He strode closer to the stones, suspecting that the old man
and his friends would be resting out of sight, lying down
perhaps. But there was nothing. He looked back over his
shoulder in case he was being followed, in case he was
too early. Jacob Lee had said come at night, but he could
have meant late on, very late on, not merely nightfall. Rob
began to feel lonely, not scared, not worried, just very alone.
He'd told no one he was coming up here. If he fell and hurt
himself, if he broke his leg and was unable to move, no one
would know where he was. He might die before they found
him, nothing would be left but a pile of sun-bleached bones
and a few tattered rags to identify him. And, he reminded
himself, patting his pocket, his whistle, at least they would
know it was him.

He made for the central stone, the flat stone, and sat
down on it. The sun was setting in a haze of distant mist, he
could see no marker stones to show the spot where it might
eventually descend below the horizon. He stood up again,
headed for the perimeter of the circle and began to count
the stones. He reached a total of thirty-eight but went round
again and this time reached thirty-nine. Another circuit told
him that there were forty stones, and another confirmed his
original figure of thirty-eight. He shivered, though it wasn't

cold. Darkness was creeping up on him; the sun had set, quietly, with none of the splendour that had graced its appearance that morning. He moved back again to the middle of the circle and sat down on the flat stone there, took out his whistle and began to play. He avoided slow airs, particularly those in eerie minor keys, chose instead jigs and reels and hornpipes which set his feet tapping against the stone. During one particularly difficult passage he closed his eyes to play; and when he opened them again wraiths were dancing before him. He stopped playing – it was all he could do to draw breath – and clambered up onto the stone.

The figures surrounding him were almost human. Some were carrying torches, and the flames prevented Rob from seeing what creatures they might be, but he caught glimpses of fur and feathers, of bones and huge white teeth. They stood between the stones in the circle, surrounding him, but not moving closer. From the moors behind other figures appeared, less substantial, clad in white, their bodies decked with twists of leaves and grass and flowers. They passed through the ring of fire and into the circle, and from somewhere a deep, resonant drumbeat sounded, and the ghosts began to dance. No two of them danced the same steps or moved in the same way, yet each had a beauty and grace of his or her own (he couldn't tell whether these strange beings were male or female). They twisted and cavorted as the beating of the drum grew faster, and another drum joined in, and another, and Rob could feel their power through the rock beneath his feet.

The dancers' elegance became a frenzied stepping from one foot to the other, and as they drew closer to him Rob could see that the figures were human, that their faces were painted white above white smocks and sheets, that they were both men and women, young and old. They wore no shoes, and their feet beat a muffled tattoo on the earth, and they came closer and closer until he could hear the harsh urgency of their breathing. They came closer still, and the drummers suddenly increased their pace twofold, but this time the dancers didn't try to keep up, they stopped altogether, extended their arms, and held hands in a circle round the stone, around Rob.

He could see their faces now, dimly; eyes that stared but saw nothing. He saw chests rising and falling; he could smell the heat of their bodies. And then the torches were moving towards him as well, and there was a sound of singing. But it wasn't singing he'd heard before. There were no words, just a sad, low melody sung in unison, male and female voices singing the same notes an octave apart, a keening, wailing, tearful tune of loss and bewilderment. For the second time that day he felt alone in the midst of a crowd, but this time he knew that all the others were sharing his solitude. He felt the tune course through his brain and his blood. He recognised it was coming to a close and he wanted it to go on, and tears came to his eyes, he wanted to scream, 'No! Don't stop!' but the words wouldn't come. The singing died; the torches were, as one, extinguished.

Rob realised it wasn't dark; he could still see the faces around him, and they were no longer looking through him but past him. He turned to follow their gaze. They were staring at two stones behind him, close to the point where he'd crested the lip of the plateau. Only one of them was still upright, the other lay on its side, tired, half buried, and above them the sky was turning silver. At first Rob thought he must have slept, that the night had slipped away and he was seeing a new dawn. But the direction was wrong; the midsummer sun could never rise here, and the sky was still light in the northwest where it had set less than thirty minutes before. He joined with the others and watched as the silver disc of the full moon slid above the horizon.

There was music again, the same music as before, and Rob found himself joining in the melody. A torch was lit, and the flame was passed round the circle. Rob saw now that the torchbearers wore masks of fur and feathers, hats decorated with the skulls and jawbones of sheep; twists of grass and flowers were hung from their belts, formed necklaces and crowns, were pinned to their smocks and dresses and tunics, were woven into their hair. The torchbearers moved round in a circle in one direction. The singers and dancers within them linked hands and moved in the other, and the stones themselves seemed to join in a far-flung farandole; and Rob was at their midst, at the centre of their world, turning slowly on his pedestal to see the faery crowds around him. And the moon, round and full and ripe, climbed higher into the sky.

From beyond the stones there came a new sound, a strange sound, and the singing, but not the movement, faded gradually. It was a musical instrument of some type, it was playing the singers' song though in a different key, and its long, grace-filled notes were reedy, wavering, as if the instrument itself were sad. Rob heard other notes as well, drones, and he knew he must be listening to some sort of pipe. He saw the musician come towards him through the ring of fire, and then closer through the circle of ghosts. It was a man playing, an old man by his unsteady gait. The instrument seemed to be a stand of long, narrow cylinders resting against the man's chest, and they were connected to a bag. The bag was being inflated by a set of bellows beneath the musician's arm, and the fingers of both hands were working at the chanter which hung down below the bag. He'd heard of, but not seen, such an instrument; like the louder bagpipes from Scotland but more delicate, easier on the ear, capable (so he'd overheard James Playford being told) of being tuned to play in different keys. The musician certainly knew how to play, his fingers moved neatly and nimbly over the chanter, coaxing trills and warbling runs from the reeds within. He stopped before Rob and looked up at him, still playing, and Rob wasn't surprised to see the old, unwashed face of Jacob Lee before him.

'I promised you'd hear real music,' the old man said, 'and see real dances. And so you shall.' He stopped playing abruptly and shouted, loud and echoless over the rolling moors. 'Come on then, lads and lasses! Let's show the dancing master what we can do!'

He moved from the air into a reel, and was joined immediately by another piper, and another, they strode into the circle to join him. With them came two fiddlers, both women, sawing fiercely at the strings, and a trombonist whose slide threatened the wellbeing of considerably more than one dancer as he passed amongst them. A drummer played a one-handed, syncopated rhythm, while his other hand fingered a three-holed pipe with ease. He was accompanied by a young girl no more than twelve years old playing the flute, by their looks they were clearly father and daughter.

As the musicians assembled, each glancing curiously at Rob before taking his or her place at Jacob Lee's side, the dancers sorted themselves into groups, forming squares of eight people, a couple on each side. The music reached the end of its sixteen bars, and as it started again the dancers began to move. They set to each other and swung their partners, they bowed and curtseyed, they formed arches and ducked under other arches, circled left and danced back again to the right. All was laughter and yells of approval, clapping and jigging and merriness, and Rob looked on with delight.

The band, for they were a band playing together, not merely a group of individuals, kept up a strong, steady pace which made Rob want to join in with the dancing. Each instrument seemed to take the lead in turn, to embellish the melody with its own variations, while the others took a less prominent part or even stopped playing for a while. Another then took over, and then another. At one point they stopped playing altogether and kept the rhythm going with yells and shouts and hand claps, then joined in again in perfect time. They moved into a tune that Rob knew. He jumped down from the stone to join them and pulled his whistle from his pocket, played along as best as he was able. He glanced at Jacob Lee who nodded his approval. 'Jimmy Allen,' the old man said, anticipating the next change, 'in G,' and the change was perfect.

They played two more sets, one of jigs, the other of hornpipes, and each time the dancers, on hearing the tunes, formed themselves into a circle or lines as the dance demanded, then performed with skill and enthusiasm and without instruction. After the third dance they stopped; musicians, dancers and watchers seemed exhausted.

'You play well, lad.' Sweat ran down Jacob Lee's forehead and dripped from the end of his nose. He dabbed at his face with a dirty kerchief.

'Not as well as you, Mr Lee,' Rob conceded. 'You were right, I've never heard such music, nor seen such dancing. Yet there's nothing written down? How do you remember it all?'

The old man laughed, unfastened his pipes from around his waist and laid them gently on the flat stone beside him.

'We don't need to remember how to breathe, nor eat, nor drink, do we? And the music and the dancin's as much a part of us as breathin', or eatin'. And certainly drinkin', and I need to drink right now. Will you join me?' He didn't wait for an answer, he took hold of Rob's arm and drew him after him. They walked across the circle, past small groups of laughing, happy people, some already carrying jars of what looked like and smelled like ale, to where there was a slight depression in the land. Rob hadn't noticed it earlier in the day, but nestling in the bowl was a large, dry-stone sheepfold, and leaning against the stone was a small byre, it's single wooden door wide open and spilling light into the dusk. As they drew closer Rob could see that the roof was turfed with green sods, and there were men and women coming and going, carrying food and drink the short walk up to the circle.

'The shepherds use it, in spring and autumn, when the sheep are taken out and it's too far to come back home. They can light a fire, use bracken as a bed, it does them for a day or two. But in summer nobody uses it; there's no need. So we bring barrels up and keep them here, just for this night. Then we come up, the whole village, others as well, from round about, there'll be about two hundred folk here altogether. We sing and we dance, we eat and we drink, we can even imagine, for one night at least, we're oor own masters. You can do that when your belly's full. We make the most of it while we can. Come on, in we go.'

They ducked under the low portal. Inside were three large barrels, it must have taken four men to carry each one up the hill. Jacob Lee filled two mugs, one of pewter, the other carved from a dark wood.

'But the singing and the music, when the moon came up, it was like . . . It was like being in church, but more than that. I can't really explain.'

'Don't try, then. It's not religion. We're not witches; we don't worship the moon, or the sun, come to that. In fact we don't much worship anythin' or anyone. God's done little for us, why should we do anythin' for him? No, it's not religion. It's tradition. We do it because we've always done it. Oor ancestors climbed up here on midsummer night long before the Taylors came to this valley, long before there was a church, long before there was even a village. The music and the dancin's in oor bones; we come here because we *have* to. We come here because it's oor home.'

'You make it sound as if you don't have any choice.'

'Perhaps we don't. There's so much been taken away from us, oor land, oor beasts, oor families, the buildin's we live in. People like the Taylors think they own us; they just move us about as they see fit. They've tried to take oor pride too, and succeeded in many places. All we have left is each other, and places like this, oor traditions. Oor songs and oor stories, oor music. It's not much. Words can't feed you when you're hungry; tunes can't heal you when you're sick. But they're oors; they belong to us.' He lifted his mug to his lips and drained it, bent to refill it straightaway.

'Are the Taylors that bad? I mean, they seem open to persuasion. I'm sure if you went to them . . .'

'And what? "Excuse me, Mr Taylor, we want better houses. We want some of the land back that you enclosed. We want to be able to keep a pig, a milk cow, grow a few vegetables. We want better wages as well. And we want a bit of protection for oor jobs. Is that alright, Mr Taylor? Starting next week, if it please you, Mr Taylor, sir." He's bound to say yes; he's bound to agree.' He drank some more, wiped his mouth with his sleeve and went on. 'What happens when old man Taylor decides he doesn't need so many people? He gets a machine that threshes for him, say. He just says, "Sorry, Jacob, you're a bit old, you can't work as well as you used to; you'll have to find other employment." But the house, for what it's worth – you've seen it, lad, you've seen what it's like – the house goes with the job. So I've got no job, no home, no money, nothing I can sell to tide me over. What do I do? Go on the parish? I stayed behind. I'm lucky, I've got family; they look after me. But I know I'm a burden on them, an extra mouth to feed, an extra bed to find.' He drank the mug dry, filled it again. Rob wondered how much the old man had drunk that evening before meeting him.

'So what do we do? Do we go to Taylor? My arse, that's just askin' to be thrown out. We manage, that's what we do. A little poachin', a little thievin'. We get by; we don't make trouble. But it's goin' to change, mark my words, Captain Swing's makin' his way north. It'll change. It's *got* to change!'

'But Mr Lee, tell me if I'm wrong, I thought Samuel Taylor was just a landlord. He only keeps a few sheep and cows himself. He rents the land out to farmers.'

'Aye, that's right. And the farmers are the ones who employ us. So it's him who's at the top of the bloody tree.'

'So why not go to him, tell him the way you feel? He's a reasonable enough man, his wife is certainly kind enough. Get them both together and I'm sure they'd listen to you, they might be able to bring pressure—'

'No! Word would get back. The ones who went to see him, they'd be the first to go. There's no shortage of labour, Mr Patterson, that's why there's this problem. And Samuel Taylor might look soft, he might even act soft, but there's steel in him. I know, believe me.'

'Well I could speak on your part.'

'Not that either! I'll have no man fightin' my battles for me. Somethin'll be done, don't you worry about it. Somethin' has to be done.' Rob was sure, even in the semilight, that the old man's eyes had misted over, that he was about to weep, but he turned, he seemed to gather himself together, his shoulders went back, his spine straightened. When he faced Rob again he was composed, calm.

'You're here to watch the dancin', to listen to the music, lad. You don't want to be wastin' your time listenin' to a bitter old man like me. Come on, we'll go back. You'll be missin' so much.'

'But I might be able to help, I might . . .' Jacob Lee ignored him.

'Back to the dancin',' he said, 'there's some people I'd like you to meet.' He strode unevenly away. Rob in tow, unable to keep up without running, unable to run without spilling his ale. He contented himself with a fast walk.

They arrived at the flat rock just as the dancers completed another exhausting round, a circle dance. They set off in search of refreshment or chatter, some seeking companionship in groups, others choosing to remain in couples and enjoy pleasures of a more personal and, to judge by the ways in which some of them were intertwined, more intimate nature. Jacob Lee ushered Rob forward.

'This here's Mr Patterson. He's been engaged as dancing master for young Annie Taylor's wedding.' There was a mutter of grumbles; 'What's he doing here then?' 'Come to teach us how to dance, has he?' 'Don't like that Annie; she knows she's got the looks,' 'Come on Jacob, I want me ale!'

'Come on, lads and lasses, let's have some hush! Mr Patterson's come to watch some good dancin', to hear some real musicians. We don't want to show him we're any less hosts than them asleep in the manor this very moment, do we?'

'I suppose not,' said a young girl clutching a fiddle, her hair long and brown and straight. She smiled at him and showed a gap between her front teeth. She must have been in her late teens, Rob guessed.

'Good lass,' said Jacob. 'You can always rely on Sarah for a bit common sense. Mr Patterson, this is Sarah.' She gave a little curtsy.

'David,' said Rob. 'Please, call me David.'

'David?' answered Jacob. 'We can't have that, we've already got two Davids here. You'll have to be Davy tonight, lad, if you're to be on first-name terms.'

'Davy'll be just grand.'

'Good! Then I'll introduce you to the rest. Adam here, he's another fiddler, popular with the lasses he is, and young Tim, he's a demon with the spoons and the bones. Martin on flute – he's not as old as he looks, he's had a bit of a hard life. David here plays the pipes, nearly as well as me, and Ben used to play the cello till he fell on hard times, had to sell it to buy food winter before last. Now he plays whistle. Made it himself he did, look at the carvings.'

A red-haired man handed him a length of wooden pipe, six holed, carved with Celtic whorls and images. Rob examined it carefully, tenderly. 'Can I?' he asked, raising it to his lips. The red-haired man nodded. Rob played a few notes; no particular tune, some slurs and trills. The whistle was well tuned and mellow, its register sweet throughout. He handed it back.

'It needs a better player than me to do it justice,' he said, and Ben blushed his appreciation.

'There's others as well, you'll meet them later,' said Jacob, 'but you'll need a lass to dance with.' He looked around, saw someone he seemed to recognise a few yards away and went over. The musicians excused themselves and went off in search of refreshment, and Rob was able to hear pieces of conversation drifting back from Jacob and his friend.

'I don't want to!'

'You'll do as you're damn well told, lass!'

'I'm not spending the whole night . . .' Rob couldn't make out the next few words ' . . . old piss-pot dancing master, specially one . . .' again there was an infuriating gap ' . . . that bloody Annie Taylor and her fancy airs and graces, and as for her sister, she's probably already . . .'

'You will! He's a reasonable enough man, you might give some thought . . .' Even Jacob Lee's words were muffled; he was trying to keep his voice low. '. . . And he's not too old. Just dance with him a few dances, he'll soon tire . . .' He kept on looking back at Rob, over his shoulder. ' . . . Chance to make some money, God knows we need it . . .'

Rob had to turn away, embarrassed that he was being talked about like this. He sat on the flat stone and gazed about him. The brands which had been thrust into the ground were still sputtering, and the moon had climbed high into the sky, so bright that few stars could compete with it. There was a distant light and noise from the shepherds' hut, and couples could be seen strolling around the perimeter of the stone circle. Rob had noticed none of the children he'd seen when he visited Jacob Lee, he'd seen no children at all, and there were few elderly people. He imagined the climb was too difficult, or the old had been set the task of looking after the young. Whatever the reason, those who were present appeared to welcome the opportunity to leave their responsibilities behind them, if only, as Jacob had suggested, for this one night of the year.

'Mr Patterson? I'm sorry, Davy.'

Rob turned round to face Jacob.

'I'd like you to meet my daughter. She's agreed to dance with you, if you'd like. Her name – come on lass, come forward – her name's Jinny.' Jacob reached behind him to tug someone forward, someone unwilling to move, someone reluctant even to look at Rob. He jumped down from the stone and held out his hand, and she turned her head to look at him, and in that moment they recognised each other.

The Tenth Bar of the Musick

<hr>

Tuesday, 22 June 1830

In which Rob learns how to dance and how to teach dancing but shows he has less knowledge on the subject of women.

'*I* know you!' they said together. Jacob Lee seemed surprised.

Rob was the first to find his tongue. 'I dreamed about you!'

She was indeed the woman, girl – he'd thought at the time she was a faerie – who'd passed him that night when he'd made his way back to the manor from Jacob Lee's home, when he'd drunk too much, when he'd lain on the grassy bank and watched the procession of little folk pass him by. She'd come at the end, chasing the stragglers away, and looked down on him. And here she was now, in front of him, brought to life.

'You're the one I saw drunk by the roadside,' she responded knowingly, 'mumblin' and groanin' about elves and goblins dancin' past. It wasn't hard to see you were in your cups. And now I find you're callin' yourself a dancin' master! Well well, may the devil take me if I see the like again. A dancin' master who can't even stand up when a lady passes him by in the night!' She laughed at him, hands on her hips, and Rob felt himself colour. She was as beautiful as she'd appeared in his dreams. Her hair was the colour of milk, purer than moonlight, and plaited into it were small flowers and long-stemmed grasses. Of the same rough materials were fashioned a necklace and bracelets, and the skin bearing these garlands was soft and pale. Her skirt was of simple cotton, its hem ripped and ragged, and her loose shirt was only partly covered by a bright blue shawl. But that blue was as nothing compared to the blue of her eyes, a blue flecked with hazel, a blue that was flint-hard and sharp and directed straight at him.

'I'm sorry,' said Rob, 'I know I'd had too much to drink, but I didn't realise how powerful the brew was, your father gave me a little too much . . .'

'He gave you some of his own ale? That's a miracle in itself, he's not noted for his generosity, are you Da? And it's strong stuff, I'm not surprised you were falling-down drunk. You hadn't spiked it, had you Da?'

'Jinny! What a thought!'

'It wouldn't be the first time, Da. You've emptied a pocket or two before now after getting the pocket's owner blind drunk.' Jacob Lee lunged for his daughter. She scampered around Rob, her bare feet easily keeping her out of the old man's reach.

'Jinny, you keep a civil tongue in you!'

She did the opposite, stuck her tongue out at him. He dived at her again.

'You're a bad lot, you are! You'll get what's coming to you!'

It was clear that Jacob Lee would never be able to catch his daughter. She was too young, too nimble, too fast; she could have run off and left them at any time. Instead she appeared to enjoy tormenting the old man, and the fact that she was laughing at him only made his temper worse. He feinted to one side and then went the other way, but the girl was quicker. Using Rob as a lever she swung herself around him, and her hand gripped his arm and swung him around. By doing so the girl momentarily unbalanced herself, and Rob was aware that her father was already bearing down on her, his hand raised to strike a blow. He knew he couldn't prevent the blow, but he moved forward, took its force on his chest, and was surprised that such an old body as Jacob Lee's could hide within it such strength. The punch winded him and he bent over, then toppled to the ground.

'Now look what you've done!' the girl screamed, and the old man gazed down in horror.

'I'm . . . alright,' Rob said, but the words were no more than a whisper, and they were hushed further by the girl's finger on his lips.

'You'd best go get him a drink,' she said, 'and hurry!' Jacob Lee nodded, scuttled away.

'I'm alright,' Rob gasped again, and the girl bent down beside him.

'I know,' she said, 'you're winded, that's all. But let him worry, it'll do him good.' She looked after her father and shook her head.

'And thank you. I saw the way you put yourself in front of me, so he struck you rather than me. I'm not sure he'd have hit me, I'm too fast for him now, I've had too much practice. But thank you anyway.'

Rob closed his eyes and let her voice wrap around him. It was round and smooth as good port, the type he'd occasionally stolen from James Playford, and just as intoxicating. It was rich and broad Northumbrian, it took a lifetime for her to pronounce the letter *r*, and when she did it was as if it had migrated all round the roof of her mouth and multiplied into a deep growl. He opened his eyes again to find her face swimming before him. He could smell her perfume, some cheap concoction of flowers and herbs. It hadn't been long since she'd stopped dancing, and the sweat from that exertion had dried on her. He could smell its slight muskiness. He breathed in deeply and lay back again on the grass.

'Davy?' Her voice seemed concerned. He lay still.

'Davy? That's your name, isn't it? What's the matter? It was hardly a punch, I saw it. You were alright just a moment ago. What is it?'

Rob reached out his fingers, took her hand, gently moved it to rest on his head. She was kneeling beside him now, he could hear her breath. He turned his head slightly and put out his tongue, ran it down her wrist, and his grip was too strong when she tried to pull away. She tasted of sweat and salt, and music and dancing. He let go of her hand and opened his eyes. She'd sat back and was looking at him. Her eyes demanded an explanation, but he said nothing. Instead he explored her face, watched as her glance moved from him to her wrist, to the trail of cool silver which he knew must still be there.

'You're strange,' she whispered, but she didn't move further away, even when he sat up and was close beside her. She remained where she was, kneeling, higher than him, and didn't flinch when his hand reached out again. She allowed him to touch her wrist, softly, to manouevre her hand so its palm was facing him. She didn't wince when his tongue flickered out again and touched her gently, just below the wrist where an island of muscle reached out to her thumb, and traced small circles on her flesh. She didn't move when his tongue moved lower, slicked a line across her palm and across the face of her middle finger. He held her hand delicately in his. She could have taken it away had she wished, but there was no sign that she desired to do so. His tongue moved again, back up her middle finger and down her ring finger, then back up once more, this time on the inside edge. The movement slowed as he reached her hand again, his nose was pressed against her palm, and his tongue played tremolos on that small area of skin where her two fingers met. He heard her breathe in sharply, but there was no exhalation to follow, and he moved her hand so that he could see her face. Her eyes were closed. He looked down and saw that her free hand was clenched into a fist, and he moved his mouth again, this time to the muscle below her thumb. He opened his lips and pushed at her hand, his teeth rasped at the swelling of her flesh, he sucked it into his mouth and was rewarded with a gasp as her eyes flicked open. He put her hand down in her lap.

'You're strange,' she whispered again, 'very strange.' Rob nodded. 'Me da wants me to dance with you,' she said. 'I told him I didn't want to. I've got friends here; I want to dance with them.'

'I'll watch,' said Rob. 'I'll watch you dance. That'll be enough for me.' As he spoke the words he knew that they were both truth and lies at the same time, that if she danced with anyone else then he'd be pleased to watch her, but his pleasure would be far greater if it was him she chose to be her partner.

'But I've changed me mind. I'll dance with you.' The thought that he might decline the honour didn't seem to occur to her. 'Look, he's comin' back, I'd better go. I'll wait over there,' she pointed at the stone circle, 'by the tall stone, where the moon rose. Come and get me when the music starts.' She gave him no chance to argue, she was away at a run, a single glance back and wave to show an arrangement had been made. And then she was lost with the other ghosts, and Jacob Lee was puffing and panting beside him, a tankard of ale in his hand. He handed it over to Rob, who swallowed eagerly, suddenly in need of drink.

'Where's she gone, lad?' the old man started. 'Left you here alone, I see, only me willin' to give you a hand. Typical of the lass, just typical. It's me brought her up when her mother died, you've seen the thanks I get – nothing but insults. But I'm forgettin' meself, you're the one who was hurt. You alright now? Fancy you fallin'. I tried to stop you but that bloody girl was hangin' round your neck, if I hadn't pushed her to one side you might have hurt yourself even more. You feelin' better now?'

Rob nodded, unwilling to argue that Jacob Lee's memory of events didn't quite coincide with his own.

'That's a relief. How would I have explained to the bloody

Taylors that their dancin' master was lyin' half-dead on the moors? And where the hell is that daughter of mine? Did she say where she was goin'?'

'No,' Rob answered, surprised that he had a voice, 'but she did say you'd asked her to dance with me, and she'd do as you asked. She did say that.'

'She did? She's goin' to do as I said?'

'That's what she told me, just before you came back.'

'Good. That's very good.' Jacob Lee seemed surprised at the news, unsure of how to react. He stood up straight. 'Right then. In that case I suppose I'd better start playin' somethin', otherwise there'll be no dancin' at all. I'll away find the rest of them; they're around somewhere . . .' He wandered off, pleased to have rid himself of his responsibility, and Rob climbed to his feet. He looked around him, picked up his tankard, and set off for the moon stone.

She was waiting for him, her back against the cool roughness of the stone, her eyes closed.

'Hello,' she said without opening her eyes, 'he'll have calmed down a bit by now, eh?'

'Yes,' said Rob, 'he does seem a bit more in control of himself.'

'It's the drink,' she answered, 'it does that to him; makes him angry. But he's a nasty old devil anyway, no doubt you've discovered that.'

'But he's got reason, surely,' Rob protested, not sure why he was taking the subject further, 'he's told me about—'

'About the land and the property, the poverty, the cows, the pig, the Taylors as well, no doubt, the way we've had everythin' stolen from us? And Captain Swing, that's his latest idea. He's going to be our saviour is Captain Swing, or so me Da would have us all believe. Is that what he's said?'

'Yes, just about. Most of the things . . .'

'He's been goin' on and on about some of those for as long as I can remember. And nothin' changes, no matter how much he rants on about them. There's only one way

to change things, and that's to do somethin' about them,
and me Da's all talk. He never does anythin'. All he can do
is complain.'

'But what could he do?'

'Does it matter? Anythin's better than standin' still.'

'What about you then, aren't you standing still?'

'No!' Her voice was insistent again. 'No, I'm not standin'
still. I'm goin' somewhere. I just haven't thought about the
best place to go, not yet. But I'm young; I've got things on
my side. I'll manage.'

Rob was intrigued at the confidence of the girl.

'How old are you?' he asked.

'Sixteen,' she answered, 'but I pass for older, don't I? You
thought I was older.'

Rob nodded his agreement.

'And I've got looks, everybody tells me I've got looks. And
I've got brains as well, and I know this is no place for me. I
know I'm going to leave somehow.'

'How?'

'I don't know yet. But I'll think of a way.' She'd been
playing with her hands, making churches and steeples with
them, staring at the results, but she raised her head suddenly
and looked at him. 'We weren't properly introduced before,'
she said in a childish voice. 'I'm Guinevere Lee, but everyone
calls me Jinny.' She dropped a brief curtsy and smiled
coquettishly at him, so blatant and over-fashioned that he
had to fight away the laughter.

'And I'm Davy . . .'

'David, you mean, that's what you're really called. David
Patterson, that's right, isn't it?'

'That's right. But I quite like Davy. You can call me Davy,
if you want.'

'I will, then.'

They stood, silent, unsure of each other, unsure of what
to say and what to do. It was a moment setting them on a
fulcrum, balanced perfectly. It would have been easy for one
to move too quickly, to upset the balance, to shift them ever

so slightly in one direction when they really wished to move in another. As if aware of this and fearful of the consequences of action, they chose immobility and longed for some external force to rescue them. And so it came, from across the other side of the circle, the sound of violins tuning to the piper's tremulous note. The sound released them. Jinny looked up and laughed and clapped her hands together like a child. She took Rob by the hand and pulled him after her, and they were surrounded by other couples moving in the same direction, towards the music.

'I don't think I'll know the dances,' warned Rob, 'I didn't recognise those you were doing before, or the tunes that went with them.'

'Why man,' Jinny replied, 'you're a dancer, aren't you, and you're a teacher? You'll learn. And besides, you've me to dance with. I'm good. I'll show you.' She pushed him into position opposite her, beaming with anticipation and excitement. Without a word of instruction being spoken, two concentric circles had been formed, the inner one of men facing outwards, the outer of women facing their partners. There was a chord from the musicians.

'Don't worry,' she said, 'I'll show you everythin'.'

The dances blurred. It was difficult to tell when one started and another finished, so fluid was the movement from squares to circles and back again. The dances were introduced not by name but by melody; a few bars of a particular tune would suffice to push the dancers into position. Sometimes this was followed by a hurried consultation as the dancers confirmed both the dance and the figures within. Jinny explained that the same dance could be performed in different ways in neighbouring villages, and that variations were tried frequently, often resulting in the figures being changed during the dance. Rob could remember the figures, the stars, grand chains and ladies' chains, figure eights, balances and swings, but they were names he assigned to movements which, so far as he could tell, were anonymous to his new companions. A certain movement would be described by the name of the individual who had taught it, or first performed it, and a simple phrase such as 'give hands' could cover a multitude of different movements. He longed for the luxury of a pen and paper so that he could commit the dances to a form more certain than his memory, but he had neither of these implements, nor the time to use them. And even if all of these had been within his grasp he doubted that he would have used them; to do so would have meant allowing another man to dance with Jinny Lee, and he was determined to keep that privilege for himself.

When she'd said she was a good dancer he'd thought that some of her bravado was due to her youth, her self-confidence, and he expected the reality to fall a little short of her claims. As soon as she began to move he realised that what she'd said was an understatement, that she danced as naturally as she breathed, that she could feel the dance flowing through her. He'd felt that Annie Taylor was a good dancer, but Jinny forced him to move every other person he'd ever seen dance one place down the scale. It was not only her natural talent which impressed him; it was the sheer exuberance she displayed, with no sign of affectation; she was dancing so well because she couldn't dance any other way, and the fact that others were watching her counted as nothing.

In the face of such a challenge Rob tried harder himself, but he was at a disadvantage. The schooling he'd had was in a more formal, restrained method of dancing, and although the figures were similar they were joined together in a seamless form which he found difficult to understand. They were not in themselves difficult, but the way the dancers, Jinny in particular, elaborated them with their own stylistic devices made them complex, involved; here a flick of the wrist, there a turn in the wrong direction which, however, made the move seem right; perhaps a double spin where the music was barely sufficient for one turn but somehow the time was found. He could see Jinny watching him and laughing at his efforts, but her laughter merely encouraged him to try harder, and so she laughed more. After thirty minutes of fast, thrilling, incessant dancing she pulled him to one side, his mind reeling with unfamiliar, addictive tunes, the names of the dances (those he could remember) jigging in unfamiliar formations; 'Sellenger's Round' and 'La Russe', 'The Morpeth Rant', 'The Ulgham Jubilee', 'Corn Rigs' and 'The Triumph'.

'You're good!' she said, breathing heavily. He saw her breasts rising and falling beneath a shirt dampened with sweat, her hair was wet. Behind her the sky was lightening.

'Thank you,' he gasped in return, 'but I'm far less able than you. And I need time to learn, to think; your dances are different to the ones I know.' She laughed again, took his hands in hers.

'Don't try too hard,' she said, 'dance with the music, not against it. Don't try to remember the steps, you don't need to, just take the lead from the others around you, from me. Come on!'

He tried to protest, to say he was too tired, but she tugged at his hands and tried to drag him after her. He shook his head. She put her head on one side, mouthed a 'please' at him, and he could do nothing but shrug and nod. She smiled broadly and stood on her toes, reached a hand up to his neck and pulled him forward slightly, kissed him gently on the lips.

'Thank you,' she said softly, and his arms were already searching for her waist, eager to pull her closer to him, but she was away, running back into the melee of dancers, and he was forced to run after her, to catch her and hold her in a swing, to try to control the hysteria threatening to overwhelm him. He lost himself in the joy of dancing with her.

As dawn approached, the number of dancers and musicians slowly decreased. They could be seen staggering and weaving, carolling and playing, each waving goodbye as they crested the rise and began their descent to the valleys below. One couple, their emotions no doubt inflamed by the dancing and the drink, had lain down together in a slight hollow;

all that could be seen of them was the woman's legs in the air and a shock of red hair on the man's bobbing head.

Rob and Jinny slipped to one side, out of the circle, and she showed him the intricacies of one figure, trying, to his and her amusement, to dance all four parts at the same time, giving each dancer a character of his or her own. First she was herself, then she was Rob, tall, slightly stiff, earnestly examining what he was doing; then she became a stout, whirling dame of forty summers and too many children, flushed and panting on fat legs and fat feet, and finally she was an old man with a stick and a limp, hobbling in time with the music, grumbling at the other dancers for getting in his way. She sang as she whirled; she was music and instruments, dance and dancers, the centre of the world, and the earth spun beneath her and the sun rose over her head and crowned her with an aura of golden mist.

The warmth brought Rob a pleasant, welcome fatigue. He was pleased to stand and watch Jinny caper and prance around him, to express mystery at how and where she found her energy. And then he broke the spell.

'I must go,' he said. She stopped dancing and looked around her. They were alone. She smiled a sad smile. Her feet were damp with dew, green and earthy brown, and she shuffled from one to the other as she stood before him.

'I enjoyed myself,' she said. 'I'm pleased we could dance together.'

'So am I,' said Rob, as awkward as she was at the prospect of this goodbye. 'I can walk down with you, if you like. There's no one else about.'

'There's no need. I know the way, and the paths go in opposite directions. You'll need to get back, you've probably work to do later on today; you'll need to get some sleep.'

'Yes.' Neither of them seemed willing to move. 'Jinny?'

'Yes?'

'I'd like to learn more about the dances, and the music. Would you help me?'

She smiled. 'I'd like that.'

'Could I call on you tonight?'

She thought for a while. 'You'll get no more than a few hours' sleep today; you'll be in no state to do any dancin' tonight. Tomorrow might be better. Come to see me in the mornin'?'

'Yes. Yes, I could do that. Thank you.'

'We'd better be going now.'

'Yes.'

'Goodbye then. Until tomorrow.'

'Tomorrow.'

Rob held out his hand in a gesture designed to be neither a handshake nor a wish to take Jinny's hand and kiss it. Its intention was purely to touch her, to give him some final sensation of belonging before they parted, and Jinny seemed willing to be compliant in this. She moved closer so that he could take her hand in his.

Rob had pursued women before; he was aware of the courtesies this demanded, the courtship, the pleasantries, the slow movement down the path of familiarity. This would allow first a chaste kiss on the cheek, then on the lips, and he'd heard that sometimes a relationship could go no further without a proposal of marriage. The company he normally kept was not fenced with such restrictions, and he knew from experience that a woman's passions were not necessarily different from those of a man. A handsome face, a ready smile, some well-chosen, flattering words and a few glasses of port could break down barriers which might have seemed insurmountable a few hours before. In this instance Rob wasn't trying to win Jinny's heart or her mind, or even to gain some sexual favour from her. He'd enjoyed dancing with her, he wanted to spend more time with her, and he was gloriously aware of the beauty of her body and, judging by the time he'd spent with her, her spirit. He considered it would be wise to wait before attempting to do more than embrace her; she was, after all, only sixteen, and her father appeared more than a little protective towards her. All he wanted to do was express a little of his feelings for her by the single act of taking her hand. He was unprepared for what was to follow.

The kiss was, at first, no different from that she'd given him earlier, and when they separated they looked at each other and smiled. He leaned forward again, but this time her hand was at the back of his neck pulling his head down, and when their lips met her tongue forced its way into his mouth. At the same time she stepped close up against him so their bodies were touching. Her other hand was behind his back pressing him harder into her. He couldn't hide his surprise, and she sensed this, backed away from him a fraction. But her fire had moved into his body, and once he was sure that she was still unafraid, once his glance confirmed that she seemed as needy as him, it was his turn to open her mouth, to explore the warm, soft folds of her lips and teeth with his tongue.

He found her moving against him. The hand which had held his neck was no longer required for that duty; it snaked down into the small of his back while its companion moved onto his waist, held him close as she described slow, circular movements with her hips. He heard, felt through her mouth, small moans of pleasure. He ventured to move his own hands. One lingered in her hair and caressed the lobe of her ear; the other travelled gradually, lest it cause offence, down her lower spine, then was allowed to descend to rest, lightly at first, on the swelling of her behind. He felt his own excitement mount, knew that she too must be able to feel it, and this gave added urgency to her movements. Her teeth captured his tongue and held it tight, not breaking the skin but preventing any movement, and her hands strayed onto his buttocks and cupped them, imprisoned them so that he was forced to join in the slow dance with her, their hips pressed together, moving together. He heard another moan, and realised the noise was coming from him.

Their mouths separated and she buried her head in his chest. Her long neck was bare, and his mouth was drawn to it, licked it, sucked at it without biting, and her hands fluttered away from his back though her body remained pressed to his. He could feel its heat through the thin material of her shirt. Her breathing was heavy now, audible, and her hands came to rest on his shoulders, exerted gentle pressure so he slid down and knelt before her. His height meant that, at full stretch, he could still reach her neck with his lips, and at first Jinny seemed content to enjoy the attention he was paying her, but then she entwined her fingers in his hair, forced him to move down, to concentrate his attention on other matters. He could smell the sweet, hot excitement of her. His hands fumbled at the buttons of her shirt and pulled the fabric aside.

Her breasts were already damp before his mouth began to work on them, and he traced their smoothness, their roundness, with his tongue. Jinny tasted of salt and musk and cinnamon, of flowers and ripe fruit, of catmint and spices, and he trailed a spiral of saliva over the skin of her breast before teasing and flicking her nipple. She groaned again, far louder this time, and pushed herself at him, almost choking him with her demands. Her nipple hardened in his mouth; he pulled at it with his teeth and she groaned again. His hand circled her other breast and performed the same task as his tongue, perhaps a little more roughly, but she seemed not to mind. Her own hands were at work now, pulling his shirt from him, reaching down to scratch at his chest and reward him for his treatment of her.

He had one hand spare now. It rested lightly at her waist then descended in a long, lazy curve over her thigh, over the rough cotton of her skirt, down until it touched the flesh of her calf. Then it moved up again just as slowly, just as cautiously, this time inside the cotton, and Jinny parted her legs slightly to prepare for its approach. He toyed with the skin behind her knee but abandoned this for the potential of other pleasures. He finger-stalked higher into the tattered folds of petticoat, into the heat, expecting to find other garments there but found none and was rewarded for his perseverance, his presumption, with a slick of moist-folded skin, and a feather-like brush of tightly curled, down-soft hair. He felt her body tighten. Her thighs imprisoned his wayward hand, and then she was pushing him away, wrapping her shirt around her.

'No!' she whimpered. 'No, I won't. Not here, no!'

Rob held out his arms to her, concerned to see tears in her eyes, amazed that there should be such a change in her mood, and so quickly.

'Jinny, it's alright. I won't hurt you.'

'I know,' she cried, 'I know that Davy, but I can't do it, and . . . and I can't explain. I need to think. I must go.' She turned and ran, and Rob started after her, easily caught up with her. She stopped.

'Please, let me be,' she pleaded, 'there's nothing you can do; the fault is mine, not yours.'

Rob said nothing, he could find nothing to say, but his worries must have showed on his face. When Jinny spoke again her voice was gentler. She appeared to have better control of her emotions, though she still sniffed and wiped at her tears.

'I can't tell you anything now,' she said, 'but I'll see you tomorrow, Wednesday, as we planned. I'll have calmed down by then. I'll need to talk to you, but I must think about what I have to say. Please, don't ask me anything now.'

Rob would have spoken, but Jinny's finger went to his lips. He kissed it, and her sorrow seemed to ease a little; he had to make do with that as she turned and walked away from him. He waved to her as she topped the rise, but there was no response, and he was left to make his way back to the manor through a dawn wet with dew and decked with overzealous skylarks. He needed to sleep but didn't welcome taking to his bed because he would be alone, and because he knew he would dream of Guinevere Lee.

The two made a strange couple. She was tall and her hair was long and she strode barefoot through the wiry marsh grass. He was old and bent at the shoulders, shorter than

her. He had a limp and he scurried alongside her like a
crab, carrying a sack from which protruded the drones of
a set of pipes.

'Well?' the old man said.

'Well what?' the girl replied. Her face was streaked with
grey where she'd rubbed at her eyes. She was staring ahead
of her, trying not to acknowledge the old man's presence.

'You didn't do it!'

'You were watchin', then?'

'You know I was watchin', it was part of the plan. I come
up and find you at it, he gives me money not to tell. That
was it, wasn't it?'

'I did what I had to, Da, no more, no less. He'll be back
again, believe me.'

'But why? We could have had money off him now if you'd
a mind to do as I said.' He sulked alongside her again. 'You're
not bein' daft again, are you?' he asked suddenly, planting
himself in front of her so she had to stop.

'What do you mean by that?'

'You know what I mean! You're not doin' somethin'
stupid like "falling in love" again, are you? You know what
happened last time.' He put his arms around himself as he
spoke, minced round her in a parody of affection. She took
the opportunity to stalk on her way again.

'No,' she called over her shoulder, 'I'll tell you that for
certain! I'm not fallin' in love with him!'

Rob woke in time for a meal at midday, knowing that he was
scheduled to teach later that afternoon. No one commented
on his absence at breakfast, and he suspected this was because
most of them had also missed the meal. Frances Arnison made
a point of introducing him officially to her husband. She'd
heard of their meeting on the stairs the previous day and
made it known (in a discreet whisper) that she would have
come to his bed the previous night had it not been for her
husband's presence. Rob hoped that his effusive shaking of
Harry Arnison's hand didn't betray his pleasure that the

husband's attendance might reduce the wife's demands on
his time. He had other business to deal with.

Rebecca Taylor told him that Annie's fiancé had been
detained; he'd sent word that he would not now be able
to attend until the morning of the wedding. She was clearly
annoyed at this, both in her own right and on behalf of her
daughter. After all, it had been Annie's wish that they learn
some new dances together, yet it now appeared that her
partner would be unable to dance with her. Rob consoled
her. He would devote some time, he promised, to instructing
the young gentleman on the morning in question. Although
his words seemed to satisfy Mrs Taylor, Rob wasn't quite
sure whether he would be able to carry out the promise.
He was, to be truthful, uncertain about almost everything
to do with dancing.

If his original intention had been to make the wedding
dance a lacklustre affair by teaching slow, uninteresting or
overcomplicated dances, then Rob was succeeding. It was
too late now for the Taylors to find another dancing master,
and he could, if he wished, ignore their protestations that
they weren't enjoying the dances he'd chosen. The music
was slowly disintegrating around him, though there would
always be the solid backbone of Harry Brown to bolster the
band's efforts. But it would remain, if he allowed it to run its
course, suitably dour accompaniment for the doleful dancing.
His job would be done, and done admirably. He would have
had his revenge on the Taylors, and the reputation of James
Playford would be compromised. Why then, he asked himself,
was he unhappy?

He hated to acknowledge the fact, but he had slowly
come to like the Taylor family. He had done them some
wrong initially, especially Annie, but there was no doubt
that Frances had subsequently enjoyed the benefits of Rob's
indiscretion; on that front all was equal. When all things
were considered it did seem unfair that he should intend
harming the Taylors for a wrong done to him by a member
of their family who wasn't even present, and it was clear

that George Taylor, the first of the clan he'd met, wasn't representative of the family as a whole. But there was more to it than that. Coming to Bellingford had convinced Rob that he had the potential to do the job he was pretending to do; he could teach people to dance. But all he'd done so far was teach them how to dance badly; what he wanted to do was teach them how to dance well. He would have liked to pretend that it was his conscience dictating matters, that the good side of him was in the process of overcoming the evil. Examination of his motives, however, led him to a different conclusion; it was his pride driving him. He knew that when he first arrived he lacked the knowledge to teach properly; his armoury of dances was insufficient. But now, after last night and dancing with Jinny, he knew what to teach! The dances they'd enjoyed were full of fire and excitement; the music was perfectly matched to stir the blood. All he had to do, within the space of four days, was to learn more dances and the music – write the music down and copy it, teach the dances, teach the music . . . It couldn't be done. Unless . . .

They were waiting for him when he walked into the ballroom.

'Good afternoon everyone,' he said. There was a mumbled response.

'I'm aware,' he went on, 'that some of you, most of you in fact, aren't happy with the dances I've been teaching you. You consider them too staid or too difficult, certainly not fitting for a wedding. Attendance at music practice has demonstrated that there are problems with the music which is, I'm afraid, linked to the choice of dances. It is now Tuesday afternoon. The wedding is to take place on Sunday.' He held out his hands and shrugged, admitting that the mistake had been made. 'But in that time I shall try to teach you some new dances that are exciting; dances that are lively, dances that move the spirit as well as the feet, dances that have tunes which come from the heart. And if all goes well we shall have a party fit for a queen,' he glanced at Annie Taylor, 'one which does justice to the good name of the

Taylor family. But we have little time. Please, form a circle. Each man must place his partner on his right. Let us start with a step, a step called a "rant". If you will be so kind as to play a reel on your fiddle, Mr Brown.'

Harry Brown played as he'd never played before. The dancers were infected with Rob's own enthusiasm and after two hours of work, during which no one sought to escape, the dancers were allowed to rest.

'Mr Patterson,' said Rebecca Taylor, mopping at her red, blooming face with a handkerchief, 'that was wonderful! You were like a different person. And such exuberant dances – far better than the formal ones we've been doing. Where did you find them?'

'A friend taught them to me a long time ago,' Rob said, 'and I suppose I use his methods for teaching them. Tweddle's his name; Rob Tweddle. He's a lot wilder than me, freer. He gets up to all sorts of tricks. I think you'd like him.'

'Perhaps one day I shall meet him. I do hope so; he sounds rather a nice fellow. But I must retire, I feel a need to sit down and do nothing for a while.'

She strolled away, her daughters fluttering about her like chickens round a hen, only Frances looking back at him with curious eyes. As he gathered his music and papers together, Samuel Taylor took the opportunity to approach him.

'Good effort,' he said, 'even I enjoyed that. Forgive me for saying this, but the music sounded . . . It sounded a little thin. I hope the rest of the musicians will be able to play alongside young Harry.'

'Yes, Mr Taylor, I'll have to work on that. My problem is that only Harry has the real – how shall I put it without offending anyone? – the real ability to understand what the dance requires, to read from the music . . .'

'You mean everyone else can't play?'

'Well, I wouldn't like to put it so bluntly, but . . . yes. Or they don't want to; some of them prefer dancing.'

'So what do you do about it?'

'Well, I did have an idea.'

'Yes?'

Rob took a deep breath.

'I'd heard that there were some other musicians; good ones, local ones. I thought I might ask them to come along to help. I'm sure—'

'You mean Lee, don't you? Jacob Lee and the rest of them, that's who you're thinking about.' His voice was suddenly stern, he emphasised his words with a schoolmasterly index finger. 'I'm sorry, Mr Patterson, it's out of the question. Jacob Lee is a troublemaker, an agitator. I'm just waiting for him to put one foot wrong and he'll be out; he'll be away. And I won't have him playing at my daughter's wedding, do you understand?'

'No. That is, yes, I think I understand the way you feel, but not why you feel that way. Perhaps if you could talk to him—'

'No, Mr Patterson, I will not. I'm afraid you'll have to make do with the musicians you've got. Now if you'll excuse me . . .' He turned to leave, had already taken two steps when Rob found his voice.

'Mr Taylor?'

'Yes?'

'I've another idea. I know some people in Corbridge, another family in Stocksfield, they can play well together. Would you mind if I sent for them? They'd be able to get here by tomorrow, I'm sure they'd do me a favour by playing for us. You could listen to them tomorrow, see what you think.'

Samuel Taylor considered the suggestion. He should, he felt, ask who these people were. Corbridge and Stocksfield weren't too far distant; he might know them. But it wouldn't be right to start an inquisition now, especially when he'd been so forthright in voicing his opinion on Jacob Lee. There was, however, one matter requiring discussion.

'Who's to pay for them, if they're good enough?'

'If you can feed them, Mr Taylor, and allow their families to come to the ball after the wedding, then I'll meet their cost from my fee.'

'That sounds fair. Very well, I agree. I hope to hear them tomorrow.' He hurried away, pleased with his bargain. What were a few extra mouths to feed amongst so many? He could only offer thanks that Annie was the last of his daughters to wed; the expense was ridiculous. Not that he would have swapped them for sons, but . . . He set off to look for his wife, to tell her his news and boast at his negotiating skills.

Only Emanuel Scrivener remained behind. He'd joined in the dancing with enthusiasm, had even removed his waistcoat, jacket and cravat.

'Well done, David, I did enjoy that,' he said.

'Thank you, I hope to see you again tomorrow. We'll be trying some more new dances then.'

'Tomorrow? I shall see you before tomorrow, have you forgotten our arrangement? To meet this evening?'

Rob had forgotten. He was to visit Scrivener's house for supper; they were to discuss their mutual friend, James Playford. Rob cursed to himself. He wanted to spend some time transcribing music. He wanted to write to Jinny (though he wasn't sure whether or not she could read); he wanted to go and see her, to talk to her, to make sure that she was well. She'd been occupying his thoughts constantly, in a way no woman had ever done before.

'No,' he said, 'I hadn't forgotten. What time would you like me to call?'

'Oh, there'll be no need to call, David. The arrangements have changed a little, I've been invited to dine here. So I'll be delighted to stroll down with you to my house after dinner, if you don't mind, for a glass or two of brandy. I am looking forward to talking with you. A fresh face, a fresh mind – they are such rare commodities in this place. Until later then?'

'Until later.'

Emanuel Scrivener left through the open double doors, while Rob made his way upstairs. It looked like being another late night; he needed some sleep.

The Eleventh Bar of the Musick

Wednesday, 23 June 1830

In which Emanuel Scrivener, slighted, tells James Playford of his son-in-law's behaviour, and Rob confesses his true identity.

*E*manuel Scrivener was a generous host. He'd enjoyed dinner with Rob at the Taylors', and since their hunger had been assuaged he judged it his duty to provide Rob with access to a wide variety of wines and liquors. They sat at leisure in the room Scrivener used as library, drawing room and office combined, comfortable in deep leather chairs. The older man smoked his pipe, occasionally sprang to his feet to search for a volume of poetry or some obscure textbook to illustrate or confirm a point he was making, reaching the top shelves with a small wooden stool which he also pressed into use as a footrest. The conversation was never too serious. Rob hadn't been looking forward to this meeting, and during the meal he'd tried to anticipate the questions he might be asked on James Playford. He'd pondered the answers he might concoct, but it was now well past midnight and the subject hadn't even been broached. He felt warm and content. The alcohol in its various guises had taken away the edge of his nervousness, but he was determined that he shouldn't lose

himself in its excesses lest he say or do something to give
himself away. Already the two were, at the poet's insistence,
on first name terms, but he felt that Scrivener was not the
simple man he portrayed himself to be, and he was wary of
his motives in seeking this meeting.

The clock in the hallway struck a deep, sonorous single
note. Rob was surprised; he expected it to chime more.
Surely the hour couldn't be beyond eleven or twelve? When
there was no further sound he rolled his shoulders, stretched
his arms.

'The hours have crept up on me, Emanuel, I hadn't thought
it so late. I really must return to my bed, the days recently
have been filled with too much excitement and too little
sleep. I've much work to do.'

'Yes, so I believe. And yet there was a pleasant atmosphere
about your instruction earlier today, I felt you more relaxed
than of late, I felt that you were enjoying yourself. Am I
correct?'

'You are indeed. I've reconsidered my choice of dances
and music and feel happier with ... with a more relaxed
and less formal approach, yes, I think that's the best way
of putting it. But this means I must prepare written music, I
must consider the best tunes to suit each dance. I must even
think about the musicians, they have difficulty in playing the
melodies I want in the way I want. And so, forgive me. I've
enjoyed myself but I must leave.'

'Wait a moment, please, David, there is so much we
haven't touched upon.' The poet was already on his feet,
refilling Rob's glass. 'I beg you, stay just thirty minutes
longer. I will confess, I have another appointment at that
time. A friend is coming to visit me, and the conversation
will be more monosyllabic than ours but with a touch more
action and movement.' He tapped the side of his nose. 'Or
that is how *I* would have it!'

'The friend of yours is a lady?' Rob asked, already knowing
the answer.

'A lady when she crosses the threshold, perhaps, but I trust

that she will be less so when she reaches my bed chamber!'
Rob joined in the laughter.

'But we spoke of your teaching, and I must confess that my
memory of James Playford is more of nights spent drinking
than days spent dancing. I am eager to know how you, a
youthful person, are able to deal with him, a man as old as
me and probably even more set in his ways. Do you teach
together, for example?'

The moment had come. The first question was innocent
enough, but it might lead to others more particular, more
vexatious. Rob decided to parry with generalities.

'Our partnership is one of business, Emanuel. We share
premises close by the quayside, and resources, but we see
little of each other. We have our own customers, our own
rooms. We pass on the stairs and bid each other good day,
but we spend little time together.'

'And how do you divide new customers between yourselves?'

'They normally come recommended to one of us in particular, and that individual retains the customer. But if someone
should contact us through, let us say, seeing our signboard,
then our clerk, a pleasant young fellow, Tweddle's his name,
Rob Tweddle, he'll go far one day, I'm sure of that ... I'm
sorry, where was I?'

'Eulogising the character of your clerk, I believe. But before
that you were about to tell me how you divide up those of
your customers, your pupils, who have allegiance to neither
you nor James. Perhaps your clerk threatens them with a
sword, like Solomon?'

'No, Emanuel, there's no need for that. He simply asks
them what type of dancing they wish to learn, we each have
our specialities, and he assigns them accordingly.' He was
warming to his subject now, his confidence increasing as
he drained his glass again. 'That's why I've had problems
here. Originally it was Mr Playford who was engaged, but
his obligations wouldn't allow him, and so I came instead.
But I thought to teach *his* types of dance, the courtly dances,

rather than the ones in which I take most interest, the *social* dances. Do you see what I mean?'

Emanuel Scrivener nodded sagely, his curiosity apparently satisfied. He leaned closer to his new friend.

'But tell me, David. I know James will be a little long in the tooth, but does he still . . .' he looked around him, as if expecting to find strangers drawing near from their secret hiding places, '. . . does he still have an eye for the ladies?' The last few words were whispered, and the question mark degenerated into a giggle. Rob found to his horror that half of the ridiculous laughter was coming from his own lips. He clapped his hand to his mouth, and the action brought another snort from the poet which he couldn't help but echo. He found himself laughing out loud and nodding his head, the words rushed from his mouth before he could stop them.

'He's fond of a well-turned ankle, is good old Jimmy, and if he can turn his attention to matters higher than that he certainly will!'

'And does he . . . does he like them . . . does he prefer them young or old?'

'Oh dear, oh dear me, I shouldn't be saying this! He prefers them . . . he prefers them to be women, and nothing more, and nothing less!'

Rob doubled up, was pleased to see that his comrade was in a similar position, his face red, rendered speechless by his own sense of humour. They subsided slowly, gradually. Both breathed deeply, caught each other's eye and began the process all over again.

'My Lord,' Emanuel Scrivener said eventually, 'it's some considerable time since I enjoyed myself so much. I do wish that James could be here now, he would so enjoy this.' The thought of James Playford being party to the conversation, of him being there with them, sobered Rob up, calmed his laughter, brought his senses back to the right side of sanity. Emanuel Scrivener subsided more slowly. While a smile was still on his lips he asked his next question.

'And what of you, David? What of your taste in women?'

'I'm married sir, to James Playford's daughter. I thought you knew that.' His voice was matter of fact, but his suspicions were raised again. Was the poet trying to catch him out, feeding him questions to which he might easily give the wrong answer?

'I know that, young man, I know. I didn't ask whether or not you were married; I asked about your taste in women. How do you like them?'

'I'm sorry, I'm not sure I understand.'

'Women. They come in different shapes, different sizes, different colours, dammit. I'm curious to know what type you prefer! You're a tall fellow; you might prefer a tall woman. But then, what's height when a body's flat on her back, eh? Same for colour of hair, colour of skin; does it make any difference when it's dark?'

Rob framed his answer carefully.

'Well, Emily – my wife, that is – she's not too tall. She's a pleasant size, well rounded . . .'

'I'm not going to tell anyone, David. I'm not going to breathe a word if you say you're married to a short, fat, dark-haired old maid but you prefer a tall, blonde, willowy wisp of a young girl. The type of woman a man marries often has nothing to do with the type he prefers!'

'I see.'

'No, I don't think you do. I'm trying to tell you that it doesn't matter if you've, how shall I put it, if you've been dallying with someone here while your wife's been at home. It would only be carrying on the ancient tradition which your venerable father-in-law often enjoyed.'

'I see.'

'I'm tired of you saying that, man! If that's the case then tell me the answer to my question! What women do you prefer?'

Rob pretended to think to himself. 'I think,' he said eventually, 'that I am of the same opinion as you, Emanuel. I enjoy women, the company of women, regardless of type. Yes, I think that's right. I like all women.'

The poet raised his eyes to the ceiling, held out his hands

in supplication then clapped them together and held them in an attitude of prayer. He spoke, slowly.

'David. Listen to me please. I'm not making myself clear; I shall attempt to do so. This village, this pleasant little place, is in truth both uninteresting and tiresome. I reside here because my pittance of an income will allow me no other choice. I had thought that the peaceful countryside would provide me with inspiration, which it has not, and safety from my creditors and the husbands of my lovers, which it has done to ridiculous extremes. I might as well be in purgatory, for this place at times resembles nothing so much as a halfway house on the road to hell. There are few things I can look forward to. One is the enjoyment I take in the company of women, though even that palls given the poor quality of those from whom I may make my choice. Another is speaking to the random stranger, the passing traveller such as yourself, who might bring me news that there is still a world outside and that I may hope, one day, to return there. And the third tid-bit, the morsel I enjoy most as the years advance, is learning what is happening within this small community. I have no interest in matters rural, I might add. The birth of lambs or the acquisition of land leaves me cold. What *does* hold my attention is news of which farmer's daughter the shepherd is tupping, and the price in favours the widow extracts from the young man renting her meadow. And so to you. Your general predilections are meaningless to me. You must give me more detail.'

'More detail? Such as what?'

'My God, David, must I be so direct? Very well then! Have you succeeded in luring Annie Taylor to your bed?'

'Mr Scrivener!'

'Oh, come now, don't play the wounded hero. You were, until last week, drooling at her every move, and she was content to flirt with you in return. You were attracted to each other. Note the past tense, because it's obvious to a seasoned observer such as myself that there has been a rift. What I want to know is, were you triumphant? Did you take her maidenhead? Or perhaps you weren't soon enough even for that. The hounds have been baying round that bitch since her twelfth birthday.'

'Mr Scrivener, I really don't think that I should be listening to you talking in such a manner about Miss Taylor. She's a lady of honour—'

'David, stop being such a prig. I need to know, I may wish to follow your path one day!'

'That is enough!' David thrust himself to his feet, too quickly. He swayed and had to clutch at the back of the chair to prevent himself being overcome by dizziness. 'I will not have you speaking that way of Miss Taylor!' he roared, he almost frightened himself with the ferocity of his voice. He hoped that Emanuel Scrivener had been drinking as much wine as he had. It might make both of them more belligerent, but it usually prevented too many blows landing accurately. But the poet's voice was as quiet as Rob's was loud, though every word could be heard clearly.

'Would you have me talk instead of Mrs Arnison?' he asked. 'Would it be better if I asked how you fared in her bed? Or perhaps she came to you?'

Rob sat down again.

'There are some things I suspect,' Scrivener said carefully, 'and some things I know. But you know not which is which. It would save time if you told me all. It's so tiresome to force information from people, and I detest blackmail. Do you understand, David?'

'I have never slept with Annie Taylor.'

'If I were to tempt her to my bed then the last thing I would want to do would be to fall asleep. Do I take it that she is still a virgin?'

'I've had no opportunity to find that out, Mr Scrivener.'

'Emanuel, please, call me Emanuel. But you tried, didn't you? Hence the frostiness of the young lady towards you.'

'Yes,' Rob admitted, 'but you mentioned Frances. How did you know?'

'I knew. I knew, David, because I was there before you.

What tale did she tell you? That she longed for a son but that her husband couldn't get her with child? That you were the one she'd chosen? That style of flattery works quite often, but when it doesn't she usually finds some lever, and the fulcrum is usually so close to her victim's heart, or his fears, that it requires very little effort on her part to move matters.'

'Then she was lying?'

'Lying? David, if Harry Arnison was a ram he'd win prizes. He's sired more bastards in this county than I could hope to count. As for Frances, I'm not sure why she takes lovers. Perhaps it's because her husband does, revenge, though I think he cares little about what she gets up to. But she's barren, there's no doubt about that.'

'She tricked me.'

'Oh yes, just as she tricked me and dozens of others. Dr Allard? Yes, him too, and Gabriel Lambert, the miller; Harold Stephenson, the mayor of Hexham. She had him when he visited a few years back. She doesn't normally descend to common folk, and she prefers strangers, but sometimes if there's a good-looking young lad she'll use him for a week or two.'

'But why?'

'It escapes me, David. I could understand it if she was a man. But in a woman it's so strange, so unusual. I've mentioned it to Allard. I thought with his medical knowledge and personal knowledge combined, as it were, he might have been able to come up with an answer. But no, he wouldn't even talk to me about it. Pity.'

'And I thought . . .'

'You thought it was your devilish handsome face, your winning ways. You thought she was falling in love with you. Alas, dear boy, she would have had you if you'd been as ugly as sin with foul breath and a wooden prick, believe me. I'm sorry if your vanity has been deflated, but it's better this way, believe me. There's nothing so unattractive in a woman as a sickly smile and a desire to talk about love. But tell me, what did you do to Annie? Did you proposition her? Did she turn you down immediately? Was there any hint of cooperation from her? A little information would be of enormous value to me, I assure you.'

'She's a whore. There's no other word for her – a whore.'

'David, please. It's my turn to be affronted now, you should not use that word to describe Frances Arnison. She is a lady of breeding; she is no whore. Did she demand money from you for her services? No, she did not. Therefore she cannot be a whore.'

'But . . .'

'No buts, David. She may have *behaved* like a whore, but you know from personal experience that there are times when I behave like a knave. That doesn't make me any less of a gentleman.'

'That's a matter of . . .'

'Believe me, David, this is a subject of which I have some considerable knowledge. You saw me recently at the bedroom window of a lady, in the village, yes?' Rob nodded. 'That lady did not ask me to pay her for the favours – yes, I admit it, the sexual favours – I received. But she may yet make some demand of me. It may even be that she desires to repeat the adventure at a time which does not suit me, and that in itself makes her a whore. Whoredom is not only about payment or the lack of it; it is about one's place in society, believe me. Any woman who gives herself to a man of a more elevated status than herself is laying herself open to the charge of whoring.'

'And if the roles are reversed, Emanuel? If a low-born man fornicates with a high-born lady?'

'There is no such thing as a male whore.'

'Physically, perhaps not. But it is possible for a man to prostitute his talents. And if he does that then does he not also prostitute himself and make himself the whore?'

'Good man! You *can* argue a case, I knew it! But you confuse morals with emotions, and your statement is concerned more with the dual meaning of words than with the veracity of the statement itself. But listen!'

Rob would have said more, but he too had heard a faint noise. It was someone knocking quietly at the main door of the house.

'It is the guest of whom I spoke earlier,' Scrivener said, rising to his feet. 'Now you shall meet a real whore. You may even, if you wish, stay and view the spectacle, I am not a shy man. The woman could accommodate you. I feel sure that we would be able to negotiate a good price.'

'No thank you,' said Rob, 'I don't think it would be wise of me. I shall leave by the back door, I have much to do on my return.'

'Very well, then. If you pass below the stairs, through the kitchen and the scullery, I'm sure you'll be able to find your way. Please take a candle. Now if you'll excuse me, I have no wish for the good lady to depart thinking me asleep.'

Scrivener and Rob parted company, Rob with his single flame, Scrivener with the candelabra. Rob remembered the buxom woman at the window in the cottage and hoped that both of them would spend an enjoyable, or profitable, few hours. He crept out of the house and blew out his candle.

The moon was almost as bright as it had been the previous night, he had no difficulty in following the path round the side of the building. He felt tired, very tired, all he wanted was the company of his bed. He walked carefully. The flags below his feet were of old sandstone and uneven, flecked with moss, grass grew from each crack and joint. His passage was silent, and he heard Emanuel Scrivener's voice before he realised that he would have to pass the open window of the drawing room.

'Ah, come in my dear. You look beautiful tonight, as you have in the past, as you will no doubt continue to do in the future. Would you care for a glass of wine before we ascend?'

Rob halted. He would either have to go on, very quietly lest Scrivener and his companion think him a Peeping Tom, or retrace his steps and go the long way round the house and garden. His fatigue decided for him. He moved forwards, even more quietly than before. He didn't hear what the woman said, the murmur of her words was indistinct, but as he approached the window Scrivener's voice boomed out again.

'No wine, my love? No laughter, not even a smile for me? Is something ailing you?' His voice became suddenly harsher. 'You don't have the pox, do you?'

'No!' came the reply, the single word high pitched, assertive.

'Then what is it? Tell Emanuel, he might be able to help, he can soothe all your cares away.'

Rob reached the window. The sash was lifted high to let in the cool air, but the curtains were almost closed, there was a gap of only two inches. Rob prepared to slide past.

'I'm not going to bed with you tonight, Mr Scrivener. Not tonight or any other night. I've made up my mind on that. I'm goin' away as soon as I can.'

Rob halted. Even through the thickness of the curtains he had heard what was said and he recognised the voice, he swore he recognised the voice.

'You're going away, are you? Touched with a streak of independence, eh? And you came to tell me that as well, when you could have just stayed away? Am I supposed to be thankful? I don't suppose your father knows of this, he'd brook no nonsense, he'd horsewhip you, he would, and that's what I should be doing. It might bring you back to your senses.'

Rob leaned forward. He needed to confirm his suspicions, his fears, but he could see nothing through the curtains save part of a chair and a table and, beyond those, shelves of books. Then Emanuel Scrivener spoke again.

'So why are you really here? It's not politeness, I'm damn certain of that. You don't come to a man's house in the early hours of the morning just to tell him you won't go to bed with him! So what is it? Do you have a secret fondness for me? Are you hoping I'll say, "Oh no, please don't go. Stay with me, live with me, be my wife"? Because if so you're mistaken. I care nothing for you, it's your body I desire, not the slut who inhabits it. And don't look at me like that, you're here because you're a whore; there's no question of that. You do this for money, that's why . . . Yes! I have it! You're after money! You came here to try, by some manner, to get money from me!'

There was silence. Rob moved his head one way and another in an attempt to see what was happening, but the protagonists were beyond his view.

'I hear no protestations, my love. Have I perhaps sailed a course too close to the truth?'

'I came only to tell you I'm leavin', Mr Scrivener. You know I saw nothin' of any money you gave me da. Indeed, I didn't know at first you'd given him anythin' at all. I'd thought there was some affection between us, even when I found out that . . . that you were paying me da for usin' me. And in comin' here tonight and tellin' you this I thought, if you had *any* feelin's towards me, then you might let me have a few shillin's, till I can get work, find me feet.'

'Find your feet?' Scrivener's laugh was unpleasant, his voice loud. 'The only way you'll find your feet is to lie on your back with your legs open, take my word for it!' There was a sound of footsteps approaching the window, Rob moved smartly to one side as the curtains were whisked open.

'Too damn hot,' Scrivener complained, 'what we need is a breeze, a drop of rain. It's unnatural, this weather.' His voice faded again. The light from the candles in the room was quite bright, although Rob would now be able to see into the room, the occupants would as easily be able to see him. He moved his head closer to the stone mullion, felt the coolness against his cheek. Slowly, so slowly, he peered round the corner. There! He could see Scrivener, standing with his back to him, and beyond him was the woman. A fraction of her skirt was visible, a hand, but little else. Rob's viewpoint was limited; he'd have to wait for the poet to move before he could confirm the woman's identity.

'You are,' Scrivener was explaining, 'a whore by any definition. Go if you must, but I warn you, the only skill you have is whoring, the only advantage you have is your youth and your looks. I'm not trying to be cruel, my dear, in speaking the truth like this. I'm trying to help you. Please, sit down.'

He moved forward and Rob tensed, but his view was still blocked as Scrivener guided his guest to a chair with its back to Rob. All he could see was the woman's hand grasping the arm of the chair as if frightened that it might come to life and throw her from its comfort.

'Now then, tell me where you intend going.' Scrivener was standing with his back to the books, watching the woman, hands behind his back. He had the look of an over-friendly uncle.

'Hexham, to start with. I can use me hands, I can get a job making gloves. Then, I haven't thought. Newcastle, perhaps. Carlisle.'

'A glover, eh? Your ambitions stretch that high?'

'What would you suggest, Mr Scrivener?'

'Me? You've already heard my thoughts on the matter. Half the glovers in Hexham are whores anyway, and the other half are too old or too ugly. And they've started work on the railway, that should provide some good trade for you. Yes, you go to Hexham. And as for something to keep you fed for a while, I'm sure I can find a little silver for you. I keep some in my pockets. Perhaps you'd care to come over here and search for a coin or two?'

'Mr Scrivener, I came for help and you make fun of me. I'd better go.' The woman rose to her feet. Rob's suspicions were confirmed. It was Jinny. He saw Scrivener step smartly forward, he took hold of Jinny by the wrists, she tried to get away. Rob ducked back to his place; her eyes had swept the room. There was no sound, no sign he'd been seen.

'Now you just listen to me, girl!' Scrivener muttered through twisted lips, 'I wanted you here for a purpose, and that didn't include talking back to me. It didn't include talking at all. Now I'll give you some money, yes, I'll do that for you, but you have to do something in return, and if you fight me I'll take what I want and give you nothing, and I'll tell your father exactly why!'

Jinny wrested herself away from Scrivener and looked around her, but Scrivener anticipated her movement and put himself between her and the door.

'Jinny,' he said, his voice soothing now, soft, his hands spread in conciliation, 'Jinny, you can't win. I know in the past I've said I liked a woman with spirit in her, but this is taking things too far. You've no choice, really. Who else will entertain you? Dr Allard? He wouldn't even give you the time of day. Who else has the wherewithal? Certainly not the farmers' sons you normally go with. Perhaps you've got your eyes on that dancing master. Not a bad-looking fellow; not too intelligent, but he wouldn't touch you. No Jinny, there's no alternative. I'll make it worth your while, I promise you. Just once more.'

'No,' she spat at him, 'not ever again! You treat me like property, your property, me da's property, to do with as you like. I won't have it! You let me go. Let me go or I'll . . .' She looked around. On the desk was a paperknife, long and slender. She grabbed it and held it firm in her grasp. 'Let me go or I'll kill you!'

Her voice was low, scarcely more than a whisper, but the words were like poison.

'You'll kill me?' Scrivener asked. 'With that toy?' Though there was meant to be disdain in his voice it was accompanied by a quaver of fear, and his eyes were fixed on the knife.

'Come, Jinny, put the knife down. Let's talk sensibly.'

'Let me go!'

Rob didn't know what to do. He wanted to interfere, he wanted to help Jinny escape, but if he did as his heart told him to do and leaped through the window to halt this stalemate then Scrivener would expect him to take his part. Rob knew he couldn't do that. But unless he did something then a fight might develop. No one would benefit from any injury caused, and it was entirely possible that more serious damage than injury might occur. Or he could leave. The matter in hand didn't concern him. It was personal, between Jinny and Scrivener, it was for them to resolve.

'Jinny, I'm warning you, my patience is not without limits. Put the knife down!'

'I'll kill you first!'

Rob made up his mind. He turned and hurried away from the window.

'Very well, then. I'll do as you ask. You can go. But back away from me. Let me move away from the door, then you can get past me, then you can go.' The words seemed reasonable and Jinny nodded, she moved backwards a few feet.

'No tricks mind, Mr Scrivener. I meant what I said,' she warned.

'No tricks, Jinny, I promise you.'

He moved away from the door and opened it, pushed it so that the dark hallway beyond was exposed to view, then retreated again. He bowed deeply, pointed at the door to guide Jinny on her way. She moved forward slowly, each step more suspicious than the last, keeping her body turned towards him and her knife outstretched.

'Please,' he said gently, bowed again. She was at the door now, and perhaps the darkness beyond confused her or his florid courtesies distracted her, but she failed to see him kick at the stool by his feet until it was too late, until the stool was propelled across the floor towards her. Had the light been better she might have avoided it, she was nimble, she could have jumped out of its way. She almost succeeded in doing so, but it caught her ankle, unbalanced her, and Scrivener was too close behind. His blow to her arm numbed her; the knife clattered to the floor. He grabbed hold of her. She made as if to kick him but he was too quick for her, a punch to her stomach doubled her up, sent her gasping to the floor. He stood over her in triumph.

'I shall have you,' he muttered, 'willing or not.' He hooked his elbows under her arms and dragged her across the floor to the nearest chair, then pulled her up and sat her in it.

She groaned. He pulled her skirt up to her waist. Beneath was a pair of soft cotton drawers, and he pulled these down and over her bare feet. He stood back and admired her with wide eyes. Only semiconscious, she stared back at him, whimpering. She put her hand down between her legs but he pulled it away.

'How much easier and less painful it would have been if you'd done as I asked,' he said, undoing the buttons at the flap of his trousers.

'Emanuel! Mr Scrivener! Are you there? It's me, David Patterson!'

Scrivener cursed as the shout echoed from the hallway, hastily buttoned himself up again. He reached the door at the same time as Rob, tried to prevent him seeing beyond.

'Good God, man, what are you doing here? I thought you left ages ago.'

'I did, but I found I'd left my hat behind,' Rob said cheerily, peering over the poet's shoulder and into the room, 'so I thought I'd better come back and . . . Goodness me, it's Miss Lee in there! Hello there, fancy seeing you here.'

Scrivener whirled around, he'd thought it impossible to see Jinny from where Rob was standing. Rob took the opportunity to slip past him. He pulled the girl's skirt back down over her knees and stood before her.

'Mr Scrivener, I fear Miss Lee is unwell. Her colour is poor indeed. Have you called for the doctor?' He spoke quickly, nervously, he carried himself with his weight on the balls of his feet, as if preparing for flight.

'No. That is, I wasn't aware . . .'

'It came over her very quickly, is that what you're saying Emanuel? I see.' He turned his attention to the girl, took her hand. 'It's alright Miss Lee, you'll be alright. Don't try to talk. Just breathe easily, deeply, that's it.'

'What happened?' he asked Scrivener.

'I don't know. She was standing there and then . . . I don't know.'

'I think I ought to take her home, don't you? Do you feel

able to walk, Miss Lee?' Jinny nodded, pushed herself to her feet with some help from Rob, bent down and pulled up her drawers. Rob looked away.

'Thank you for looking after Miss Lee, Emanuel. I'll let you know how she is. The fresh air will do her good, and the walk, I've no doubt.' He put his arm round Jinny's waist and they headed for the door. 'Don't bother to see us out. You look a little flustered yourself; perhaps you ought to consider retiring. I'll see you tomorrow, at the manor. Goodnight!'

They left. Emanuel Scrivener heard the door slam. He sat down and drained his glass, persuaded his heart to cease its wild beating. His fingers drummed at the leather arms of the chair, he shook his head once or twice, then stood up and moved to his desk. He searched for pen and ink and paper and began to write, mouthing the words as he did so.

My dear James,
I trust you will remember me, your old friend Emanuel Scrivener, now living in the village of Bellingford where, by coincidence, your son-in-law has come to teach dancing. I felt I must write to you on a matter concerning Mr Patterson which directly affects your good name, and which I fear may distress your daughter. Mr Patterson has had liaisons with a number of women while he has been staying here this past fortnight. Please allow me to tell you details of his behaviour. He has . . .

The couple held each other close. Jinny had recovered her strength and could support herself, but still her arm reached up to rest on Rob's shoulders. He was aware she no longer needed his assistance but had no wish to take his hand from her waist. They reached the village green without saying anything, lost in their own thoughts, but each knew there were words to be spoken.

'Do you want me to walk back with you?' Rob asked.

Jinny shook her head. 'No,' she said, 'I'm not goin' back.

I told Mr Scrivener I wasn't goin' back.' She looked up at Rob. 'You heard me didn't you? You were there?'

'Yes, I was there. I heard everything. I'm sorry, I didn't mean to eavesdrop . . .'

'No, I'm glad. If you hadn't been there I don't know what would have happened. It was clever of you to do what you did.'

'I had to do something.' He reached his spare hand round and tucked her under the chin, bent his head to kiss her, but she turned away from him. 'Jinny? What is it?'

'I don't want you to kiss me. I'm pleased you were there to help me. I'm grateful, but . . . but I'm not easy, despite what you heard in there. And . . .' There was a tremor in her voice, she sounded close to tears. 'And you're a married man. I could have loved you, but you're married. You're going back to your wife in a few days' time. I won't have anything to do with you for that reason alone. I'm sorry, David, but I can't.'

Rob sighed, took his arms away. Jinny didn't move; she was lost in her own self-pity.

'Look at me,' he said. She shook her head.

'Jinny, please?' This time she raised her eyes. He smiled at her. 'I'd like to ask you some questions. You don't have to answer them if you don't want. You don't have to do anything. And then I want to talk to you, because I've things to say as well. And then we might be able to think better about what to do. Does that make sense?'

'Aye, I suppose so.'

'And will you answer my questions?'

'If I can.'

'Good. I told you before I was outside the window, listening. I'd been to see Mr Scrivener. We'd been drinking together, he told me he had a woman coming to see him, and I had to leave by the back door when you came in at the front. The path led by the window, that's why I was there. I heard just about everything. I heard him call you a . . .' He limped to a halt.

'A whore? There's no need to be afraid of the word, Davy. It's not a pleasant word, but it's true. I went to bed with Scrivener, aye, and with others, and they parted with money for that privilege. I saw none of it; me da kept it all. But the word's right.'

'Why? Why did you do it?'

'Why not, Davy? That's the question you should be askin'. What other way is there of a girl makin' money round here? Especially when her da's old and crippled, and drinks too much, and there's no work. What else could I do?'

'You could have gone away. You say you're going away now; why couldn't you have done it earlier?'

'You make it sound like I'm runnin' away from somethin'. I'm not proud of what I've done, but I'm not ashamed either. And till recently I didn't even know that some people consider it wrong. You're lucky, you're almost a gentleman. You earn a livin' doin' somethin' you're good at. You didn't starve when you were a bairn, you didn't see your mother die for want of food and warm clothin' and a little medicine. I did. Me da was all I had to look after me, and he did, for a while, in his way. But then he couldn't work. He got bitter, he started drinking too much. He'd cry at nights, and I'd go to him and try to comfort him, but he'd push me away.'

They skirted the village, sat down on a patch of grass close by the river. The moon was high now. Only lovesick owls and distant, nervous sheep threatened the still night. Jinny went on.

'One night, I must have been ten or eleven, no more, he didn't turn me away. He held me close and I could feel the tears on his face, and his hands on me. It was summer, as hot as this, and he began to stroke me through the shift I was wearin', and then underneath it. I didn't know what he was doin', not to start with, but he told me it was alright. I must have gone to sleep. I woke next morning and he looked worried. He stared at me when I got dressed, but I was just the same as normal. The next night he called me to him, and I went, and he showed me where to touch him. But he made me promise not to tell anyone what we did together. He said it was oor secret.

'It went on like that for a while, till I was fourteen or so. Then some of the lads started showin' an interest in me, but they were frightened of me da. They didn't do much. One night a stranger came to stay, he was a friend of me da's. We only had one room and when I went to my bed I could hear them talkin' and drinkin' and playin' cards. Next thing I know this man's wakin' me up, he's fumblin' with me clothes. I was frightened, but I saw me da there. He's noddin', he's sayin' alright, so I let him do what he wanted, this stranger. I was awake when he left the next mornin'. I saw him give me da some money, but I thought it was just for stayin' the night.

'It happened again and again. Sometimes I didn't like it, the men would be old or sweaty and they'd smell, or they'd be too rough. Sometimes it was good and I'd enjoy it; I couldn't help it.'

'But what about Dr Allard?'

'He's a man, isn't he? He's got his needs, same as anyone else, same as you. And what about you? You were keen enough last night, yet you're a married man. And there's a rumour you've been with that Mrs Arnison, though you won't be the only one. Who's the whore there? Me, who turned you down, or her? Or even you?'

Rob chose to ignore the question. 'And your father, does he still . . . you know?'

'No, I won't let him. I think he feels guilty.'

'So why stop? Why leave?'

'Because I want to. Because . . . I'm sixteen years old and I want to get away. Because I know there's more to life than what I'm doin'. Because . . . Oh, I don't know, does there have to be a reason? Can't you just accept the fact that I want to go?'

'Yes, I can accept that. But it worries me to think of you alone, trying to get by. Life's hard enough without trying to do everything yourself.'

'So what are you suggestin'? I come back with you? I'm sure your wife would like that. Have you got a big bed? Would we all fit in it?'

'Jinny, don't be silly. And anyway, how do you know I'm married?'

'Da told me, I don't know where he learned it, but nothing's a secret round here, believe you me.'

'It didn't seem to hold you back last night, up by the stones. You seemed keen enough then.'

'I know, I'm sorry about that. But . . .'

'Yes?'

'There was a reason. I was . . . I was doin' as I was told, by me da. He told me to be nice to you. That's what he says when he wants me to go with a man. "Be nice to him." But I'd danced with you all night, and you'd been kind to me, and I liked you for the way you were, and . . . and if the truth be told I could have gone with you because *I* wanted to, not because me da told me to. That was why I didn't.'

'You mean you felt something for me? You would have gone to bed with me because your father told you to, but then, because you thought *you* wanted to, you didn't? One of us is mad, and it isn't me.'

'Listen, Davy, if we'd done anythin' me da would have come on us. He was watchin', he would have found us, he would have threatened to tell people what you'd done; he would have demanded money from you.' Rob laughed out loud. He fumbled through the grass at his side and found some small stones, threw them lazily into the river.

'It's not funny, Davy.'

'Oh yes it is, Jinny, really, it is. In the first place I've no money, not until I get paid by the Taylors. Then there's the fact that you didn't go with me for my own good, to protect me. And also I'm not quite sure who he'd threaten me with, who he thinks I'd want to keep information from.'

'Your wife, of course.'

'My wife? Oh, yes, my wife.' He started laughing again.

'Davy, I don't see the joke.'

'The joke, Jinny, is that I don't have a wife. I'm not married.'

'You are. Her name's Emily, I think that's what me da said.'

'No, you're mistaken. Emily Playford as was, little, round, fat, roly-poly Emily Patterson as now is, she's married to David Patterson.'

'And that's you.'

'Wrong again. My name's Rob, Rob Tweddle.'

'I don't understand.'

So Rob explained. He told her who he really was, he explained why he'd come to Bellingford, that his intention was to take his revenge on both the Taylor family and on James Playford by doing his job badly. Jinny listened carefully, nodding occasionally. There were certain details he omitted, such as Frances Arnison's visits to his room; he was aware that Jinny suspected just such an occurrence but he felt he needed to retain some secrets. He mentioned his unsuccessful assault on Annie Taylor's virtue as evidence of his bad intentions, but then came his confession.

'But now I find I want to do well. I want to teach everyone dances like the ones we danced last night. I want them to experience the excitement of the music and the movement. And there's vanity there as well, I want the pleasure of showing I'm good. I want recognition, I want applause. And I don't want to go back to being Rob Tweddle. I want to continue being David Patterson. Does that sound stupid of me?'

'No, it doesn't sound stupid. The whole story sounds . . . Well, it sounds unbelievable. But I suppose it fits together. And you say no one else knows you're not the real David Patterson?' Rob shook his head. 'Then I can't see why you've a problem. You just keep goin', you get your money, you leave. It's easy for *you*.'

'No. it's not easy. To begin with, I don't know enough dances. And secondly, I don't know the music that goes with them. Third, even if I did know the music, even if

I had time to write it out, the musicians couldn't learn to play it in time.'

'Get some different musicians then.'

'I'd thought of that. I'd thought that I could ask your father—'

'No! He wouldn't do it, he hates the Taylors too much.'

'What about the rest of them, then? He seems to be their leader. Would they play without him?'

'No, I doubt it. I'll say this much for him, he can play the pipes well, and musicians respect him for that. If he said no the others wouldn't do it.'

'You could talk to him. Persuade him.'

'Me? I wouldn't do it. He's one of the reasons I'm goin'. He'll whip me if he knows I've told you about him, and he'll whip me again for not stayin' the night with Mr Scrivener. I don't want to see him again.'

'What if I was to say you could come with me when I go, after the wedding? I'd take you as far as Hexham. And you could have some money, three pounds, say, and in return for that you teach me the dances you know so I can teach them at the wedding. What would you say to that?'

'Old man Taylor loves Da as much as Da loves him. He wouldn't have him playin'.'

'I'll worry about that. Could you do it?'

'Will you come with me, to see me da?'

'Yes, if you want me to.'

'I'd feel safer.'

'I'll come with you then, when it gets light. Is there anything else?' Jinny shook her head. 'Then we'd better shake hands on the agreement,' Rob added.

'I won't shake hands,' Jinny answered, then added hesitantly, 'but I will kiss you now, if you want me to. Now I know you're not really a married man.'

Rob smiled. 'I'd like that,' he said, reaching out for her, but she stood up swiftly before he could make contact. She motioned him to his feet and he rose stiffly.

'You're tired,' she said, 'and so am I, though I know what

you're thinkin' about, because I'm thinkin' the same thing. But there's somethin' else I want to show you, to tell you. I'm going to stay up at the shepherds' bothy tonight, by the stone circle. Come up for me tomorrow when you can so we can go to see me da. We can think about how we can persuade him to play, we can talk about the dancin'; and we can do other things as well, if you still want to. Here's me kiss to seal the arrangement.'

She stood on her toes and brushed his lips with hers, the softest of touches, but it reached down through his body and sent every nerve alight, every muscle surging. And then she was away, running up the hill, and he followed her with his eyes until she disappeared into the silver mist of the moon. For the third day in succession he was up to see the sunrise, but none would seem as wondrous as this. He longed for his bed, he longed for sleep, he longed to dream of Jinny Lee.

The Twelfth Bar of the Musick

Thursday, 24 June 1830

In which Rob enjoys the pleasures of a woman's company, and a woman who has been denied the pleasure of his company prepares to exact her revenge.

Rob woke to the scent of sweet grasses and singing, the singing of larks and a woman. He rolled over on a bed of bracken and hay covered with a light blanket. The bothy was pleasantly cool, a slight breeze was blowing through the open door, and through it he could see the woman walking towards him. She was naked, but her walk was natural with no sign of embarrassment. Her hips swayed, her hair was blowing about her head. She spun on the spot and jumped in the air, laughed out loud, then recommenced her song. He looked at her as she approached. He'd heard tales of Guinevere of legend, Arthur's queen, the beloved of Lancelot, but he knew that no queen could compare with his Jinny. Her hair was soft and pale; it hung long and straight from her head, though this morning she'd decorated it with small golden flowers and tied it back with a black ribbon. Last night he'd gently kissed her eyes and her nose, her cheeks, her chin, her lips, and each caress convinced him that that particular part of her was the most beautiful, that her face was perfectly formed because of those eyes, or those lips, or that nose. But looking at her now, physically beyond his reach but with his skin still able to recall the touch of her body, his mind still drunk with her presence, he became aware that she *was* beauty. A painter who had spent years studying the works of the old masters to discover the way one achieved perfect skin tones, the way another depicted a hand and an arm just so, how a third used the finest of brushes to detail every single hair, could have saved so much time by gazing on Jinny.

She danced not for him but for herself, with an assurance, a confidence that belied her sixteen years. Her legs were long and lithe, her feet nimble; the swell of her hips and, when she turned, the taut muscles of her behind aided her agility as she capered and span. Her waist was narrow and her stomach flat, and the wedge of hair that lay below was so fine, fine as thistledown, that it did little to hide from view the flesh beneath. She leaped into the air then turned a cartwheel, laughed out loud from the sheer joy of the day, then resumed her step-hop back to the bothy and to Rob. He thought he could see the faintest bruise on her left breast, and another on her neck, but they could as easily have been shadows, and if he'd been the cause then the injuries would have been due to passion and not anger. Her small breasts moved lightly with her step; they confirmed her youth, and her nipples were pale pink and erect in the morning breeze. She looked directly at him and saw he was awake. She smiled and ran towards him. He thought she would run straight into the hut, but she slowed and stopped at the threshold.

'It's a good day,' she said, 'sunny and warm and fresh.'

'It's a beautiful day,' Rob said. 'I could see that from here, but not so beautiful as the dawn maiden who was dancing for me just a moment ago.'

Jinny smiled, raised her arms so her hands rested on the head of the door frame, spread her legs so her feet were pressed into its bottom corners. She blocked out some of the light, appeared dark against the sky.

'Won't you come and join me?' Rob asked. 'I feel in need of your company.'

'So I see,' she countered, sliding her eyes down his body. 'But I thought you wanted me to teach you some dances? That's right, isn't it?' Rob nodded. 'Well then, now's as good a time as any. Let's dance while there's still dew to cool us and the sun's smiling with us, not laughing down on us from on high.'

'You want to dance now? Out there?'

'Aye, Rob. I do.' She tasted his name; it was new to her. He climbed to his feet.

'If you want to dance, then I'd have no other man be your partner.' He reached for his trousers and thrust one foot into them, then another. He was about to pull them up when he caught sight of her shaking her head.

'Now what?' he said. She said nothing, but looked at his breeches, continued the slow, sideways movement of her head. 'No trousers?'

'I've no trousers. Why should you be any different?'

He stood up straight. The trousers fell to the ground of their own accord, and he stepped from their crumpled body and took her in his arms. They kissed each other, and it would have required little persuasion for them to have returned to their bed. Had Jinny tried to pull Rob outside, then he would probably have picked her up and deposited her on the nest of bracken, and once there she would have been unable (neither would she have wanted) to escape. But Jinny's move showed that she was less resolute than she believed. She lowered her hands to Rob's waist and tried to pull him back into the room, so he, with a perversity of nature which came from being in love, led her in the opposite direction and took her firmly in a ballroom hold.

'Shall we dance?' he asked with an excess of politeness, and felt Jinny press herself close against him. How different, he thought, from the last time he'd tried to dance this figure, only the day before . . .

*   *   *

Rob took Annie Taylor in a ballroom hold.

'Shall we dance?' he asked with an excess of politeness. She avoided looking at him.

'We're about to demonstrate a progression,' he instructed the others watching, 'which allows two couples to change places by polkaing round each other, and all within an eight-bar phrase of music.'

The couples were in two lines, men in one and ladies in the other, each facing his or her partner. Annie had been about to dance with her brother, Charlotte Stephenson having returned to Hexham to collect her dress for the wedding, but Danny Taylor had found a sudden need to excuse himself, a call of nature, he told his sister, and Rob had stepped into the gap without thinking.

'Gentlemen, your right hand should rest lightly on your partner's waist, your left hand should support your partner's right hand, thus. Ladies, your left hand should be on your partner's right shoulder. Those who are *first* men will be facing the presence, those who are *second* men have their backs to the presence. Yes?' He glanced up and down the set. They all seemed to have mastered that part of his instructions. 'Good. Now the progression. A single polka step takes up the same musical time as a rant step. Each couple should imagine a square on the ground, and should dance one polka step along each of the four sides of the square *but do not attempt this yet!*' His raised voice succeeded in halting those who anticipated his instructions; one or two couples almost overbalanced as they checked their movements, but amidst a background of giggles they all resumed their places.

'One polka step along each of four sides of a square will bring you back to your place. A further two steps will take you into the place of the couple you've just been dancing with. And then two rant steps will let you separate from your partner and resume your place in the line. Please allow me, with Miss Taylor's assistance, to demonstrate.'

He nodded at Harry Brown, the only musician present, who drew his bow across the strings of his violin in a chord and then led straight into the second part of the tune of 'The Morpeth Rant'. Rob and Annie polkaed elegantly round four sides of a square, then two sides further, then ranted into their new places in their lines.

'Now let's all try that,' he shouted as Danny Taylor hurried back into the room. Rob gave up his place to the young man, to Annie's obvious relief, and hurried around the set to push and prod individuals into their places. Satisfied, he gave Harry the sign, and the dancers began to move after the chord. They were reasonably well coordinated and, prompted by Rob's yelled instructions and warnings, helped by his vigorous clapping, they performed the figure with, in most instances, a degree of elegance and enthusiasm which surprised them.

'Keep going!' Rob bellowed, and they swung into the main part of the dance itself, passed through it, and once again entered the progression which had a little while ago given them so much trouble. This time was better than the previous one, and they went into the dance anew without being told to. Four more times they wheeled and polkaed and ranted, then Rob waved at Harry. Harry finished with a chord, the dancers bowed and curtseyed, and then, for the first time, burst into a round of applause. Rob smiled at them.

'There will be more,' he announced, 'tomorrow.' But he refrained from adding that he would have to have Jinny instruct him first. 'Thank you all for coming.' He wandered over to Harry Brown and clapped him on the back.

'Well done, lad, I don't know how I'd manage without you. I don't suppose you've been able to speak to any of the other musicians?'

'I have, Mr Patterson, but you won't like what I've had reported to me.'

'Go on then.'

'They won't play.'

'None of them?'

'Not one.'

'Did they say why?'

'Aye, they did, but there were many different reasons. Some said they were too busy, the miller for one, and others said they didn't have enough time to practise the tunes. Others said the tunes were too difficult to play anyway, they couldn't manage them even if they *did* practise. Quite a few said they wanted to enjoy the wedding, they wanted to be able to talk with their friends, they wanted to dance themselves. They all sounded sorry, but none of them said they'd play.'

'Except you.'

'Except me. But I'm not enough, am I? You need more musicians, and time's running out. Have you tried . . .?'

Rob hushed him; Samuel Taylor was hurrying over, mopping his hot, red forehead.

'Mr Patterson,' he beamed, 'David, that was capital, thoroughly enjoyable. These new dances are much more enjoyable than the old, much livelier. I can feel the urge to move even in *my* old bones.'

'I'm so pleased, Mr Taylor. I can sense everyone's pleasure myself,' said Rob.

'Yes, quite. There is, however, one thing which still concerns me.'

'And what's that, Mr Taylor?'

'Music. Or rather, the lack of it. Or to be even more precise, the lack of musicians to play it.' Harry Brown coughed, and Samuel Taylor looked across at him. 'Present company excepted,' he added quickly. 'Young Harry's doing a grand job. If only we had six or seven more like him. But we haven't, have we?'

'I agree, there does seem to be a lack of enthusiasm amongst the musicians you selected for me,' Rob said, lightly emphasising the fact that it had been Samuel Taylor who had done the choosing, 'but I'm working on that problem and I feel sure that a solution will be found.'

'Good. Very good. I knew you'd have things under control, but the truth is . . .' he leaned closer to Rob's ear and whispered conspiratorially, with much dramatic glancing about him, '. . . the truth is, it's not me who's worrying. It's Rebecca. She does so want the day to go well, and she's been a little disturbed about the way things have been going, as I mentioned to you a day or two ago. Now the dancing appears to be on the mend, but the music . . .' He shrugged. 'I told her you'd mentioned musicians from Corbridge, that you had plans . . . I'll tell her everything's under control. Keep it up, David my boy, keep it up.' He chugged away to join his wife, whistling a tune which might have been one that he was dancing to earlier but was not really identifiable as such.

'What will you do?' whispered Harry to Rob.

'I have my plans,' Rob smiled back at him. 'Just as Mr Taylor said, I have my plans.'

Those plans first involved escaping Frances Arnison. There was a note waiting for him, sealed in an envelope this time; she obviously considered it too dangerous to leave messages which could be read by others. It accused him of avoiding her, of spending time away from the manor when he should have been there. She had apparently been to his room at night and, finding him absent, come to the conclusion that he was in the arms of another woman. She threatened that she would reveal his true identity, or what she knew of it, to her father unless he made sure that he was available for her pleasure that same night.

Rob sat down and scribbled his own reply. He told her that he knew of her secret, that she was in the habit of bedding any male visitor to the manor and others in the community at large. He explained that he was occupied in his work, that her accusations were absurd, and that unless she desisted from thrusting herself on him then *he* would have no choice but to tell her father, and her husband for all the good it would do, about her night-time wanderings. He sealed the letter in her own envelope, slipped it under her bedroom door, then hurried away up the hill to the stone circle.

Jinny was waiting anxiously for him.

'I thought you weren't going to come,' she said as she threw herself at him. Rob accepted her greeting willingly, then pushed himself away to look her in the eyes.

'You mean you don't trust me?' he asked.

'No,' she answered, then corrected herself. 'That is, it's not that I don't trust you, just, well, I mean I don't know you well enough yet.'

'I can think of a good way for you to get to know me much better,' Rob suggested, and he pulled her back towards him and kissed her, his tongue forcing open her lips. His hands wandered over her behind as hers clutched at the hair at the back of his neck.

'No, Rob, not yet, please. You said you wanted to get some musicians; you wanted to learn some dances. If you want to see me da we'd better go now. He drinks in the evenin' and if we don't hurry we won't get him to talk any sense at all. Come on.'

Rob acknowledged that Jinny was being reasonable, that his priorities should have been exactly as she'd stated, but that didn't stop the faintest feeling of frustration clouding his mind. She'd taken the lead in wakening his sexual feelings for her (Was it lust or love? He wasn't sure; all he knew was that he wanted her), and yet she discouraged him whenever the opportunity to satisfy his needs arose. He wanted to believe that her logic, her reasoning, was justified, but he needed to know that his feelings for her were mirrored by hers for him. The thought of her with other men, lying with them, coupling with them, was a strange aphrodisiac to him; but at the same time the circumstances of the relationships she'd had made him suspicious of her motives in dealing with him. Perhaps she saw him only as a means of escape from the village, from her father, from the life she was leading. But when she took his arm in hers and her fingers idly teased the hairs on the back of his hand, when the sway of her body encouraged him as they descended to the village, when she laughed and sang alongside him and encouraged him to do the same, he felt guilty that he should have suspected her of any deviousness at all.

Her happiness diminished as they approached the cluster of dwellings she called home. She let go of Rob's hand, walked a step away from him.

'He won't be pleased,' she told Rob. 'Mr Scrivener will have told him what happened last night, and he'll be wonderin' where I am. If you come in with me he'll jump to a conclusion, I promise you. He'll try to blackmail you.'

'He's got nothing to blackmail me with,' Rob insisted, 'not yet. All I want is for him and his friends to play at the wedding, nothing more. You've offered to help me with the dances, I want him to help with the music. It couldn't be simpler.'

'It could; it could be a lot simpler, but it isn't, so we'll just have to get by. It might be best if I see him alone first . . .'

'I don't think that would be a good idea,' Rob said. 'I'd rather get it over with, and if he gets unpleasant I'd rather be in there with you. Don't worry, I won't hurt him.'

'Hurt him? It's the other way round I'm worried about. He's a mean man in a fight, me da, if he starts gettin' violent we run, both of us, you hear? He's used a knife in the past. He's even threatened me with one, so watch out.'

'I'll watch out,' Rob said, 'for both of us.'

They scattered dogs and piglets and small children before them as they trod the path to Jacob Lee's house. The noise advertised their coming and the door was open for them. Jacob Lee was inside, his tankard on the table.

'You'd better come in,' he yelled at them, 'both of you, though I can guess at what you'll be saying, and I can't promise I'll be pleased. Take a seat, both of you.'

Rob and Jinny sat down, he on the remaining stool, she on the bed.

'Mr Lee,' Rob began, 'I've come to ask . . .'

'I know what you've come to ask,' the old man said, 'I know what the two of you have been up to. Scrivener's told me everythin'. You, Jinny, you want to go away. And you,

Mr Patterson, you want to help her. I can guess why, I can
guess the things she's said and done to you. She's a clever
woman, lad. She takes after her da in that way; aye, she
does that.' He took a deep draught of ale, and Rob took
the opportunity to begin his speech again.

'I think you've misunderstood—' he began, but could get
no further.

'I've misunderstood nothin', lad, nothin' at all. It's you
who doesn't understand what's happenin', but I'll tell you,
I surely will.'

'Da, please, it'll do no harm to listen to—'

'It'll do you no harm to listen either, for a change. You
always did talk too much, just like your bloody mother.
Both of you can listen. You can listen to me, and then you
can say your piece, but not before!' He drained his tankard
and banged it down on the table.

'My daughter, Mr Patterson, is a whore. She'll sell herself
to anyone who'll have her. I'm not proud of the fact, no,
not proud at all, but I'll admit she does it to help out, to
bring in a few pence which we need, we really need. She's
good at her job, so I've heard tell. No dissatisfied customers
for our Jinny, eh lass? And I've heard she enjoys herself in
her work. She's no hard-faced strumpet is my daughter, no
need for her to act. Or perhaps she really is a good actress.
You'll know that better than me, Mr Patterson. What's your
opinion?'

The old man gave no time for nor expected an answer.

'But there's not much need for someone of Jinny's talents
in a place like this,' he continued, 'not enough people with
money, not enough people with the *need*. So she has to hook
others too; people like you, strangers, those passin' through.
The only qualification's havin' a few pennies to rub together.
The other night, up at the stones, I didn't ask you up there
so's you could hear the music. I didn't want you to see the
dances. The only reason was to get you with Jinny so she
could hook you, and she did that, right enough, didn't she?
That goodbye – I was watchin'. I saw you bite, lad; I saw

her play you in. I can see the hook in you now. Barbed, it is. You won't get that out easy.'

'Da, that's not true, you know—'

'Be quiet girl, or I'll make you be quiet. This is men's talk.' He turned back to Rob. 'Trouble is, Mr Patterson, you're not like Jinny's usual men. You're young, you're almost handsome, you can dance, you can play music, you're in a position of responsibility. You're married, true, but a man like you can probably afford to keep a mistress, at least that's Jinny's way of thinkin'.'

'That's lies, complete lies!' Jinny was on her feet, but one look from her father quieted her, pushed her back to her seat.

'Or it might be that she's done somethin' really stupid. It might be she's fallen in love with you. But it doesn't matter; the end result's the same. She wants to leave. And that's bad news for me, me only daughter leavin' me, leavin' me alone here, no one to care for me, no one to support me. So what we need to do, Mr Patterson, is discuss the compensation you'll see your way to payin'. A little sum to help me keep the wolf from the door. A regular little sum, as it were. But now I'll be quiet, I can see you're both keen to say somethin', and you'll want to be considerin' what it's worth, this little sum, to stop me tellin' about you. I'm sure Mrs Patterson would be most upset to hear about your dancing partner, lad, about the particular jiggy-jigs you've been doin'. So I've had me say; it's your turn. Please, go on. I'm listenin' now.' He leaned back in his chair smiling triumphantly.

'Da, you're a bastard! You're the nastiest—'

'Miss Lee, I think you ought to let me speak first. Mr Lee,' Rob said, using his Sunday voice, the one that ironed out the most obvious burrs of his Tyneside ancestry, 'I'm aware of the fact that your daughter is a prostitute. She and I discussed this, and many other matters, last night when I accompanied her from Mr Scrivener's house. This was immediately before I returned to my own bed – late, it's true, but entirely alone. I may add that I've never had intimate knowledge of your daughter nor will I ever pay to do so.' He looked across at Jinny; she was quiet, her head low. She was sitting on her hands.

'But at the stones, I saw you both. You were all over her—'

'I was very tired,' Rob continued, his manner as officious as he could make it. 'I'd been drinking, and it doesn't concern me that my wife might find this out since I've already written to tell her of these events. I tell her everything, Mr Lee. She's fully aware of the strains and temptations under which a man such as myself works. As you said, I'm not unattractive, my employment often involves me working with impetuous, immature young women . . .' He paused and stared at Jinny who was now looking back at him, her face curious. '. . . Young women such as your daughter, though usually, I might say, of a better class. I'm used to these women forming emotional attachments; I'm used to being the focus for these attachments. When I say, therefore, that I've talked with your daughter, you may rest assured that I've done only that and nothing more. The attraction between us, if there is one, is purely in one direction, from her to me. I care nothing for her, how shall I put it, her physical attractions. I've never consorted with loose women and I don't intend beginning to do so now.'

Jinny's mouth had fallen open in disbelief. Her father was alert to the possibilities Rob's monologue had opened.

'You mean you're not goin' to take her away?'

'I'd never intended doing so, Mr Lee.'

'But she wants to go. Scrivener told me.'

'True, Mr Lee. And I'll say now, lest you begin to feel that you can keep her here under your control, that I'll give her some money as payment for services rendered, and she'll accompany me . . .'

'I knew it! You *have* had her!'

'Mr Lee, let me finish! I'll allow her to accompany me to Hexham when I leave, and if she chooses she may then use her own money to travel further. That money will be payment for the instruction she's given me and will give me in the dances I saw performed recently, dances which are new to me and which are therefore of some value. Do you understand, Mr Lee?'

'And you came here just to tell me that? To tell me you were takin' her away? Even if your words say different, it's the same meaning in the end, isn't it? She goes, I'm left behind.'

'Yes, I go,' Jinny interrupted, 'and not before time, either! You think I'm your property, you do. I'm like that chair and the table, somethin' you can buy or sell or hire out to somebody. Well I'm not, I'm a woman. I can look after myself, and I'm goin' whether you like it or not!'

Jacob Lee rose to his feet angrily. He wasn't used to having his daughter speak to him in that way. He reached for his stick but Rob's hand was there first, he pulled it away from the old man's grasp and rose himself, towering tall over the other two.

'I think we'd all better sit down,' he said, 'and calm down. Jinny?' She sank back to the bed. 'Mr Lee?' The old man tried to stare him out, but Rob was certain of himself. He stared straight back, and Jacob Lee reluctantly resumed his seat.

'Thank you,' Rob said, and sat down himself. 'I've a proposition to make to you, too, Mr Lee. That's the reason I came here today, not, as you think, to gloat over the fact that your daughter is leaving home. It's a proposition which involves you working for me, and which, if you accept, will earn you a small sum of money. But it may also help you in other ways. It may raise your position in the community and perhaps make it easier for you to find other work.'

'Get on with it, man, and talk normal, there's no need for that fancy voice with me. You didn't talk like that the last time you were here, why should you now? Go on then, tell me what it is, this work of yours. Labourin'? I can't work fast enough with me leg the way it is, and I've no skills other than in labourin'.'

'You have,' said Rob. 'You can play the pipes.'

Jacob Lee looked at Rob, then across at his daughter, as if asking her to confirm that he'd heard correctly.

'You mean you want me to play for you? And you'll pay me?'

'Yes. But it's not just you. I need others; some of the men and women I heard the other night at the stones. You can pick them, six or seven, say. I'll pay you half a guinea; you pay them from that. Agreed?'

'No, not agreed. Not yet, anyway. You haven't told me where I'm to play, or why, or who I'll be playin' for. You'll be finished here by the weekend. Is it to be in Hexham? Newcastle's too far, and Carlisle – nobody'll travel that distance to play.'

'No, it's not that far, neither in distance nor in time. I want you to play at Annie Taylor's wedding.'

Jacob Lee showed no sign of having heard Rob. He looked at him as if waiting for more words, but his face didn't change. Then Rob noticed a slight twitch of the lips, and it became clear to him that the old man was trying to hold back his laughter. He clenched his fists, squeezed his eyes shut then opened them wide, sucked his bottom lip into his mouth, but it was all ineffective. The laughter was born deep inside him. It built up slowly, then burst out in a torrent of raucous, raw spluttering and braying. He slapped his knees; his head went back and then forward, his cheeks moistened with tears. Rob could see that Jinny was smiling too, and he couldn't help grinning at her. That grin was a mistake – it was the gateway to his own laughter, and soon the three of them were joined in a chorus of hooting and snorting which threatened to burst down the walls and throw the roof high into the air. It was Jacob Lee who was first able to gather his senses together. He took a deep breath and then another, shook his head, and found enough strength to speak.

'You want me to play at Annie Taylor's weddin'? You want me to play for that Samuel Taylor? You must be bloody mad!' There was no humour in the statement, rather it was filled with resentment and hatred, but its result was to start the laughter anew. The calm was quick to follow, however, and it was Rob who spoke first.

'Why won't you play?' he asked forthrightly.

'Why won't I play? Let me ask you first; what makes you think old man Taylor'll have me playin'? He hates me as much as I hate him. He won't have me or mine . . .' he threw a nod at Jinny '. . . in his house.'

'Let me worry about that. I'm asking why you're refusing to play.'

'I've told you, I don't like the man. I'll do nothin' to favour him, nothin' at all. You'll have to think again.'

'But suppose you do play, Jacob. It'll be seen that you're a better man than him. It'll be seen that you were generous and came to his aid when he needed you. And you'll be paid for doing so!'

'You didn't hear me, man. He won't have me in his house. I won't do it, I won't even try.'

'I think you should, Da,' Jinny said.

'And what does your opinion matter?' Jacob Lee spat back.

'It matters a lot,' Rob said slowly. Now was the time to show his hand. 'It matters because Jinny told me a lot about you. She told me how *you* made her what she is today. But she also told me that you practised on her yourself—'

'You little bitch! I told you never to—'

'Mr Lee, you don't seem to have many friends here, and you'll have even fewer if I tell them what I've learned. Surely you can see. Jinny's a liability to you now, the best thing you can do is let her leave with your blessing. And then you can do what you can to draw your neighbours around you, to try and use your music to build a bridge with those at the manor. I'm giving you the chance to do that.'

Jacob Lee shook his head again and sighed. 'It sounds easy when it's just words, lad, so easy. But you're not listenin' to me, are you? Even if I say yes, even if you manage to sneak me into the house, even if I play with me head in a sack, he'll throw me out!'

'I've told you, Jacob, I'll deal with that.'

'Do I have any choice?'

'No, not really.'

The old man spat on the earthen floor of his house, the gobbet of phlegm was quickly absorbed by the dry, dusty soil.

'In that case,' he said, 'when do you want us? And where? And it's a guinea, no less, even if old man Taylor won't let us play.'

'Friday night, at the manor. I'll let you know the times.' Rob tried to hold back his excitement. The first part, the easy part of his task, had been successfully achieved. 'And I'll pay you a guinea even if you don't play. How you split it is up to you.'

'I'll be there,' said Jacob Lee. 'But I think you'd better go now, before I change me mind.'

As Rob and Jinny left him they could see there was almost a smile on his face. During the climb back up the hill Jinny was quiet, and she kept her distance from Rob. There was none of the easy familiarity she'd shown on the way down. He didn't ask her what it was that troubled her, though he saw that she was troubled; he waited for her to speak. When she did her voice was trembling.

'You said some things to me da that were hurtful.'

'Hurtful to you,' Rob asked, 'or to him?'

'To me!'

'And?'

'And I need to know the truth. I need to know the way you feel about me.'

'Why? Does it matter?'

'Yes, of course it matters! You were tryin' a few hours ago to get me into your bed, and I was close to goin' with you. Then you said you had no feelin's of affection towards me, and it sounded as though you meant it, even though you were sayin' it to me da. I thought perhaps you were actin', that it was part of your plan, but then I thought it wasn't an act, that you really felt that way. And now I don't know.' She stopped and looked at him. Her eyes were misting over, but she blinked, determined not to cry. Rob tried to remember how he'd felt when he was sixteen.

'The things I said were partly true,' he explained. 'I said I cared nothing for your – what were the words I used? – your "physical attractions". I said you were attracted to me, but that the reverse wasn't so. Was there anything else offended you?'

'You said you'd never consorted with loose women, and you weren't plannin' to do it in the future.'

'I said that?'

'Yes.'

'Well in that case I must confess I wasn't entirely truthful. I *have* had occasion to spend time with women whose morals might be considered loose. But as for the rest . . .'

'Yes?'

Rob held her. She couldn't escape his grip, he forced her to look at him.

'Jinny, the feelings I have for you are too intense to be considered a mere attraction. And it's not only your body I admire but the person who owns it, and if I do spend time with you, which I certainly hope to do, then I wouldn't be willing to share you with anyone else. I don't believe you're a loose woman, and even if you were in the past, if you feel about me the way I feel about you there'll be no need for either of us to look at anybody else. Does that explain matters a little better?'

'I hear the words,' she said, 'and I know what they mean, but I don't think I understand you, and I don't know if I ever will. But I'd like to try.' She took him by the hand and led him to the bothy, and there they spent the night together.

They danced naked in the fresh day, and then Rob picked her up and carried her back to their bed. She seemed different; softer, more compliant than she'd been the night before. Then she had led him. She'd pulled the clothes from him, pushed him down and mounted him. She'd woken him in the night, her warm hands working their magic, and again she'd taken according to her need and, sated, slept beside him. But now she lay quiet, eyes closed, and waited for him to move.

He watched her stillness, the gentle rise and fall of her breasts, the way her fingers were outstretched, her toes pointed. He tried to memorise her, and so intent was he on absorbing her in this way that she turned her head and opened her eyes, wondering why he hadn't yet touched her. But she saw his face, saw his smile, and trusted him. She lay back again and waited.

Beside their bed was a jar of cool water which Jinny had fetched that morning from the stream. Rob dipped his left hand into it and cradled a few drops of the liquid in the palette of his palm, he used the fingers of his right hand as a painter would a brush and stroked the water across Jinny's lips. She opened them slightly, and her tongue snaked out to confirm the identity of the balm. Rob moistened the down on her upper lip, he traced her nose and the bones of her cheeks, he painted the helix of her ears, coloured the pillared muscles of her neck with the plain, colourless water. Each time his fingers moved, each time they passed over an area of peach-smooth flesh, they added light and texture to her skin. They delineated the curves of her shoulders, they drew pale pinks to her breasts, they circled and surrounded her nipples and gave them form and Jinny gasped as they brushed her, but lay still. Rob traced her ribs and laid his hand flat on her stomach, allowing his wet hand to cool her, then to warm her. He pressed and took his hand away, watched the pale stigmata disappear.

He became a sculptor. With both hands he fashioned the bone and flesh and muscles of her legs, softly kneaded the smooth clay of her thighs and calves and ankles, moulded each toe with care and precision. His nails coursed the rough skin on the soles of her feet, his thumbs pressed firm into her arches, his fingers moved up her body again, negotiating the tracery of veins and nerves.

With the heel of his hand on her navel, his fingertips made

play with the pale hairs on her body. He dampened them with more water, made warm by the heat of his palm, and twisted and tendrilled them into dark seaweed shapes. He made a V of his fingers, and slid them forward. Jinny parted her legs, and the fingers met warmer flesh, darker flesh, flesh made moist by other than water. Rob pulled his hand back gently, slowly, and the mound of her sex moved with it to reveal fold within fold of petalled lips. With a single finger of his other hand he reached down and touched the rough blanket between her legs, then ran the finger leisurely up her body, allowing it to linger where it pleased him and her, until it rested, slick with fragrant nectar, at her apex held open by his hand. It found the well-hidden secret kernel of her desires and her freedoms, coaxed it into tumescence.

Jinny could no longer be still. She opened her legs wide and placed her feet and her hands flat on the mattress. She pushed hard against his hands and urged him on with her whimpers and groans. He teased her, slowed when she quickened and quickened when she slowed, made his movements gentle when she would have him coarse and hard, then when she lay back he would lean over her and hold her with his weight, and his fingers would delve and dive, encourage and inflame her so that she begged for the freedom to move herself against him.

She excited him. Her hands reached out to feel him, they cupped him and caressed him; they took hold of him firmly and worked a rhythmic spell on him. It was Rob's turn to moan, to protest at the pain of this pleasure, to fight against it while begging that it shouldn't cease. They could smell each other's excitement, the hot sweat of passion. At some wordless moment they ceased their torment of each other's body. Rob clambered eagerly over Jinny. Their eyes locked. He positioned himself and slid gently forward. There was no resistance, only a welcoming sigh and her fingers at his back, his head bent to her lips and her breasts, and the increasing thrust and tempo of her body against his.

The stones echoed with their one cry. Some new beast had

claimed the moorland and was exulting in its possession of this land, its valleys and hills, its pinnacles and its lush grasses. And then there was silence, broken only by the wind and the tumbling lapwing.

Rob was in good form that night. He was in control; he knew it, and his pupils knew it. When he encouraged them with a small joke they laughed, when he demonstrated a figure or a step their attention was focused on him alone, when he pointed out an error in style or carriage then the individual concerned practised straightaway until the error was eliminated. His enthusiasm, his exuberance, carried the evening through to a triumphant close when he and Harry Brown were applauded to the echo. Even Annie Taylor smiled at him.

'Ladies and gentlemen!' he said loudly, holding up his hands to silence them, 'Thank you very much. It is indeed heartening to find that you appear to be enjoying yourselves as much as I am. I know that some amongst you have expressed concern that there should be more musicians on the day of the wedding, and I must admit that I too have been worried at this. It's with great pleasure, therefore, that I can inform you that tomorrow, Friday night, we will have with us a company of musicians whose ability is beyond question, whose music will thrill you and inspire you to such dancing as you've never experienced before! Saturday will, as you know, be taken up with preparations for the wedding itself, so this will be the first, and the last, opportunity to practise your dancing before the great day itself. I hope to see you all there. Thank you and goodnight.'

Once more there was applause, and Rob quickly gathered his music together. He wanted to escape before he could be captured by a curious Samuel Taylor, and he was eager to head back to the shepherds' bothy where Jinny would be waiting for him. He couldn't help grinning at the thought of her. They'd stayed together for most of the day, bathed in the cold stream then returned to their bed. It was with great reluctance that she'd persuaded him to leave her and attend this practice. But she'd been right to do so, and their parting at least brought with it the anticipated pleasure of their reconciliation. He hurried from the ballroom and turned the corner for the stairs, only to find Annie Taylor ascending ahead of him. She turned at the noise of his feet.

'Mr Patterson,' she said, 'your dancing is proving a revelation. I would not have thought you capable of such spirited instruction given, please forgive me for saying this, the comparative mediocrity of your first few days here. I feel sure you will do us proud on the wedding day, and I know that word of your success will spread.'

'Thank you, Miss Taylor. I'm pleased that after such an inauspicious beginning I'm able to satisfy your needs.' She looked at him, suspicious that in his choice of words he was playing with her again, but she could find no trace of sarcasm in his polite smile. At the top of the stairs he turned right and she left.

'Miss Taylor?'

She turned at his voice. 'Yes Mr Patterson?'

'Forgive me, you mentioned doing you proud on your wedding day, and I'm sure you were referring not necessarily to your parents but to you and your fiancé. And I think I recall you saying he would spend a little time here before the wedding, isn't that so?' Annie Taylor nodded. 'But I'm not aware that he's been to any of my classes. Is he well?'

'Oh, yes, Mr Patterson, he is well. His letters do not complain of ill health. They do, however, mention how busy he is at his work. He is a gentleman farmer, and I regret that he will be unable to attend until Saturday. I'm afraid that I shall have to rely on others for company in some of the more difficult dances—'

'I should be pleased to offer *my* services,' Rob interrupted.

'— but he has a good sense of rhythm and is a quick learner. I feel sure that we shall manage the simpler circles and squares.'

'I trust that will be so, Miss Taylor. But if you will excuse me? I really am rather tired.'

'Of course, Mr Patterson, but first, if you don't mind, I have a question for you.'

'A question? Please, ask away.'

'It is of no great importance, Mr Patterson. You may have noticed that my sister was not present this evening.' Rob nodded, though he hadn't been aware that Frances Arnison had been absent. 'Yet she was asking after you all this morning and this afternoon, she seemed very keen to speak with you. Has she managed to find you? Did you speak to her earlier today?'

'No,' Rob shook his head, 'I've had no sight of your sister for, let me see, two days now? Do you happen to know why she wanted to see me?'

'She mentioned, in passing, something about personal instruction, but beyond that I know nothing. Ah well, if I see her I shall tell her you have retired early. Goodnight, Mr Patterson.'

'Goodnight Miss Taylor.'

Rob hurried to his room, deposited his music, then left again. It was almost dark as he hurried up the path to the stones, but still light enough for the woman who had just entered his room to stand at the window and identify him by his tall, gangling passage, and curse him in a fashion which belied her upbringing. Frances Arnison stormed back to her own room, reached for pen, ink and paper, and sat down under a flickering candle. She imagined as she wrote that her pen was a dart and her ink poison, but her target was still the dancing master.

My dear Uncle George,

Please forgive the brevity of this letter, but heed its content and act upon it with all due urgency.

I am aware that you had not wished to attend my sister's wedding, but I implore you to reconsider. I suspect that the dancing master you engaged for us is not all he appears to be and may even be an imposter. My evidence is circumstantial, but you should be able to investigate matters speedily in Newcastle and act accordingly. The man who calls himself David Patterson is over six feet tall and exceedingly thin. He can dance well and he can play flute passably, but his voice is common. I fear that he has won over the people here, but your presence may help uncover the truth.

There is little else to say other than that I miss you still and, should you feel able to travel here, would welcome the opportunity to renew our special relationship.

With fondest affection from your niece, who loves you now and forever,

Frances Arnison.

The Thirteenth Bar of the Musick

—◆—

Friday, 25 June 1830

*In which Samuel Taylor dances to Jacob Lee's tune,
and Rob learns that revenge can last a lifetime.*

*T*he day was hotter than any Rob could remember, despite
the unrelentingly fine weather that had accompanied
his stay at the manor. He looked out from his room over
lawns stained with a yellow-brown patina, like that of old
parchment, dry and dusty. Sheep and cattle lay sprawled
beneath pasture oaks whose leaves were turned by the
faintest of breezes, and there was an unnatural silence in
yards and stables. Ducks sought the muddy waters of a
shrinking pond, hens scratched lethargically or squatted,
beaks gaping, like fat puffballs beneath wide-doored coops.
Only the swallows seemed possessed of energy as they divided
their time between clay-basket nests hung precariously under
barn timbers (now filled with bat-squeaked young) and the
insect-laden air above the slow-moving, deep-watered river.
It was too hot even for the children of the village, who could
often be found gracing the cool waters with their shouts and
exuberance. Today they were elsewhere.

Rob knew where they were. Although the world outdoors
had been left to bake, inside, in every house in the village,

all was busy. In the manor, to stand still was to risk being given a job of cleaning or decorating, dusting or polishing or scouring. Long bolts of linen had been hung from the ceiling of the ballroom close to the walls. Fastened to them were sprays of evergreen and frameworks of thin twigs which would be decked with flowers early on the Sunday morning, ready for the festivities to come. Guests would be arriving throughout this day and the next, and there was insufficient room to keep them at the manor. Close relatives or friends, those of high status, those who were owed favours, were to be kept within the building. Others would be sent out to the village to stay in the farms and houses there, and the children who ought to have been laughing and cheering, shouting and jumping at the sun, would be helping in their homes, pressed into service by parents in the same way that servants in the manor were being chivvied and harassed into working harder and faster and more efficiently.

Members of the family were not excused their duties. Rob had seen Danny heading for the stables, grumbling that *he* had been given the job of preparing the four-wheeled coach and its tack and instructing the stableboy in how to groom the two mares for their role. Rebecca Taylor and her daughters, hair tied back and sleeves rolled up, aprons protecting their oldest dresses, were helping in the kitchen. Rob thought it best to avoid that particular area of the house; the heat was bad enough. The smell of roasting meat assaulted his nostrils, and three commanding officers were four too many for him.

Even Samuel Taylor had been given a job. With pen and quill – and the assistance of Harry Arnison and a bottle of port – he was organising the seating plan for the wedding meal, keeping separate those who would argue; mixing friends with family, young with old; promoting individuals to seats close to the bride and groom and their entourage. This vexing task was made more difficult by his not knowing some of the people whose names his wife had written down for him. His solution, cutting up the sheet of paper and

drawing them at random from his hat, was as likely, Harry
Arnison assured him, to produce a satisfactory result as any
more objective approach. And it would leave them more
time, they agreed, to stretch back in their chairs and close
their eyes and collect their wits and their strength for the
days ahead.

Rob himself had no physical tasks to perform. His duties
had been shelved until the wedding but for one further
evening of dance, to take place that very night, when he
was due to produce his new musicians. His original band
had showed nothing but pleasure at this news. All of them
had, they revealed, been searching for ways to avoid being
conscripted to this task in the first place. None felt him- or
herself to be a natural musician, and it was only their loyalty
to Samuel Taylor which had allowed them to be volunteered
in the first place. Now they could relinquish this burden and
enjoy the evening as dancers and guests. The only difficulty
would be persuading Samuel Taylor that Jacob Lee and his
colleagues should be allowed to play. Rob had made gentle
enquiries; none of the labourers had been invited to the
wedding, not to the church service or the meal that was
to follow, or to the dance. He was unsure whether this was
general custom or perhaps the result of the animosity which
existed between the two men. Whatever the reason, getting
the musicians into the ballroom to play would be difficult
enough; overcoming Samuel Taylor's objections would tax
Solomon's wisdom.

The musicians and the dances weren't the only matters
claiming Rob's attention. His thoughts turned frequently to
Jinny Lee, and in a way that troubled him deeply. He'd
agreed that she could accompany him as far as Hexham
on the day following the wedding, and that the money he
would have received by then would pay her for teaching
him some dances. She'd thought of finding a job in Hexham.
The glovers and hatters were always, she told him, looking
for nimble-fingered girls. Her questions regarding his future
plans brought an admission that he had none, that he'd

thought no further ahead than completing his deception, albeit with results somewhat different to those he'd originally intended. This didn't worry him. He would have money. He could return to Newcastle or travel west to Carlisle, and then his options were limitless. He was young, he had a certain talent to please and an ability to deceive, and his self-confidence was growing daily. Why should he worry about the future?

He admitted that it wasn't the future he was worried about. It was Jinny Lee. And it wasn't her ability to succeed in whatever life she chose for herself; he had no doubts that she would be as successful as he hoped to be. His problem lay in the feelings that were growing between them. Acknowledging that there were feelings was a first step towards realising that he had a decision to make. His options for the future had originally only been for him. In his daydreams he saw only himself, as a dancing master in Manchester or courting a rich young widow in London. But now there were other possibilities, and they all included Jinny. To his horror he found he welcomed them. He could see a life where they would be together and happy in each other's company. He saw them setting up home with their own bed, acquiring pots and pans, sheets and pillows and blankets, furniture and carpets. But he wasn't used to such all-pervading domesticity; he'd never had to share anything with anyone.

The nervousness he felt would have been made bearable had it been without foundation. If it had been Annie Taylor who'd occupied these dreams then he would have been able to laugh and put down the aberration to strong beer or undercooked wild mushrooms, secure in the knowledge that she would have laughed at the thought of spending any part of her life with him. But Jinny was different. Everything she did showed that she felt at home with him; she enjoyed being with him, enjoyed caring for him and his needs. When they lay together and he stirred she was straightaway asking him what it was he needed. Water? She would fetch some. Food?

There was some in her basket; only bread and cheese, but it would do until she could prepare something else. If he had an itch she would scratch it, an ache she would soothe it; if his hand moved to her breast or cupped her behind then she would be ready for him. At first he'd assumed that this readiness to satisfy him was a result of her immediate past, that she'd become so used to being a man's plaything that she could imagine no other role. He soon realised his mistake; in their conversations, in her desire to explain her life to him, it became clear that she was falling in love with him, and her actions were a physical manifestation of that love. And Rob suspected, though he'd never admitted to the emotion before, that he was falling in love with her.

Neither of them went so far as to express this feeling to the other. But Rob felt sure that if he suggested that she come away with him she would have no hesitation in agreeing to do so. He tried to tell himself that this was vanity on his part, but he had no wish to test Jinny by asking her if she loved him; he wasn't sure which answer he would fear most, yes or no.

He'd tried to persuade her to accompany her father and the other musicians that evening, and she'd gone so far as to agree to come down to the manor, to secrete herself outside one of the windows and watch the excitement. But his suggestion that she should make her presence known, that she should perhaps dance with him in a demonstration, was met with a plain refusal. She wouldn't be welcome, she said. And so Rob lay in the afternoon heat, dressed only in his soft cotton breeches, windows open wide, his hands behind his head, and wished that he were on the high moors with Jinny.

Jinny Lee was packing and unpacking her bag for the third time. She had little in the way of clothes and even fewer possessions. Two skirts and a dress, two shifts, a blouse, two pairs of long woollen stockings (all clean, though worn and patched), a woollen smock, an old coat, a pair of leather shoes too small for her and boots too large; that was the total sum of her apparel. She held and then put away a crucifix which had once belonged to her mother, kept more for comfort than devotion, and a twisted crown of dried grass and flowers, now far too small for her head. There was a bible, which she could read only slowly and without comprehension, and a small wooden box, no more than an inch square. She opened this gently. Inside was a ring, a simple band of gold. She took it out and placed it on her finger, the ring finger of her left hand, and stared at it for a while, turning her hand to and fro so that the dull yellow metal caught the light. Then, with a wry smile, she removed it, put it back in the box, and put the box away.

There was only one more item, a small knife, its blade hidden in a scuffed leather sheath. Its hilt was cast from brass and wrapped round with a wire of some other more malleable metal. It wasn't attractive. There was no doubt that ceremony had never been part of its role, but when she pulled the blade out its sharp edge glinted. It had been ground flat and true, and Jinny smiled as she raised it to her lips and kissed it gently.

'On Sunday,' she said, running her fingers up and down the flat of the blade, 'you just wait till Sunday, then you'll have your reward. You'll taste blood then, oh yes you will. After the dance when he's had too much to drink, you'll have him then. A strike under the ribs, into the heart, that's all the revenge we need. And then away, away with Robbie. We'll do it, oh yes we will, we'll do it this time. He'll pay, he will. He'll pay with his life.'

The knife was put away, wrapped in her clothes. The bag itself was made of leather but had no handle. A length of rope held it closed and acted as a strap so that it could be slung over her shoulder. She tied the rope and put the bag under the blanket, then stepped outside the bothy door.

It was mid afternoon. The clear air of the previous few days had been replaced with a heavy, leaden atmosphere. The hills were shimmering ghosts, bleached of colour and shape. Jinny lifted her hands to her eyes and surveyed the land around her, turning to absorb each viewpoint as if it were the last time she would gaze on the moors and hills, the distant forests and hidden marshes. It was here she felt at home, not in the hovel she shared with her father, and until recently it was here and only here that she felt happy. But now she was leaving, and she suspected she would never return. The decision to leave had come easily – there was little to make her stay – but she still didn't know where she would be going. Hexham was the immediate destination. She could cope with that, Hexham was manageable; it was near enough for her to imagine the miles and the scenery between them. But she wasn't sure her journey would end there. She could find a job, she was sure of that, she could probably take care of herself. After all, hadn't she been doing that, to a certain extent, for most of her life? But . . .

She sighed. She knew how easy it would be to turn to the life and the trade she'd already come to know. Her body had been used by men in the past and she was aware they found her attractive. It would require little effort for her to earn more money as a prostitute than she ever could as a seamstress in a glover's sweatshop or a felter in a hat factory. It was something she feared. She'd been told so often that she was good for nothing but pleasuring men that she was almost ready to believe it herself. Almost, but not quite. She had another vision, a more dangerous vision, one in which she rose to respectability, where men paid her compliments for her beauty and her taste in dresses, her style and grace, her poise, her dancing. She laughed out loud. Her dancing! The last time she'd danced both she and her partner had been naked, and they'd honoured each other at the end of the dance with a degree of intimacy reserved for the bedroom, not the ballroom. She knew how to behave in the former, but not the latter. She could act the part of courtesan, strumpet, lover even; she could gasp and groan when required, she could shudder and shake and toss her hair about in a manner most convincing, she could coax and compliment her partner and make him believe that her need for him was as great as his for her. But she didn't know how to be a lady. She didn't know how to conduct herself in private, let alone in public. Her morals belonged to the bawdyhouse. She contemplated this while walking up to the standing stones.

She'd confessed her background to Rob and he hadn't cared. For this alone she was grateful; she felt she deserved far less from him than understanding. And he'd admired her, that had been the very word, for more than her skills in bed, for more than her body. Yes, they'd been part of the attraction – it would have been foolish of her to consider that it would ever be otherwise – but he'd talked to her and listened to her, and that would have been enough for her. But more than that, he'd encouraged her. He'd asked her advice on dancing when he already knew so much about it, he'd agreed she ought to leave the valley, he'd given physical help when she needed it and supported her with other than blandishments. He'd offered to take her with him to Hexham, to pay her for the dance instruction. No man she'd known in the past had ever wanted to give her so much.

Once before she'd thought she was in love, and the object of her affection had sworn he was in love with her. He'd lied; she would have her revenge, and that would be the matter dealt with. But Rob, he confused her. He hadn't said he loved her, although she suspected it might be the case. Neither had she confessed the depth of her feelings for him, partly because she wasn't sure of those feelings, but also because she didn't want to drive him away from her. She suspected he wasn't ready for any commitment, not while his mind was occupied with the grand deception he was carrying out. But once it was over, once they left together, once they got to Hexham, what would happen then?

Jinny decided that the question was best, for the moment at least, left unanswered. She walked the circle of stones, touching each, saying her goodbyes. She knelt in the shadow of the tallest and absent-mindedly plucked wild cotton from the small tussock before her, singing as she did so – a song without words, sad with lost dreams of the past and the future. Then she made her way down the hill. Rob had asked her to meet him after the dancing, the dancing at which her father would be playing, and she pictured Rob's eager, smiling face and silly, awkward grin, and realised with a strange thrill in the pit of her stomach that she was looking forward to seeing him, looking forward to the night.

Rob had asked the dancers to assemble at eight o'clock, hoping that the heat of the day would have diminished by then, knowing that their labours would have made them tired, that they would probably arrive late. That gave him time to organise the musicians. He'd told them to come early and he waited for them, Jacob Lee and seven others, in the garden. He recognised one or two of them, was formally introduced to them all: Sammy Devlin and Col Butterworth, both slightly older than him, eager to shake his hand and engage him in conversation, fiddles clutched in their hands; Jamie Charlton and his son Charlie, the first on flute, second on pipes, variations on the same theme of deep-browed reticence; Sally McIntyre, a wide, blowsy woman with a broad, toothless grin and a viola (her husband, Geordie, a thin, ferret-faced man, had come along to watch, he said, and to be there 'just in case'); and another piper, Susan Blamire, a shy young woman with a stoop, who wouldn't look Rob in the eye. He welcomed them all, then explained how the evening would progress.

'I want it to be a surprise,' he said, looking at Jacob Lee, 'so I'll—'

'I've told them,' said Jacob. 'They know old man Taylor's feelin's about me, and mine about him. They don't reckon there's much chance of carryin' this off, but they're willin' to try.' He paused, then went on. 'For my sake.'

Rob shrugged. 'You're here, that's more important than why you came. Follow me. I'll show you where you'll be playing.'

'What exactly will we be playin', Mr Patterson?' asked Sally McIntyre, her small, thin voice sitting uneasily on such a large frame. 'I mean, we don't read music, leastways I don't. Charlie can a little, and Jacob, or so I believe, but not me. I can play the tunes I know well enough, but I'm not so good on the new ones, though Susan's got a good ear. Whistle her something once and—'

'Sally, be quiet,' said Jacob Lee firmly.

'Oh, beggin' your pardon, sir, sorry for existin',' she retaliated and continued to mouth at him behind his back.

'You just need to play the tunes you know,' Rob explained. 'They'll be for familiar dances, "Morpeth Rant", "La Russe", "Corn Rigs", "The Square Eight", others such as that. And Harry Brown, you know him I believe, he'll be there as well to give a hand. Don't worry about it.'

'It's not the music I'm worried about,' said Jacob, and his dour words and manner seemed to affect the others. Even the boisterous fiddlers reduced their chatter to an infrequent whisper.

'I'll tell you how I've got things arranged,' said Rob, keen to raise their spirits, 'so you'll know what's happening. There's a main door into the ballroom. That's how everyone else will get in. But at the far end there's some doors lead into the garden. That's where you'll be waiting.'

'They won't even let us start,' objected Jacob. 'As soon as they see me we'll be ordered out and that'll be it.'

'It won't,' said Rob. 'I've thought of that. There's some wooden fencing screens already in the ballroom. They're going to use them in the garden to hide the privie. I've set them up so you can play behind them. By the time they find out who you are they'll have realised how good you are as well. And, of course, it'll be too late to find any other musicians. So don't worry, just concentrate on playing your best. Play the way you did at the stones and you'll have them roaring and yelling for more, believe me.' Although they all nodded, Rob doubted that his words did much to counter Jacob's pessimism.

He led them through the gardens, keeping to the paths that would hide them from the house, moving ahead of them and shepherding them through the more exposed areas. They reached the doors to the ballroom without discovery, and Rob checked inside to make sure no one had arrived early. Finding the place empty, he showed the musicians inside, stood by the doors which led into the main body of the building and kept watch as they investigated the room. It was the first time, so far as he knew, they'd been inside the manor. Only Jacob Lee showed no overt signs of curiosity, but even he, Rob was pleased to see, glanced from the corner of his eye at the paintings of Rebecca and Annie Taylor.

Rob called the others to their places and arranged the screens, woven from branches and bark, around them. He hurried around the room to make sure they couldn't be seen and was eventually satisfied. Under Jacob's instruction they tuned up, played once through the Hexham Races to make sure all was well, then put down their instruments and went outside.

'I'll come and get you when I'm ready to start,' Rob explained. 'I'm not sure what'll happen after that. I don't know how long the Taylors will be able to hold back their curiosity. And when the screens are eventually taken away, well, I can't imagine what'll happen. We'll play it by ear.'

'What about the tunes?' asked Susan Blamire quietly. 'Who'll tell us what to play?'

'Mr Patterson'll call out the name of the dance, lass,' Jacob Lee explained, 'and I'll tell you the name of the tune. Just play as you normally would. Take the rhythm from me. We'll keep playin' till Mr Patterson shouts to stop. After all, he's in charge. Isn't that right, Mr Patterson?'

'Whatever you say, Mr Lee,' Rob answered, annoyed by the old man's tone. It was as if he was determined that the venture should fail, just to prove he'd been right.

From round the corner there came the sound of running feet. The musicians faded into the shrubbery as Harry Brown hurried into view. Rob ushered them out again. Harry had met everyone except Susan Blamire at one or another of the local inns where they gathered to play. He was greeted by them as an equal, one capable of joining them without the need for lengthy preparation or instruction. Rob left them to talk amongst themselves, warning them to stay hidden, then went back into the ballroom to await his pupils.

They arrived in ones and twos, obviously tired from the day's exertions but looking forward to expending energy in a more entertaining manner. There were smiles and laughter as distant relatives were greeted, old friends hugged or slapped on the back, memories embellished and exchanged. Rob began to think that it hadn't been a particularly good idea to have a practice on this night. Surely people wouldn't want to dance; they'd be more interested in talking. His worries were dispelled as he was introduced to the strangers in the room, all of whom said how much they'd been looking forward to the evening. Even if half of this was mere politeness it still boded well for him.

The arrival of Samuel, Annie and Rebecca Taylor meant that the company was complete, and Rob clapped his hands loudly to attract their attention.

'Ladies and gentlemen,' he declared loudly, 'my name is David Patterson. And I am a dancing master.' The words sounded good to him. He felt sorry it wasn't his real name he was using but, he told himself, there would be time enough in future days. 'For the last two weeks,' he continued, 'it's been my pleasure, my privilege, to have been a guest of Mr and Mrs Taylor and to have tried, as much as my ability would allow me, to teach them, their friends, neighbours and family, some new dances in the English style. These dances are to be performed and, I hope, enjoyed on Sunday at Miss Annie Taylor's wedding.' There was a muted whisper of approval. Heads turned this way and that to search for the blushing Annie and, finding her, nodded their approval of her maidenly beauty, her elegant charm.

'But we're gathered here tonight so that those of you who haven't yet had the benefit of instruction may find out a little of what we've been doing. To that extent it would be helpful if those who know the dances select their partners from those who've recently arrived. To begin with we'll try a straightforward dance, "The Cumberland Long Eight", and we need sets of four couples in the longways fashion, up and down the room, each person facing his or her partner.'

Rob wasn't quite sure how he should think of them; students, audience, customers – they were a mix of all of these. While they formed themselves into the desired sets he hurried out, beyond the screens, and whistled for the musicians to make themselves shown.

'It's "The Long Eight",' he said. 'When I've finished instructing them Harry can start playing by himself for, let's say, sixty-four bars, twice through the dance. Then, without Harry stopping, the rest of you come in. Agreed?'

'Jigs or reels?' asked Jacob, his voice surly. 'You can do it to either.'

'Jigs, I think,' Rob answered. 'Now come in quietly, when I'm talking them through. I'm not sure when I'll make you known, but let me do the talking, the persuading. Samuel Taylor won't be an easy man to bargain with.'

'Don't I know it,' muttered Jacob, fixing his pipes together, but Rob didn't hear; he was back in the ballroom.

'Does everyone have the required number?' he shouted. There were murmurs of assent.

'Good. Now then, if I explain something you already know, please have patience. There'll be others who haven't yet risen to your position of grace.' There was a polite communal smile at his comment, and Rob smiled back. Everything would work out well, he told himself; all would be just as he planned.

'This, then, is how we do the dance. Couple number one in each set, the couple nearest to me, should cast. The lady turns out to the right, the man to the left, and each dances to the bottom of the set, followed by the others, lady following lady, man following man. Good. That's very good, yes, you may skip the step, like Daniel and Charlotte. Then, first couple, link hands with your partner at the bottom of the set and promenade back up to the top; everyone follow. Excellent!

'When you get back to your places, don't stop. Just cast to the left *as a couple*. Once again, all follow, go down to the bottom and lead up to your places. The top two couples then right and left hands across, bottom two couples the same, that takes eight bars of music, eight steps in each direction. Then first couple swings down to the bottom of the set, and that's it! We start again with a new first couple each time, do the dance eight times through, each pair gets to be first couple twice. Come back to your original position and we'll start with a chord from young Harry Brown. He's rather shy so he's going to play from behind these screens, isn't that right, Harry?'

'Yes, Mr Patterson.' The bodiless voice brought a ripple of laughter.

'Very well, then, off we go for "The Cumberland Long Eight"!'

Rob continued to bellow the figures over Harry's violin, and it was clear that the dancers who already knew the figures were helping those who didn't. They all found it difficult to keep in time, not because Harry's rhythm varied but because they couldn't hear him clearly over the noise of their own skipping feet. Samuel Taylor beckoned to Rob as the first couple in his set began their journey to the bottom.

'Where are these musicians you promised, then?' he gasped, already out of breath, 'This won't do for Sunday, will it?'

He was urged away by his wife's push as the dance wound round to another cast. Rob skipped alongside him.

'I gave my word, Mr Taylor,' he said, 'and I'm as good as my word. You just wait and see. You just wait and hear.'

'I'm waiting, Mr Patterson, I'm . . . Ahh! Rebecca!' This time his wife pulled him towards her, flashed a smile of sympathy at Rob, then cast again, holding firmly on to her perspiring husband. Rob moved away, surveyed the other sets. Twelve of them, that was ninety-six dancers,

and they were all performing reasonably well. Then there
were at least two dozen still sitting round the perimeter of
the room, and on Sunday there would be double that number,
say two hundred and fifty altogether? That would be a good
number; a good number to have under his control, a good
number to have doing just as he wished. He watched all of
the first couples swing down to the bottom and waited.

There was an almost imperceptible pause, like an intake
of breath, then Jacob and the other musicians joined in. It
was the same melody but in a different key, a tone higher,
much louder, and there was a drive, an enthusiasm that lifted
most of the dancers and caused them to roar their approval.
There'd been no increase in tempo, but everyone seemed to
be moving faster while keeping in time with the music. Each
skip was higher, each swing wilder, each smile broader. Rob
couldn't hold back his own grin. There was no doubt the
dancers approved of the music. Samuel Taylor was nodding
at him, clapped his hands together three or four times to
show his accord.

'Mr Patterson!' It was one of the spectators, Parson
Westborne, his wife on his arm, moving rapidly down the
room towards him.

'Mr Patterson, I owe you an apology. It was most remiss
of me to cease attending your music classes, but I *did* despair
of playing the tunes properly, and I know I ought to have
explained the matter to you – Mary said you would have
understood – but the others felt the same and . . . Anyway,
none of us could have done as well as the musicians you've
found for us, so perhaps it was God's will I behaved as I
did! But who are these angels who play so sweetly? I must
see them.'

Rob held out his arms. 'All will be revealed, Mr Westborne,
in time, I promise. But please, the dance is drawing to a close.
I think you ought to join in with the next, I feel you'll enjoy
it.' He ushered the parson away only to be accosted by others
who complimented him on his success in finding such talented
musicians and asked why they played behind screens. Rob

fended off their queries politely and, as the dance came to a close, positioned himself at the bottom of the hall so no one would be able to pass to satisfy his or her curiosity. Sure enough, Samuel Taylor was the first to bear down on him.

'David, Mr Patterson, that was magnificent!' His face was red and leaking, he was dabbing at it with a large handkerchief. His wife, more sedate, followed behind.

'Yes, Mr Patterson, Samuel and I are in total agreement about that.' She pronounced the statement as if the couple's total agreement was an infrequent occurrence.

'I must thank them,' continued Samuel Taylor, 'I must offer them my personal congratulations, though I know, of course, the effort you have put into this, David. Why are they hiding? Are they shy? Disfigured?'

'They want you to appreciate their music above all else, Mr Taylor, but I will introduce you, I promise. But now we're about to begin again with "Ninepins". You mentioned that this is your favourite dance, I'd hate to see you miss it.'

'Yes, dear,' Mrs Taylor added, taking her husband's arm. 'And you may be the pin, allowing me to rest a while. Come, you may escort me to my seat.' Rob swore she looked back at him and winked, but he could have been mistaken. He put the thought to one side and formed the sets for the next dance, squares of four couples plus an extra man in the middle of each set as the pin. The dance was as much a game as anything else. The couples had to gallop across the set and back in an attempt to bowl the pin over, and the dance culminated in all five men dancing in the middle of the set. The music would cease abruptly, usually in the middle of a phrase, and the men had to find a partner quickly. One was left to be the pin next time through the dance. Rob didn't like the dance much, it was inclined to become a brawl as men fought to gain a partner or the pin was knocked flying by a galloping couple. But it was undoubtedly popular, and as the music started he was pleased to see that the dancers had been paying enough attention to render his shouts unnecessary. Instead he was able to listen to the music.

He knew the musicians were playing from memory, not from music. No, that wasn't actually the case. They'd memorised the tune, that must have been true, but each was playing his or her own variation. Some kept close to the melody line, others took it in turns to spin away in sweet harmonies or complex arpeggios, but the fiddles always drove on with a relentless rhythm, and the pipes' haunting wails, their slight dissonance, added an air of melancholy. Sometimes they moved from one tune to another, always in a different key, always complementing that which had gone before and providing a lift to the dancers at a time when strength and spirits might be flagging. They needed no prompting from Rob about when to stop, and he could hear no instructions from Jacob on when to change tunes or start again. They were playing as one, sensing the others' feelings, and the dancers, no matter how inexperienced they might be, could recognise this.

The dance ended, but the final chord was drowned by the cheers and applause of the dancers. Now, Rob thought. Now was the time; there'd be no better. He held up his hands to hush the room.

'Ladies and gentlemen, allow me to introduce our musicians!' He knocked the screens to the ground, they fell with a theatrical crash and the applause began again, then died swiftly away. The guests who didn't recognise the musicians were silenced by those dancers who did. Rob looked around him. Samuel Taylor's face ought to have been red with the exertion of the dance he'd just performed, but all blood had been drained from it. It was pale and contorted, and its owner bore down on Rob like a leviathan, scattering flotsam before him. Those in his way moved quickly or were washed to one side; Rebecca Taylor, caught unaware, floundered in her husband's wake, pulled after him by the vacuum of his passing.

'Mr Patterson!' he bellowed. 'How dare you bring these people into my house! Remove them immediately!'

'Mr Taylor, please. Only a moment ago you—'

'I'll have no bandying words with you, Mr Patterson. Remove them, or by God I'll do it myself, and I won't be half as gentle as you might be!' He was in front of Rob now, breathing heavily, his face only inches from Rob's. His wife had caught up with him and was holding on to his sleeves, fearful that his anger might cause him to strike Rob.

'Samuel,' she whispered, 'everyone's watching you, calm down. I'm sure Mr Patterson meant no harm. We can talk about this privately, I'm sure we can resolve the matter—'

'Resolve be damned, woman, I want that man out of my house!' His trembling finger was levelled at Jacob Lee who stared back at him, an expression of sullen contempt on his face. He shrugged and looked at Rob. No words were needed; he'd said this would happen, he'd known it would happen, and it had happened. Rob tried again to intervene, spoke quickly but firmly to avoid being shouted down again.

'Mr Taylor, I assure you no harm was intended. You said only a moment ago that the music was excellent. I fail to see how the identity of the musicians can alter those feelings.'

'Mr Patterson, this man is a troublemaker, a malcontent, a source of dissatisfaction amongst his fellow workers. And the others, they're as bad as him, I can tell by the look of them. You had no right to bring them here and ... and you knew it! You did, that's why you had them hidden. You set out to deceive me, admit it Mr Patterson! You're as bad as they are, I've a good mind to set you packing as well!' Jacob and his companions were silently gathering their instruments together, making ready to leave. It was Rebecca Taylor who, unexpectedly, motioned to them to sit down again.

'Samuel dear,' she said, 'you're behaving badly, and everyone can see you're behaving badly. Please, calm down.'

'Father?' It was Annie who spoke, who had hurried up to join them. 'Did I hear you right? Did I hear you threaten to send Mr Patterson away?'

'I did. He set out to deceive me.'

'He set out to help you as well, surely you can see

that? Didn't you enjoy the music? Didn't you enjoy the dancing?'

'Yes! That just makes it worse!'

'Why? I'm sorry, I don't understand.'

Samuel Taylor balled his fists and raised his tight-shut eyes to heaven. 'Lord preserve me from dancing masters,' he muttered, 'from worthless musicians and from women, both wives and daughters.' He opened his eyes and stared in turn at each of his tormentors, but saved his family for last. 'Has a man no say in his own house?' he demanded. 'I've requested that these musicians leave, yet they're still here. Must I do more than raise my voice?'

'You should not even do that,' Rebecca Taylor said, 'if you wish to retain the goodwill of those around you, your friends, your neighbours,' she lowered her voice so that only he could hear, 'and your wife and daughter.'

There was silence, a silence no one dared interrupt. Frances and Harry Arnison moved to join the group, it was clear from their expressions that they hadn't heard all that had been said. They were closely followed by Daniel Taylor and Charlotte Stephenson, equally curious to find out what had happened. But no one spoke. They waited for Samuel Taylor to pass judgement. His breathing grew more easy, his muscles relaxed sufficiently for his wife to let go his sleeve. He swallowed and turned to the room.

'Ladies and gentlemen,' he said calmly, 'if you will excuse me, I wish to consult with my wife and children over a matter of some importance which, as I'm sure you realise, has disturbed us a little. We shall repair to the garden, but in our absence, please avail yourselves of the refreshments which are available, and rest assured that we shall return quickly. I do apologise for these ... for these unforeseen events.' He turned back to his family. 'Let us go outside,' he said and led the way past the musicians, staring fixedly at Jacob Lee as he passed. The rest made as if to follow, but Rebecca Taylor halted them.

'I think that this would best be discussed by family only,'

she said. 'Harry, Charlotte, it would be of great assistance to us if you reassured our guests, spoke to them, calmed them. Annie, Frances, Daniel, please come with me.' She set off after her husband, then paused and looked back. 'Mr Patterson, this affects you considerably. I feel you ought to be present also. If you don't mind?'

'If you wish me to be there then I'll certainly do as I'm asked,' Rob replied, 'but I'm not sure Mr Taylor—'

'I shall take care of my husband, Mr Patterson. Please, come with us.'

Rob did as he was told, somewhat sheepishly. It was still warm outside, though the sun was hidden behind dark, threatening clouds and the western horizon was less than a memory. There was a distant rumble of thunder.

'Auspicious weather,' he heard Frances Arnison saying. The family was waiting for Rebecca Taylor to join them, and when Rob appeared behind her it was Frances who spoke again.

'Mr Patterson, my husband and my brother's ...' she searched for the right noun to describe the relationship Charlotte Stephenson might have with Daniel Taylor, but came up with nothing she felt appropriate, '... and my brother's friend, his close friend, have been excluded from this discussion. I hardly feel that your presence would be welcome.'

'I asked Mr Patterson to attend,' announced Rebecca Taylor, 'since his actions have provoked this outburst. Does anyone intend arguing with my decision?'

'It matters little to me,' said her husband, 'since I will not be gainsaid in this matter, and I care little who hears that opinion. I will not have that man Lee play at my daughter's wedding.'

'Why not, my dear?' Rebecca's tone was gentle, solicitous. It took Samuel by surprise.

'I beg your pardon?'

'Why will you not have Jacob Lee play at Annie's wedding?'

'Because . . . You already know why, I've said it before. The man's a scoundrel!'

'Please, Samuel, there's no need to raise your voice. If you feel that Mr Lee is such a bad character then there is no alternative, he shan't play.' Rebecca turned to Rob. 'Will the other musicians play if Mr Lee isn't there, Mr Patterson?'

'I don't think so, Mrs Taylor. He's their leader, both in music and, it would seem, in the community. I doubt they'd play without him.'

'And do you know of any other musicians able to play for these dances?'

'No, Mrs Taylor. The parson and his wife; Dr Allard; the miller; they've all said they don't really want to play, and the tunes are too difficult for them to learn even if they were pressed into playing.'

'I see. So who would we have left?'

'Harry Brown. I could assist, I suppose, though my whistle will add little to the quality or the volume. And I don't feel Harry would want to carry the whole evening by himself.'

'Thank you, Mr Patterson.' She turned back to her husband. 'We appear to have little choice in the matter, Samuel. There is no alternative.'

'We could cancel the wedding.'

Annie Taylor was even faster than her mother in her objections. 'Father, how could you suggest such a thing? After all the preparations, people will think there's some other reason. They'll wonder what it is; there'll be speculation, there'll be talk. No, I won't have it!'

Frances Arnison was determined to have her say. 'We could cancel the dance,' she suggested. 'Since it's Mr Patterson who's at fault here why should he not be the one to suffer? We should send him away without payment, immediately.' She stared triumphantly at Rob. Her smile showed that she felt the logic of her argument was inescapable.

'Just a minute,' interrupted Danny, 'why should David be held at fault here? How could he know that Jacob Lee and Father didn't get on? He was just trying to help, to get the best possible music and dancing for Annie's wedding. I say it would be a good time for forgetting the past, whatever the cause of any falling out, and thinking about the future. You know the men are restless, Father, all our tenants tell us so. It would be a good gesture on our part to let them join us on this occasion. Don't you think so?'

'No, I do not.'

Rob was amazed at Danny Taylor's eloquence. It wasn't just the words that were surprising, but the thoughts behind them. They appeared to show Danny in a far better light than Rob would have thought possible. And then he caught a glimpse of Danny's raised eyebrow, aimed at his mother, and Rebecca Taylor's nod of approval, of appreciation. In that moment it became clear that though the voice was Daniel's, the words and thoughts were his mother's.

'Perhaps, my dear, you'd care to explain exactly why you dislike Mr Lee so?'

Samuel Taylor looked at his wife with horror. 'I will not!' he said swiftly.

'Why is that, my dear?'

'You know the reason, Rebecca. I will not discuss this in public—'

'Then perhaps I will, Samuel, since it concerns the rest of us here.'

'Rebecca, I forbid you!'

'I'm not sure how you can prevent me, unless you gag me, unless you drag me away now. Are you prepared to do that?'

'Why, woman, why? It will do no good to air old grievances, especially before our children. I beg you, if you love me, say nothing.' Samuel Taylor's bluster had fallen away entirely. In its place was left an old man pleading for a boon he knew he was unlikely to receive. His wife went to him, put her arms around him, kissed him gently on the lips.

'It's because I love you that I have the strength to speak,' she said softly, 'though I know I ought to have spoken before now. Much wrong has been done, by both of us, and this may be the opportunity to put matters right. I *will* tell this tale, but the words would come more easily if you too agreed to its telling.'

'What difference does it make? You'll have your say regardless.'

'Regardless of the fact that I love you? Yes, that's true. And I'll still love you, as I've loved you from the day of our marriage. Nothing will change that.'

Samuel Taylor looked down at his wife. His eyes were moist, his nose red, though it was difficult to say whether this was through sorrow or self-pity or anger. He shook his head slowly from side to side like a baited bear, acknowledging that he could never win this argument.

'Speak on,' he said, 'speak on. And then I'll abide by your decision, Rebecca, and you too Frances, and Annie; Daniel too. But listen carefully to your mother's story, I urge you, and try to understand.'

Rebecca stepped forward.

'Do you wish me to leave?' asked Rob, unsure whether the words he was about to hear were for him as well.

'No, Mr Patterson.' Rebecca smiled at him. 'You're young; you may learn something. I hope you will all learn something. It's an old story but a true one, a story from my youth, and one I haven't told before. In those days I was an attractive girl, so I've been told, and had no shortage of suitors, though I was from yeoman stock. My father was ambitious, I suppose. He had the notion to marry me off to some rich gentleman, a landowner, perhaps, or a well-to-do merchant. But I was as strong-willed then as I am now, and I told him that *I* would choose my husband, not him, and that money would not necessarily count for a lot. Oh, he argued with me. He kept introducing me to men he thought would make good husbands, but I always said no. And I kept my eyes open. I suppose I flirted a lot, but some men presented themselves to me of their own accord, and some of them I liked.

'Two of them in particular. They were good friends, farmers' sons both of them. They took to seeking my company. I suppose I ended their friendship. What started as joking and fun-making ended as rivalry, as competition. I couldn't really choose between them, but they insisted. I was of a marrying age, and my father had two younger daughters waiting for me to marry first. So I chose; for right or wrong, I chose. The one I was to marry, he was in good enough spirits, but the other, he went away, disappeared, for nigh on seven months. But he came back again.

'He came back the week of the wedding. He had a woman with him, a common woman she was, and she was pregnant. Not long to go, I'd have said. They came to see me and my father. We were surprised. We noticed neither of them had a wedding ring, but we made them welcome. We offered to let them stay. The woman was tired; she didn't look too strong, and she retired. Then the man I was to marry came to call. He saw the other, his rival as was. He was shocked but after a while they started talking again and it seemed just like it used to be, all good friends. My intended got up to go. It was late, I remember that, my father was asleep in his chair. But the other said to wait, he had a wedding present for us. He went out, and came back in with the woman. She just said hello – nothing else, just hello. But she knew my intended, and he knew her. He didn't say anything at first, then he stood up and went over to his former friend and felled him. He dealt him such a blow I thought he'd never get up, but he did and he threw himself into the fight. My father woke up at the sound, it was as much as he could do to separate them. He had to call for help.'

'Mama, I'm confused,' said Annie. 'You haven't told us any names. I don't know which one hit the other.'

'Names are easy enough, child. One of the men was called Samuel. The other was called Jacob. The man I first chose to marry, that was Jacob. The other, your father, I rejected. He went away and found this woman; she was pregnant by Jacob. The two of them had gone into Hexham one market day and met her. She was a slip of a thing, your father had been too drunk to do anything, but Jacob had evidently had enough strength in him to get into her bed, to get her with child.'

'I'll finish the tale, Rebecca,' interrupted Samuel Taylor, 'as I ought. You were right, it does need telling, though it won't change my feelings.' He spoke softly, stared at each of his children in turn, sought their support. 'Your mother is still beautiful. I don't tell her often enough but she knows the way I feel. In the days of her youth she was even more beautiful. Jacob Lee, you've seen him tonight, he used to be my friend and my rival. It was him your mother said she'd marry. He could play the fiddle and sing; he could write her love songs. I could never do that. But I was steady, I was dependable, and I thought if Jacob was out of the way then your mother would be certain to choose me instead. So I found this girl. I intended bringing her back to tell what Jacob had done. But she told me she was with child, so I kept her, I cared for her, and then I brought her with me when it was too late to do anything about the bairn. The way Jacob went for me was enough, it was a sign of his guilt. If he'd gone down on his knees and begged forgiveness your mother might have listened to him. If he'd denied the child was his, your grandfather, bless his soul, would have believed him. But he didn't do either of those. He attacked me, and then he cursed me, and then he took the girl by the hand and he fled.

'I knew I'd done wrong, but I couldn't think of anything else to do. I loved your mother so much. I didn't think whether Jacob loved her or whether she loved him.'

'But what happened to him?' said Danny. 'You said he was a farmer's son. What happened to his land, his family?'

'What happened to the young girl? What happened to their child?' asked Annie.

'Do you want me to tell them?' asked Rebecca Taylor of her husband. He nodded, unable even to speak.

'Jacob Lee and his young woman disappeared. I was distraught, I cried, nothing would console me. But your father came to see me, to comfort me. He explained how much he loved me and why he felt he'd had to do what he did. He asked me to marry him, three times I said no, but the fourth time I said yes. Part of the rest you know. Your father's father did well, bought land cheaply and sold it dear, bought this place and left it to your father. We married and had children. It's been a good life together.'

'Then he came back to haunt me.'

'Let me finish, dearest. Jacob had been a good worker, his father's only son, and without him the farm fell into disrepair. Old Mr Lee took to drink and gambling. Eventually he sold the farm to your father and moved away. But then Jacob came back, oh, sixteen years ago. He had another woman with him. She was pregnant as well but she died in childbirth. Jacob managed to get a job with one of your father's tenants. He didn't do anything wrong, not that we knew of, but—'

'He was there, that was the thing. He was there.' Samuel Taylor's voice was black with anger. 'He'd be looking at me, looking at Rebecca, leaning on a fence and staring but not actually saying a word. One day I caught him playing with you, Annie, dandling you on his knee and singing to you as if you were his own child. I told him to leave you alone. I told him I never wanted to see him again. So he kept away, but still he was there. And he started agitating. He started making the other workers unsettled. He made them dissatisfied with their lot. It wasn't so's you could blame him for anything, but I knew it was him. And now he's in my house, and you, and you . . .' he looked at his wife and at Rob, then at his children, '. . . all of you, you want him to play at my daughter's wedding. Well I'm telling you, I'm not having it.'

If Rebecca Taylor had thought that telling the story would weaken her husband's resolve then she could have had no consolation from those last words. But still she remained calm.

'You said, Samuel, that the decision rested with the rest

of us. I must ask the children how they feel, having heard both of us. What do you think, Frances?'

'I think Papa was right. I think he loved you then as he loves you now, and we ought to send Mr Lee . . .' she turned to look at Rob, '. . . and Mr Patterson packing, since the last is, by his own confession, no use without the first.'

'And you, Danny?'

'I don't know, really. I don't know. How can I say? It's wrong to expect me to judge my own father . . .'

'I'll say, then,' said Annie. 'I'll say clear. I love you both, Mama and Papa, and I can see how much you must love each other. I can't say whether you did right or wrong, Papa, in bringing that girl back when you knew what would happen. I can't judge you on that. But I believe in forgiveness, and whatever Mr Lee did in the past, he's come along to play at my wedding, and that in itself shows a deal of courage, or stupidity, or whatever it was that made him come in the first place. I think you'd be more of a man than anyone could ever be if you were to go back in there and shake his hand and say forget what's happened, and ask him to stay, ask him to play. I won't go so far as to say you should ask his forgiveness because I'm not sure you've done anything which needs forgiving. But you were friends once. Why can't you be friends again?'

'I agree with my little sister,' said Danny straightaway. 'She said what I wanted to say but . . . but she always knows the words better than me. And it would make her happy on her wedding day as well, which is something we should . . .' He ground to a halt under his elder sister's baleful glare.

'That's three onto one,' said Annie. 'Me and Daniel and Mama on one side, Frances on the other. What do you think now, Papa?'

Samuel Taylor's immediate thoughts were never to be revealed.

'Just a moment,' said Rebecca Taylor, 'you've counted my vote before it's been cast.'

'But Mama, you said—'

'What I said and the way I vote might not be the same thing. I agree with you, Annie, that Mr Lee should be asked to stay . . .'

'Well then, we still win. Three to one, like I said.'

'Quiet child! But I vote against. I vote to have Jacob Lee leave.'

The silence was broken by a crackle of lightning and another boom of thunder, nearer now, and the sky gathered close to listen darkly.

'But Mother, why? That means two each, a tie. Now what happens?'

'Now? Now your father must decide. His vote is the casting vote. He must determine whether Mr Lee goes or stays.'

Samuel Taylor looked at his wife with horror, unable to comprehend why she was tormenting him in this way. She didn't need him to say as much; his eyes asked the question.

'Many years ago, Samuel, you made a decision which altered your life, and mine, and Jacob Lee's. You made that decision alone, without listening to anything anyone else said, without even talking about it beforehand. But this time you've heard what your children think, and you've heard what I think. The only thing I can add is that I believe you to be a good man, an honest man. At least you've always been so with me. Your dislike of Jacob Lee is prompted, in my opinion, more by your own guilt than by anything he's done to you or to your family. And if you feel jealous because of my affections for him, they're long gone, long forgotten. I'm not the young girl I was then; neither are you the same youth, nor Jacob. I love you as you are now, not as you were.'

Samuel Taylor reached out and took his wife's hands in his.

'Have I been foolish all these years?' he asked. 'Why didn't you tell me?'

'I tried, dearest one, I tried, but they were the wrong words at the wrong time. But now . . . Now the time is

right, and the right words may do more to help all of us
than they could ever have done in the past. You are a very
powerful man, my love. You have it in you to do much good
to many people, but you might also do much harm. You see
things differently from me, and it may be that in morals and
in actions we must agree to have our different viewpoints.
Because of that I will love you regardless of what you say
or do, though I may sometimes argue with you, as I have
today. The decision, however, is yours and yours alone.'

'Mr Taylor!' The shout came from the doorway, it was
Harry Arnison. 'Are you ready to return yet?'

'We're on our way, Harry,' Rebecca Taylor called back.
She took her husband's arm, kissed him on the cheek, then
turned his head with her hands so she was looking into his
eyes. She raised her eyebrows, and he nodded. It was as if
they were talking to each other without words.

Rob had largely played the part of silent witness. He
watched Rebecca and Samuel Taylor head slowly back to
the ballroom, their children linked in a trio behind, and felt
suddenly alone. He had no family, he had no real identity,
and within two days he would be returning to a life as . . .
He wasn't sure what. If all went well, if Samuel Taylor
allowed Jacob Lee to play at Annie's wedding, then Rob
would be paid. And then there was Jinny. What would he do
about her? He suspected that accompanying him to Hexham
would be only the first part of what she saw as a longer
journey, where the destination was less important than the
companion. He wasn't certain he was ready for that degree
of commitment. He set off after the Taylors, arriving at the
door to find that Samuel Taylor, his wife still by his side,
had hushed the crowd within. The musicians were gathered
to one side, eyeing everyone else with suspicion. They seemed
on the point of leaving, their instruments were packed away
as if they were sure of the outcome of the discussion. Jacob
Lee's glance fluttered from Samuel Taylor to his wife, then
to Rob standing at the door. Rob could do nothing but shrug,
then listen as Samuel Taylor began to speak.

'Ladies and gentlemen. Please accept my apologies for
this disruption. Some of you know the reasons for my
outburst, others will no doubt have questions to ask, and
I shall endeavour to answer them in due course. The crux
of the matter is that, a long time ago, I fell out with a good
friend. I'm not sure where the blame lies for this; I'm not
sure any of us will ever know. But this happy occasion,
when preparations for my daughter's wedding are close to
fruition, would not have been my own choice as a good time
to bring them out again. I'd thought them hidden; not gone,
but locked away. But I was mistaken.' His voice was low.
He faltered, his gaze wandered the room and rested often
on his wife.

'The friend who became an enemy is here tonight. His
name is Jacob Lee, and in recent years I've not mentioned
that name without a curse attached. I suspect the same may
be said of his talking of me. Some of you may have heard me
say before that I would not have him in my house. My wife
has spoken to me and asked me whether those are Christian
words, whether they're moral words, whether they're good
words for one man to say about another. I've listened to her.
She's talked of forgiveness. And yet ... And yet I can't find
it in me to forgive this man.'

There was a collective intake of breath. Even those who
knew nothing of the original argument were held by Samuel
Taylor's speech. Rob looked at Jacob Lee, he was shaking
his head. He turned and whispered to the musicians behind
him, signalled to them to gather their instruments together.
Rebecca Taylor squeezed her husband's arm. Annie's mouth
fell open, her sister's smile was one of triumph. Danny shook
his head wearily. Their father raised his hands to silence the
murmur which had grown to cloak them.

'How can I forgive a man,' he said gravely, 'who has done
me so little harm when compared to the grievous hurt I have
caused him? How can I condescend to bear his presence when
I should be asking whether he can bear to be in the same room
as me? I am the one who should be seeking forgiveness. I am

the one who should be accepting the laurel branch already proferred.' He turned to Jacob Lee.

'Jacob, will you play for my daughter's wedding? Will you take my hand in friendship once more?' He held out his hand, Rob could see it shaking. 'Will you forgive me?'

It began to rain, heavy, tearful drops which hissed and died on the cracked, baked soil. Lightning and thunder danced overhead in the dark sky, the long drapes of curtains danced in the sudden breeze which swept into the ballroom. It was as if heaven was weeping, though whether with joy or anger Rob couldn't tell.

The Fourteenth Bar of the Musick

Saturday, 26 June 1830

In which Rob learns that revenge is to be exacted upon him and must decide whether to flee or face the consequences.

'Tell me again what happened,' said Jinny, 'tell me what me da said.'

Rob sighed. She was like a little girl sometimes, dancing round him, her face filled with excitement, urging him to go on.

'I've told you twice already,' he said, shaking his head with amazement.

'Tell me again, then. Please?'

'Last time then. And that's it – no more.'

Jinny nodded her agreement.

'Alright then. Here we go. I thought your dad was going to take Mr Taylor's hand,' said Rob, 'but he didn't. I can't remember his exact words, but he looked at old man Taylor, and he looked at Mrs Taylor, then he said something like, "I won't take the hand of a man who's done me so much harm. I won't forgive someone who's an enemy," something like that. Everybody gasped. They thought they'd come to blows, I know I did, because your dad moved towards Samuel Taylor and I couldn't read his face at all.'

'I wish I'd been there.'

'But then he stood in front of him. He drew himself up, and he said in a loud voice, "But I'll take the hand of an old friend. And I'll forgive someone who thought he was doing right," and they shook hands and everybody cheered. Then we got back to the important things like playing and dancing.'

'Oh, Rob, you can't tell a story, can you? Where's the drama, the excitement? There must have been other things said, other things done.'

'There's enough drama and excitement in my life already without making any extra, Jinny. What happened, happened. What's more important is that your dad'll play at the wedding. Oh, there was something else as well. Mrs Taylor asked all the labourers and their families to come as well, to the dance. That includes you.'

'Really? That was kind of her.' For the first time her voice showed no sign of enthusiasm.

'And we'll be able to dance together.'

'No, Rob, we won't. I won't be goin'.'

'Why not? You'll be the only one not there.'

'That doesn't worry me.'

'But why won't you go?'

'You don't want to know.'

'I do. If I didn't want to know I wouldn't be asking, would I?'

'That's as may be, but if you *did* know, you'd probably wish you didn't.'

'I wouldn't.'

'You wouldn't what?'

'I wouldn't wish I didn't know. That is, I wouldn't be angry if you told me. I think.'

'You're talking nonsense, Rob Tweddle.'

'And you, Jinny Lee, are changing the subject. Look, I told you about me. I told you who I really was, why I came here,

I told you everything. But you're still hiding things from me, keeping secrets.'

'And what if I am? That's my business, isn't it? It's not as if we're married. It's not as if you're me husband.'

Rob stopped walking. It was early evening, they'd escaped together. Everyone else seemed caught up in some last-minute preparation for the wedding next day. For some reason they'd decided to go for a walk, though it had rained steadily through the previous night and halfway into the day. The clouds had still not retreated. There were pools of water lying in the ruts and cart tracks of the path they were following, but at least it had stopped raining, and the air was cool and fresh and clean. They'd talked about many things and covered at least three or four miles, and all of that time they'd enjoyed each other's company; at least Rob had, and Jinny had shown no sign that she felt any different. She'd been affectionate towards him, holding his arm, pressing herself close to him, kissing him and cuddling him, but suddenly, at the mention of her attending the dance, she'd cooled to him. And then there was that line she'd thrown, the one about being married. Had it been a baited line, well cast, in the hope that he'd rise and take it? She was, without doubt, an attractive lure. Or had it been a reaction to his pressing her for information, with no meaning behind it at all? He looked ahead of him, further up the track. Jinny was kicking at stones, it was clear she was waiting for him to catch up, waiting for him to say something. Rob was tempted, because she was expecting him to do this, to do the opposite, to turn round and head back to Bellingford, but even as the thought entered his mind he realised he wouldn't, couldn't do it; it would hurt her too much. He laughed out loud. Would he have felt the same way about anyone else? He'd been prepared to lie his way into Annie Taylor's bed but she wouldn't have him; he'd allowed Frances Arnison to use him as he'd hoped to use her sister, and then he'd ignored her; neither of them meant anything to him. But Jinny was different, that was why he couldn't bring himself to hurt her.

He cared for her. And yet he might have to hurt her if she was searching for something he was unable to give. He suspected she loved him; and he wasn't sure if he loved her.

The elements were undoubtedly on Jinny's side. It began to rain, a flurry of drops which set her dancing ahead to shelter under the branches of an oak, then a downpour which caused Rob to run after her. He was breathing heavily and was quite wet by the time he joined her in the cool, green shade. She'd settled with her back to the trunk, her knees drawn up to her chin. She was twisting a grass stalk in her fingers and watching the rain cascade from the outer leaves of the oak. There was space for Rob beside her. He sat down, not touching her, and waited.

'Shouldn't last long,' she said. 'The rain, that is. There's blue skies comin'.'

'Good,' Rob replied, 'I wouldn't want to get any wetter than I am already.'

There was another long silence. Small dots of insects shared their shelter, danced in front of them, and Jinny idly wafted them away with her grass stalk.

'Rob,' she said idly.

'I'm listening,' he answered, prepared to do exactly that. It was clear she was going to say something important.

'I don't want to be a burden on you.'

'You're not. Not at the moment, anyway. What makes you think you are?'

'Not are, Rob, might be. It was kind of you to do what you've done for me, in the last week, and I don't want you to think that . . . well, you shouldn't think that what followed was just me saying thank you. It wasn't; it isn't. I didn't go with you for payment. It was because I liked you.'

'I wouldn't have wanted it any other way, Jinny.'

'But I'm grateful as well, because you know what I've done in the past, and why I've done it, but you've still stayed with me.'

'Your past made you the person you are today, and I like

the person you are today. If your past had been different, you'd have been different.'

'You're good with words, Rob, you always seem to know the right thing to say. But you said you wanted to know why I wouldn't come to the dance, and the reason's in my past, and I'm worried that if I tell you it might change the way you feel about me.'

'And what way do you think I feel about you?'

She turned to look at him. He could feel her eyes on him, but he couldn't bring himself to return that look.

'I can't be certain, Rob. The way I feel about you depends on the way you feel about me.' She sat still, quiet; Rob knew it was his turn to speak.

'I don't know you,' he answered. 'I don't know you at all, not really, I just know about you, and even then not very much. I find you attractive, I like being with you, I feel . . . It may be wrong of me, but I feel sorry for you. And I'm confused, I don't know what to do.' What he wanted was for Jinny to come to him, to put her arms around him, to comfort him. He wanted her to tell him what he ought to do, what he ought to think, what he ought to feel. But there was no movement from her, not even the lightest touch. All she could give him was the sound of her voice.

'Last year,' she said, 'I had a baby.' It was his turn to look up, to seek out her eyes; and it was she who avoided his gaze, stared straight ahead of her.

'The father was an important man – not a farm worker, a gentleman. I told him as soon as I knew, and he gave me a little money, said I was to get rid of it. He wanted nothin' to do with it. But I loved him, at least I thought I did, and I wanted the child, and me da wanted the money I'd been given, so I didn't get rid of it. I carried it. I lived out at the bothy and the shepherds brought me food. No one else knew, no one in Bellingford at least. The baby was born in December last. A boy; a handsome lad. I called him Tom. In the new year he fell sick. It was bitter cold, so I wrapped him up and went down to see Dr Allard. He wouldn't come straightaway, he was eatin', having his dinner, and he made us wait for two hours in his hallway. There was no heat, no light. He looked at the baby, said he needed some medicine and could I pay. I had no money. He looked at me. He said, "I know who you are, I know what you are. You can pay me in kind." He made me do it with him, there and then, with me baby there in the same room. Then he gave me some medicine, said if I needed more I could pay in the same way.' She sniffed, but Rob could see no tears in her eyes. 'I didn't need any more medicine. The bairn died next day.'

'Jinny, I'm sorry . . .'

'I took him down to the church but the parson wouldn't bury him, he said he hadn't been baptised. He said the child was a bastard. He sent me away. I buried him myself up at the stone circle, it was the only place I could think of that was . . . that was holy enough. That was why I wouldn't have you up there. It would have been wrong.'

'Yes, Jinny, I can see now.' He put his arm round her shoulder and she leaned into him, and he could feel her body shaking.

'It's alright,' he said, 'don't cry.' He would have gone on, but he realised how stupid his words had been. 'No, hinny, you just cry away. There'll be times when you can't cry, or you won't cry, but now isn't one of them. Cry while you can, love, cry while you can.'

'I didn't want to tell you,' she sobbed, 'in case it turned you against me.'

'Now why would it do that? It hasn't altered my feelings at all.'

'I haven't finished yet, Rob. There's more.'

'More? How can there be more? You're only sixteen, lass. You haven't lived long enough to pack any more into your life.'

'It's not in the past; it hasn't happened yet. But it will, you'll see; it will. I'm goin' to kill him, Rob. I'm goin' to kill the man who murdered my baby, and I'm goin' to do it tomorrow, at the weddin'. He'll be there. He'll be at the dance, but if I make meself known to him he'll suspect me. I'm goin' to wait for him, wait till he's alone, then I'll get me knife – it's a small knife but it's sharp – and I'll cut his throat.'

Jinny's voice was quite calm. She appeared to be in control of herself, but her eyes held a strange fire which caused Rob to think carefully before speaking.

'Is that the right thing to do?' he asked. 'Does this man deserve to be killed? After all, he got you with child, but it was your decision to keep the baby. And the doctor, could he have done more? And what about Parson Westborne? Turning you away at a time of need wasn't a very Christian thing to do. Will you kill them as well for their part in this?'

'Rob, I'm sixteen years old. I'm a whore, I've already mothered a bastard, and some people might think that means I've not got much in the way of brains. But I can see things, I can understand things. I know the men you've mentioned could be blamed in some measure for me bairn's death. But then so could me da, and Mr Scrivener; any of the men I've taken to me bed who've made me the way I am. You too, Rob Tweddle, I could include you in me list. Men by their nature tend to take without thinkin' of givin', or they give you somethin' without value, or they give you somethin' you do want, like love, or babies, or a home, then they take it away. Perhaps it's men in general who are at fault. But I can draw a line. I can say that this man – and no, I won't tell you who he is; he might even be somebody I've already mentioned – this man has caused me more hurt than anyone else, more than all the rest put together. You see, he was the first man who ever told me he loved me, and I believed him. I was a fool, I know, and I wouldn't fall for the same trick again. But I swore I'd kill him. And I will. And nothing you can say'll stop me doing that!'

'You do it if you want, Jinny. Don't let me keep you from a dance with the gallows.'

'It won't come to that. I'll be gone by the time they discover him, and there'll be plenty others who could have done it. No one'll cry at *his* funeral.'

She seemed unconcerned at the enormity, the finality of her ambition. Rob shrugged. He didn't know what to say, what to do. He didn't even know if he was right to try to prevent her doing this, since he didn't know who the object of her revenge would be. He wondered what else might happen to confuse his life. At least it had stopped raining.

'Come on, Jinny. We need to talk, but it's getting late. We should be heading back now. Will you take my arm?'

She wasn't listening to him. She was staring along the track to the green hillside ahead, a hillside where white dots of sheep were scattering before an object creeping slowly down the slope towards them. As Rob followed her gaze he saw the amorphous shape become an animal. A large animal. A cow, perhaps, or a deer? No, it was a horse, but not a horse being ridden, a horse being led.

'We should be getting back, Jinny,' he said again. 'Jinny, it's just a horse and a rider, nothing more.'

'But he's walkin'. He should be able to ride down that field, it's not too steep. And it's late for someone to be out. Let's wait a while, he's sure to be comin' this way.'

She was right. The horse, a big, clumsy-looking bay, could soon be seen over the hedge, its progress remarkably slow. Presently the man leading it came into view as he rounded the curve into the lane. He slowed further as he neared the tree under which Rob and Jinny were waiting. It was obvious that his horse was lame or had cast a shoe.

'He's not a local lad,' whispered Jinny as he halted in front of them.

'Evenin', Sir, Miss,' he said, touching his hand to his brow. Jinny giggled; she wasn't used to such deference, but the rider was young, no more than ten or eleven. He was a gangling youth, ill dressed, his face wore a worried expression.

'Good evening, young man,' said Rob politely. 'Is there a problem with your beast?'

'Aye, she's cast a shoe, daft bugger, and me in a partic'lar hurry. But you might be able to help me, sir. I'm looking for a Mr Taylor's place, a Mr Samuel Taylor. Is it near here?'

'It might be, for a man on a horse. But it wouldn't be for a young lad with a lame mare, I fear. But tell me, what's the reason for your hurry?'

'I shouldn't really say, sir, but seein' as you're a gentleman who might point me in the right direction, I've a letter for this Mr Taylor, an urgent letter. It came by coach to Hexham earlier today with instructions to bring it straight out, so me dad sent me.'

'A wise man, trusting his best messenger with a difficult task.'

The boy couldn't help show his pride at the compliment, though Jinny had to turn her head away to stop herself laughing. Rob glared at her.

'It so happens that I'm returning to Mr Taylor's house at this very moment. I can take the letter with me if you wish. There's a smithy a further half-mile down this road. He'd be able to see to your mare and you might just be back home before midnight.'

The boy considered the offer. Rob could see that he didn't relish the journey ahead either way but that he would have preferred to be heading home.

'That's very kind of you, sir, but my instructions were to hand this direct to Mr Taylor. How far is it to his house?'

'Oh, a good six miles,' exaggerated Jinny. 'We'll be there before dark but we can walk faster than your horse. But Mr Taylor's son here, he can tell his father there's a messenger on the way, though I doubt he'll wait up half the night for you to arrive. He'll get your letter in the morning, I suppose.'

'You're Mr Taylor's son?' said the rider. 'I don't suppose it would matter . . .'

'Your instructions were to give the letter to Mr Taylor?' asked Jinny.

'Aye.'

'Well then, this *is* Mr Taylor. Come on, we'll show you where the smithy is.'

The three ambled slowly down the lane, Jinny dancing
impatiently to and fro, determined to have the boy hand
over his message. The blacksmith's forge was set back from
the road in a clump of trees, and Rob pointed it out to
the boy.

'We might see you in the morning,' he said. 'I'll warn my
father that urgent news is coming.'

'At a snail's pace,' added Jinny.

The boy felt inside his jacket, brought out a package and
looked at it.

'I don't suppose there's any harm—' he said.

'Of course there isn't,' said Jinny, snatching the letter away
from him. 'Now you get your poor mare seen to and off you
go. And tell your dad he shouldn't be sending lads as young
as you on such long journeys.'

The boy seemed pleased to have the responsibility taken
from him. 'I wouldn't normally come on an errand like this,'
he explained. 'Me dad has others he can turn to, but they
were already out and about carryin' news. I was the only
one left, and this damn beast the only one in the stables.'

'And what was this important news to be spread about
the countryside?' Rob asked.

'Oh, yes. Me dad said to mention that as well. The
king's dead.'

Rob and Jinny walked on, Jinny forcing the pace. She was
eager to be out of sight of the messenger boy so she could
open the letter.

'Interesting news, that,' said Rob.

'How do you know? We haven't opened it yet.'

'No, not that. I meant about the king dying.'

'What? Why should it be interestin' that Fat George
is dead? From what I've heard about him it's a miracle he hasn't gone earlier. What's more interestin' is this
letter.'

'Why's that?' asked Rob. 'That is, I went along with your
story, but I couldn't see why you were so concerned to get

hold of it. And what do you mean about opening it? It's not yours to open.'

'I know. And I'm not goin' to open it. But you are.'

'No I'm not. I couldn't open someone else's letter.'

'Oh, Rob, after all your other deceptions? What harm would it do?'

'I'm sorry, Jinny, but Mr Taylor deserves a little respect in my books. It's through him and his wife that there's a chance of a reconciliation with your father. The least we owe him is to respect the privacy of any private correspondence he receives.'

'Oh. I suppose you're right, then. We'd better just hand it over when we get back.'

'Yes, I believe we should. And anyway, we've some talking to do, you and me, about what you said before.'

'Interestin' writin' this, on the letter.'

'You're ignoring me, Jinny.'

'Scrawly writin', I can't read it too clearly. I can't read well at the best of times. Here, Rob, you read it, tell me what it says.'

Rob took the letter from Jinny's hands.

'It's addressed to Mr Samuel Taylor, Esquire, Bellingford. That's all. Now what you said before, don't you think—'

'No, the other side. Tell me what the other side says.'

'Jinny, really. You're behaving like a little girl. The other side says . . . Oh, dear Lord!'

'I didn't think he wrote letters. Angels, prophets, that's what he uses.'

'It says "Urgent: from James Playford, Dancing Master."'

'But you won't open it, will you Rob? It wouldn't be right.'

Rob was already tearing at the envelope, caring little that the seal would be broken.

'You knew!' he said angrily.

'I can read well enough to pick out the letters of a name, Rob. Come on, read it out. You're better'n me at that. Tell me what it says.'

Rob did as he was told. In the dying light he pinched his eyes at the familiar, inelegant script, it's letters wandering drunkenly this way and that across the page.

Dear Mr Taylor

Please forgive the haste with which I write, but the content of this letter is of great import. We, you and I, are the victims of a treacherous deception. The man you believe to be my son-in-law, David Patterson, is an imposter. His real name is Rob Tweddle and he was, until I was forced to dismiss him, in my employ as a common clerk. He was to arrange my son-in-law's visit to your home but has left me with the wrong dates. The real Mr Patterson is due to arrive next Monday, 28 June, by which time Tweddle would, no doubt, have left.

I urge you, do not pay this man, but detain him until my arrival. I expect to be with you on Sunday, 27 June and I shall bring with me my daughter and my son-in-law and a constable from Hexham. As well as deceiving both of us, Mr Tweddle has, I believe, taken money and books from me, and I suspect that he will have been making mischief of some type while staying with you. Beware, he is an evil, impious fellow who has a way with words and, so I am informed, with women.

I have discovered this terrible affair by means of letters sent to me by Mr Scrivener, and to your brother, Mr George Taylor, by his niece Mrs Arnison. Mr Taylor will accompany me on my journey. He is most keen to see this rascal Tweddle apprehended and jailed.

I am, as always, your humble servant,
James Playford

'Oh dear,' said Rob.

'Oh dear? Is that all you can say? And you an evil, impious fellow who has a way with words? And with women? No wonder I fell under your influence. How could I have escaped when I was faced with this magician and his charms.'

'Jinny, this is serious.'

Jinny stopped capering around and stood in front of Rob, preventing him from moving any further.

'No,' she said, 'this is serious.' She reached up and took him by the neck, bent his head down towards her and kissed him. It was a kiss which demanded no response but was more than a sign of friendship or affection. It was a kiss which told of understanding and asked for the same in return.

'We'll go back and get our things,' Rob said, 'then we can leave straightaway. We can take the dogcart if we're quiet. There'll be so many people about we could take the coach and four and it wouldn't be noticed in the confusion. Then we can go to Carlisle. I'm sure we'll be able to find work; travel down to Manchester, perhaps. But we'll need to move quickly.'

'Rob, you keep on sayin' "we". Is that you and me, together?'

'Well who else would I be talking about?'

'But what am I meant to do? Come with you as far as Hexham? No, you mentioned Carlisle, so it can't be that. Come with you till I'm no use to you any more, till I'm a hindrance? And what part do I play? Companion? Mistress?' She looked at him carefully, trying to see into his eyes. 'Or your wife, perhaps?'

'Does it matter?' said Rob, almost angrily, 'isn't it enough that I want you there?'

'It's enough that you haven't asked me if I want to be with you. You can't just assume somethin' like that. After all, I might be a common whore, but you're a thief, a criminal, an imposter. You're the one the constable's coming to arrest, you're the one who should be in jail. Have you considered that I might not want to come with you?'

'No,' answered Rob. 'No, I haven't. I listened to what you had to say before, about the way you feel about me being affected by the way I feel about you. And it came naturally, when I was thinking about leaving, that you'd be there too, that you'd come with me. I didn't think about it any other way. Look, Jinny, it might not be easy. We hardly know each other, but I *would* like you to come with me, to stay with me, to . . . to live with me.'

'Why, Rob?'

'Why?'

'Aye, it's a straightforward enough question. Why do you want me with you?'

'I've just told you.'

'No you haven't. You've told me it felt natural to think of me with you, whatever that means, but that's not a reason. Leastways, it's not the reason I need to hear.'

'What do you want to hear then?'

'Damnation, Rob, if I have to tell you that then it's not worth you sayin' it!'

She stamped her foot and tossed her hair, flounced away in a manner that would have been funny had both of them not been so intent on being serious.

'What do you want me to say, then? Do you want me to say I love you? Do you want me to ask you to marry me?'

'It isn't what I want that matters, it's what *you* want!'

'And you! What you want matters as well, doesn't it?'

They were shouting at each other as they marched down the road, Rob's longer legs allowing him to keep a more measured pace, Jinny's energy keeping her slightly ahead of him, sometimes speaking back at him over her shoulder.

'Just say what you mean, Rob, I can put up with whatever it is. I'm beginnin' to think that letter was wrong. Your way with words isn't up to much, and as for the way you treat women, well, you could do with some lessons in that direction.'

'And I suppose you're the one to teach me, eh? With all your experience, with knowing men so well, you could teach me a lot.'

'I could. I could teach you about sayin' what you think instead of wanderin' around the subject like a little girl scared of jumpin' across a stream. First you come close, then you back away. Then you take a run at it, but you stop just before the bank. Then you reach out to see if the water's cold, then you screw up your face, then you start bubblin' like a bairn. That's what you are, you're a little girl!'

'And you're just as bad, Jinny Lee. You're talking about me not saying what I mean, but you're just the same. If you're so bold, so fearless, so *forthright*, you tell me. You answer my question. Do *you* love *me*?'

She stopped in her tracks, and Rob bumped into her.

'Sorry,' he said.

'That's alright,' she answered, 'no harm done.' She looked up at him. 'And yes, I do love you.' She kept his gaze, refusing to let him go until he responded.

'Good,' came the reply eventually, 'I love you too.'

'I'm pleased.'

'That's it settled, then, we'll get our stuff and leave. We can get married in Carlisle.'

'No we can't.'

'What? Jinny, you said . . .'

'I said I loved you, and yes, I want to marry you, but I'm not leavin'. If you'd asked me before we saw that letter I might have agreed, I might have been away with you by now. You see, there was no certainty that the man, the one I said I'd kill, would be at the wedding. I thought he might be, I felt he ought to be, but I couldn't be certain. I hadn't seen him since before the baby was born. He didn't come round much anyway, just when he was visitin' his brother. But that letter confirmed it. I can't go with you, Rob, not yet. I've work to do tomorrow. I've sworn I'll have revenge on George William Frederick Taylor, and tomorrow's his day of reckonin'. The last day of his life.'

The Fifteenth Bar of the Musick

Sunday, 27 June 1830

In which Rob Tweddle admits the errors of his past, and the true dancing master triumphs over his false rival.

Nature had taken a hand in matters. The rain of the previous days had taken away the dry, dusty, dirty edge of the gardens and hedges and lawns. It had brightened the flowers, it had cleaned the manor house and the church, it had left the air sweet scented and clear. The distant hills had been burnished green and purple, the bees had been instructed to provide a gentle buzzing harmony to the skylarks' high melody, and hidden linnets crooned secret love songs from gorse bushes polished bright yellow for the day. Blackbirds and thrushes sang on every green spray as if they were being paid for their performance, with an extra gold sovereign for the best tunesmith. It was a day made for a wedding, a glorious wedding, and what nature couldn't provide man had been working to supply through day and night.

Young maidens had crept early from their beds to gather meadow flowers while the dew was still on them, and these had been taken to the church and arranged carefully at the end of every pew, around the font, through the nave and over the balcony. Long stalks of grass had been twisted and woven into rings and crowns and ribbons, garlanded with cornflowers and oxeye daisies, marigolds and foxgloves and honeysuckle, then hung and draped on every available surface. The air was warm and heavy with drowsy perfume, and as the girls worked they laughed and giggled and whispered to each other, and talked of young men, and blushed as their secret thoughts were loosed to career round the echoing, vaulted roof.

The objects of their desires, boys and men alike, were hurrying through their tasks on farms and in mills, feeding fowl and polishing tack, moving beasts from one field to another, dwelling on the excitement to come and the delights of dancing and drinking and eating, and enjoying female company. Some had been detailed to report to the manor and could be found in the ballroom. They cut branches of bright-green holly and twists of ivy to decorate the cloth hung from the ceiling, and the material spun and danced like windmill sails in the cool air. Trestle tables leaned against walls, piles of tablecloths were ready to be pressed into service, knives and forks and spoons had been begged and borrowed from every house in the village and from miles beyond.

Those with speaking parts in the day's proceedings, aware of their own importance, hid backstage. Their entrances were already planned and practised. Even the groom had arrived and was being polished and decorated by his colleagues. Annie Taylor was being bustled over by her mother and her sister and Charlotte Stephenson; Samuel Taylor was hiding in the library, pretending to be asleep but planning his long journey to Cornwall; he did want to see those choughs. Danny Taylor and Harry Arnison were checking, for the third time, that the coach and four would be ready, while the groom was cursing behind their backs and muttering about interference.

The cooked meats were being brought from the cold room, vegetables were rubbing shoulders with each other in pots of

boiling water, kegs of ale and bottles of wine marched up
from the cellars under the careful, rheumy eye of Andrew
the butler. All was going well; everything would be ready
on time. Nothing would be allowed to spoil the day.

In the stone and clay houses down by the river where Jacob
Lee and his musicians lived there was as much excitement as
in Bellingford itself. The clothes on display may not have been
as grand – there were undoubtedly more patched trousers and
altered hems as boys and girls grew into their siblings' castoffs
– but the smiles were as genuine, the faces were as clean, the
boots and shoes (where worn) were as polished. There was
a hubbub of noise and conversation as hair was brushed
and combed, ribbons tied, waistcoats fastened, watches
brought out from dusty chests. Cravats were knotted and
reknotted as unpractised fingers attempted to mimic what
they thought was fashion. Hats were taken out of old
wardrobes, examined, frowned over, then put away again.
There was a constant straggle of visitors to Jacob Lee's front
door, asking for advice on what to wear and how to wear
it, how to behave, what to say if they were approached by
the loftier guests. Jacob dealt with most of these enquiries by
nodding or shaking his head and grunting, but he displayed
little emotion. To those who came to thank him for allowing
them to be in the position of attending the wedding, however,
he effected a smile and a look of disdain as if to acknowledge
their thanks but imply that the privilege was not as great as
they believed. But for the first time since he returned to the
valley so many years ago there was an air of happiness, of
content, of common purpose. He'd felt it the very same day
he'd shaken hands with Samuel Taylor. He'd looked at the
dancers and then turned to look at his musicians and realised
that most of them had never known what it used to be like,
when labourer and tenant farmer, farmer and landowner,
landowner and squire and gentry had all acknowledged each
other's part in the great plan of things. It was too early to
be certain, but perhaps talking to one another again might
help. Perhaps together they might change things.

He was aware that David Patterson was responsible for this in a small way, and he assumed that his daughter was away with him somewhere. He wasn't upset at this. She was too much of a handful for him; too strong-willed, too much of an embarrassment. He'd always preferred life as a loner, and if she was to go off with Patterson, well, good luck to her. They could sort out the problem of Mrs Patterson between them.

There were others who didn't know where the dancing master had got to. Frances Arnison had spent a few moments looking for him, if only to ensure that he was about so she would be able to gloat over his coming downfall, for she was sure that her uncle would find some way of bringing it about. She wasn't worried when he wasn't in his room, or when questions to servants and family brought the response that he hadn't been seen that day. Everyone was too busy to worry about him. He'd always appeared when he was meant to appear, why should matters change now? Perhaps he was coaching his musicians. Had she been a little more diligent in her enquiries she might have discovered from the chambermaid that his bed hadn't been slept in the previous night and that his clothes and flute and music had all been taken away. But she didn't ask the question direct, and the chambermaid was unwilling to volunteer information. The dancing master's disappearance went unnoticed.

The wedding itself went as expected, promptly at two in the afternoon. There was insufficient room in the church for everyone, but the labourers were happy to wait outside and comment on the poor quality of the hymn playing (the musicians were being led by Dr Allard) and the lack of feeling and harmonies in the singing. They joined in the prayers when they could hear them, they smoked and chatted, and their children played amongst the gravestones. They all cheered dutifully when the bride appeared and they said how beautiful she was. When she threw away her posy of flowers, Charlotte Stephenson blushed to catch them, and Danny Taylor's face was decked with smiles as he watched her.

The bride and the groom played their parts according to
the script. She was both happy and modest; she smiled yet cast
down her eyes when custom required her to do so. She held
her husband's arm and gazed at him with pride, she dusted
his shoulders when his frown showed that those scattering,
fragrant petals had been over-energetic in their enthusiasm.
She looked into his eyes and stroked his dark, red hair. She
was a dutiful wife.

He had no need to act; tall, handsome, confident. Few
of those watching knew him well, but he smiled to show
bright teeth and he won affection by bowing deeply, even to
the most unattractive women. Some giggled, some blushed,
some curtseyed, and some nodded to show that they had
identified a ladies' man. He slapped his male friends on the
back and laughed heartily, and his handshake to strangers
was as firm as his chin, as direct as his gaze. He looked
down on his wife with the air of a man who has bought a
substantial country property or negotiated an advantageous
business deal. And even the most cynical of observers would
have believed his eyes to have held nothing but love.

Everyone followed in procession as they headed from the
church to the manor, and Jacob Lee and his musicians
provided lilting tunes to accompany them. It was almost
impossible to walk out of step and common for the younger
folk to start jigging or ranting figures from dances they knew.
One or two looked around to see where Mr Patterson was,
surprised they hadn't seen him at the service, more surprised
to find he wasn't with his musicians. He'll be preparing his
dances, they said to one another. After all, the church service
is all written down, there's not much can go wrong with that.
But the dance, that was entirely in the hands of one man,
and the day's success would be measured by the enjoyment
people gained from the night's entertainment.

The seating arrangements were not too complex. The
wedding party sat at the top table; the rest fought for their
places. There was little argument. The majority selected a
seat by rank, only Jacob Lee sat proudly out of place close

to the bride's parents, and even Samuel Taylor grudgingly acknowledged his right to be there. The food was served promptly and enjoyed fully, and there was no difference between what the highest and the lowest were offered to eat. At the end of the meal Annie Taylor whispered to her father that she could see no sign of David Patterson. Her sister mentioned that she'd looked for him earlier that day but found no sign of him. Danny Taylor was extracted from the company of Charlotte Stephenson and sent on his way to find the lost dancing master and return with him or with news of his whereabouts. He came back half an hour later with neither.

There was still no panic. Toasts had to be made and replied to, the tables had to be cleared away, space had to be found for the musicians and, more importantly, for the dozen casks of ale. Work on this began while the guests took their ease on the lawns. Couples, fortified by generous servings of wine and the sweet scent of love which lingered in the air, sought quiet, shady spots to indulge in private recreation. Emanuel Scrivener and Frances Arnison found themselves keeping one another company by the gate in front of which passed the road to Hexham.

'Mrs Arnison, how pleasant to see you.'

'And you, Mr Scrivener. I trust you've enjoyed the day.'

'I have indeed. I'm sorry I wasn't able to speak to you earlier, but I know how busy you've been, helping your sister and your parents. It will be quite pleasant for you once the day is finally over.'

'Yes, it has been a tiring fortnight. But I shall stay a day or two longer, just to help tidy up, see things through. And, of course, there is still the evening's entertainment to look forward to.'

'So I believe. I must admit that I've been anticipating this with relish for one or two days now, but I haven't seen Mr Patterson about.'

'No, he seems to have vanished. No one has seen him for quite some time. Such a pity.'

'Yes.' They were quiet, each caught up in their own thoughts.

'Forgive me, Mrs Arnison, your eyes are so much younger than mine. Am I mistaken or do I see a carriage coming down the road?'

'Mr Scrivener, your eyes must be very good indeed. There is a carriage, travelling uncommon quick as well, by the look of it. How strange that we should both be here to witness it, as if we were expecting someone to arrive. Who do you think it might be, travelling at such a rate?'

'I'm sure I have no idea, Mrs Arnison. Do you have any thoughts on the matter?'

Frances Arnison's reply, if there was one, was lost in the clatter of wheels and hooves as the coach slewed to a halt in front of them. They raised their hands to their eyes and mouths to protect themselves from the dust it brought with it. The driver, his head hidden in a scarf, leapt from his seat and opened the door nearest to the spectators.

'Damned uncomfortable ride,' said a voice harshly.

'You did say you were in a hurry,' countered the driver.

'Don't answer back,' continued the voice, 'not if you want to be paid! Damn dust. Can't see a damn thing!'

Frances Arnison stepped forward to greet a shadowy figure.

'Uncle George,' she said, 'how pleasant to see you again, and in such good temper.'

The dust settled slowly, and a tall figure stalked the dying billows.

'Frances!' exclaimed George Taylor, moving forward, his arms outstretched to hug his niece. 'Your father received the letter then. I suppose he's too busy to greet me himself.' He drew Frances close to him, kissed her cheek, held her slightly too close and too long; she didn't struggle to escape. She saw Emanuel Scrivener looking across at them, curiosity in his eyes. She motioned him closer.

'Mr Scrivener, you've met my uncle before, I believe.'

'I have indeed, Mrs Arnison. Mr Taylor, sir, it is good to see you again.'

'Mr Scrivener, I'm delighted to meet you once more, and I must thank you for your correspondence. It is that which, together with Frances's note, brought me to ...' He halted, puzzled by the strange looks on the others' faces.

'You wrote to my uncle?' Frances Arnison asked the poet.

'No, I did no such thing,' replied an equally perplexed Emanuel Scrivener.

'And you mentioned a letter to my father,' continued Frances Arnison, turning her attention to her uncle. 'To my knowledge he has received no letter recently, or if he has then no mention has been made of it.'

'There was a letter, though I took no part in its writing. I did, however, see it written. It told my brother about his so-called dancing master, and urged him to restrain him. The man is an imposter ...'

'I knew it!'

'... and the constables from Hexham will be here tomorrow morning to detain him.'

'*I* wrote to a friend of mine, James Playford, on the subject of Mr Patterson,' said Emanuel Scrivener. 'Has Mr Playford perhaps been in touch with you to precipitate your visit?'

'In touch be damned,' came another voice from the far side of the coach. 'It was *my* letter Mr Taylor is speaking of, and I'm not content merely to write. I'm here in person and angry as a hellcat! Where is he? Where's Tweddle? I'll rip him in two. He's stolen money from me and besmirched my good name. And as for that good-for-nothing he left in his place, that lecherous imbecile, that dirty, smelly reprobate. Why, he—'

'He made advances towards me,' added another, shriller voice. 'He made improper suggestions.'

Three figures rolled around the coach. The first was James Playford, red in the face, his eyes so narrow they threatened to cut his head in two. A step behind was his daughter, her

father made female, and a step further behind, clutching two
large bags, came another man, small, slim, almost dapper,
his neat face curled into a grimace of disgust as he tried to
avoid the dust descending around them.

'Frances,' said George Taylor painfully, 'please allow me
to present Mr James Playford; his daughter, Mrs Emily
Patterson; and his son-in-law, Mr David Patterson. I have
shared the journey with them from Newcastle . . .' he wiped
his forehead with a large kerchief, '. . . and I must admit to a
great fatigue, coupled with a great relief that we have, finally,
arrived.'

'James!'

'Emanuel!'

The two oldest men dissolved in a hug which told of
interesting times shared long ago.

'But Uncle George, this man, this Rob Tweddle, he's
disappeared. We haven't seen him all day. We thought he
might be preparing himself for the evening's entertainment,
resting even, but there is no sign of him anywhere.'

'I knew it,' crowed James Playford, 'just not up to it, that's
Tweddle all over. He knew he wouldn't be able to carry it
off so he's run away. It's a damn good job I'm here, at least
there'll be some dancing tonight. All is not lost.'

'Mr Playford,' Frances Arnison pointed out, 'Tweddle has
succeeded in deceiving all of us for almost two weeks. I hardly
think he would run away unless there was a reason for doing
so. Perhaps he found out that you were coming.'

'Impossible, how could he do that? He's a coward; no
backbone. Never did think much of—'

'Mr Playford, please be quiet.' George Taylor's voice
commanded silence. 'I believe my niece to be correct. Tweddle
must have discovered our plans, perhaps by intercepting your
letter. I can think of no other reason why he should leave
so precipitously. But I would talk with my brother, find
out a little more about the events of the past few weeks.
Tweddle may have left some clues as to his destination.
Please, follow me. Frances?' He held out his arm for his

niece to take. She linked with him and they led the procession into the ballroom, James Playford, his daughter and Emanuel Scrivener following at a respectful distance, David Patterson bringing up the rear.

The happy, gentle hubbub of conversation died as they made their entrance. George Taylor advanced to the top table and reached across to Rebecca Taylor, took her hand and kissed it. He did the same with Annie, then bowed to his brother.

'George,' said Samuel Taylor, his voice and his face puzzled, 'I thought you were unable to ... That is, you said that you couldn't ... You would be away. You wrote to me ...'

'I found myself able to attend after all, dear brother. How could I miss my favourite youngest niece's wedding? And I've brought some friends along. You'll have heard of Mr James Playford, of course.' At the mention of his name the dancing master bowed deeply. 'And he has brought his daughter, Mrs Emily Patterson.' An inevitable curtsy followed. 'And lastly, Mr Playford's son-in-law.' He paused briefly, then raised his voice. 'Allow me to introduce Mr David Patterson.'

The silence deepened. Even the children in the ballroom, the youngest babies, ceased their noise and motion, aware that something important was happening but unable to decide what it was. And then it began, a sibilant whisper like some distant seashore, but it grew. No person in the room could remain quiet. Each contributed to the murmuring, which became a querulous, questioning, open-mouthed disquiet, then a more urgent, more strident braying and barking of individual voices which combined in a crescendo of uproar, of yells and shouts and clamorous pandemonium. Samuel Taylor joined in the tumult, but his screams for quiet couldn't be heard. It was only when his wife rose to her feet and held her hands in the air that a semblance of order was restored.

'Ladies, gentlemen,' she cried, 'friends, I beg you, remain

calm, remain quiet.' Her words soothed the crowd. Expectant faces followed hers to look at George Taylor, to glance sideways at the man who had been introduced as David Patterson, then to look at her brother-in-law again.

'This man,' she asked slowly, 'is David Patterson?'

'None other,' bellowed George Taylor, 'David Patterson, *the* dancing master! Anyone else claiming to be David Patterson is an imposter.'

'But what of the man,' said his brother, 'who has been with us for two weeks, who was sent by Mr Playford at your instigation, who has enjoyed our hospitality, our friendship?'

George Taylor shrugged his shoulders, but the gesture signalled not a lack of knowledge, but an absence of concern. He glanced at the consternation around him – looks of horror, Annie Taylor's pale face, her mother shaking her head. He saw Frances Arnison's triumphant grin and reached across to her, squeezed her hand briefly in his, and her eyes stared into his own, overflowing with gratification and promises. It had worked out better than he'd ever dreamed, and he was there to share in the delightful confusion, the wonderful chaotic bewilderment, with a sense of power, of knowledge, of control. He turned to hear James Playford, in his best borrowed voice, address the crowd.

'Mr and Mrs Taylor, ladies and gentlemen, please allow me to explain. The man who has endeavoured to teach you dancing, who has masqueraded as my son-in-law, is in reality Robert Tweddle, a former clerk in my employ. He was dismissed because of gross insolence and sought his revenge against me by stealing from me, and by this ridiculous pretence of being a dancing master. But, thanks to the diligence of Mrs Arnison and Mr Scrivener, he has been found out!'

'He has, for the moment, escaped, my friends,' continued George Taylor, 'but he will be found and brought to justice. Even now the Hexham constables are on their way.'

'Too bloody late, the bird's flown,' cried a deep-burred

voice, a local voice, and the words carried respect, sympathy even, and approval. Heads turned in the direction of Jacob Lee, but he wore an expression of innocence.

'He is a stranger, he cannot know the area well! He will be found!'

'But what about the dance?' cried Annie Taylor, her eyes wet with tears about to fall, 'what can we do now?'

'Never fear,' boomed James Playford, 'you are fortunate to have with you the best dancing master in England, and I shall be pleased to demonstrate that fact if you will allow me.' His eyes moved from Annie to her father. He nodded briefly.

'It is decided then! My daughter and her husband will assist me in playing—'

'Mr Playford,' interrupted Rebecca Taylor, 'we already have some musicians.'

'You do? Do I know them?'

'They are local people, Mr Patterson ... That is, Mr Tweddle arranged for them—'

'Then I hardly think I need concern myself with them if that reprobate had anything to do with them. What instruments do they play?'

'Northumbrian pipes, I believe, and fiddles; a flute ...'

'Enough! Bagpipes? Any group of musicians containing a piper deserves to be horsewhipped. Pipers are rogues and criminals by definition. No, my daughter will play piano, Mr Patterson violin, and I shall play violin and instruct the dancers. Now if you will excuse me, I will need to arrange some music. Until later, then?' He bowed and bustled away, his family trailing after him.

'I don't like him,' said Rebecca Taylor to her husband.

'We have no choice, my dear. I too prefer our old dancing master, but if what we hear is true, and I have no reason to doubt it, then the man is a scoundrel. And I don't have the same faith in the constables that my brother has. But here comes Mr Stephenson, he'll have something to say on the matter.' He switched on his smile.

'Harold! What an upset. I do hope it doesn't spoil your enjoyment . . .'

Amidst the bustle of noise James Playford organised himself, his family and anyone else who came within ten yards of him. He ordered the piano be moved, he requisitioned seats still occupied, he had tables moved despite the fact that plates and food were being used on them. Those who dared complain were silenced with a glower. Only his daughter and son-in-law were oblivious to his efficiency. They sat down to become acquainted with a bottle of wine and allowed the rest of the world to move about them. Harold Stephenson, mayor of Hexham, father of Charlotte, justice of the peace, conversed earnestly with his host, alternately raising or lowering his eyebrows to convey displeasure or gross displeasure. His daughter watched him from across the room, hiding from his glance, though aware that, since he wasn't wearing his spectacles, he was unlikely to be able to differentiate her from any of the hundred or so other young ladies present. It gave her a good excuse to hold on to Danny Taylor, to move him around her so that she remained in his shadow.

'It doesn't bode well,' she muttered. 'I shall need to find him in a better mood than this before he'll consent to you marrying me.'

'And I asked him,' her charge replied, 'this David or Robert or whatever his name is, I asked him to try hard to make the day especially good, to impress your father, just so that he would say yes when I asked for your hand. After all I've done for him, he's deserted me. And I thought he was my friend.'

The bride and groom moved around the room, alternately reassuring their guests and then indulging in urgent, whispered, private conversation.

'I knew I should have come along to meet this fellow,' hissed the groom, nodding his head in agreement with his own statement. 'I would have realised that he was an imposter straightaway.' His unruly red hair had been oiled into place earlier in the day, but Annie could see it was beginning to reassert its will, to revert to its natural wild state.

'Well why didn't you come?' she spat in reply. 'There was plenty of opportunity, but you were always too busy with farm work. I've hardly seen you for a month.' She reached up to pat an unruly wave back into position and her husband brushed her hand away thoughtlessly.

'One of us has to work, my dear, to allow for your expensive taste in clothes and . . .' he searched for another noun, '. . . and dancing masters!'

Her grip on his arm tightened, as did both of their smiles as they neared his grandparents and prepared once more to soothe worries and answer questions with platitudes and false confidence.

Emanuel Scrivener and Frances Arnison were locked in a corner, discussing how each of them had suspected the dancing master was not who he claimed to be. Harry Arnison approached them once but was unable to make his presence felt; his throat clearing was ignored. He left with his tankard of ale in his hand, rolling round the room in search of some unattached female to breathe over.

George Taylor stood alone, watching, listening, nodding an acknowledgement where necessary, smiling broadly at pretty young girls. He was happy to be present and was looking forward to seeing the dancing commence. He'd spent a long journey with James Playford and had come to the conclusion that the man was an insufferable egotist, in love with the sound of his own voice and dogma. He was therefore ideal for the occasion, would probably be only marginally better than his fool of a clerk would have been. On receiving Frances Arnison's letter his first impulse had been to ignore it, to pretend that it had been lost or that he was away on business when it arrived. That plan was short-lived. Within hours Playford had appeared on his doorstep, clutching his old friend Scrivener's missive and

demanding that something be done. It required little time
for him to realise the delicious potential of the situation; he
would ride to the rescue, unmask the deceiving Tweddle,
provide the successor in James Playford (who would still
be incapable of doing the job), and be present to see the
whole unravelling of the flimsy cloth that was his niece's
wedding. He watched Annie on her peregrinations. Perhaps
she would have need of her uncle's soothing comfort and
company later that evening when her boorish husband had
drunk too much. She was a little too mature for him, but
the satisfaction he would gain from having bedded both of
his brother's daughters more than outweighed his personal
tastes. He smiled, was rewarded with a wave and resolved
that he might well stay in Bellingford a day or two.

Jacob Lee and his musicians had retreated with their
instruments to the back of the hall where they watched the
goings-on with fascinated bewilderment, like rabbits before
the fat dancing weasel who was James Playford. Sammy
Devlin and the Charltons, Jamie and Charlie, had wanted
to leave as soon as James Playford made known that he
didn't need their services, but Jacob had persuaded them to
stay. The beer was free, he reminded them, and there was
no knowing what entertainment might arise.

Sound and motion ceased as the violins took their A from
the piano and James Playford, perspiring freely, looked
around.

'Ladies and gentlemen,' he said, and his lips and eyebrows
capered merrily around his nose, 'it is indeed a pleasure to
be here in . . . to be here in . . .'

'Bellingford,' his son-in-law whispered.

'. . . to be here in the home of Mr and Mrs Taylor,
in Bellingford, to celebrate the wedding of their daughter.
My name is James Playford. I am a dancing master. And
I hope that you will join me now in our first dance, "The
Twenty-Ninth of May".' He tapped his foot on the ground
to signify the speed, took a deep breath, then bowed his head
to encourage the thin chord which followed. The tune was

undistinguished. The musicians were able enough but lacked enthusiasm, and when he signalled a stop and looked up he found that the floor was still empty.

'Please, ladies and gentlemen, bring your partners onto the floor.' There was no movement. He looked across at Samuel and Rebecca Taylor and nodded eagerly. Begrudgingly they led the way onto the floor to stand facing him. Annie and her husband followed, then Mr and Mrs Allard, the parson and his wife, until forty or fifty people stood, scattered around in pairs, looking expectantly at James Playford.

'Very well, then,' he said hastily, 'form the set.'

'What set is that?' asked Danny Taylor.

'The set for the dance, of course. What other set would I mean?'

'No, what shape? Is it to be a square, a circle, a set of four or five couples?'

James Playford lowered his violin to his side, scratched at his head with his bow. 'You mean you don't know the dance?' he asked incredulously. There was a collective shake of heads.

'But everyone knows this dance. It's one of the first I teach.' He turned to his musicians, 'Just what has Tweddle being doing with his time?' he complained, then glued his smile back to his face as he turned to his audience again.

'Then I shall teach you the dance, from the beginning. The form is longways for as many as will. Please form a set – two sets perhaps. Yes, move the seats back a little to give more room.' He fussed and puffed and moved couples around, then began the instructions. The dance was not straightforward. It involved movements such as the poussette which were strange to some, and quick changes of place. At various times in the dance men were meant to dance on the ladies' side of the set and vice versa. They were meant to move up and down the set in lines of four, and couples were meant to progress up or down the room according to their allotted number. Those who thought they understood the instructions became impatient with those who felt they hadn't quite grasped it, though some of the latter were more right than the former. Confusion became their partners and tripped them as they skipped, made them cast when they should have turned, and the dance became a battle. But James Playford would not be diverted. For twenty minutes or more he pushed and pulled, bellowed encouragement, turned his eyes upwards in exasperation, then finally announced that they would try the dance to music. And they tried.

The dance was in three parts. By the end of the first part a third of the dancers had sat down; by the end of the second part those remaining were wandering around, unsure of direction and intention. Halfway through the third part all motion had ceased, save for an old couple swinging happily in the middle of the room with an elegance and style which belied their grey hair and crooked bodies.

The dance would normally have been played six or eight times through, but once was enough for James Playford. He knew he must find dances that were easier to understand, but could think of none. His thoughts were interrupted by the old man and woman who staggered up to him.

'Why'd you stop?' the man asked in a tremulous voice, his head bent down parallel to the ground. 'Me and the wife was enjoyin' that, 's that right Agnes, me dear?'

'Aye, you're right there, Gordon me owd lad.'

'But you weren't dancing the right steps,' said Playford. 'You were just swinging, and it wasn't a good swing anyway. The balance was wrong.'

The old man snorted. 'The swing reflected the dance, in that case,' he chortled, 'and the music, and the instructions, eh me dear?'

'Aye, you're right there, me owd lad.'

James Playford ignored their comments. 'Ladies and gentlemen,' he began, 'perhaps we should try something a little simpler to begin with. Perhaps we should try—'

'Aye, let's do "The Morpeth Rant"!' shouted the old man, surprisingly loudly. There was a mutter of approval from certain corners of the ballroom, and Jacob Lee and his musicians looked up, surprised to hear the name of a dance they recognised.

'No, me owd lad,' said the lady, her head sheathed in a dirty grey bonnet, '"La Russe" is a better dance by far.'

'And what about "Corn Rigs"?' demanded her partner from behind thick glass spectacles, his collar turned up and hiding half his face.

' "Square Eight"?' she countered.

' "Long Eight"!'

' "Ploughboy"!'

Amidst this argument James Playford looked first at one, then the other of the odd couple in front of him. Despite the warmth of the evening they were dressed in long coats, as if protecting their fragile limbs. His face showed curiosity, then annoyance, then anger. Behind him Jacob Lee had risen to his feet and was making gestures to his musicians, urging them for some reason unknown to them, to find their instruments. Few noticed this; the attention of the room was fixed on the old couple and the irascible Playford.

'For God's sake, be quiet!' he yelled. They appeared to do as they were told, turned to face each other, then turned back to face him.

'Which is it then?' asked the man.

'Which is what?'

'Which is the best dance?' said the lady, holding her hat firmly on her head.

'How should I know?' growled Playford. 'I've never heard of any of the damn dances you mentioned!'

The old man turned again to face the crowd. His hair was thick for his age and dappled with uneven grey patches, as if it had rained flour on his head.

'Well dearie me, 'e calls 'imself a dancing master, but 'e doesn't even know the dances.' There was a ripple of laughter.

'If you can do better, old man, then you just do so!' countered Playford.

The old man drew himself together, as if summoning strength. 'Aye,' he said, 'thank you for the invitation. I think I'll do just that.' His bowed back straightened. He shrugged himself out of his coat and pulled off his spectacles, shook his head to let a cloud of dust fly from his long hair. It was left to James Playford to speak aloud the words others were murmuring softly.

'Rob Tweddle!'

'Aye, none other!' yelled Rob. He threw his coat to the floor and leaped onto the nearest table. Jinny Lee gazed up at him after removing her coat and hat and shaking her long hair down. Those watching were mixed in their response; some made as if to move forward, to catch this thief, this liar and cheat, while others smiled and applauded the most recent deception. Some were unsure how they ought to behave and glanced at their neighbours for guidance. One or two, distant relations of the groom, were clearly unsure who this young man was and why he was standing on a table in front of them.

'So you'll admit that's your name, Rob Tweddle?' asked Samuel Taylor, silencing all other questions.

'I'm Rob Tweddle, Mr Taylor, and proud to be so. Getting rid of that false David Patterson is a relief, like taking off a hair shirt. I won't deny I'm Rob Tweddle.'

Harold Stephenson whispered urgently in Samuel Taylor's ear; Taylor nodded.

'I'm sorry, Mr Tweddle . . .' he began.

'Please, call me Rob. I feel sure you know me well enough.'

'What? Yes, I see. Well, Rob, I'm afraid that by your own admission we must arrest you. This is Mr Stephenson. He's a justice of the peace. His constables will be here tomorrow to take you for trial and he advises me—'

'But I've committed no crime, Mr Taylor, no crime at all.'

'Preposterous!' yelled James Playford. 'What about the money you stole from me? And you've deceived the Taylor family. You intended taking money from them under false pretences, that's fraud without a doubt.'

'And my dancing books,' offered the real David Patterson, quietly, meekly. 'He stole my dancing books.'

'Be quiet!' snapped his father-in-law.

'There appears to be a case to answer, Mr Tweddle,' said Harold Stephenson. 'I have many friends here, many men who will restrain you if you attempt to escape.' He motioned to both sides of him. A dozen young men stepped forward, unsure of the duty they would be required to carry out but confident that the odds would be with them.

'Wait, I beg you, allow me to explain.' Rob's arms were oustretched. Harold Stephenson nodded his permission.

'You've heard me accused of certain crimes. Had I committed these crimes, would I have returned here this evening? Would I have entered this room, seeing Mr Playford here, seeing Mr George Taylor here, knowing full well that they would recognise me? Is this the behaviour of a criminal? Yesterday it was my fortune, good or bad, I know not, to come across a messenger boy carrying the news that Mr Playford and his family and Mr Taylor were coming here to unmask me, to have me arrested. I could have fled. I could be in Carlisle by now, heading for Lancashire or the coast. No one would find me. Instead I chose to stay, to come here tonight. Are these the actions of a criminal, a guilty man?'

'They're the actions of a lunatic,' said George Taylor, 'or a very clever, and very dangerous, individual. And you don't seem mad to me, Mr Tweddle.'

Rob looked around, trying to gauge his support. He knew from experience that he ought to be able to outwit his old master, but George Taylor was a different matter, and he hadn't allowed for the presence of Harold Stephenson. But there was no going back now.

'No, I'm not mad. I'm innocent . . .' There was a rumble of dissatisfaction. Rob spoke up louder. '. . . I'm innocent and I shall demonstrate that! Mr Playford has accused me of stealing money from him. I would ask him what money I stole.'

'What money? Why, the money from my safe. You saw where I kept the key and you took it all, every last penny. There must have been fifty pounds there!'

Rob smiled. There had been a little over thirteen pounds, he knew it and Playford knew it. 'You run a business, do you not Mr Playford?' he asked.

'What a damn stupid question. Of course I do, you know that; you used to be—'

'And you keep records of your income and expenditure?'

'I do. At least I did, until that imbecile you recommended to me laid his hands on the ledger.'

'But your records show you had no such sum in your safe. Your records show you had no cash balance whatsoever. Your records—'

'But you're the one who completed the records! You know that sometimes amounts weren't entered, that they were spent without records being kept. I told you that—'

'You told me I was not to inform your son-in-law, your partner, of this "special income", so you wouldn't have to share it with him.'

'Father!' Emily Patterson hissed, 'How could you?'

'I didn't, it's a lie!' her father protested.

'But if it's a lie, Mr Playford, then there was never any cash in the safe. And if it's true, then you were trying to cheat your partner. So I'm innocent, because there was no money to steal, or your actions were themselves those of a thief. Which is it to be?'

'Your argument is illogical, Mr Tweddle,' said George Taylor. 'Clever, elegant even, but illogical. You attempt to shift attention from your actions to those of Mr Playford, when it is your actions that are under question. But I appreciate the way your mind is working. I admire a mind that works.' He glanced disparagingly at James Playford. 'But you cannot deny that you attempted to deceive my brother and his family, or that you impersonated Mr Patterson in an attempt to extort money from my brother. But no doubt you have an explanation of some sort. May we hear it?'

Rob nodded, looked down to where Jinny had been standing, but she was gone. He looked around, saw her blonde hair marking her passage through the crowd as she headed for George Taylor, standing at the far end of the room. He had obviously not recognised her when she removed her disguise. Either that or he had no suspicions that she wished to harm him. But it was Rob's task to keep attention on him, that was the bargain he'd made with Jinny.

'I have received no money from Samuel Taylor. I've taken nothing from this place save hospitality, which was freely offered.'

'Freely offered to a man we thought was David Patterson,' shouted Frances Arnison.

'No, madam, not to David Patterson. That name is no more than a label. All I have been given, be it food, wine, lodgings – friendship even,' he sought Danny Taylor out, 'good company, comfort and pleasure,' he stared at Frances Arnison, 'pleasant conversation and discourse,' he caught Annie's eye, 'were offered to a young dancing master. And in return that dancing master fulfilled his part of the contract. He taught you all to dance, and—'

'Dancing master?' James Playford couldn't hide his derision. 'You're no dancing master. You're a tuppenny-halfpenny clerk, a ne'er-do-well, a rogue and a scoundrel, as we can all clearly see. You're no dancing master.'

'I'm more of a dancing master than you'll ever be, James Playford, and I'm willing to put that claim to the test. Everyone here has had a taste of your instruction, of your music, of your dances. Let them try mine now. Let me take charge, and then we'll see who's the true dancing master. Or perhaps you're frightened of the comparison.'

George Taylor stepped forward again, cleared his throat. He could see what was going to happen, and his admiration for this rascal Tweddle was increasing by the minute. The challenge was laid down and Playford would be unable to resist responding. His conceit would allow Tweddle to lead a dance or two and there would be overwhelming support for the young man. And then? There were many possibilities, but it seemed most likely that Playford would skulk back to Newcastle and Tweddle would be acknowledged the true dancing master and be allowed to go free. George Taylor couldn't permit that. If he spoke up now, if he pre-empted Playford's acceptance of this duel of dances and forbade it, then, with Harold Stephenson's backing, Tweddle would be locked up until the constables arrived to take him to justice. He could do it, he knew that. His voice carried sufficient authority in this bleak congregation where individuality was as rare as intellect. He cleared his throat.

'You think it's a good idea,' whispered a voice, a woman's voice, from close beside him. 'You think it would be a fair test to have a dance competition.' George Taylor wasn't aware that the words were directed at him. They were the buzz of a passing gnat, to be swatted to one side then ignored.

'You'll say as much out loud as well, or I'll sting you good and proper.' He felt something sharp at his side, just above his waist. He would have turned but the voice continued. 'It's a knife, Geordie lad, a sharp knife. It'll be under your ribs and tickling your heart before you can cough, and I'm not afraid to strike the blow. You can turn round, slowly, and look at me face now. See if you remember me.'

Another sharp pricking made him do as he was told. He saw a smiling face and bright blue eyes, blonde hair hanging loose.

'I remember you,' he said softly.

'Good,' Jinny replied. 'I'll tell you quickly. Part of me wants you to scream you're bein' pressed into this. I want an excuse to twist this knife into your liver. I want to spill your guts all over the floor. D'you understand? I want you to die, just like my baby died. Just like *our* baby died. Am I gettin' through?'

He nodded.

'But I know that what Rob wants you to do is speak up and say you approve of him taking some dances. Either way I get some satisfaction. It's your choice, Geordie. Make your decision now.'

'Ladies and gentlemen!' George Taylor's voice rolled around the room. All eyes turned towards him. 'Ladies and gentlemen, you've heard this man, this Rob Tweddle, answering charges pressed against him. This is not a court of law. We are not a jury nor can we act as judges. Some of you may think that his proposal, that he be allowed to prove himself a dancing master by being allowed to lead a dance or two, is preposterous.'

'Get on with it!' hissed Jinny.

'I, however, feel that, since this is a wedding, and since we all wish to be entertained, we should allow Mr Tweddle the privilege of taking us all through a dance before we offer not our judgement but our opinion on the matter. I'm sure Mr Playford will say he has nothing to fear in this?'

James Playford nodded his head vigorously. There were loud cheers from the guests. This was entertainment indeed, far better than they could ever have wished for.

'Well then, Mr Tweddle, it would appear you have your chance. Please, give us your instructions.' The tone of sarcasm in his voice was lost as Rob turned and urged his musicians forward. They pushed through the crowd to stand in a semicircle behind him, instruments ready and in tune.

'I thought you'd lost it that time, lad,' said Jacob Lee, 'and you're still not out of the fire. So what's it to be?'

'Ladies and gentlemen,' shouted Rob, 'please form square sets with four couples in each set, each couple with their backs to a different wall of the room, each man with his partner on his right-hand side, for a local dance, a dance I learned here in Bellingford. Take your partners, please, for . . . "La Russe"!'

The crowds rushed onto the floor and became dancers as the musicians, with no need for persuasion from Rob, launched themselves into the tune for the dance. By the time they'd finished their allotted forty bars the room was filled with expectant couples forming compact squares, and Rob was holding his hands aloft signalling that he wanted silence.

'Ladies and gentlemen,' he said, looking warmly about him. 'Lads and lasses. You know this dance, those of you who've been coming along to practices. I imagine most of the rest of you know it as well, but I'll talk you through it, once, just to make sure. This is what you do . . .'

'Do you intend standing here for the rest of the night,' George Taylor said to Jinny, 'threatening to make a hole in me?' He flinched as the knife was pushed harder into his side. 'I ask only because this waistcoat was rather expensive. I'd hate to see it damaged.'

'No,' Jinny answered, 'I'll take it away shortly. At least I think I will. Things are goin' well for us, I believe. Rob's goin' to carry the night. He will, look at him. He's a man who believes in himself.'

'And does he believe in you also?'

'More than you ever did, Geordie lad, far more than you ever did.'

'You have a poor memory, girl. I took nothing from you without payment, and generous payment at that. When you came to me—'

'When I said I was goin' to have a bairn you gave me more money. That's all it meant to you, money.'

'You were happy enough to take it.'

'I'd little choice in the matter, did I? Men, you're all the same; you think money and position and good looks can buy anythin', includin' women. Includin' me.'

'Is he the same as well, then, your latest man, Rob Tweddle? You know him better than me, better than anybody here. He has much in common with quite a few men here. He's had his way with you – No! You've no wish to stick me now, surely, in the middle of a dance? It would distract from his triumph, would it not? And I spoke only the truth. That's better, girl, ease the pressure a little. And you haven't answered my question. Is he any different to the rest of us poor mortals?'

'Aye, he is! He cares about me. He wants me to gan wi' 'im, to stay wi' 'im. He loves me.'

'And has no one else told you that?'

'They were lyin'! You were lyin'!' Her voice softened. 'He's not, though, he means it.'

'My God, true love! I believed it to exist only in the imaginations of poor poets, and now I find it rampaging before me in the heart of a peasant's daughter.'

'You poor man. Not even a man, if you can't understand love. Come on, outside, into the garden. I've business with you no one else should see.'

George Taylor began to object, but the knife pierced his flesh and he yelped.

'Lead the way, Geordie lad. There's nobody watchin' you or me. Look at them all.' She urged him to look back into the room. The dance was in full swing. Rob was beating time on the table and surveying his charges, yelling words of encouragement to those dancing well, throwing instructions at the confused. The musicians were enjoying themselves, grinning at those sweating and gasping on the dance floor, expressing admiration (in the case of the men) when a trim ankle passed them by or (in the case of Sally McIntyre and Susan Blamire) a handsome young man ranted round the outside.

'He's beaten you, hasn't he?' Jinny crowed. 'He's won already, and nothin' you can say or do can change that. Go on, out you go.'

He preceded her into the garden. Twilight had crept up unnoticed. The candles in the hall had been lit without anyone's attention being drawn to the fact, and the sun had set a half-hour before behind blue-grey clouds. It was cool after the warmth of the ballroom. The hedges and shrubs were damp with the promise of rain and dew.

'Weather's changin',' said Jinny, pushing George Taylor ahead of her.

'For the worse,' he muttered.

'Some people prefer it cooler,' she replied. 'Some say a change is long due anyway. You can have too much of anythin'. Some of us have had too much.'

'If I didn't know better, girl, I'd swear you were talking about more than the weather.'

'Oh no, Geordie, that can't be right, can it? After all, I'm just a poor country lass. What do I know? Now turn right, round the corner, into the farmyard. Watch your step, you don't want to get those nice clean shoes dirty. That's a good lad. Now in there.'

'In there? But it's a barn.'

'Aye, a byre, just right for low, menial animals. But don't worry, there's nothin' in there, save for some rats or mice, an old bit of straw. In you go, that's a good lad. Now turn round. You're a proud, grand cockerel, aren't you? So I think you'd better learn a bit humbleness. Take your clothes off and hand them to me.'

'I'll do no such thing!'

'Geordie, lad, just because you're in there and I'm out here doesn't mean I can't do just what I want. I can't reach you with me knife, I know that, and you think you're stronger than me, which you might or might not be. But I've a brain in this head. I've thought things out. There's still a bit light left so's you can see, I know you can see. Look carefully, Geordie.' She reached to one side without looking and her hand fell on a long length of wood triple pronged with metal. 'This here's a pitchfork, and I can reach you with that easily enough. So you'd better hand your clothes out, starting now, and be damn quick about it. I might just decide to be impatient.'

'Why? Why are you doing this?' he said as he removed his jacket.

'I told you, Geordie. Revenge for the wrong you've done me.'

'But why this?'

'Why not? I wouldn't worry, it's better than bein' dead,

isn't it? And that's still an alternative. Now come on, faster.'

More items of clothing were thrown from the barn. A waistcoat, trousers, shirt and collar and cravat, silk stockings – 'Aye, shoes as well,' said Jinny – cotton breeches.

'Let me see you,' said Jinny. 'Come forward.' George Taylor did as he was told, shuffled towards the door, his face pained with each step on the grimy, straw-covered stone floor. His hands were folded in front of him, his shoulders hunched, his head lowered. Any spirit he'd shown in the previous few minutes had disappeared. The removal of each item of clothing had taken with it a layer of self-reliance, of defiance. He was naked and no different now to other men in his manner and his bearing. Jinny brandished the pitchfork at him and he halted in the doorway. There was barely enough light to see him, but the paleness of his body, his shivering (though it was not particularly cold) and his low, helpless whimpering, like that of some small animal, helped fix his position. Jinny shook her head, then smiled and began to laugh. It wasn't wild, uproarious laughter, but in it there was ridicule and derision, malice, hatred. But no pity; no sympathy. George Taylor heard all this.

'Did I ever do you this much harm?' he cried, backing away from Jinny, who followed him into the barn until he was pressed against the rear wall. She held out the pitchfork and let the spines rest on his belly, then raised it slowly, softly, leaving dark, rusty marks on his chest, up to his chin, forced him to look up. Still he avoided her eyes, but she could see there were tears falling down his cheeks.

'Yes,' she said, 'and worse, much worse. Now move away. Go on, quick!'

He scuttled to one side, fell over and yelped.

'Be quiet, Geordie! I need to think. I need to think what to do with you. Now listen carefully. Are you listenin'?'

'Yes,' he sobbed.

'Good. Now there's a strong lock on this door, so you won't be able to get out. There's nobody around, they're all

havin' a good time dancin'. That gives me time to think. I'll
be just across the yard there, and if I hear one word from
you, one single squeak of a word, I'll be over. I was goin' to
cut your throat in the ballroom, but it would have been too
good for you, too quick. I quite like the feel of this pitchfork.
It's solid, got a decent heft to it. I could just see it sticking in
your belly and you squirmin' like a stuck pig. All I need is
an excuse, d'you hear me, Geordie?'

'Yes.' A whisper.

'That's the last word I want to hear from you, then; 'cos if
that one isn't, the next one will be. Goodnight, Geordie.'

Jinny slammed the door shut and engaged the padlock,
strode across the yard and into the shadows opposite. There
she laid down her weapon and crept quietly away, round the
corner, along through the gardens again and back into the
loud, swinging, dancing ballroom. She could have been
away no more than thirty minutes, but Rob was still on his
feet, still on the table, still yelling instructions, his long hair
damp with sweat. But this was another dance, another set
of tunes, and as she glanced round the room she could
see that only the very young and the very old were still
sitting down. Harold Stephenson was mopping his brow and
laughing while being hurried round a set by Rebecca Taylor,
her husband was dancing with his newly married daughter,
Danny and Charlotte Stephenson were holding hands in a
manner suggesting more than friendship. Jinny walked the
perimeter of the room until she was beside Rob, reached out
and touched his leg. He looked down to see her, raised his
eyebrows. She nodded. His smile was one of victory.

The dance came to a fast spin of an ending. The room
was filled with whirlpools of colour and excitement, and
then applause, such applause as Rob had never before
witnessed. There was no doubt in his mind that he'd won,
and his competitor seemed unwilling to re-enter the fray.
James Playford and his family were sitting, hunched and
uncomfortable as a trio of windblown crows, staring at
the floor in search of nonexistent crumbs of comfort. Rob

held up his hands to silence the yells and whistles, and at his command they ceased. He wiped his forehead with his handkerchief.

'Thank you,' he said. 'Thank you for listening, for dancing. Thank you for enjoying yourselves, if indeed you have.' The applause started again. There were cries of 'We have!' and 'Don't stop; let's have some more!'

'Oh, there'll be more, I promise you. I hope I've demonstrated that I am, indeed, entitled to be called a dancing master. I hope I've shown that the charges laid against me were malicious, that I've been the injured party, that I've done my job here in Bellingford to the best of my ability.'

'Hear, hear!' shouted Danny Taylor enthusiastically, and there was yet another burst of applause. Rob noticed, from his vantage point, a ripple of movement in one corner of the room. Frances Arnison and Emanuel Scrivener were clearing a way through a knot of people. They thrust their way to the front, but neither of them said anything. Instead, from between them, stepped a young man with red hair, the bridegroom. Rob realised he still didn't know his name, but the frown on his face wasn't encouraging.

'May I have silence please,' he yelled. 'Silence please! I have something to say!' Rob looked at him. There was something about him, something familiar. Perhaps it was his demeanour. He seemed to share with his two companions a dour look, the three of them owned the only unhappy faces (apart from James Playford and family) in the room. Rob saw in the groom's eyes a hint of jealousy. Jealousy? Had Annie told him of his advances towards her? No, it couldn't be that. He trusted Annie, that was their secret. But Frances Arnison might have said something! Yes, that could account for the look in his eyes. But there was something else as well, Rob could sense that. He climbed down from his table and waited. The groom moved forward one pace and held up his hands again.

Rob looked around him. Someone winked; a hand reached out to pat him on the back; a woman mouthed 'well done!'

and nodded. Then it came to him. He realised that the night was his, that the reason for the celebration may have been a wedding, but the real jubilation was for him, his achievement in belittling Playford. He was the catalyst, the conduit for the enjoyment of hundreds of people. It didn't matter to Annie; she wasn't his competitor. But her husband saw Rob as a rival. So what was he going to do? What was he going to say?

'Ladies and gentlemen,' he began, swaying slightly. He was quite drunk. 'Thank you all for coming to my wedding. No, no, I didn't mean that, I'm sorry. Thank you for coming to *our* wedding.' He searched for his wife with unfocused eyes but couldn't find her, missed the worried look on her face which others could plainly see. 'I don't want to interrupt, but . . .'

'Get on with it then!'

'I will! I have something to say. It concerns this man in front of us, this . . . this Tweddle person. He may have won you all over with his clever words, his clever actions, his *dancing* . . .' he spoke the word as if it were dirty; he spat it from his mouth. 'But I must tell you something else about him, something about his behaviour to my . . .' He halted, the thread lost, and Frances Arnison leaned forward to hiss at him.

'Yes, quite. This Tweddle's behaviour to my wife, that's what I must mention.' He took another step forward, into the middle of the room, and Rob did likewise, strode to meet him. There was a rush of breath from those watching, a sudden inhalation. Was there a fight in the offing? That would be too good a way to end what had already been an eventful evening.

'What my good friend wants to say,' Rob began, 'what he'd like to tell you all, is this.' He draped his arm round the groom's shoulder, not an easy action since the man was backing away from him at the time, sure that he was about to be attacked. Had he been less in his cups he might have escaped, he might even have struck a blow, but instead Rob was able to whisper urgently in his ear. The groom shook his head; Rob whispered again. Then the groom nodded, sullenly.

'If a man can't drink at his own wedding, when may he drink?' Rob shouted. There was a low, heavy cheer from the men present. 'And if my friend here has taken that advice a little too much to his heart, then it hasn't affected his emotions. Listen to him, I pray.' Rob silenced the crowd again with one hand, the other still grasping the groom about the shoulder. The groom began to speak.

'Concerning my wife Annie, and Mr Tweddle,' he said unsteadily. 'I merely wished to say that . . .'

'In my absence . . .' Rob prompted.

'In my absence, over the past few weeks, Mr Tw . . . Mr Tweddle, he's been, that is, he's helped my wife . . .'

'And her family . . .'

'And her family, of course. He's brought music, and dancing, and music . . . No, I've said that once. Anyway, he's brought music and dancing into this house . . .'

'And friendship . . .'

'Yes, quite. And friendship. He's been a gentleman of the first order, and I wish only to thank him for his . . . for his . . .'

'Publicly. Thank him publicly . . .'

'Yes, I wish to thank him publicly for his . . . That's it, for his kindness and his generosity. That's it. I wanted to say thank you.' There was a pleasant round of applause during which Rob could be seen whispering friendly thanks on his part to the groom.

'And I also wanted,' the groom continued, 'to offer him my support. He's a good man, I know that now. I won't have a word said against him, he . . .' His words died slowly to even more muted clapping, and Rob helped him stagger into his wife's arms. She had a puzzled expression on her face.

'I think you should take him to bed,' Rob said, 'before he becomes ill. He's had a busy day.' He was off again, signalling to his musicians, introducing another dance before anyone else could interrupt the goodwill he was sure was his. Jinny was waiting for him beside his table.

'What was that?' she asked urgently.

'Oh, nothing much. Our drunk friend was about to suggest I'd made advances to his intended. It might have turned people against me, so I thought I'd better stop it.'

'And had you? Made advances, that is?'

'I behaved as any gentleman would, Jinny, no more and no less. But I must get on now. There's hours of dance left in this crowd yet.'

'Wait on. What did you say to him, then, to make him change his mind? The way he was talkin' it was like he'd married you.'

'I just told him I'd seen him before, that was all.'

'You'd seen him before?'

'Yes. But it wasn't the fact that I'd seen him that did it, it was what I'd seen him doing.'

'Go on.'

'That night, up at the stones when we danced, he was there. I didn't recognise him at first because I hadn't seen his face, but there can't be many people with hair like that, red hair. He'd been in the grass with some girl, you can guess what they were up to, and I just told him it wouldn't go down too well if people got to know about it. He agreed. Now I must get on, I've work to do.'

Rob Tweddle had never worked so hard in his life, but it didn't matter, it didn't seem like work to him. He was enjoying himself as much as the dancers, more than the dancers. Just before midnight it became clear that the dance would shortly be over. A mixture of alcohol and fatigue was driving and drawing guests and participants to their beds. Harold Stephenson was one of those leaving. He came up to Rob, hand and smile extended, Samuel and Rebecca Taylor in tow.

'Mr Tweddle,' he said, 'I must congratulate you on your efforts this evening and during the past fortnight. My daughter has been very impressed with your instruction, and though

I was a little disturbed by the revelations earlier this evening, I feel you have demonstrated that you deserve to be credited a dancing master. Since Mr and Mrs Taylor have no wish to press any charges against you concerning the possibility – the somewhat vague possibility, I would add – of your deceiving them or behaving in a fraudulent manner, then I feel there is no case to answer.'

Rob smiled. He'd won. Jinny was by his side. He felt her hand squeeze his and he returned the gesture.

'There is, however, the matter of the alleged theft from Mr Playford. I have spoken to him and, despite my attempts to persuade him to the contrary, he does wish to press charges.' Rob's hand fell to his side. Had he come this far only to lose after the finishing line had been crossed? He swallowed, forced back the panic that overwhelmed him, that prepared him for flight. He breathed deeply. Harold Stephenson's face was surely too friendly, too happy to impart such bad news. He leaned closer to Rob, put his arm round his shoulders. Rob could smell wine on his breath, and something stronger.

'It is, however, questionable whether I, as a Justice of the Peace, or my constables have any jurisdiction over a crime supposed to have been committed in . . .' he wrinkled up his nose, '. . . Newcastle. I have therefore told him there is nothing I can do to help him.' He smiled at Rob. Rob smiled back. They both turned and smiled at Samuel Taylor, whose face was already framed with a huge grin. There was a cheer behind them, and Rob turned to see Danny Taylor leap into the air. Jinny was looking up at Rob with pride in her eyes.

'I hope,' the mayor of Hexham continued, 'that I shall meet you again. It is some considerable time since I enjoyed myself so much while dancing, and even longer since it made me so infernally tired. But forgive me, my carriage is waiting, and it is a long journey . . .'

'Wait!' It was a bellow of a voice, filled with anger and indignation. It echoed round the ballroom, almost empty now, and turned all heads.

'Where are they? I'll have them for this!'

The figure which burst into the room had hair knotted with straw. Its arms and legs were streaked with mud and dirt and its eyes were wide and wild. It was obviously male. It wore only a cloak which flapped open as it ran into the room. Samuel Taylor was the first to recover his voice. He drew his wife close to him.

'George,' he said, 'is that you? Cover yourself, please, there are ladies present!'

'Ladies be damned!' his brother replied. 'That minx had me locked away naked in the stables!' He levelled a shaking finger at Jinny, turned as the rhythm of running feet and panting breath told him that another had entered the room. 'If it hadn't been for this good lady,' he stepped to one side to allow Frances Arnison to take her rightful place as his saviour, 'I might still be there. But she let me loose, lent me her cloak, and I am here now. I demand you arrest this imposter and his hellfire bitch of an accomplice, they have done me great harm.' He stared at Rob and Jinny, a comical sight wrapped in a lady's cloak.

Rob found himself fighting the urge to laugh, surely nothing would come of this ridiculous suggestion. After all, if he could escape prosecution for theft and deception then he'd be able to explain away this silliness. A game, a prank, a drunken jest which went wrong; all were possibilities. Or Jinny would be able to say that he lured her into the stable yard on some false pretext, that he tried to assault her, to have his way with her. How else would he explain his nakedness? It would be too easy.

Harold Stephenson looked at the scene before him, then turned to Samuel Taylor.

'Samuel, I urge you to hold this man Tweddle and his friend until I can arrange—'

'No!' cried Rob, 'you haven't even asked me or Jinny for an explanation, you can't—'

'Until I can arrange,' the mayor continued, 'to have them taken to Hexham where they will stand trial.'

'This is sheer stupidity,' Rob said. 'Look at him. Are they the words of a sane man? Why listen to him when you weren't prepared to listen to Mr Playford?'

'Mind, Samuel, keep him secure. I shall send the constables as soon as I get back to Hexham. And in answer to your question, Tweddle, as to why I have decided that you will answer these allegations in a fair trial, then I can say only one thing to you. In deciding to ignore Mr Playford's accusations I was aware of his place in life. He is, after all, only a dancing master. But Mr Taylor, Mr George Taylor, why, I've known him for years. Mr Taylor is a gentleman!'

The Sixteenth Bar of the Musick

Monday, 28 June 1830

In which Rob Tweddle and Jinny Lee consider whether the future will see them at liberty or in bonds.

*I*t was perhaps fitting that Rob and Jinny should find themselves captives in the same barn from which George Taylor had made his escape. At least they'd been allowed to remain clothed, and for that they were thankful; the night had turned cold, rain fell intermittently and beat out a sad tattoo on the roof of the barn, and a chill wind teased the straw at their feet. They sat in one of the wooden stalls, saying little, caught in their own thoughts. Rob had paced to and fro at first, searching for a means of escape, but Jinny told him there was none; she'd made sure of that prior to locking up George Taylor. The only way out was through the padlocked double doors, and they wouldn't be opened until the morning when the constables came to take them to Hexham.

'We were almost there,' said Rob. Jinny nodded. He could feel rather than see the motion, she was cradled in his arms for warmth and comfort.

'What'll happen to us?' she mumbled into his chest. Rob

snorted in reply. He knew nothing of the ways of courts and judges.

'Prison, I suppose. Deportation?'

'Perhaps, if they send us to Australia, they'll let us stay together.'

'It would be better, from what I've heard, if they kept you here.'

'No,' she said firmly. 'I want to be with you, wherever you are. I love you, Rob.'

'I love you too,' he answered sadly, wearily, as if admitting the emotion meant little now they could do nothing about it. There was silence for a while. In the depths of the barn the rustle of a mouse passed their ears, and then a cockcrow, too early, but signalling the dawn which would come too soon.

'Rob?'

'I'm here, love. I'm listening.'

Jinny sat up, fished inside her skirts, sought his hand and held it open. The clouds scudded away from the moon and allowed a keyhole of light to enter, and that was enough for Rob to see Jinny place a small golden ring in his palm.

'It was me mam's,' she explained. 'It's the only thing I've got that belonged to her. It's the only thing I've got of any value at all. I want you to have it, Rob.'

'I can't take that, Jinny, how can I? Not if it belonged to your mother.'

She refused to listen, curled up his fingers so the ring was locked away safely. She held his hand closed until he could feel the warm metal within. He couldn't find the words to reply. No one had ever given him a gift of any type in the past, yet here he was being offered something by someone who could least afford to give it away. He put out his free arm and held Jinny close, pulled her into him yet again.

'All I have to give in return is myself . . .' he began, then stopped. That was no longer true. 'Give me your hand,' he whispered, 'your left hand. Hold it out. I do have something for you, Jinny. Here.' He placed his hand under hers, supported it gently, then slid the gold band she'd just given him onto her ring finger. 'It's more than a gift,' he said, 'more than something to remember me by. It's a promise, a promise that one day, when we're both free, we can celebrate our love for each other properly. I can't call you my wife. I doubt I'll be able to do so for a long while, but one day I will. If you'll have me.'

'Oh, Rob, I'll have you. I'll wait for you, I promise I will. I love you.' She turned her head to meet his, intending to kiss him, but in the darkness their mouths missed and their noses collided instead, and they began to laugh.

'I don't know why you're so happy,' said a harsh voice from outside the barn.

'It's at the thought of you having to sit there in the cold to keep watch over us,' answered Rob. 'Do you think someone's going to help us escape? Don't you trust your own family?'

'I trust no one, Tweddle. Nothing would surprise me,' said George Taylor, 'except to find that you're concerned over my warmth.'

'You mean you've found your clothes?' said Jinny.

'No thanks to you, girl, I found them lying in the mud. They're ruined, of course, but that's only one extra item to add to the list of insults and injuries you've caused me. You will pay, both of you. You *will* pay. I know there are certain parties here and in Hexham who are sympathetic to you, but I shall apply to have your case heard in Newcastle where *I* have friends, and where I can rely on a verdict and punishment more in keeping with my opinions of the damage done to me. I shall enjoy seeing you both squirm.'

'He's the type who pulls wings off flies,' Rob said to Jinny, 'and torments kittens.'

They sat in silence again, awake, until they became aware they could see each other, dimly, and could hear birds in the distance. Thrushes and warblers celebrated the new day, and footsteps on the cobbled yard announced the approach of someone, a woman, who called out a greeting as she clattered towards them.

'George? Where are you?'

'Rebecca? Is it you? What are you doing up at such an early hour?'

'I bring news for you, George. The constables have arrived from Hexham. Mr Stephenson must have shaken them from their beds himself as soon as he reached home. They're taking a sup of mead before they return, Samuel is lending them the dog cart to transport their . . .' there was a catch in her voice, '. . . their prisoners. If you want to go and greet them . . .'

'Thank you, Rebecca, but I shall stay here. No doubt they will come here in due course. But what is that?' He pointed to a basket she was carrying, leaned forward and sniffed it.

'Breakfast for Mr Tweddle and Miss Lee, George. Since you don't trust me not to let them out in your absence, please let me in to talk to them. You may lock the door behind me.'

'If that is what you wish. But first, if I may, I would like to examine the contents of the basket.'

'Are you suggesting, George, that I may be smuggling in a pistol? Or a knife, perhaps? A saw to cut through a spar within? Really!'

'A precaution, dear sister-in-law, merely a precaution.' He folded back the linen cover to reveal a jug of steaming coffee, a warm loaf, some cheese and bacon, six apples, a pat of butter and a twist of salt.

'Breakfast?' he said. 'There's enough there for a week of breakfasts! And there's nothing for me?'

'It's all for them. They may be hungry on the journey. My hospitality to you extends as far as inviting you to join the rest of the family when we sit down at eight o'clock. I cannot, however, be sure of the reception you'll be given.'

'You're a fool, woman, just like your husband. Go on, give your pups their meal, they'll receive no more where they're going.' He unlocked the door and ushered Rebecca Taylor inside. Rob could see he was holding a pistol and that

another was tucked into his belt. He stood well back. There
would be no rushing him, no escape in that direction.

'There's food enough here for you both, my dears,' said
Rebecca Taylor, 'and enough for a day beyond, if you're
careful. And here, this is for you also.' She reached into her
coat – it was cold enough for her to wear that – and brought
out a purse which she handed to Rob. He felt the weight of
it, pulled it open to see the gold coins nestling inside.

'I don't understand,' he said.

'Payment, Mr Tweddle. Payment from my husband to the
dancing master for services rendered. He always keeps his
word, does Samuel, and you did your duties well. I've a
feeling the money may come in useful.'

'Useful? As bribes, perhaps, that's all we'll be able to use
it for,' said Jinny. The older woman raised her fingers to
her lips.

'Some words of advice, my dears. First, don't always
anticipate the worst. You have friends. And second, I must
explain something to you so you know why certain things
have happened and may happen in the future. Please, eat
and drink while I talk. It won't take long, and the constables
will be here presently.'

Rob and Jinny did as they were told, tore hungrily at the
food, washed it down with strong black coffee.

'My brother-in-law is a jealous man. I don't know why.
Perhaps my Samuel was given all the kindness in the family,
all the humanity, because George has always been like this.
Mr Tweddle, you heard my husband and I tell the tale of our
courtship, of Jacob Lee's part in that. We told the truth, I
must say that, but there was a part of the story we missed out.
It had no importance at the time. But now I feel it ought to be
told, since its relevance might concern you in the future. You
see, there was a third man who pursued me, a man I never
cared for and to whom I gave no encouragement. That man
was George Taylor. It was he who took Samuel and Jacob
carousing that fateful night. He introduced Jacob to the girl
he got with child; he encouraged Samuel to reveal her to me.

He made advances towards me, improper advances, when no one was there to witness them. He came to visit when Samuel was away, after we'd married, he told me his low opinion of my husband, suggested that if I made myself available to him, for his pleasure, then he could make Samuel's fortune. And if I didn't do as he asked, then matters could become poor for us. Despite the manor and the trappings of luxury we are not wealthy, I swear that, and I feared what he might do. But I was steadfast, and from that day I have not made him welcome at this house, though I have told my husband nothing of what he has said. Until the early hours of this morning, that is.' She shook her head as if unsure that she had done right, then took a deep breath and went on.

'That is the type of man my brother-in-law is. He is jealous; he always seeks revenge. I have told you this tale to illustrate that fact, because . . .' she leaned closer to them and lowered her voice, '. . . because the opportunity may arise for you to escape the fate you both fear. If that happens you must flee. He will pursue you in deed, if not in person. Change your names, your appearances, your trades. And remember, this conversation did not take place.'

She stood abruptly. Beneath the hood of her coat her face was worried but also flushed pink, and she wore a triumphant smile. She bent to kiss Jinny on the lips, shook Rob by the hand, then was at the door, asking to be let out.

'And what was all that about?' George Taylor asked.

'You,' she replied, 'and there'll be no need to lock the door again. Look, the constables are here.'

The yard outside was suddenly alive with motion. Andrew, the butler, a torch held high above his head, was leading the dogcart and pony out, while the two constables, hoods low over their faces to protect them from the drizzle, one large and tall, the other wide and much smaller, were being preceded by Samuel Taylor, hunched against the cold.

'Did you get everything I told you?' Samuel Taylor asked the servant.

'There are blankets, and Mr Tweddle's luggage, and a

bag which I believe belongs to his friend. They're all there, Mr Taylor.'

'Good.' He turned to his wife. 'And they've had breakfast, and food for the journey?'

'They have, dear. I've spoken to them both.'

'Then I feel we should get this over with.' He pulled open the door to the stable. 'Mr Tweddle? Miss Lee? Would you care to come out?'

Rob and Jinny stepped into the cold yard, its cobbles slicked with damp, the torch flame guttering in the wind.

'I am indeed sorry that our association must end in this way.' Samuel Taylor stared at his brother, then looked back to the young couple before him and took Rob's hand. 'And you may rest assured I shall do all I can to assist you in proving your innocence.'

'You'd be better employed burning your money,' said his brother. 'Now then, where are the chains. They're a dangerous pair, these two, they should be bound to prevent their escape.'

'No chains, no bonds,' said Samuel Taylor, 'they won't be needed. And if there were any here, George, then you would be safest if they were applied to me, because my feelings towards you have been changed by what I have seen and what I have been told in these past twenty-four hours. We must talk, we two, and I trust that your words will ease the desire I feel at this moment to cause you great injury.' He turned to the constables. 'Go then, take your charges away!'

'No!' cried a voice, a female voice, from the door in the corner of the yard. It was the Taylors' younger daughter. She ran across the yard to stand in front of Rob. Her hair was loose, it held droplets of misty water like a cobweb's dew, and her feet were bare. She was wearing the same white shift she'd worn when Rob had first seen her a fortnight before, all those years ago. He felt Jinny's hand seek his, hold it tight. 'Mr Tweddle, I thought you'd gone.'

'You see me before you, Annie, still here. Though not for long.'

'I wanted to say thank you. Thank you for everything.'

'Everything, Annie?'

'Everything.' She lowered her eyes then looked up at him again, used his proper name for the first time. 'Rob.'

'Perhaps one day we'll meet again. I can teach you . . .'

She shook her head. 'I think not, Rob. We both have other commitments.'

'How is your husband?'

'Sleeping. He'll feel ill when he wakes.'

'I hope he appreciates how lucky he is.'

Annie shook her head again, turned to Jinny Lee. 'Look after him. You won't find another so easily.'

'Dear Lord,' interrupted George Taylor, 'this isn't the curtain of some one-act play. Constables! Be on your way, and guard these criminals carefully.'

Rob and Jinny were ushered into the rear of the dogcart. The smaller of the constables followed them and sat sideways in front of them, and the larger mounted a horse which the ever-efficient Andrew had led from the front of the house. The cart pulled away with a jolt, and looking back Rob and Jinny saw Samuel and Rebecca Taylor, Annie between them, waving them away.

The track led round and in front of the manor. Candles had been lit in some of the downstairs rooms. Smoke was curling from several chimneys. The house seemed smaller, less threatening than it had been the first time Rob had seen it, as if it had gathered its coats close about it in preparation for bad weather.

In one upstairs room light shone from within. There were two figures silhouetted there, a man with silver hair and a woman, shorter than her partner, with red hair. As the cart reached the point nearest to the window the couple kissed, and the man's hand reached inside the woman's robe.

'Emanuel Scrivener,' said Jinny.

'And Frances Arnison,' added Rob. 'If ever two people

were made for one another, that's a couple who'll meet
again in hell.'

The shorter of the constables, the one holding the reins of
the dogcart, turned to see what it was Rob and Jinny were
discussing. He saw the couple at the window, spat into the
roadway, then turned his attention once again to driving.

The fields around them came slowly to life. Trees, heavy
oaks and tall beeches, slim whipped birches and fronded
rowans, loomed out of the mist and drizzle. The delicate
monotone shades of grey which had coloured the landscape
were touched with the faintest hues of blue and green and
brown. Curious bullocks steamed and stamped in the field
alongside them, trailing a dark passage of wake in the wet
grass. The rumble of wheels disturbed a flock of pigeons
from their roost. They thunderclapped their way skywards,
their passage provoking a raucous chorus of complaint from
one of Samuel Taylor's distant rookeries.

The hedgerows were filled with a chorus of birdsong.
Filigrees of spiders' webs vibrated in the breeze and amplified
each note, threw them out to join others in a glorious
confusion of sound. Rob inhaled. He could smell earth and
moisture, flowers and perfume, growth and decay, and he
realised he was enjoying these sensations of sight and smell
and sound in a way he would have believed impossible two
short weeks before. Was he really the same person who had
lain on the grass in the middle of the village green and longed
to be back in Newcastle?

'I could get used to living somewhere like this,' he said
to Jinny. She was looking behind them as they crested the
hill, looking behind to say farewell to a place she'd never
left before.

'Somewhere like this, yes,' she said, 'but not the same as
this. It's changin' Rob. It doesn't look like it, but it is. And
the people, they'll have to change as well, and people don't
like change.' She turned to look at him, holding back tears.
'Bellingford's a better place for you havin' been there, love,
and I pray it'll keep on gettin' better. But I don't know if it

will; I just don't know. And it's out of our hands now, out of our reach.'

The larger constable, the one riding the horse, was close beside them, and he ventured his opinion.

'It will get better,' he said, 'believe me. As long as enough people want change for the better, that change will come around.'

'And what's it got to do with you?' Rob asked, affronted that a stranger should interrupt his thoughts and opinions. 'After all, you're from Hexham, aren't you?'

'Hexham? No, not me. Terrible place, Hexham. There's only one good thing in Hexham, and do you know what that is?'

'No,' said Rob warily, 'what's that?'

'The road leading back to Bellingford!' He guffawed and slapped his thighs, amazed at his own wit, surprised that the line had been fed to him so perfectly. The second constable joined in, shook with laughter so that the pony, taking the movement of the reins for a sign that she should go faster, began to trot. The driver reined her in, overcompensated, and the trap ground to a halt, allowed the constables to bring their mirth under control.

'No,' said the first, 'I don't like Hexham at all. In fact, I'd advise you two to stay well clear of it if you can.'

'There's not much chance of that, is there?' said Jinny. 'That's where you're takin' us, isn't it?'

'Us?' said the smaller constable, tying the reins to the cart and climbing down, 'Take you to Hexham? Why would we do that?'

'No, we couldn't do that at all. And there's a very good reason for that as well.' The taller, wider constable climbed down from his horse to join his companion. They stood together, pinching and pushing each other like schoolchildren daring each other to tell a secret, their hoods still hiding their faces from sight. Rob was confused, thoroughly confused, and suspicious. Perhaps the men had secret instructions from

George Taylor. Perhaps he and Jinny would be knifed and thrown into a ditch.

'Why's that, then?' he asked warily. 'Why aren't you going to take us to Hexham?'

'Because,' the tall one said, 'because ... Shall I tell them? Now?'

'Go on,' said the smaller, 'put them out of their misery.'

Rob steeled himself. Only injured dogs and lame horses were put out of their misery, usually with a bullet.

'We're not taking you to Hexham because, along the way, we might just meet two men who could, if they knew about us, arrest us, take us away and put us in Hexham jail.'

'I don't understand,' said Jinny.

'Well, you see, the two men we might meet, they could be,' he tittered, 'they could be constables. Real constables. And they could arrest us for impersonating them. For pretending to be constables. Now do you understand?'

'No,' said Jinny, shaking her head. Rob was equally bemused.

'Oh dear. Oh, dear, dear. Perhaps it would be easier if we just did this, then.' He took down his hood; the smaller constable did the same.

'Danny!' yelled Rob. 'Danny Taylor!'

'And Mr Arnison!' added Jinny.

'None other,' smiled Danny, hopping delightedly from foot to foot.

'And please,' said his partner, less mobile but broader mouthed, 'call me Harry.'

'How ...?' began Rob.

'Why ...?' asked Jinny.

'It's a long story,' said Danny, 'it really is. I suppose it was my mother who thought of it, a way of getting you away. We all met ...'

'It's only a long story when he tells it,' interrupted Harry Arnison, 'and we don't have much time. Suffice to say that Samuel and Rebecca, Danny and Charlotte, Annie and I, we all felt you were being treated unfairly. We sat for a while, thought about what we could do to help you and, at the same time, take our revenge on George Taylor, my wife and that damned poet.'

'But you saw them at the window,' said Jinny, 'as we were leaving.'

'They won't have been doing anything they haven't done in the past, my dear, and I've become used to her flaunting her indiscretions. It will do her good to find she's associated with idiots like Scrivener and villains such as George Taylor. She'll be laughed at in public rather than behind people's hands. Perhaps it will do her some good, though I doubt it. But I digress. We sat down and thought up the plan which you've seen us accomplish. So far as anyone else is concerned, you were taken away by two men claiming to be constables. We can't be blamed if they were imposters!'

'But don't be caught!' warned Danny. 'I'd hate to deny I'd seen the look on your faces when you found out who we really were.'

'But what do we do now?' asked Jinny.

Rob answered the question for her. 'We drive to Hexham. Even better, just outside Hexham.'

'Haydon Bridge,' suggested Harry Arnison, 'leave the cart there. There's a coaching inn, they'll look after it until we can be informed about it.'

'Haydon Bridge it is, then. And we take the coach to—'

'No, don't tell us. The less we know the better. But you'd better be moving. There's no knowing when the real constables will arrive.'

'Quite some time, I'd say,' ventured Danny. 'I saw Mr Stephenson's face last night, he took quite a shine to you, Rob. It's just a pity you won't be around to guide us all in the dance when Charlotte and I are wed.'

'You mean you asked him?'

'He gave his consent last night, just before my uncle reappeared. Just think, I'll soon be able to call him Papa!'

He doubled over with laughter again, stopped, then stood

up and grabbed Rob, hugged him close. Rob saw he was crying.

'Thank you,' he said. 'Thank you for everything. And good luck. Take care of each other.'

'We will,' said Jinny, as Danny bent down and took her in his ample arms. She kissed him gently on the cheek and did the same to Harry Arnison, who smiled and strode over to Rob, shook his hand boldly, slapped him on the shoulder, then turned to pick up the horse's reins and began the walk back to the manor. Danny made as if to follow him but halted. Instead he watched as Rob and Jinny climbed back into the cart and started on the journey to Haydon Bridge. He was still there, waving at them, as they topped the next rise, and the sun shimmered into the sky behind his outstretched arms.

Rob sang a tune to himself.

'That's a good tune,' Jinny said. 'I've not heard it before. What's it called?'

'I'm not sure. I heard it in a pub on the quayside, oh, two months ago. Couldn't get it out of my mind. I haven't thought of it since and . . . Yes! I *can* remember the name. The fiddler, the one who was playing it, he *did* mention it.'

'Come on then, what's it called?'

'A strange name. Quite fitting really.'

'Tell me then.'

'It's called "De'il among the Tailors".'

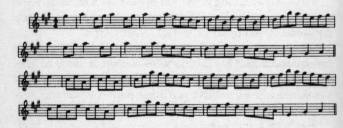

The Final Chord Of The Musick

━━◆━━

Tuesday, 29 June 1830

*In which the dance comes to a close, but the dancers
agree that such a pleasant, pleasing pastime must be
repeated. Soon.*

Rob and Jinny lay in bed together. The inn was comfortable, the food and drink both filling and warming.
They'd even managed to stroll past the castle and the
cathedral before thunderclouds threatened them and they
deemed it safer to return to their room, and their bed.

'There's a coach leaves tomorrow for Lancaster,' said Rob,
'how does that suit you?'

'Isn't this far enough?' answered Jinny, half asleep. Rain
and wind hammered at the roof above them, but they were
dry, content, happy to be in each other's arms.

'I don't think so. They'll find the dogcart at Haydon Bridge
and ask about us. They'll know we took the coach to Carlisle.
We need to go further yet.'

'Oh, what a pity. I like Carlisle.' Jinny's voice was soft
and dreamy.

'Why's that, my love?'

She opened her eyes and smiled at him. 'Because you're
here,' she answered. He laughed at her. 'You're not laughing

at me, are you?' she said, sitting up straight so that the sheets
fell away from her. She wore no nightdress.

'Yes, of course I am. There's no one else here to laugh at.
Just as well, really.'

'I'll let you off, then. After all, if a man can't laugh at his
wife, who can he laugh at?'

Rob frowned, but Jinny had let her head fall back again
to the pillow. Her eyes were closed once more. He wanted to
speak. He wanted to say that they weren't married, not yet
anyway, so she wasn't his wife. But his insistence on accuracy,
whatever the reason, probably wouldn't be welcome. And
they would get married, some day, when they settled down,
when they found somewhere to live. He could work as a
dancing master, he knew he could do that, and Jinny could
demonstrate the dances with him, and they would be invited
to society balls, they would have beautiful clothes . . .'

'Rob, Mrs Taylor, she said we should change our names.'

'Probably a good idea, especially if George Taylor comes
after us.'

'What should we change to, then?'

'I don't know. Anything's better than Tweddle, I suppose.
I've never liked it, people always get it wrong. They call me
"Twaddle" or "Twiddle". What do you think?'

'I think you should choose a name that describes the way
you are.'

'The way I am?'

'Mm. Like "brave" or "handsome". D'you know what I
mean?'

'Robbie Hansom. I like that. I like the sound of that; it's
a good name for a dancing master.' He looked at her again.
Her hand was at her mouth; she was trying not to laugh.
'You were joking,' he said, 'you didn't mean it at all!'

'I did!' she protested, 'but you looked so funny when you
said it, "Robbie Hansom," and you stuck your chin out. You
looked really noble. But I don't think . . .'

'What, then?'

'I don't know!'

'How about "fearsome"?' he cried, leaping from the bed with a fierce grimace on his face and prowling round the room like a wild, naked animal. Jinny scrambled away from him, across the bed.

'I think I prefer "gentle",' she said with a trembling little girl's voice.

'Dancer!' exclaimed Rob, stepping lightly from one side to another. Jinny laughed and clapped her hands together, ran round the bed to join him in an impromptu waltz which slowed and slowed and dissolved into a kiss. Rob picked her up and took her back to the bed.

'Hm,' she whispered, 'Strong, because you're exactly that. You hold me so easily, so tight; your arms are so strong.'

'Yes,' agreed Rob, 'I could live with that. "Armstrong". Robert and Jinny Armstrong. It's a good name, that; I like it.'

'We'll be Armstrongs from now on then, Rob, my love.' They kissed again, stretched out on the bed beside each other, his hand on her breast, hers on his thigh, all smooth, soft movement.

'And what about our son?' she whispered in his ear.

'Our what?' he said, stiffened and pulled away from her.

'Our son. We'll have a son, Rob. I can feel him inside me already.'

'Already? But it's only a week . . .'

'I can tell, Rob. He'll be a son to be proud of. He'll grow up strong,' she giggled, 'with strong arms, son of Armstrong, and we'll call him . . .' She stopped. 'The baby I had, Rob, the one who died . . .'

'I remember,' said Rob, pulling her close to him again.

'I called him Tom. Would you mind if . . .'

'It sounds a fine name to me, love. "Tom Armstrong". A good name; one of the best.'

'Well, perhaps we'll actually call him "Tommy". It comes off the tongue better, "Tommy Armstrong", don't you think?'

'If you say so, love. Tommy Armstrong it is.'

'And you know something? With you as his father and me as his mother, I can tell you one thing for certain.'

'What's that?'

'He'll be one hell of a fine dancer.'